AMANDA
CADABRA
AND THE FLAWLESS PLAN

HOLLY BELL

Other titles by Holly Bell

Amanda Cadabra and The Hidey-Hole Truth
(The Amanda Cadabra Cozy Mysteries Book 1)

Amanda Cadabra and The Cellar of Secrets
(The Amanda Cadabra Cozy Mysteries Book 2)

Other books published by Heypressto

50 Feel-better Films
50 Feel-better Songs: from Film and TV
25 Feel-better Free Downloads

AMANDA CADABRA

AND THE FLAWLESS PLAN

HOLLY BELL

To Alwyn

There are more things

in heaven and earth, Horatio,

than are dreamt of

in your philosophy..

William Shakespeare
Hamlet

CONTENTS

THE VILLAGE OF SUNKEN MADLEY

KEY
1. Amanda's House
2. Sunken Madley Manor
3. The Sinner's Rue Pub
4. The Library
5. St Ursula-without Barnet
6. Medical Centre
7. Priory Ruins
8. Playing Fields
9. The Snout and Trough Pub
10. Post Office/Corner Shop

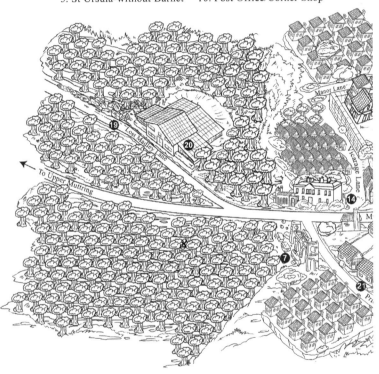

AND LOST MADLEY

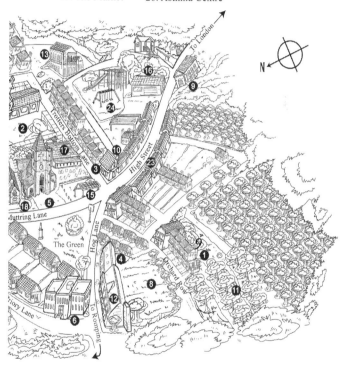

St Ursula-without-Barnet

KEY
1. The Rectory
2. The Church Hall
3. The Manor
4. Car Park

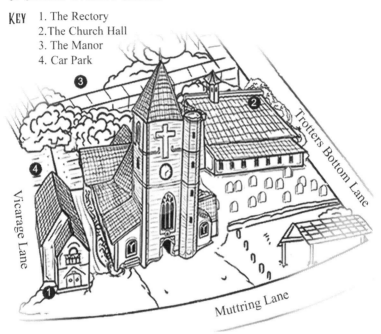

Trotters Bottom Lane

Vicarage Lane

Muttring Lane

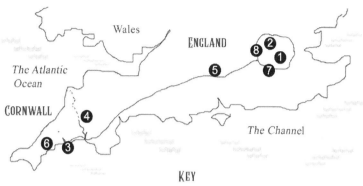

Wales

ENGLAND

The Atlantic
Ocean

CORNWALL

The Channel

KEY

1. London
2. Sunken Madley
3. Parhayle

4. The River Tamar
    & the border
5. M3 Highway

6. Bodmin Moor
7. M25 Orbital Road
8. Heathrow Airport

MAP OF CORNWALL AND THE SOUTH OF ENGLAND

Introduction

Please note that to enhance the reader's experience of Amanda's world, this British-set story, by a British author, uses British English spelling, vocabulary, grammar and usage, and includes local and foreign accents, dialects and a magical language that vary from different versions of English as it is written and spoken in other parts of our wonderful, diverse world.

For your reading pleasure, there is a glossary of British English usage and vocabulary at the end of the book, followed by a note about accents and the magical language, Wicc'yeth.

Chapter 1

༄

CRYPT AND CELLAR

Amanda found her lying on the floor of the crypt. Her head was up against a medieval stone coffin where it must have struck. One arm was hidden beneath the long raised form of the sarcophagus.

She hurried down the stone steps, her soft soles silent as the grave.

'Please, no, not another body, oh please no,' she murmured, gazing in dismay at the sight of her friend's black cassock-clad body.

Amanda knelt beside the fallen rector of Sunken Madley church. There was no blood in the dark brown bobbed hair. Perhaps there was still life. Amanda laid a hand on her shoulder.

'Rector!'

The body convulsed. The head turned. The alarmed face of the shepherd of St Ursula-without-Barnet looked up with alarm.

'Good heavens, Amanda! You gave me the shock of my life. You really mustn't creep up on people like that.'

'Oh Rector, I am sorry, I just saw you lying there, and I thought …'

'Of course, dear, after that dreadful affair at … aha!'

The Reverend Jane Waygood withdrew her arm from beneath the sarcophagus and knelt up, looking at Amanda's feet.

'Yes. Trainers. I see why you apparently stealthed up. Well, you're just the person I wanted to see, and even more so at this moment. I believe your arms are slightly longer, not to mention slimmer, than mine or, at least, those craftsperson's fingers of yours may be more agile.

'You were trying to get something out from under there?' asked Amanda, leaning down.

'It's the keys to the church hall. They slipped out of my fingers and slid away into inaccessibility, and I wanted to have them ready to take you down there. I'm hoping that you'll be involved in my plot,' said Jane, in mysterious but hopeful accents.

Amanda was mindful that 5th November, Guy Fawkes Night, was soon to be upon them, celebrating the attempt, or possibly failure, of a group of 15th-century activists to put paid to the Houses of Parliament by the use of then state-of-the-art explosives.

'If you're planning to blow it up, don't you think we should visit it under cover of night?' suggested Jane's parishioner helpfully.

'Oh, if only we could,' sighed the rector wistfully. 'Claim on the insurance and rebuild the wretched thing from scratch. Unfortunately, my calling prevents me from engaging in such deception even if it wasn't a listed building. Meanwhile, do you think you could be a dear and get those keys out from under there?'

Amanda looked at the floor with concern.

'It's as clean as a whistle in here,' Jane assured her. 'You don't need to worry about dust setting off your asthma. Mrs Scripps cleans down here regularly. You could eat your dinner off those flagstones. Not that anyone else comes down here but there's always hope of a rare visitor.'

'Then of course,' Amanda replied cheerfully and lowered herself onto her stomach. She reached between the coffin's carved bears' feet.

'Here,' said Jane holding her phone with the torch app on shining a light into the narrow space.

'I see them! Thank you, Rector.' Amanda slid her arm in the direction of the glint. 'Yes … oh, there's something else … it's small … I can reach both … ah! ... got them!'

Amanda pulled out her arm and stood up. She opened her hand, passed the keys to the rector and frowned down at the remaining item sitting on her palm. 'Whatever do you suppose ...?'

'Bless my soul. It looks like a tiny little gold … cup or something. It's quite thick, and look at all of these close-set wavy marks. Do you think it's something to do with the sea? A fitting on an instrument that maybe was used on one of the old ships? An ornamental screw cover on a … sextant or something?'

'Well, whatever it is, it's the property of the church,' said Amanda holding it out.

'No,' Jane replied thoughtfully. 'No … you keep it. I have a feeling …. I think it's an apport.'

'A what?'

'An apport. Hmmm. Ask your Aunt Amelia. She'll tell you about them.'

'Oh. Ok. Well, thank you, Rector.'

'And now to business. You got word through the grapevine, yes?'

'Sylvia said you wanted to see me about something.'

'Well, thank you for popping in, dear. Got your car with you?' asked Jane, leading the way up out of the artificially lit crypt into the daylight in a corner of the west end of the church.

'Yes, as it happens.'

'Good. Go and fetch a dust mask.'

'Oh?'

'I'm taking you down into the bowels!'

With the mask secured, they took the path between the mellow stones of the higgledy-piggledy graveyard to the hall at the boundary of the church property. The rector used one of the newly retrieved ornate keys to open the side door.

'I had no idea that this door existed,' commented Amanda.

'I know, we always herd people through the front. But here we are now. Come inside so I can push the door to, and get to this.' There, at right angles to it, was another one, also locked. The rector opened it, switched on a light and led the way down some wooden stairs into the space below.

With difficult progress and in insufficient light, they passed between old rolls of carpet and backdrops, cardboard and wooden installations, trunks, suitcases, boxes, crates, a basket of stage swords, a golf bag of spears, and a large vase of Japanese parasols, as well as all manner of paraphernalia that it was hard to identify.

It was unexpectedly high-ceilinged for a cellar, and roomier than the hall because there was no stage or anterooms as there were above. Eventually, they came to an area that was even more challenging to traverse. A group of upright posts of wood were set at intervals, piled around with crates and cases that barred the way.

'Right,' Jane began briskly, 'look up there. See those joists?'

'Yes.'

'They're rotten. Not too bad for most of it, but along this section here, they're as weak as water. That's why the hall has been closed for as long as it has. It's all a bit unsolid, but here it was dangerous.'

'I see,' said Amanda.

'Well, I've been wanting to repair and reopen this hall for years, but, of course, the church roof had to come first, and now it has … and, well, I didn't want to ask the kind benefactors to put their hands in their pockets again, especially so soon, without some effort on my own part and contributions from the community, towards restoring this lovely old hall. Except … no one was interested.'

'I suppose the church with its medieval pedigree and the famous St Ursula stained glass window —'

'— and the bell tower, yes,' concurred Jane. 'That was comparatively easy to attract donations to. Well, I said, "If you want this church to still be here for your enjoyment in 100 years, or even 50, you have to be willing to support it," and so they were. But this hall. You see, it's only late 1800s or even later and that's no great shakes, is it?'

'Not really,' agreed Amanda.

'So, what would make people realise the worth of the hall?'

'Using it?'

'Yes, but what's the most exciting thing people can do on a floor?' asked the rector blithely.

'Erm.' Amanda was unprepared for the question, and her mind boggled.

'Dance!' uttered Jane enthusiastically.

'Ah.'

'But no one could dance on a dangerous floor. So … I had it repaired! See, these wooden posts are supporting that group of floorboards above? Taking over from where the joists are rotten.'

Amanda squinted into the gloom. 'I think I need a better light. Let me go up to the car and get a torch.'

'No, no, you stay there,' Jane insisted. 'I'll get one.'

The rector hurriedly picked her way across the stored goods and up the stairs. Amanda stood alone in the dusty silence, her breath contained and amplified by her mask. She felt a little dizzy, her vision fuzzed. Suddenly it was as if something shot down through the ceiling of floorboards above and would have hit her if she had not dodged back, tripping over a wooden case and stack of props. She got to her feet. But there was nothing there. Nothing above or below that had not been there before.

But now there was the faint sound of music. Maybe someone had a car radio on loudly nearby. And yet … there was singing too …. It was a waltz … an old song … Grandpa used to sing it … yes, to Granny … 'Roses are shining in Picardy … in the hush of the silver dew', and there was thumping above — no, not thumping exactly — feet ... walking — no, they must be dancing … waltzing across the boards above her head, and people singing their hearts out. It wasn't frightening … there was something wonderful and free and heartbreaking about it all at once. She wanted to be up there with them ….

'Here we are, dear!' came the rector's voice, and, at once, it stopped. The music, the singing, the waltzing feet. As if it had never been.

Chapter 2

≈

THE RECTOR'S PLOT

'Rector, did you hear that?' Amanda asked urgently.

'The ambulance? Must be coming from the residential home. They do very occasionally come through the village if the A1000's blocked up.'

'No, the … the ….' Amanda suddenly thought better of saying any more about her strange experience moments before. 'Oh, yes, of course, that must have been it.'

'Here's the torch,' said Jane. It flashed briefly over Amanda's face. 'You shine it where you want. Are you all right? Have you been away with the fairies while I was gone?'

Amanda gave an unsteady laugh. 'Yes, I'm afraid so. Never mind. Let me have a look at this woodwork.' She directed the beam along and up.

'Er ….' Amanda took a closer look at the supports. Each was made up of apparently random lengths of wood bracketed together to make a long post, tall enough to reach the floorboards above them. Amanda tested the stability, and they were wedged in tightly between the floor and ceiling of the cellar.

'Rector, I don't know much about building, but I'm pretty sure that this isn't quite …'

'Oh Amanda, I got all sorts of quotes, and they were all far more than I felt the church could afford. And then someone recommended these two lovely gentlemen, and they were so understanding and so affordable!'

'Really?'

'Yes, and they were all done in no time at all, and they only charged £40!'

'What were the names of these "lovely gentlemen", Rector?' asked Amanda suspiciously.

'Let me see, one was Ronald and the other was er … Philip.'

'Ron and Phil?'

'I suppose so.'

'Ronald Recket, by any chance?' asked Amanda, fearing the worst.

'Yes, I think so.'

'Recket and Bogia? Rector, you didn't!' implored Amanda.

'Why whatever's wrong?' asked Jane, anxiously.

'I may not know much about building, but I know most of the builders around here. And those two are notorious scoundrels. This is almost certainly not the way to support a floor, and these bits of wood and the brackets were almost certainly not honestly come by.'

'What! But … but, oh my, whatever will the bishop say?'

'It's all right,' soothed Amanda. 'These seem sturdy and tight enough to do the job. It's only temporary, and, once there's enough money, the floor will be done properly, and no one need know.'

'Oh, but I feel dreadful deceiving —'

'You're not deceiving anyone. If I thought for a moment that it wasn't safe, I'd say so, but these are tight and will certainly hold, although you should ask Mr Branscombe to look at them because he is a builder and will know.'

'Thank you, Amanda. Oh dear,' Jane said mournfully.

'So tell me your plan,' she urged to give the rector's thoughts a happier direction.

'Well, I thought: dancing! Dancing classes and dances. The hall will cost nothing, and we just have to find a teacher who'll be willing to charge a low rate, and then the extra will go into the fund, and the dances will bring in a good bit. It may take a while, but we'll, at least, be on our way to a brand new floor; a proper sprung floor, new joists and, new boards. Perhaps parquet flooring. And then we can hire it out for classes of all sorts.'

'I think it's a wonderful idea, Rector. But why have you honoured me with your confidence? To check the er …?'

'Well, partly, but mainly because you're the only dancer I know of.'

'I'm not a dancer, Rector.'

'I mean, you like to dance. You do go dancing.'

Amanda frowned. That was something she did with her friend and next-door neighbour, Claire, and they did it well away from the village.

'May I ask how you know?'

'Everyone knows,' replied Jane, as though stating the obvious.

'How?'

'Um … let me see … I heard it from Irma Uberhausfest who said she heard it from … ah yes, Penny.'

'The doctor's receptionist?'

'Yes, she said she bumped into you with her fiancé one night in a bar in Camden. The Blood Bath?'

'The Bubble Bath. Ok. Well, I suppose it only took that one person and that one time,' remarked Amanda resignedly.

'Anyway, will you help?'

'Of course,' answered Amanda willingly, 'but how?'

'Whip up enthusiasm, spread the word.'

'I think the grapevine will do that,' said Amanda knowingly.

'And you will come along to the classes and the dances, won't you?'

'Of course I shall, Rector, and yes, I'll encourage everyone I know to join.'

'Thank you, dear. Now let's get out of this dusty place.'

'What's the story behind this hall? What is all this stuff?' Amanda enquired casually.

'Now, you'd have to ask Mrs Pagely because I'm not really up on all of this, but it was built at the turn of the century, I believe. Funded by someone who was very fond of theatricals. They wanted lots of space for storing props, and, over the years, they accumulated through one production after another. And then, I think, other things collected in here.'

'What about during the war?'

'Which one?' asked Jane.

'The first.'

'Probably used as a hospital. A lot of halls were. But I think the floor here has never been right. It's been repaired over the years, until things got too bad and the hall had to be closed.'

They reached the comparative safety of the stairs.

'You go up first dear, and I'll lock up behind you,' said Jane. She secured the door at the bottom of the flight, then the one at the top and finally the side entrance. 'Would you like a cup of tea? And then I must get on with some paperwork.'

'Thank you, Rector, but I need to get home too.'

'Perhaps later in the week I can show you the space above?' asked Jane with renewed excitement.

'Yes, of course. I'm on site tomorrow with a couple of builders. I'll mention the floor to them and bring them over to check it.'

'Wonderful. You are a dear,' said Jane giving her a hug.

'I'll be in touch tomorrow,' promised Amanda.

But tomorrow had other plans.

Chapter 3

༶

TRAINING AMANDA

Former Chief Inspector Hogarth, lately of the Devon and Cornwall Police, leaned on the wooden handrail of his sister and brother-in-law's luxurious Spanish villa and looked out with pleasure. The sun was rising over the orange flushing vista of the Balearic Sea.

'Tea up,' called Vera, his older sibling. He moved towards the cream-padded cane furniture around the table, where she was setting out the pot and cups. As he sat down, she pushed a tin of pre-breakfast Hobnobs towards him and remarked casually,

'You haven't told me how the youngsters are getting along.'

'They're well enough. Amanda's asthma still troubles her, but she manages, you know. Thomas, he's as fit as a fiddle, and still enjoys his work.'

'That's not what I meant, and you know it, Mikey. How are they getting along with each other?

'Cautiously.'

'Are they friends yet?

'I'd say friendship is a component in their complex relationship of detective-witness, covert wi— well you know what she is — playing against his rampant scepticism and deep-seated unease with all things supernatural. Mutual suspicion is, I think, being very slowly eroded.'

'Hmm. Is it too soon to hope?'

'It is never too soon to hope, my dear.

* * * * *

Amanda, some 700 miles to the north, was likewise up betimes. She had magical training to start before she began her day's furniture restoration work. Granny and Grandpa, Senara and Perran Cadabra, were sure to be found in the workshop this morning, although they had been nowhere to be seen when Amanda had got home the day before. However, Amanda was used to that. Since their transition to whatever dimension they now inhabited, commonly known by the word 'death', and the details of which they were vague about, they came and went apparently at random.

Unless, that was, Amanda called on them. As Granny had often pointed out: the dead cannot harm the living, and they cannot help them either unless they are asked.

Today they would begin helping in a specific way. Amanda had resolved to begin a new stage in her spell-casting development. Only days before, her levitation skills had been tested to the limit and, if she had not had help, Amanda would not have survived. It was time to get serious.

Tempest, her familiar, had been served breakfast, and Amanda assumed that he was out irritating the local wildlife in typical cat style. But she was in error. Having traversed the garden between the spent fruit trees and entered her work domain, her gaze was drawn to the seat of a Sheraton shield back that was waiting to be dispatched to the upholsterers.

On the chair, reposed a bundle of fur in a selection of greys. It opened one baleful yellow eye at Amanda's entrance. 'Hello, Sweetikins,' she addressed him lovingly. The one cat to which she was not allergic, he had been an important part of her life since she was a frustrated 15-year-old struggling with the physical limitations of her asthma. Granny and Grandpa, deciding that the moment had come, had closeted themselves one night in the workshop and conjured the irascible feline that was none too pleased about being reincarnated. Within moments of meeting, Tempest and Amanda had established a unique bond, the magical nature of which, in the past year, had become more important than she had ever imagined.

Tempest surveyed his witch impassively and, tacitly but successfully, communicated, 'Where have you been? Where is my workshop treat?' He released an audible sigh expressive of, 'You can't get the staff these days.'

She came over to kiss his fluffy head and give him a cuddle, which he endured as the inescapable lot of the glamorous and adored.

'Mrowwl,' he uttered shortly.

'Your wish is my command, oh Fuzziness,' said Amanda and went to a drawer under the work surface by the window. She was delivering a Magnificent Morsel for The Discerning Feline when Senara and Perran Cadabra appeared and solidified.

'Good morning, Ammy dear,' Granny said affectionately.

'Mornin' bian,' said Grandpa in his gentle Cornish accent. He had called her his bian, his baby, ever since she could remember.

'Granny, Grandpa, glad to see you. Yesterday —'

'— Yes, we know, dear. You did well,' Senara commended her.

'Oh, you know?'

'Well, we popped by while you were in the church hall. You were right not to say anything to the rector.'

'And you made a nice recovery,' added Perran. 'Lucky about the ambulance going past.'

'Yes, well, I do realise that not everything I can see is visible to the Normals,' said Amanda.

'We trained you well.'

'You did,' she agreed whole-heartedly.

'Speaking of which, shall we start, bian?'

'First, aren't you going to tell me what all that was about? That thing falling in front of me and then the music and singing and dancing?'

'You'll work it out,' said her grandfather reassuringly. 'This one is going to be more complicated than the last one. Possibly ... probably. Definitely.'

'The last one? The last one what?'

'But you'll be fine. And you do need to remember more about your childhood. But you'll have help.'

'What?'

'Now time for your training. You only have half an hour,' Grandpa pointed out.

'Well, I think that'll be enough,' replied Amanda. 'I don't want to go to work exhausted. And doing the banister won't be so easy as I won't be alone in the house today to use spells to help me.'

'Yes, you'll have to be circumspect,' Grandpa agreed. 'But that's always good practice.'

'So you're not going to tell me anything about anything?' asked his frustrated granddaughter.

'You won't need us to. You did so well last time.'

'And the time before that,' Granny added.

'Now your levitation. We'll build up slowly. No house-lifting to start with!' joked Grandpa. 'That chest of drawers, let's start with that.'

'With or without the wand?'

'Let's start with.'

Amanda put her hand in her left-hand pocket and withdrew an apparently normal IKEA pencil. But this was no ordinary writing implement, and she was not about to make notes. With a flick of her thumbnail, she opened the top of the pencil. The light caught a yellow stone set in a recess. She pulled it out, revealing that it was attached to a slender length of orange-red wood. For this was one of Dr Bertil Bergstrom's patent Pocket-wands, presented to Amanda by the doctor himself. Bertil and Kerstin Bergstrom were the Swedish inventors of magical assists that were known to all magical folk. As it happened, this couple also made up fifty per cent of all the other magical folk that Amanda knew, apart from her grandparents.

The wand looked like it would barely assist a fly, but Amanda had learned the power of petite, and this was her most potent tool.

She pointed it at the heavy oak three-drawer chest and pronounced in the magical language, Wicc'yeth, 'Aereval.' It raised gently off the floor.

'Now, how about the small workbench?' suggested Grandpa.

Holding the chest of drawers in position with her mind, Amanda directed the wand at the workbench and repeated the spellword. As it rose, the chest wavered slightly, but she kept it level.

Perran commended her. 'Now raise them both another six inches ... Excellent. Now go over and turn on the hob.'

Amanda kept her eyes darting between the two objects as she crossed the room and felt for the switch in the socket on the wall.

'Just look at the switch,' said Grandpa.

She turned her gaze away and felt the bench waver. Amanda looked back to see both items of furniture tilting.

'That's natural. Don't worry about it'' Perran encouraged her.

She corrected the angle, turned back to the hob and switched it on.

'Now set the glue pot stirring.'

'Mecsge,' Amanda uttered.

'Now look back,' said Perran.

The chest had sunk, and the workbench was upending like the Titanic. The chisels on it were sliding to the edge ready for the fall into the blue of the vinyl below.

'Ahh!' cried Amanda, hurriedly correcting them.

The gluepot brush had given up and was leaning once more against the rim.

'Oh no!'

Thud! The chest landed. Clang! The workbench had leaned forward and tipped its unattached vice to the floor.

'Good grief! How am I ever to get the hang of this?' Amanda exclaimed despairingly.

'Patience,' replied Perran. 'You're getting too intense about it all. This is not an exam. It's just Day One.'

'Yes, Grandpa,' she sighed, 'you're right.'

'Now let's try it again. And this time, calmly. Set your intention, not your force of will.'

Twenty-five minutes later, Amanda emerged with Tempest from the workshop, moderately pleased with her progress. It wasn't great. But it was progress.

Amanda locked up the house as they went, and boarded Grandpa's legacy Vauxhaul Astra in racing green, bearing the legend in gold down the sides: Cadabra Restoration and Repairs.

They drove up Orchard Lane, turned left into Hog Lane, past the library on the left, and opposite the Sunken Madley school next door to it, turned right into Priory Lane, past the medical centre on the right and parked in the driveway of the Reiser's House. Tempest went about his own affairs, and Amanda rang the bell. Ruth, Amanda's favourite teenager, whom she occasionally helped with her homework, had already left for school, but her mother opened the door.

'Oh good. Thank you, Amanda, for being on time. You don't mind if I rush off now, do you? I'm sure you can find your way around the kitchen, and you know where the bathroom is. I'll be right next door if you need me.'

'Of course, that's fine, Esta.'

'See you later. In case you want to ask me anything in person, I'll be popping back this afternoon.'

Which, as it turned out, was very fortunate indeed.

Chapter 4

✑

HORACE BOTTLE

The banister ran from converted attic to the ground floor, with newel posts at the top and bottom of each flight. When the Reisers had moved in, it was already painted, and, with the expense of the upgraded house and cost of the move, they had merely added fresh coats of gloss, matt and eggshell over the years. Now, thanks to a bequest from Mrs Reiser's mother's cousin, they had the means to make some long-overdue repairs and refurbishments, including finally revealing the wood beneath the layers on the handrail and newel posts.

The improvements to the house included a new basement, which needed heating, lighting, storage units, shelves and carpet. Horace Bottle was seeing to that ably assisted by Bryan Branscombe, who was dark, short and slightly portly but agile and light on his feet.

On Amanda's arrival, Horace lifted his narrow face, under thinning strawberry blond hair, and called up a cheery flirtatious welcome. Branscombe mounted the stairs to greet her pleasantly and to assure her they would not get in her way. However, occasionally Bottle and Branscombe did pass Amanda on the stairs when going up and down to the water tank in the loft.

It wasn't until the afternoon that it happened. Trying to get paint free from a particularly persistent crevice, Amanda went to fetch her multi-tool to help deftly dig out the residue. However, it was nowhere to be seen. Not in her toolbox, not in the boot of the car, not on the stairs. She had definitely packed it the night before. Or had she?

Amanda was standing in the hall, wondering if she should go home and check, when Branscombe came up from the basement. He was holding her multi-tool in his hand. Or was it his? No, there was the burn on the handle where she'd left it too close to the soldering iron and a 'C' at the end, which Grandpa had put on all of his tools.

'Erm … Mr Branscombe,' Amanda said hesitantly, 'Ah, I think you have my multi-tool there.'

'Oh sorry,' he replied anxiously. 'Horace lent it to me, said it was his.'

'Really?' asked Amanda in surprise.

'Yes. I said, "That's a handy gadget," and he said he paid a pretty penny for it. Didn't realise he'd erm ….' Branscombe, blushing, handed it over.

'You're welcome to use it when I've finished with it,' said Amanda amicably. 'Don't worry. It's not your fault. I'll have a word with him.'

Amanda descended to the basement with only slightly raised pulse. After all, Bottle had been friendly, almost to the point of over-familiarity, in the past. He straightened up from his task at her approach.

''Allo, lovely. Come for a visit?'

She took a deep breath. 'Actually, I'd like to make a request,' she said, in the most diplomatic tone she could muster.

'Yes, darlin', what can I do for you?'

'Well, next time you'd like to borrow one of my tools, I'd appreciate it if you'd ask me first. It did give Mr Branscombe an embarrassing moment when I noticed that he had my multi-tool, thinking it belonged to you, as you had claimed.'

At once Bottle's hackles rose, the corners of his thin mouth pulled down and his eyes shrunk into a menacing glare.

'Wot you sayin'?' he asked, jutting his head forward. 'That I stole it?'

Amanda leaned back. 'Well, it did rather look —'

'I was just jokin'! It's people like you that take orl the fun outta the trade. We're all sposed to be in this together, aren't we? It's people like you,' he repeated, stabbing the air in front of her with his forefinger, 'goin' on about ownership that spoil it fer everyone. Comin' round 'ere, tryin' to do a man's work, taking someone's job an' lookin' so innocent. Well, someone's onto you. Got their eye on you, so just you watch out. Now look wot you done! You've upset me, look at me 'ands. I can't work around people like you!'

'Well really, Mr Bottle, I didn't intend to upset you, but you did —'

'I'm goin'!' he shouted, throwing down his spanner and stamping his feet one after the other so loudly that the sound of Esta Reiser's key in the door was drowned out.

'Whatever's going on?' she called down the stairs.

Bottle went stomping up, bellowing, 'It's 'er. I'm goin', and I'm not comin' back till she's outta here. It's 'er or me. See?'

With that, he pushed past Mrs Reiser and flounced out of the front door. He slammed it behind him, making the panes of stained glass rattle in their leads.

Amanda, white-faced, emerged from below, and turned to the startled lady before her.

'Esta,' she began, but Mr Branscombe intervened.

'I'm sorry about the hullabaloo, Mrs Reiser —'

But it was not over yet. A yell sounded from the road outside. The three hurried to open the front door and peer out. Bottle's van was parked right opposite the gate. He was standing with the driver door open, looking down at the seat, roaring, and his complexion reddening.

The cause was not far to seek. A bundle of grey fur, set at one end with livid yellow eyes and a tail at the other, was sitting smugly on the roof of the vehicle while the owner was hit by the reek of feline micturition and the sight of a large moist patch on the seat.

The shiny paint on the offside of the van was indented with sets of three parallel lines of scratches. Horace leapt, clawing at Tempest. But Amanda's familiar sprang nimbly to the opposite corner of the roof, out of the man's reach.

The air turned blue with expletives, before the man thrust himself into his seat, banged his door shut, started the engine, grated into gear and stamped on the accelerator. Tempest had jumped to the ground long before Bottle's sole connected with the pedal and stared after the retreating vehicle with the air of a job well done.

Amanda bit her lip. Her familiar gave her a saucy glance over his shoulder and sashayed off, tail waving like a plume.

'Naughty kitty,' said Amanda unsteadily. 'He's —'

'Mrs Reiser,' said Mr Branscombe, 'the truth is that Bottle stole one of Miss Cadabra's tools and that's the long and short of it. She was very nice about, but he didn't like being caught out red-handed, so to speak, and started shouting at her. I don't know as he'll be back.'

'I wouldn't have him back!' replied Esta with spirit. 'I'm not having any of that sort of conduct in my house. Mr Branscombe, can you take over?'

'Yes, of course, I can,' Bryan answered eagerly. 'I'll do the best I can for you.'

'That will be quite satisfactory. Amanda dear, I deeply regret that someone behaved toward you in such a manner on my premises. Come and have a cup of tea and a gingernut biscuit. Would you like one too, Mr Branscombe?'

'No, thank you, I'm good. I'll go and see about the work.'

'Well, perhaps later. Come into the kitchen, dear.' She settled Amanda down with refreshments. 'I'm just going to water the pansies while I remember. You'll be alright if I leave you for a few minutes?'

'Oh yes, I'll be fine.'

In fact, Amanda was glad to have a quiet period of reflection. Bottle's behaviour had undoubtedly taken her by surprise, even alarmed her. But amongst his sound and fury, had been, at the bottom of the storm in a teacup, a nugget of gold. A piece of information. Someone was watching her. Uncle Mike —no, it wasn't him, it was the inspector — had asked her if she'd ever felt under surveillance and she'd waved the suggestion away. And, years ago, she'd asked Amelia if someone had her in their sights, and her aunt had thought not at the time. But now ... Amanda knew for certain. Someone did.

The first thing to do was tell Uncle Mike. She checked the time. It was 3.30.

'How are you feeling, dear?' asked Esta solicitously, coming back in from the garden.

'Much better, thank you. Would you mind if I popped home?'

'Why not call it a day? The light's pretty much gone, and I can see you're getting on well.'

'Thank you, Esta, I think I shall.'

'And don't you give that horrid little man a second thought. I believed he was so nice, but, well, he's shown his true colours, and I shall make sure all of my friends and neighbours know about it, you can be sure! I doubt you'll ever be working around him again, mark my words!'

Amanda went to thank Mr Branscombe for his support.

'That was very kind of you,' she said sincerely.

'My pleasure. To be honest, I had the feeling he was a bit of a scrounger, always wanting something for nothing and not paying me as I should be. But he had a way of backfootin' me, so to speak. Didn't think he was an outright thief. Now I know, and now I've got this job, and I know Mrs Reiser will recommend me, 'ope I won't be workin' with him no more.'

'I think we'll get on fine without him,' replied Amanda. 'If you want to borrow any of my tools you just have to ask.'

'Likewise, if you need a paintbrush, I'm your man,' answered Branscombe with a grin.

Amanda collected her lunch bag and joined Tempest at the Astra. As she got in and settled herself, her mood began to change. The more Amanda thought about it, the more indignant she became.

'They're right!' she exclaimed. 'How dare he speak to me like that! I can't believe I apologised to him.' Her indignation was heating to rage. 'He made me feel like I was in the wrong. When he was the one who stole! And lied.' Amanda banged her hands onto the steering-wheel. 'And he's done this to other people. And he gets away with it.' The flame of her anger was morphing from hot red to cold blue. 'Well, not this time …' Her energy was darkening as she started the car. 'Someone has to stop him.'

Tempest's interest was aroused. He licked his lips and flexed his claws, his eyes glittering like yellow diamonds as he savoured the delicious anticipation of just such mischief as he relished.

'And today …' said Amanda, 'it's going to be me who stops him.' She pulled out in to the road. 'Just a little visit to where he lives. An innocent stroll past his van to pop the lid on every tin of paint and varnish, they'll be solid by tomorrow, and

… yes … open the locks on the doors. The local thieves can help themselves. I might as well jam the starter motor in place while I'm at it. Oh, I'm sure there's a few things under the bonnet that I can move around. And then … there are other things I can do ….' Amanda's breathing became more deliberate as her intent focused, and she flexed her fingers. 'Sooo easy, Tempest, sooo easy.' She turned right onto the High Street heading for chez Bottle. The ire was bubbling within her … so much that it was heating the car, and she lowered the windows. That's when it struck her, the silence in the village. Suddenly it was broken by the sounds of the children in the playground behind the houses ….

Chapter 5

༖

ANGER

Amanda was seven years old. Her magical gifts had manifested in a very small way the previous year, and she had been in training with Granny and Grandpa since then. It was a fine day. They had taken her to the park behind the High Street and Trotters Bottom. She liked to play on the swings. It wasn't too energetic and so didn't set off her asthma, as greater exertion could so easily do. However, little Amanda was uncomfortable around her peers. They attended Sunken Madley School, unlike her who was home-educated. To them, she was a rara avis of strange and possibly dangerous plumage. Amanda walked between her grandparents holding a hand of each of them. It made her feel safe.

And she was safe physically, but Amanda was not proof against words. As eight-year-old Gavin Whittle ran past them towards the gate, he shouted,

'Look at that baby, holding gruesome Granny's hands! Weirdy weirdy, Mad Mandy!' Her lips tightened. She pulled her hands from her grandparents, spun on her heel, glared towards him and uttered with furious intensity:

'Understeppith!'

At once the boy tripped and fell. Amanda turned back quickly to see, to her horror, that her grandparents were steadying each other as though against a blast of wind. Both five-a-side football teams on the grass to the left were on their bottoms, three mothers in the playground found themselves on the ground, and two ducks by the pond were looking about in dismay at finding themselves abruptly sitting down. Fortunately, all of the children in the playground had been seated on the swings, slide or jungle gym and had remained unaffected.

As luck would have it, between Amanda and those affected by the spell, there was a large old horse chestnut tree. It was right in the path of the Cadabras, and, quick-thinking, Perran told her to go to it. He and Senara appeared on the other side, and joined together arm in arm as though taking a stroll by themselves. Those affected by the blast radius were picking themselves up, brushing themselves down and looking about in dismay, trying to identify the freak gust that had blown them all clean off their feet.

Amanda kept herself flat against the tree, waiting for her grandparents to reverse course. They went to sit on a bench. Perran pointed out a perfectly ordinary pigeon flying overhead, which distracted some of the onlookers. After a few minutes, they rose and made their progress back to the chestnut. As they neared it, Perran bade her get in front of them quickly. Amanda did so, and they managed to progress unseen to the gate, the car, and home to 26 Orchard Row.

Once home, the unwelcome surprise of what she had done began to tell. Her breathing became shorter and more laboured. Knowing she could go into shock, with a subsequent asthma attack, Perran bundled her up in blankets, lit the fire and cuddled her while Senara made her a hot drink.

'It's all right, *bian*,' he soothed her. 'You've got quite some power under your hat, haven't you?'

'Plenty of power, no control,' called Senara. 'And your eyes, remember what a giveaway they are?'

Amanda looked up anxiously at Grandpa, who said gently, 'They've gone completely brown, love.' It was an unfortunate side-effect of using magic that caused the tiny chestnut islands in the sea of her blue irises to expand.

'Fortunately we were in the open-air so the smell soon wafted away,' he added optimistically. The smell of magic: the odour of sandalwood and the taste of tin. Grandpa had safeguards in the workshop to account for it: solder and incense.

'And where did you find that spell. I didn't think it was in *Wicc'huldol Galdorwrd Nha Koomwrtdreno Aon.*'

Witchcraft: Spells and Potions: 1 was an hereditary grimoire of the Cardiubarns, Senara's unsavoury family. It was written in Wycc'yeth, a magical language, which Amanda was quickly grasping. It had only been weeks since Granny had unearthed it from a secret hiding place in the attic, and, with reservations and certain pages hidden by Perran, introduced it to their little granddaughter.

'It was on a piece of notepaper between the pages. One of Great-great-great-great-great-grandmother Jowanet's,' answered Amanda informatively.

Grandpa tutted. 'We told you never to use spells against humans anyway, but we didn't think that one was in there. I should have guessed something like that would have been, after that nasty lizard spell we found. I'll wager that Jowanet was no more 'n nine when she wrote it out, by the hand-writing.'

'But no harm done. Fortunately, no one was hurt,' said Senara, coming in from the kitchen, with hot chocolate made with coconut milk. '*This* time.'

'Sorry, Granny and Grandpa,' said Amanda in distress,

'I never meant to, not all of those people, just that boy. It's just that I got so … so …'

'Angry,' finished Granny.

Amanda nodded mutely.

'I understand. I understand all too well. And I saw the Cardiubarn Darkside come out in you, and there's a side of them, believe me, that you *don't* want.'

'But,' mitigated Grandpa, 'anger isn't always a bad thing. There's things that happen or go on that we should feel angry about, so that we do good things to put them right.'

'So I did a good thing?' asked Amanda, looking at them more hopefully. 'That boy did such a bad thing; he called you a bad name, Granny, and he said a very mean thing, so I made him fall over, and he stopped shouting. And maybe it'll stop him being mean to someone else,' she added reasonably.

Grandpa chuckled, and helped her take a sip of her hot chocolate, but said, 'While I can't fault your logic, that's not quite what we mean. Why do you think that boy said those things, *bian*?'

'Because he's a bad person?'

'Because he's *afraid*.'

'Of what?'

'Of us, the way we live. It's different you see.'

'You mean I don't have parent parents, and I don't go to school?'

'That's the sort of thing.'

'So what he was doing was like a sort of spell? To protect himself from me? From us?'

'Kind of.'

'But,' said Granny, 'did you think he could do a real spell with those words of his?'

Amanda shook her head.

'But you knew that *you* could do a real spell.'

'Yes,' said Amanda confidently.

'So you used your magic against someone who could not retaliate or defend themselves. And any of those other innocent people could have got hurt falling down, into the bargain. So was it a good thing to do?'

Little Amanda, much struck by this, widened her eyes and shook her head solemnly.

'That's awful. I didn't think, Granny. I just got so… so … angry!'

Senara nodded. Amanda's eyes were filling with tears of remorse.

'Now, now, there's no need to get all emotional and worked up about it. Just take from it this lesson about spell-casting. Are you listening?'

Amanda sniffed and looked earnestly at her grandmother. 'Yes, Granny.'

'Remember this: a witch does not cast in anger. What is the lesson, Ammy?'

Amanda repeated, 'A witch does not cast in anger.'

* * * * *

Amanda murmured, 'A witch does not cast in anger.' Suddenly she turned the steering-wheel to the right, and, instead of heading out of the village, drove down Orchard Row.

'No, Tempest, we're going home.' Her feline companion rolled his eyes in boredom. 'Yes, I know you're disappointed, but you've already done what you've done to his car. No. We're going home, and I'm going to call Uncle Mike.'

Within minutes they were back at the cottage. She closed the door, and, even before removing her jacket and boots reached for her phone.

'Uncle Mike?'

'Ah, if it isn't my favourite newly adopted niece,' replied former Chief Inspector Michael Hogarth.

'Yes, it's me.'

'You don't sound all right. What's happened?'

'Some nasty man on a job was rather vile, but that's not the point. In his rage, he let slip a piece of information that I suspect he was supposed to keep under his hat.'

'Oh?'

'Yes. He said, "You look so innocent, but someone's onto you, got their eye on you, so just you watch out."'

'Ah,' remarked Hogarth with interest.

'Well, the inspector asked me if I felt I was being watched and I just brushed off the suggestion, but now I know I *am*.'

'Yes. Indeed.'

'Should I make some discreet enquiries? Perhaps I could get him in a temper again and see if he reveals more?'

Hogarth chuckled. 'No, that's not something I'd necessarily advise. There may be other ways of getting more out of him. But for the moment let me have a think about the best way to do it. Meanwhile, do and say nothing to show that you took in that piece of information as anything more than a mote in the stream of insults, OK?'

'OK. I shan't be working around him anymore.'

'Good.'

'His assistant, who is a very nice man, is taking over his job at the client's request.'

'Excellent. Leave it with me. Are you all right now?'

'Yes, Tempest avenged me in the most disgraceful fashion. He raked his claws down the man's car and er … baptised his driver's seat!'

Hogarth's laughter rippled down the phone.

Amanda expounded, 'Bottle got in such a temper that he turned *puce*! I had no idea a complexion could *be* that colour.'

'Oh, well done, Tempest. That's my boy. Bravo! I'll bring him something special back from Spain when I come home, and that's a promise. What are you going to do now?'

'I feel much better, but hot bath, dinner, hot chocolate and *School for Scoundrels* I think.'

'OK. Wait for my call, all right?'

'Yes.'

Amanda tapped off and looked down at Tempest ,who, with his sharp ears, had been listening in.

'I wonder what he'll come up with to get more information.'

Her familiar stared back uncommunicatively … but knowingly.

Chapter 6

❧

KARMA

That night, possibly because the Hunter's Moon was roaming the sky, but more likely just because he could, Tempest decided that he no longer cared for Monarch's Superb Salmon Specialité. He could now be tempted only by Empawrer Gourmet Tuna Filet.

Consequently, his dutiful attendant human was obliged to return to the corner shop to change her special order of cat food. This, naturally, could be obtained only from three small and select suppliers in the entire United Kingdom.

With a ding! from the shop door, Amanda entered Mrs Sharma's domain. Tempest had gone with her to ensure that she made the alteration correctly. He and Mrs Sharma regarded one another with respect — to say 'admiration' would be going too far but, — definitely, respect. They understood one another. Mrs Sharma knew that there was more to him than cat, and he knew that she knew and gave her credit for that.

Mrs Sharma kept a store of Orijen Tundra Kitty Treats

for the sole reason that they were the best. She offered them only one at a time and one per visit. In return, anyone who thought of shoplifting or showing Mrs Sharma anything but the utmost courtesy was speedily and summarily taught the value of honesty and good manners.

Amanda approached the counter with the grumpy mobile grey fluff at her ankles and uttered a cheery, 'Good morning, Aunty.' Mrs Sharma returned her greeting affectionately and, gracefully lowering her willowy form, simultaneously reached for the treat packet. Mrs Sharma had babysat Amanda when she was little, her mother enthralling the little girl with tales of India.

'How are you today, dear? Recovered from your shock?'

'My shock? Oh, you mean …?'

'Disgraceful conduct. I never believed all that charm,' remarked Mrs Sharma severely.

'Well, it's all water under the bridge now,' Amanda replied breezily. 'I don't expect we'll cross paths again.'

'What can I do for you, dear?' said Mrs Sharma warmly.

'I'm terribly sorry, but could I, please, change my order of —'

'— No need to tell me. The raj has decreed an amendment to the menu,' discerned Mrs Sharma, with years of experience behind her of the cat's vicissitudes.

Tempest regarded her benevolently. He liked it when his wishes were anticipated and he was addressed with proper respect.

'Yes, please,' replied Amanda apologetically. 'We're back to Empawrer Gourmet Tuna Filet, please.'

Mrs Sharma had a hotline to all of the select cat food suppliers. 'I'll see to it.'

'Tha —'

Ding!

'Good morning, Dennis.'

'Good morning to you, Nalini,' responded Mr Hanley-Page of Vintage Vehicles, gallantly tipping his tweed trilby. 'Amanda. How are you faring after your ordeal? Shall I call the cad out? At twenty paces on the green? Though I do believe dear Miss Armstrong-Witworth is the better shot,' he added impishly.

'Thank you, Mr Hanley-Page, but I don't think that will be necessary,' replied Amanda with a smile.

'I see you've brought your minder.'

Amanda glanced down at her familiar.

'Oh yes, he's very protective.'

'I was addressing the cat,' he quipped.

The ladies chuckled, which affronted Tempest.

'Your cigars were just delivered,' said Mrs Sharma.

'Splendid, splendid,' replied Dennis.

Ding! This heralded the entrance of the village's oldest and most respected resident, Miss Cynthia de Havillande of The Grange. She held the door open as she called into the street in stentorian tones:

'Churchill! Heel! Come along now. Don't dawdle!' An elderly terrier, distracted by a fascinating scent in the gutter, unwillingly wandered in.

'Good morning Nalini, Amanda. Ah, Dennis! Excellent! The very man I wanted to see. About your vehicle —'

'Well, I really must be on my w—' began Mr Hanley-Page.

Ding! Joan the postlady burst in, evidently big with news.

'Oh! Everyone!'

'Are you all right, Joan?' asked Mrs Sharma solicitously.

'I am, thank you, Nalini, but I can't say the same for *other* people.'

The ongoing traffic feud between Miss de Havillande and Mr Hanley-Page was forgotten.

'Whatever has happened?' asked Amanda.

'Well!' said Joan, looking around at her audience. 'I thought I'd give the new salon a try. It's just opened, and I thought, "Support the local shops," you know how you do?'

'Yes,' agreed Dennis, 'quite right.'

'So,' continued Joan, 'in I went to make an appointment. They seem nice enough. A brother and sister. She's the older one, the more qualified, and he's got the business side of it with his background, and it's been a dream of hers.'

'Yes, Joan, but what happened?' enquired Cynthia patiently.

'So, there I was at the reception while we arranged a day and time, when the phone rang.'

Joan paused for effect.

'Yes?' encouraged Dennis.

'And, of course, it was for the funeral parlour as was. You know, Mr Blackaby's. Well, it was there for 30 years at least, and they hadn't changed the number but then why would they?'

'Quite,' agreed Cynthia.

'As I was standing right there, I couldn't help but hear the caller. Not intentionally you understand.'

'Of course not,' soothed Mrs Sharma.

'The voice said, "Mr Blackaby?" and of course, Donna, that's the hairdresser, said, "I'm sorry, but the funeral parlour is no longer here."'

'But I said, "Hold on, please. I recognise that voice. Is it all right if I have a word?" And she hands over the phone, and I say, "Deirdre? Is that you?" and she says, "Yes. Joan?" And I say, "Are you all right, dear?" and she says, "Yes, but I need funeral services." "Whatever for?" I say. And she tells me … he's kicked the bucket. She was calling from the hospital!'

'Who?' the assembled cast asked in unison.

'Horace. Horace Bottle!'

'But … but how?' exclaimed Amanda. 'I saw him only

yesterday.'

'What time would that have been?' asked Joan.

'He left the house where I'm working at about 3 – 3.30.'

'Yes, that would be right. She said he was driving down the A1000 when he had a heart attack, the doctor said. And drove into a lamppost. It was curtains. Someone stopped, of course, but he was a goner. Just like that!'

'Oh dear,' said Amanda penitently. 'He was in a lather when he left. I'd never seen a complexion that colour before.'

'Well, it finished him,' stated Joan.

'Poor Mrs Bottle.'

'Oh, she didn't sound "poor Mrs Bottle",' Joan replied. 'Glad to be rid of his foul temper, I shouldn't wonder. I asked what she'd do now, and she said she's got the death certificated all right and tight, and she's seeing a solicitor friend of Erik's this very morning to get probate started. "As soon as I get it," she says, "I'm putting the house on the market. I've got two weeks compassionate leave from work, and as soon as I've got his things to the charity shop, I'm off to my sister's in Derbyshire." You know? Where she comes from. "I've had an offer to go into partnership with her," she says. Yes, and she was only holding off for that husband of hers, and no way was he going to budge and move up there for her. So there! What do you think of that?'

'So she's leaving?' Amanda confirmed.

'Yes, I think she's planning to be gone by this afternoon.'

Oh no, said Amanda to herself. How will I question her about what Horace said yesterday, about someone watching me? Or question *him* for that matter! It was all very inconvenient.

'So there you go. All's well that ends well,' Joan summed up.

'Except for Horace Bottle,' commented Dennis wryly.

'I wouldn't like to comment,' said Cynthia with equal dryness.

'Karma,' pronounced Mrs Sharma judicially.

'I don't think anyone will argue with that, Nalini,' agreed Joan.

'Dear, dear,' murmured Amanda. 'Well, I must be off. Goodbye, everyone. Come on, Tempest.' Once outside the shop, she added, 'We need privacy!'

They hurried back to the Astra and bolted for the cottage. Amanda had no sooner shut the front door behind Tempest than she pulled out her phone and tapped the number.

'Amanda?'

'Uncle Mike!'

'Whatever is the matter?'

'Something dreadful has happened.'

'Calm down and tell me all about it,' urged Hogarth gently.

'Horace Bottle is dead, and his wife is leaving today. I won't be able to question either of them again!'

'I see. Did his demise take place in questionable circumstances?'

'I think it might have been my fault,' Amanda replied anxiously.

'Dear me. Did you brain him with the lead piping in the kitchen or the candlestick in the library?'

That surprised a smile out of Amanda.

'Neither, but he was in such a temper when he left, after what happened, that he had a heart attack while he was driving and went into a lamppost.'

'How inconsiderate of him,' condoled Hogarth. 'My dear, you cannot be blamed for someone flying into a pucker when you point out, ever so nicely no doubt, that they have purloined one of your tools.'

'No. No, you're right, Uncle Mike.'

'However, it does mean that that route to further information has now been cul-de-sacked. Alternative measures are required that I shall now arrange. Leave it with me. There is nothing more for you to do. Enjoy your Horace-Bottle-free day, Amanda. Besides which, if anyone is to be blamed it is not you, is it? The Furry Fury is the impenitent culprit.'

'Thank you, Uncle Mike. I do feel better talking to you.'

'Good.'

'Sorry to bother you with this when you're on holiday.'

'Not at all. On the contrary, I shall enjoy setting the next train in motion,' he said with delight. 'Off you go to work now, my dear.'

'Yes, bye for now.'

'Cheerio.'

Hogarth had been standing on the decking and now sat on one of the loungers. Vera came out with tea.

'You look pleased with yourself,' she remarked affectionately, handing him the cup, and putting the biscuits down in front of him.

'Ah good. Hobnobs. You are a princess of sisters. Yes. I am pleased. Bottle has departed this life, and his widow is departing posthaste for The Midlands. There is now no reason for me not to follow the course of action that has been appealing to me for the past 18 hours. All right if I invite a guest?'

'Is it who I think it is?' asked Vera, shrewdly.

'It is.'

'He'll be very welcome. I'll get the other spare room ready. Sure he'll say yes?'

'I can be very persuasive,' said Hogarth.

But, on this occasion, he didn't have to be.

Chapter 7

༂

THOMAS IS PERTURBED

On the previous Saturday evening, just four days ago, after a late night finishing off some admin in the police station at the small port of Parhayle on the Cornish south coast, Detective Inspector Thomas Trelawney had received a domestic SOS from his mother.

'Darling, I'm so sorry to ask, and you can say no, but are you busy tomorrow?'

'Er, I don't have to be,' replied her son helpfully.

'Could you possibly come up to London? Marcus has let me down. He was supposed to help me to get the old dining suite out of the attic for the Heart Foundation to come and collect in the afternoon. They're doing a special run, but his mother is insisting that he join the family gathering, as his sister is suddenly coming down and … well!'

'Of course, Mum,' said Thomas affably. 'I'll throw some things into a bag and come now.'

'But it's 8 o'clock.'

'I'll be there around midnight, and there won't be much traffic.'

'You're an angel.'

'You don't have to wait up. I'll let myself in.'

'Of course I'll wait up. I'll have cocoa and shortbread biscuits ready for you.'

Thomas chuckled. 'You know the way to your son's heart.'

'So I should hope,' rejoined his mother cheerfully.

'See you presently.'

The following day, the furniture was removed from the attic at Penelope's house in Crouch End, North London, and successfully collected. Companionably, she and Thomas cooked dinner: roast beef, Yorkshire puddings, roast potatoes, carrots and parsnips with peas, cabbage and gravy. Penelope opened a bottle of Super-Tuscan Chianti.

Thomas inspected the label.

'Good heavens, Ma-maa, bit extravagant, isn't it?'

'Not at all, my lamb, I got a case of six at a discount.'

'Hm, I shall have to help you move furniture more often!'

After dinner, replete, washed up and contented, mother and son collapsed on the sofa, pushed the fair-trade coffee table a little away from them, and talked of meals shared in the past.

Thomas slid down in his seat, and they leaned companionably against one another. Penelope's hair was blonder than her son's light brown but it was easy to see where he got his hazel eyes. The height he owed to his father and his gentleness and courtesy too. His incisive mind could be traced to both parents, but cultivated by himself in a scientific, practical and deductive direction since the age of twelve.

Thomas was one of the best police interviewers in his area, and if there was one thing he knew, it was how to pick his time. The time was now. He broached a sensitive subject.

'Puddings, Mum.'

'Yes, love?'

'Do you think some time you could make me jam roly-poly? It's not that I don't appreciate the spun-sugar basket of passion fruit and pineapple compôte. But I do like the old-fashioned stodgy stuff once in a while.'

'You and your jam roly-poly. You've loved that since you were a tot!'

'Really? I don't remember.'

'And spotted dick and marmalade roll.'

'I did?'

'Oh my word, yes!' recalled his mother, affectionately.

'Mum .... '

'Hmm?'

'What was I like?' Thomas asked tentatively.

'When you were little?'

'Yes. You know I have practically no memory of anything before I was about ten.'

'Oh, you were adorable,' Penelope answered at once. 'Even as a baby, you usually slept through the night as long as you knew your father and I were OK. If we were restless, you'd wake up. It was very sweet. And you always seemed to know if I was sad or worried, and you used to comfort me, put your little arms around my neck and your head against mine.'

'I did?'

'Yes, darling. And once or twice you even verbalised it, although you didn't say many words yet. I remember this one occasion. There you were with your tea ...'

'Tea?'

'Oh yes, you loved your tea from a very early age. I suppose I shouldn't have let you have any, knowing now, as we do, how much caffeine there in it! But there you are. You used to drink mine or your father's, so we gave you your own. And then as soon as your tiny fingers were strong and dexterous enough to hold a cup, if I put your tea in your beaker, you cried.'

'Oh dear,' Thomas remarked apologetically.

'You'd have water, milk or juice in your beaker, but tea had to be in a cup, and no ordinary cup either, your special cup.'

'Good heavens, what a demanding child!'

'Oh no, it was no trouble really. It was the only thing you were ever insistent about, and I liked to please you.'

'Thank you, Mum. So what cup was this?'

'Wait … I'll go and get it. In a minute. But, first, let me tell you about that day.'

'That day?'

'Yes. You see, your father was very late, and I was getting worried about him. He'd usually find a way to call, and eventually, he had a car phone, you know. Anyway, you wouldn't go to sleep, and there we were in the sitting room at the house, and I made tea for us both. And there you sat, staring into your cup — oh, it used to fascinate you when I poured the milk in; the patterns it would make. You'd take a sip and gaze at the tea, and you liked tea leaves too, and you'd drain the cup, and, — anyway, there you sat staring into your cup, and suddenly you said, "Mummy. Daddy OK". Oh, it was so endearing. And he *was*, you know. He came home about an hour later, and he'd been stuck in dreadful traffic and couldn't get near a phone box.'

'I'm glad that I was a solicitous toddler to make up for my fussiness.'

'Oh, you were an angel,' said his mother, ruffling his hair and getting up. Her still lissome form, clad in a black yoga outfit, moved toward the kitchen. 'Now let me find that cup …. It was one of a pair,' she called from the pantry. 'Your great-grandmother's. Eggshell china ….'

Penelope came back into the room in triumph. 'Here!

A bit dusty but …,' she wiped it with a piece of kitchen roll and handed it to Thomas. 'It's so fragile that it's a miracle you didn't break it, but you never so much as cracked the glaze.'

'Hm,' said Thomas receiving it from her. It wasn't familiar at first. There was a clank from the kitchen where utensils disturbed in the search had keeled over.

'Oh!' exclaimed Penelope, and headed off to restore order, leaving Thomas with his old friend. On an impulse, he slid off the sofa onto the floor in front of the coffee table, to child height. He cupped his hands around the delicate porcelain.

In a flash, he was there. Tiny hands, the warmth of the liquid, the still surface at first reflecting only the ceiling. And then … the picture formed … there *he* was … his father … but not in a car as he'd told Thomas's mother, but in the house, the old house, Flamgoyne, seat of Thomas's paternal grandmother's powerful family. Kytto, his father, was with the old woman and the other men in black that Thomas had seen in a dream and then remembered. His father was fine. He looked intense but calm.

Thomas came back to the present with a gasp. How on earth had he been able to do that? His father was, as Thomas's little self had said, 'OK'. But Kytto Trelawney had not told the truth to his wife about where he was. And it had all been playing out in the surface of the tea, as clear as day… and Thomas had seen it … how? Why? He didn't believe in all that mumbo jumbo paranormal nonsense. It must have been his imagination. His hands shook as he placed the cup on the table and sat back up on the sofa as his mother came back in.

'Are you all right, darling? You look as white as a sheet,' said Penelope, concerned.

'I'm fine,' Thomas assured her with a smile. 'I was just thinking how happy we all were, and what a shame it —'

'Water under the bridge, my sweet.'

'Yes, of course, and it was all for the best. I got used to

it. And you know, in the end, it was better having two homes and you being happy, rather than one where you weren't. And Dad seemed to relax after. He wasn't so … so scared. Maybe because he knew that the person he loved most in all the world was safe from his family.'

'Oh yes, you were the apple of his eye.'

'Not me, Mum. You. You were safe in London.'

His mother, for once, was lost for words. She plumped up the cushions on the sofa and rearranged the throw. Finally, she said,

'Well, we are where we are. And look how fine you've grown up to be. Your father and I are both very proud of you, you know. You've done very well for yourself, and you were right about the career you've chosen, in spite of our reservations.'

The diversion in the conversation had calmed Thomas considerably. His hands were steady once more.

'Would you like some tea in that cup?' asked Penelope.

'No,' he said at once, then more slowly, 'a mug will do fine for me, thanks, Mum.'

He followed her out to the kitchen, as though to put some distance between him and the egg-shell china on the coffee table.

-

Chapter 8

੭

PENELOPE ENQUIRES

'You do seem to enjoy your work,' observed Thomas's mother, pouring tea into each of two British Museum mugs. 'Oh, I know it has boring bits but … it suits you, Thomas.'

'Thank you, Mum.'

'How's your witness?'

'Which one?' asked Thomas.

'That girl a few miles north of here that's so important to you.'

'She's, er … fine.'

'What's her name? I can't keep calling her "that girl". It's not polite,' stated Penelope.

'You don't have to call her anything,' Thomas replied firmly. 'It's an ongoing investigation, and you're not —'

'Yes, yes,' she agreed, handing him his tea, 'but, come on, she's not on witness protection, is she? Or working for MI5? You don't have to give me her real name, any name will do,' cajoled his mother.

'Of course not. Oh, all right,' capitulated Thomas long-sufferingly. 'Amanda. Her name is Amanda. Thanks for the tea, Mum.'

'Amanda,' Penelope repeated thoughtfully. 'Latin for "loved"… and is she?'

Thomas considered. 'Actually, yes, I rather think she is … you should have seen the villagers looking me over like a bull at the county fair when I was in the local with her! Sizing me up and most likely finding me wanting!'

His mother chuckled. Thomas continued,

'The two who own the local coffee shop obviously dote on her. Even one of the local toddlers greeted her like a long lost friend.'

'That speaks well of her,' remarked Penelope, leading the way back into the sitting room. 'Is she pretty?'

'Well, that's an irrelevant question!' countered Thomas, taken off-guard by the enquiry. 'Whether a witness is … is neither here nor there.'

'Well, is she?' his mother pressed home, sitting on the sofa.

'I don't know,' he replied testily. 'No … yes ….' Why did he always think of her as she had looked when he first met her? The first two times …. 'She's usually in dusty overalls with clunky work boots, and her hair done up in a messy plait, and wearing glasses,' Thomas said, taking a seat beside his mother. But then suddenly, Amanda came to his mind as he'd seen her the night of the storm …. 'Lili Marlene,' he murmured.

'Lili Marlene?' asked Penelope. 'She looks like Marlene Dietrich?'

'No, no, she …. more of a pixie-face, more a touch of Monroe perhaps … no, that's perhaps … but … all I mean is, that she can look really quite ….'

'Quite?'

'Nice,' he ended lamely.

'Nice?'

'Never mind that,' Thomas, adjured his parent adamantly, realising he had been led down a path he had had no intention of exploring. Ever. Penelope, surprised at how much data she had managed to extract, diplomatically changed her tack.

'What is she a witness to? A murder?'

'It's a cold case.'

'Was it in the papers?' enquired Penelope, tucking her feet under her.

'Yes. Actually, it was the case that put me on the road to becoming a detective. I read about it on the train here. I must have been about twelve at the time.'

'Well, if it was in the papers, surely you can remind me of it. I can work out that it was in Cornwall, if you read about it in the rag on the way here, and you've given me a year to go by.'

'All right,' agreed Thomas. 'It was the minibus; the family whose minibus went over a cliff.'

'I don't remember that.'

'All of them were killed.'

'Well, accidents do happen,' said Penelope philosophically.

'But the cause was never identified,' countered Thomas. 'Someone reported something on the road at the time but … the family didn't die as a result of the injuries incurred in the crash.'

'What *did* they die of?' asked Penelope, her curiosity aroused.

'Unknown.'

'How strange!' Penelope mulled it over, then asked, 'What has Amanda got to do with it?'

'It was her family.'

'But she survived?'

'Yes, because she and her grandparents, who were supposed to join the party, didn't go. The entire family was wiped out except for the three of them.'

'Good heavens. But that was about 30 years ago. How come you've got the case?'

'It was passed to me by Chief Inspector Hogarth before he retired,' Thomas explained.

'I see. He must have thought it was important,' surmised Penelope.

'I didn't think so when he gave me the file. But since then ... I've begun to think ...'

Penelope looked at her son carefully, and hazarded, 'Thomas, is this somehow personal?'

'Yes, Mum,' he said, seeming to stare into an unseen distance, 'I rather think it might be.'

Penelope didn't like to see her son so perturbed and said comfortingly, 'Well, you know you're welcome to stay here any time, and for as long as you want to, when you're coming and going from wherever your interviewee is.'

'Thanks, Mum, I know,' he said with a smile.

'And if it means I get to see more of my son, then I've to thank the young lady,' his mother announced cheerily. 'I take it she is? Young?'

'Mum, you're incorrigible,' he replied, shaking his head. 'Thirty-something. No, not young and yet .... she'd pass for 20 when she's presentable, and then again, there's something child-like about her. Smart and yet with flashes of naiveté ... I suppose it comes of always having lived with her grandparents in that village ...'

'Well, *you* look good for 40! I wouldn't put you a day over 30,' stated Penelope hearteningly.

'Thank you, mother,' replied her son in failing accents. 'You comfort me.'

She laughed. 'Nonsensical boy!'

'Would you mind if I had some coffee and drove back to Parhayle tonight? I've only had the one glass of wine and I'd like to be in the station on time tomorrow.'

'Of course not, darling.'

In the silence of the car, the October night mild around him and the moonlight reassuringly bright, Thomas Trelawney wound south, anticlockwise, on the M25 London orbital highway, wondering if he should have told his mother who Amanda's family was. He knew her well, and by tomorrow she'd have unearthed the story, found out where it was printed, and would probably have obtained a copy of the newspaper.

And she'd have a name. A name she wouldn't like: Cardiubarn.

They were long-standing enemies and only occasional uneasy allies of the Flamgoynes. The two great Cornish houses, Flamgoyne and Cardiubarn Hall, stood staring at one another across a bleak space of Bodmin Moor and the cold grey waters of the Dozmary Pool.

'Cardiubarn' linked the case to Flamgoyne, and the name Flamgoyne to him. Flamgoyne, the clan that had divided his parents. Their uncanny gifts and hold over his father had rent them in two, and given Thomas, thenceforth, a home in London in the holidays and one in Cornwall during school term. No … his mother wasn't going to like it at all.

However, Thomas had more troubling matters on his mind, and on the M3, the highway heading west to Cornwall, the memory of the cup danced in his mind. He pushed it away, insisting aloud, 'It doesn't matter; whatever I could do then, I can't do now.'

But that only begged the question, 'Why and how did I stop being able to do that?' He was a sensitive, intuitive child … wasn't that what Hogarth always said about him though, as an adult? How much he trusted Thomas's intuition? He had to talk to Mike Hogarth! But his mentor and closest friend was in Spain, uncertain of when he'd return. If only he could talk to Mike … the one person who ... Mike ….

Chapter 9

ൟ

CLASS

On Tuesday when the phone rang, and the invitation to Spain came, Thomas responded will alacrity and relief. That evening he was on the plane flying south.

Amanda went south too, but by car and only a few miles from Sunken Madley to Muswell Hill, for her weekly dinner with Aunt Amelia.

She had fully meant to ask about the … what was it?... the apple? No … apport. Yes, the apport. But with all the excitement surrounding the affair of Horace Bottle, it went clean out her head.

After a morning's work on the banister rail, more scraping and boiling away with toxic chemicals of the old varnish and paint, Amanda needed some fresh air. She took her lunch box, with Tempest in attendance, to the bench on the green. From there she was in sight, if not natural, certainly with binoculars, of the rector who grabbed a banana from the rectory fruit bowl and hurried out join her parishioner.

'Hello, Amanda,' Jane greeted her enthusiastically.

'Hello, Rector.'

'Shall we lunch together?'

'Yes, of course,' responded Amanda, politely making room for her by sliding herself and Tempest further along the bench. He inevitably chose to climb onto his human's lap, where he had better access to the lunch box and could scan it for desirable food items.

Amanda wisely extracted a piece of smoked salmon she'd brought for him, closed the flat lid of the box and placed the food on top of it. She was hoping it would occupy her familiar long enough for her to engage in uninterrupted conversation with the rector, who would undoubtedly have some diplomatically couched cause for complaint to broach regarding the unruly feline.

She prepared herself, but unnecessarily.

'I have news, Amanda!' said Jane with delight. 'Thanks to a kind recommendation, I have found dance teachers for us. Well, teach*er*, I should say; Victor doesn't do much in the way of dancing now because of his limp, but he helps Majolica.'

'Majolica?'

'They're Majolica and Victor Woodberry.'

'Does he have a dance-related injury,' asked Amanda solicitously.

'Well, he is 82, although, you wouldn't know it to look at him.'

'So his wife must be —'

'Oh, she's considerably younger. In her 60s I'd say, but very fit and able. And experienced, of course. They actually have a dance studio built onto their house and hold private lessons and workshops there. Though, of course, that would not do for us, just adding to the expense and involving travel, although not far. But still, we want the class to be here in the village, on the spot that we're raising money for.'

'I agree, that does make sense,' replied Amanda. 'When you say not far ...?'

'Romping!'

'Romping-in-the-Heye?'

'Yes, I know, just up the road. So it's very convenient for them. And consequently they're charging a generously low rate for the classes. As it's for the church.'

'How did you find out about them?'

'Oh, word of mouth. I always think a personal recommendation carries so much more weight than something you find online, but, then again, if there are testimonials on the website, that goes a long way.'

'Yes, I thi—'

'Ja-aaane! Amandaaaa!'

The two women on the bench exchanged speaking glances, then turned and rose politely at the approach of their illustrious fellow villager.

'Hello, Miss de Havillande,' said Amanda courteously.

'Hello, Cynthia,' Jane greeted her parishioner warmly.

'Good afternoon to you both. Churchill! Heel!' The terrier was snuffling by the pond. 'So you found someone suitable? I trust that they *are* suitable. I hear some of these *tango* instructors are not at all to be trusted around the ladies!'

'This is a mature married couple, Cynthia,' replied the rector, 'and they will be teaching a whole range of classes. And Mr Woodberry is 82 and I am quite sure will treat the ladies professionally.'

'Woodberry?'

'Yes. Majolica and Victor Woodberry.'

'Hmm ... now, where do I know that name?'

'Oo-oo!' came a voice from the other side of the lane.

'Hello, Sylvia,' Amanda hailed the lollipop lady. She was so called because of the disc-shaped stop-sign on a pole that she carried to stop the traffic when escorting the local school children across the road. Although not with as many summers to her credit as Miss de Havillande, at only 78, Sylvia was on her fourth husband and respected, even by the teenagers in the village, for her experience in areas generally thought to be outside Cynthia's purview.

''Ello, ladies all,' replied Sylvia, ruffling her short pale blonde curls. 'So it's settled then? It's goin' ahead? The classes?'

'Yes, Sylvia,' confirmed the rector joyfully. 'I hope I may count you among our happy number?'

'Oh, me and my Jim'll be there like a shot. Always fond of dancin', we was. So who's this couple who's going to teach us?'

'Their name is Woodberry. Victor and Majolica.'

'Majolica?' asked Sylvia slowly, with creased brow and note of suspicion in her voice. 'Where from?'

'Romping,' replied Jane.

'Ha!' replied Sylvia. 'Well, if it's the Majolica, *I* know, she wasn't always Woodberry.'

'You know her?'

'Hmm. Majolica Flitton, as was. Yes, and no better than she should be!'

'I've never understood what that meant,' said Jane.

'I think,' said Amanda diplomatically, 'that it means she was considered to have elastic principles in the romantic department.'

'Very nicely put, Amanda.' Miss de Havillande commended her.

'So she's back in Rompin', is she?' asked Sylvia, hand on hip.

'Yes,' replied Jane, 'she and her husband have a house and studio there. In Suidae Row.'

'Oo, got 'erself very nicely set up, I daresay. Well, I shall withhold my judgement,' said Sylvia inaccurately. 'She may have changed. She'll be my teacher, and I shall treat 'er with the respect that she deserves, don't you worry now.'

'Good. Well, I'm sure we're all very appreciative of having teachers,' said Jane pacifically.

'Not but what,' intoned Gordon French, the retired headmaster of Sunken Madley School, who had joined the ensemble largely unnoticed, 'as I have mentioned to Amanda before, one must be cautious of strangers, people who,' and he punctuated the words with taps of his stick, 'are … not … Village. Especially when there is such an influx of them.'

'Only two have actually moved in, Mr French,' Amanda pointed out respectfully.

'When do the classes start?' called Dennis Hanley-Page, who had driven up and was parking his red 1959 MG sports car, hood down as it was a dry day.

'Hello, Dennis,' they greeted him.

'Ladies,' he replied touching the peak of his Harris tweed patchwork cap deferentially.

'Saturday week,' said the rector, in answer to his question.

'Guy Fawkes night weekend?'

'Yes, the Sharmas are providing fireworks for after the first class, and I expect we'll have the bonfire on the green.'

'No, that will be on the actual night,' corrected Miss de Havillande.

'Oh, very well but we can have sparklers,' conceded the rector. 'I thought it the best day; people are free, and it's not like Sunken Madley is a thriving centre of nightlife.'

'There's always Barnet. It's so close,' commented Amanda.

'Seriously?' said Joan, the matronly postlady who'd arrived unseen in the intensity of the conversation.

'Hello, Joan,' came the uneven chorus.

'Hi, all. Seriously, dear? You'd go to Barnet for a

Saturday night?'

'Well, no, not actually personally,' Amanda answered awkwardly, 'and I'm not being a snob or anything. After all, there are some nice —'

'The point is,' intoned Jane, coming to her rescue, 'that I think most people will be happy to spare a couple of hours on a Saturday to get out of the house and learn something new.'

'There'll be socials, won't there? Dances?' asked Sylvia.

'Yes, indeed there will,' the rector assured her. 'Once a month to start with. The first will be on 17th November, at the Feast of St Ursula of the Orchard, another for a Christmas Dance, and, of course, one for New Year's Eve.'

'It'll be fun!' said Joan excitedly.

'It'll be a lark!' exclaimed Sylvia.

'Very pleasant,' agreed Cynthia.

'Delightful,' concurred Dennis, 'and an opportunity to get my dinner jacket out.'

'Excuse me, please, may I chime in?' asked an unfamiliar feminine voice.

They opened the circle to discover the petite, wiry form of Donnatella Weathersby, the new hairdresser.

'Ah, here's one of our new villagers,' said Jane, welcomingly. 'This is Donna. She and her brother were kind enough to drop into the rectory to introduce themselves.'

'Hello,' said the other ladies.

'Good afternoon, Miss,' added Dennis and Mr French.

'Hello, everyone,' said the newcomer. 'I hope it's OK that I came up like this. Only, you're talking about the new classes and dancing, right?'

'Yes.'

'Well, I'm offering to do anyone's hair on any of the dance nights for half price. Anyone in the village.'

They murmured approval. 'That's very neighbourly of

you,' said Jane supportively.

'Well, I want to do something for the village,' explained Donna, clasping her hands nervously. 'Everyone has been really nice and welcoming, so I want to do something in return — I mean *we*, of course, my brother and I. You're all such lovely people.'

This was Amanda and Dennis's first sight of Donna. Neat, high-waisted, turned up jeans and peasant blouse proclaimed the 1940s fan. The long rippling dark hair artfully highlighted in auburn shades bore testimony to the coiffeur's skill. It rose in a high wave curving back in a defined curl on her forehead. Brown eyes with winged eyeliner gazed frankly out at them. Rose red lips smiled beneath a Roman nose.

'We'll spread the word,' said the rector warmly. 'We'll see you on 3rd then for the first class? You and your brother?'

'Of course. Maybe, not both of us as it's a Saturday and the salon might be busy. But yes, of course, we'll try.'

'Do your best,' commanded Cynthia.

'We will.' She turned to Amanda. 'Are you … er … Cadabra Restoration and Repairs?'

'It's the overalls, isn't it?' replied Amanda, with good-natured humour. 'A dead give-away.'

Donna laughed. 'Well, Mrs Sharma did point me in your direction. We have some wooden-framed antique mirrors that were damaged in transit, and the insurance people referred me to you as the local repairer.'

'Oh yes, I do quite a lot of insurance work,' Amanda assured her.

'Would you mind popping over some time to give us a quote? Any time is good.'

'Of course. In the meantime …' Amanda reached into her breast pocket, '… here's my card.'

'That's fantastic,' said Donna, taking it.

'Not at all.'

'Thank you to both you and your brother for your generous discount offer,' the rector repeated.

'Our pleasure. I must be getting back now,' Donna excused herself.

'Of course,' said Cynthia.

They bid her farewell politely and regarded her retreat, manifestly reserving judgement on their new neighbour.

Chapter 10

೪

FLAMGOYNE AND CARDIUBARN

'Rector, how much will the dance classes be?' asked Amanda practically, distracting the ensemble from their speculations about the new hairdresser in Sunken Madley.

'Just £5 each,' Jane answered.

'Oo, that's good,' approved Joan. 'They charge more than that in most places.'

'And I'll be suggesting a £5 donation toward the new hall.'

'I expect we can stretch to that.'

'Thank you, Joan. And it'll be a chance for the two at the salon to meet the village, and for the village to meet them.'

'Has anyone here other than the rector seen the brother yet?' asked Sylvia.

'No, ' answered Miss de Havillande, 'but Nalini says he seems gentlemanly.'

'Oh, I'd say he was a decent sort,' opined Dennis. 'It can't be easy for them settling into a new community.'

'We must do our best to make them welcome,' urged the rector.

They indicated acquiescence.

'Just think, Amanda,' said Sylvia, brightly, 'the brother might be a *possible*, and other people wanting to learn might come from far and wide; a chance for you to meet some nice men. Might put your young man's nose out o' joint, but it'd give 'im some competition since he's not making 'is move.'

'What young man?' asked Amanda wearily.

'You know! That Ryan Ford up at Madley Towers.'

'He's not my young ma —.'

'— No, no, 'er *other* one,' Joan corrected her friend.

'Oh no, there's no chance there, I don't think,' responded Sylvia with certainty. 'After all, he's gone ba—'

'— Yes, that was a shame,' commented Jane, 'we all liked him.'

'Yes, we did indeed,' concurred Dennis.

'He's not my... he *wasn't* my young ma —' began Amanda.

'— And that other one, he wasn't 'alf 'andsome, wasn't 'e?' said Sylvia.

'He was,' agreed Jane.

'But he was too flighty,' remarked Joan.

'No,' insisted the lollipop lady. 'I mean the one that's got his eye on 'er *now*. I like the look of him.'

'Who are you talking about?' Amanda asked mystified.

'Your nice policemen. The inspector!'

'He's not my young man, I do most sincerely assure you.'

'Oo, come now,' said Sylvia, looking at her waggishly.

'And look at the time, ladies!' Amanda urged them, getting up and edging away. 'I really must get back to work. And why don't you go and share the news about the classes with Mrs Sharma? I'm sure she and Mr Sharma would come along.'

'Oh, she already knows,' said Joan.

'*She* told *us*,' added Sylvia.

'Well, see you Saturday week then, if not before.' Amanda hurried off knowing that it would undoubtedly be 'before'. What was she thinking, taking her lunch to the village green?

* * * * *

It had been late when the plane landed at Barcelona airport. Later still when the cab Hogarth had arranged delivered Trelawney to Vera and Harry's villa, some miles south along the coast.

The couple made Thomas welcome, but Vera perceived he was anxious to hold a colloquy with her brother. She made him comfortable, showed him his room and told him where things were in the kitchen. Then, together with Harry, she tactfully left Thomas and Mike alone on the moonlit deck with tea, Hobnobs and shortcake.

Hogarth gave Trelawney a few moments then prompted,

'Come on, lad, out with it. What's troubling you? It's not like you to snap up an invitation that takes you away from your beloved station desk.'

Thomas acknowledged the truth of his friend's remark with a grin. Then, relapsing into seriousness, related, as factually as he could, the conversation and strange experience he had at his mother's house. At the end of it, he picked up his tea, as though he now needed it.

Hogarth heard him out and nodded. 'You want to know how come you could do that?' he said coming to the point.

'Well, yes. That isn't normal, is it?'

'Hm, probably more little children can do things that are regarded as "not normal" than we give credit for. Only they can't tell us, and we all too soon start telling *them* what's normal, and what they *should* be doing and seeing and hearing, and they soon learn to keep their mouths shut, and, soon after, to forget what they once could do. But no. It's not normal. Except, in your case, given your antecedents, it is.'

'Flamgoynes?'

'There's a gift, you might say, that runs in your father's maternal family.'

Thomas looked at him enquiringly. Hogarth explained,

'You might call it insight, intuition, divination. Seeing things in liquid, tea leaves is one way of mediating or amplifying that insight. Now, not every Flamgoyne would have it, and not everyone who has it is a Flamgoyne, but —'

'Wait, Mike. The old woman and the men in my dream, they kept asking my father about me! I would be in the house — yes, at Flamgoyne! — I was a child, and I'd be standing or sitting apart from the adults, but I could hear her, my grandmother, I suppose, asking my father … asking … "*Can* he …?" And my father shaking his head. There were asking if I had … I could do …'

'What, in fact, you *could* do,' said Mike.

'Do you think my father knew?' asked Thomas.

'I'd say yes. You see, he'd know what to look for. Your mother wouldn't, being a Normal. I think he kept the Flamgoyne gift from her.'

'Yes, she hated all of that stuff,' corroborated Thomas. He fell silent, processing what was, to him, an awful truth. Finally, he said, 'So I had it.'

'So it would seem,' Hogarth responded gently.

Trelawney's detective mind switched back on.

'So *where* did it go? *Why* did it stop? And why didn't I *remember* I had it until Sunday night?'

'I don't think it went entirely,' said Hogarth. 'Your intuition has always been exceptionally strong. Oh, you can call it "hunches" or "going with your gut", but I saw it early on, Thomas, and I've always trusted it, even over my own judgement.'

Something fell into place in Trelawney's mind.

'That's why you sent me to the Cadabras, why you passed that cold case to me.'

'Yes,' admitted Hogarth.

'Everything seems to come back to them … to her. To Amanda Cadabra,' Trelawney mused. A thought presented itself. 'If the Flamgoynes and the Cardiubarns were such enemies, why did they intermarry? Miss Cadabra remembered two sets of ancestral portraits that her great-grandmother Cardiubarn showed her when she was tiny. Every one of whose subjects came to a grisly end at the hands of a relative, as far as I can tell. But I distinctly remember two Flamgoyne-Cardiubarn marriages.'

Hogarth remained silent, letting Trelawney follow his mental lead.

'What is the Cardiubarn gift?' Thomas asked. 'Do they have one?'

'Oh, they have one all right,' Hogarth answered, leaning forward to add hot water to the teapot.

'What is it?' urged Thomas.

'By rights, I should make you seek out this information yourself, but I'm not entirely sure Senara and Perran would have told Amanda.' He gave the pot a stir and said,

'Spell-weavers.'

Thomas nodded and said, 'I have a theory.'

'Yes, I have the same one,' responded Hogarth.

Trelawney's bloodhound spirit was up. 'I have to get back to Sunken Madley. I need Miss Cadabra to remember the rest of the portraits at Cardiubarn Hall!'

'Yes, but not tonight,' Hogarth replied firmly. 'I'm not driving you to the airport in the small hours of the morning. Have your tea, go to bed and sleep on it all.'

Thomas smiled and relaxed back in his chair.

'Here. Have some shortcake,' Mike recommended.

'You're right, of course,' agreed Thomas, accepting one of his favourite biscuits, and dunking it in his tea..

'And I haven't got round to work. Which is why I asked you here,' added Hogarth.

'Oh, yes,' said his young friend with interest.

'Tomorrow, Thomas, tomorrow.'

'Very well,' he conceded. 'But tell me this — and I'm still not at all comfortable with the thought of having … powers of … of … as a child — but, hypothetically, how could a child like that *lose* its powers and its *memory* of those powers?'

Hogarth poured himself another cup of tea, then said, 'Why don't you ask Miss Cadabra?'

Comprehending that this was as much as he was going to get, Thomas assented, 'All right.'

'But if you do follow this line of enquiry, and I think you should, be prepared for answers which you may not like. You may not like at all,' Hogarth warned him.

At that, Thomas fell silent for a moment, then said slowly,

'Yes, I may not like it. But I'd rather know the truth.'

'And there's another thing: if you want useful answers from Miss Cadabra you must make her feel comfortable giving them.'

'What do you mean? How am I to do that? How am I to know what makes her comfortable or otherwise? I'm not psych—'

'Not psychic?' replied Hogarth with amusement. 'It seems you once were, Thomas, and I think you've got enough left for the purpose. Use your intuition!'

Chapter 11

୭

SALON

Meanwhile, back at number 12 Priory Lane, Amanda was enjoying a fortunate circumstance. The sink that had been delivered for the basement had been discovered to have a crack in it, and Mr Branscombe had gone out to collect a replacement some distance away. Hence, Amanda was free to use the magical assistance so necessary to save her from the overexertion that so often brought on her asthma attacks.

Nevertheless, as the day wore on, the stress of being alert to his possible reappearance at the scene of the spellcrafting began to tell. In addition, Mrs Reiser was at work, but who was to say she would not return unexpectedly?

By 3.30 Amanda was exhausted from the vigilance and had made sufficient progress to clock off for the day. She packed up and left a progress report note for Esta Reiser.

Tempest, who had been inspecting the back garden, engaged in an exchange of insults with a squirrel and warned the frogs in the pond several times about splashing his fur, was more than ready to leave. They drove to the top of Orchard Way and parked.

'Let's get this quote over with,' said Amanda.

Tempest had already toured the premises of the salon. He knew the layout intimately from funeral parlour days. Mr Blackaby used to keep a bowl of nuts and raisins for the sustenance of the bereaved. Tempest didn't want them often, but, when he did, he knew where to find them where he wouldn't be challenged.

Amanda had worn her work-wear straight from home, not having expected to go elsewhere. As soon as she opened the salon's glass-paned door, she felt like a bull in a china shop. Her mustard suede, polish-stained, steel-toe-capped boots echoed on the waxed wood floor. Her untidy mouse-brown plait contrasted radically with that of the customer in the white leather chair receiving the finishing touches to her luscious waves of soft ash blonde hair.

Tempest stood at Amanda's side sniffing the air redolent of coconut, vanilla and ylang-ylang but there was the sharp edge of hairspray. Her lungs reacted slightly against the chemicals. She controlled her breathing, but could not prevent a cough or two.

There was a small tray of gold and silver-wrapped chocolate hearts on the shelf before the client. Tempest's interest was aroused. He was only an occasional partaker of chocolate and was extremely particular as to quality.

Amanda looked around for Donna. The hairdresser conducting the finale to the appointment in the chair was male. The brother, no doubt. He was of medium height, lithe, and some years younger than his sister. Amanda was struck by the ready smile in his blue eyes and the sweetness in his expression that he turned towards the newcomer.

'Hello. Miss Cadabra, is it? My sister told me to expect you. Sorry, she had to pop out. Please do take a seat, I'll be right with you.'

He gave a last spray of fixer, a final primp, and reached for the mirror to show the lady the back of her head. She responded with satisfaction, untied the gown protecting her clothing, and stood up, revealing the familiar face of the proprietress of the Snout and Trough. It was known as 'The Other Pub' but with acknowledged gastro excellence, and situated at the southern entrance to the village.

'Sandra?'

'Amanda!' replied the lady with pleasure. 'Yes, it is I, of the straight, flat hair and sensible bun! My dear, this man is a genius! You must give him a try.'

Amanda, who preferred to do her own hair, made a noncommittal noise, and asked,

'Special occasion?'

'Yes, my sister and I are having a rare night off and going into town to see *Harespray*, the new musical by Poppea Watership and Barry O'Down.'

'I'm glad you're taking some time out. You work so hard, Sandra.'

'But I love it. Still, it is also nice to get glammed up and take the publican's hat off for a while.'

Sandra paid, tipped and was helped into her jacket.

'Must get back. Do pop by, Amanda, always pleased to see you. Pudding on the house for you, and, of course, the kitchen will be pleased to provide sustenance for the prince there.'

Tempest looked at her with approbation. Sandra was another one on the list of those who showed him due deference. Her kitchen consequently went unraided, and nary a rodent was permitted to pass any of her doors. Sandra made him a flourishing bow, and, with a farewell and a wave, quit the premises.

'Now, Miss Cadabra,' said the hairdresser, 'proper introductions. I'm Leo, Leonardo. I know. Product of an Italian mother, I'm afraid.'

'It's a distinguished name. How do you do, Leo. Welcome to Sunken Madley,' Amanda said warmly.

'Many thanks. Would you like a drink? Coffee, tea, before we begin?'

'Perhaps afterwards,' she answered with a cough and a hand to her chest.

'Are the products annoying you?' he asked with concern, going to the door and opening it. 'I'll do the back door too. Just to change the air.'

'That's most kind. I have asthma. Just a little oversensitive to certain chemicals. Sorry.'

'Not at all.' He returned shortly. 'So, refreshments afterwards. OK, here is the damage.' He led her to a mirror towards the back of the premises.

The salon was a strange mixture of rustic and feminine, almost frou-frou. Oak floors and exposed brickwork played against ornate gold-framed antique mirrors, swagged voile curtains in the window, white leather chairs and a chandelier. There were touches of gold in the wall lights.

Amanda inspected the frame Leo was showing her. One corner was smashed, presumably where it had been dropped, but the glass was intact. On the opposite edge was a gouge, where likely another piece of unprotected furniture had collided with it.

'I might be able to build up this corner with filler then stain or paint it,' said Amanda, 'and this deep scrape here I can probably fill with hard wax and paint. It's not a huge job. I'll email you an estimate this evening.'

'Thank you. Tea now?'

'Please,' Amanda accepted politely. 'How are you and your sister — Donna, isn't it? — settling in?'

'Pretty well. I entirely understand and respect the reservations of our new neighbours regarding strangers. After all, this is a tightly knit community in some ways, and it will take time for them to get to know us and us them.'

'That's generous of you. It's not as tight as it seems. Most of the villagers work outside of Sunken Madley. It's just the notables really who are more visible.'

'Ah, I see. Excuse me while I just go into the back room to make the tea. English breakfast?'

'Builder's tea, yes, please. I am in the industry after all,' said Amanda cheerily.

'I would say you're more of an artisan, aren't you? A craftsperson.'

'So is any brickie, joiner or plasterer worth their salt. I'm sure I've seen some of the best in houses I've worked in.'

'I meant no disrespect to the trades,' he protested lightly. 'Don't call the union!'

'I won't, at least, not this time,' she jested.

There was a conversational silence, broken by the reassuring sounds of cups chinking, lids unscrewing, a fridge door opening and shutting. And then the warm bubbling of the kettle, the burble of pouring hot water, the ting of a spoon stirring. As if drawn by the sound of tea in progress, Senara and Perran appeared. They looked carefully at the interior of the premises.

'Some nice bits of wood in here,' said Grandpa.

'Décor odd. Very odd,' pronounced Senara. 'Reminds me of the dancing hippos in *Fantasia*, for some reason.'

Their granddaughter frowned at them, and they seated themselves, in two of the salon chairs lining the opposite wall. Amanda did her best to ignore them.

'May I say something?' Amanda asked Leo, as he returned with the tea in two hand-thrown green and brown mugs, giving no sign of being able to see Senara or Perran.

'Of course,' he responded readily.

'You don't seem the type to … that is, you seem more

like the City type – movers and shakers – the financial sector – dinner at Quaglino's, Sketch …'

'Yes, I know,' agreed Leo, 'And I look younger and perhaps fitter than I am. I have done that scene. Straight from uni with a degree in business and economics, I joined up with a friend I'd known since school days. He was a furniture maker. Real-deal artisan. We were successful to the point of burnout. Then my friend quit – met a fellow crafter and moved to the coast to set up a studio with her. They invited me down, and when I saw what they had, how happy they both were, it made me rethink my life.'

Leo paused and looked around. 'It's getting rather too cool in here.' He got up and went to close the back and front doors.

'He does like to talk, doesn't he?' remarked Senara. Amanda did not react but waited for Leo to return and continue his story. Tempest had found a shadowy corner in the window, between the wall and one of the boxy display stands, and was regarding Leonardo with his citrine eyes aglow.

Aglow with what, Amanda could not tell.

Chapter 12

༄

GOODWILL

Leo returned from closing the salon back and front doors against the autumn chill.

'Where was I?' he asked, taking his seat again on one of the white leather chairs beside Amanda.

'You were saying that your friend and business partner changed from upscale furniture designer to coastal artist.'

'Ah yes. It was around that time that Donna's relationship ended. She'd been a hairdresser for some time, and I think she was divided between keeping the domestic on the simmer and really going for the career she wanted.'

'Hm,' said Senara disapprovingly, 'if the man had been any sort of support, she wouldn't have had to choose.'

'So Donna and I got together,' Leo went on, 'and I said, how about it? Go into business? She loved the idea. I did an intensive eight-month course in hairdressing, would you believe, discovered my creative side, and she found this place. It took a while for the previous owner to come to terms, finalise and wind down —'

'Mr Blackaby?'

'Yes. But Donna made good use of the time. She wouldn't tell you this herself, but she went to the residential home, er …'

'Pipkin Acres?'

'That's the one. She offered her services for free to the residents and staff, to cheer them up, the ones who were down, and save a bit of money for the already light of heart.'

'How kind!' Amanda was touched. 'That must have meant a great deal to them.'

'Well, that shows character,' pronounced Senara. 'Good woman.'

'And,' added Leo, 'she went to the school here and offered hair and makeup classes once a week. The school just had to foot the bill for heating and lighting a classroom after hours.'

'She sounds like a caring soul' approved Perran. 'Looking after the young and old alike,' commented Amanda.

'She's done everything possible to create goodwill,' Leo concluded.

'Yes, she offered fifty percent off hair appointments on the dance event days,' Amanda told him. 'I must say, she didn't get the response I, for one, think she deserved.'

'I'd reserve judgement too,' stated Senara, examining the hairbrush on the shelf before her.

'It takes time,' Leo said. 'They're not sure if she's genuine yet, I suppose. We understand.'

'Thank you for telling me, though. I'm moved by your sister's kindness and generosity.'

'She has a good heart; I'm sure of it. She might come across as a bit edgy or brittle at times or gushy. But this is all a bit nerve-wracking for her. I think she was very popular with the staff and clients where she worked. And, of course, the relationship ending was rather a blow to her confidence.'

'I'd like to know what the whole story behind *that* is!' Senara remarked, folding her arms across her chest.

'Of course,' Amanda agreed with Leo. 'Well, I certainly will do all I can to make your sister feel welcome.'

'Thank you, Amanda. I know she'll appreciate it, even if she doesn't say how much. But what about you? Have you always been a furniture restorer?' he asked reaching onto the shelf behind him and presenting her with a dainty, white, rose-patterned Wedgwood plate, of what Amanda identified as Hotel Chocolat Foiled Hearts. These would pass muster with Tempest, who would expect her to accept them.

'Thank you,' said Amanda, picking one from the dish. 'Yes, I've been very fortunate in that regard. My grandfather trained me. My grandparents brought me up, you see. They adopted me after my parents died.'

'I'm sorry,' Leo condoled.

'Oh, don't be,' Amanda said at once, with a smile. 'I don't remember them, and Granny and Grandpa were wonderful.'

'Thank you, *bian*,' said Grandpa affectionately.

'They've passed on, I take it?' asked Leo.

'Yes,' answered Amanda, 'but I feel there're still with me as much as ever,' she added with the veriest hint of gritted teeth.

'So you've always lived in Sunken Madley?'

'Pretty much.'

'Would you ever move?' Leo enquired

'No, no I don't think so. Everything I want and love is here. I have a house, a garden, a workshop, a business, good neighbours and friends.'

'So …, any man who wanted a future with you, hypothetically speaking, would have to move here.'

'We'll check his bank statement,' said Senara, 'Make

sure he's not after your goods and chattels, dear.'

'He's going a bit fast isn't he?' remarked Perran. Amanda agreed.

'Yes, he would,' she said discouragingly, in response to Leo's enquiry.

'Oh, I didn't mean ... I'm sorry ... that was far too personal a question. Please, forgive me. I'm just trying to understand what's it like to be part of a village, that's all, to grow up in one, live one's life in one place. We've moved about so much, you see.'

'Yes, of course,' she said more warmly. 'That's something I would like to understand, but I should be going.'

'Perhaps we could meet for coffee sometime. I haven't been to the hub of the village yet.'

'The Big Tease?' asked Amanda.

'That's right. Here. Please, take my card. If you ever fancy a chat during a tea break from work, send me a text, and we can spend 15 minutes "havin' a chin wag over a cuppa," as I believe Joan the postlady would say.'

Amanda laughed as she took the card.

'Thank you. I will.'

'And ... if you ever feel like doing something different with your hair ... it would be on the house.'

'My hair?' said Amanda, suddenly self-conscious.

'You've actually got good hair.'

'Mouse-brown and fly-away?'

'Well, it's not heat damaged or product damaged.'

'I do prefer to do it myself.' Amanda didn't like the feeling of a stranger's fingers in her hair, being so close to her.

'If you change your mind. For one of the dances perhaps. Maybe for the New Year's Eve Ball,' suggested Leo.

'Thank you. I'll let you know. It's very nice of you. Yes, perhaps. That dance will be a very special occasion. Well, goodbye for now. I'll get the quote to you as soon as possible.'

'No hurry.'

Amanda returned to the car, remarking to Tempest, 'He seems nice. Not show-offy or pushy or anything, and he is actually quite …'

'… hot. I believe is the current vernacular,' finished Senara, striding along beside her.

'Granny! I thought you were still in the shop.'

'Oh, Da Vinci's just tidying up. Nothing to see.'

'No harm in having a "cuppa with 'im" in public,' said Grandpa.

'Yes, that's just it,' replied Amanda, 'Public. By this time tomorrow …'

'You underestimate our neighbours,' countered Granny, 'if you think it's going to take 24 hours for the world to receive the news that you spent half an hour tête-à-tête with the new man in the village!

Chapter 13

჻

THOMAS GETS A MISSION

Vera knew that her brother, Mike, was choosing his moment. She did nothing to steer the conversation in a helpful direction or drop hints. However, after a gourmet meal of Harry's confecting: a twist on a 14th-century recipe for Catalan paella followed by panallets, sweet almond and potato balls, she did suggest to her husband that they tackle the washing up before they subsided into the alcoholic haze that an excellent Rioja was tempting them toward. Harry had been married too long to his Vera not to recognise a Sign when he saw one, eased himself out of his chair with a good-natured quip about no rest for the wicked, and ambled off to the kitchen after her.

Mike Hogarth and Thomas Trelawney sat, wine glass in hand, gazing out at the calm Balearic Sea and sighting occasional passing ships bound for Tangier and Genoa. There was no one in whose company Trelawney felt more relaxed than his mentor and friend. Since that first day, a decade and a half ago, when the young detective constable had walked nervously into then Inspector Hogarth's office, he knew he had found a kindred spirit and guiding light.

As for Hogarth, there was no one whose instinct he respected more than that of his younger disciple. He recognised that Thomas tended to take a rather serious view of life, understandably a result of his father's imprint, but that was leavened with humour that lurked beneath the deceptively grave surface, and was not always easy to discern. He did not need to advertise his sharp intelligence nor to be the smartest person in the room. Thomas's quiet courteous manner and by-the-book approach had been the net in which many a villainous foot had been snared.

No wonder he and Amanda inevitably bemused and somewhat frustrated one another, reflected Hogarth. Thomas was in some ways as much a mystery to her as she was to him. It was all vastly entertaining, and Hogarth was about to enjoy himself further.

'Are you choosing your moment?' asked Thomas humorously.

'Yes, lad,' laughed Hogarth.

'You know you do have to tell me eventually: why you invited me out here.'

'Apart from the much-missed pleasure of your company, you mean?' Mike asked jovially.

'Yours was missed just as much, I promise you,' his protégé assured him.

'Thank you. Yes, in answer to your question.'

Trelawney waited. Hogarth put down his glass and said, 'I wanted to ask you something,'

'Yes?'

'How's your dancing?'

Thomas choked on a sip of wine.

'My what?' he asked, when he had recovered and put down his glass.

'Your dancing.'

'Why? Is Vera throwing a shindig in my honour?'

'If you like,' replied Hogarth cordially.

'Thank you, but no, thank you,' Thomas responded firmly.

'You haven't answered the question,' Mike pursued.

'My dancing? Well … it's all right. I can … what do they say these days? Throw shapes? Or is that "so last season" now? But yes, I can acquit myself without excessive embarrassment to most things from the last four decades, I suppose. If I have to. Why? Oh and yes actually … when I was a teenager, my mother used to recruit me to partner her around the dinner-dance floor, so she taught me that formal sort of thing: waltz and foxtrot or whatever. Then she accrued a bevy of eager squires, and I managed to wriggle out of it.'

'That sounds not unhopeful,' said Hogarth encouragingly.

'Hopeful for what?' asked Thomas suspiciously.

'For an undercover mission,' stated Hogarth.

'Undercover?' queried Trelawney with interest, leaning forward. 'Tell me more.'

'I've had confirmation from our sole remaining witness to the day of the minibus incident —'

'Miss Cadabra?'

'Quite — confirmation that she is being watched,' said Hogarth. 'Unfortunately, the person who let slip this valuable piece of information has shuffled off this mortal coil, and his wife has departed post-haste to the Midlands. Your mission, therefore, should you choose to accept it, not that I'm offering you a choice,' Hogarth added with a wink, 'is to go and observe the villagers of Sunken Madley, find out who is keeping a close eye on our Miss Cadabra, and why.'

'But I can't go undercover. The village knows me.'

'It knows you as "the Inspector",' Hogarth pointed out.

'What do you suggest? I don Groucho Marx moustache

and glasses?'

'No,' Mike replied succinctly. 'You go as a student.'

'Of what? *Dance*?' asked Thomas incredulously.

'Exactly.'

'Why would I come all the way from Cornwall for a dance class, for the love of Pete?' Trelawney objected.

'Because you're far too occupied with your duties when in Cornwall, whereas when you pay your regular visits to your sainted mama in Crouch End, you are frequently at a loose end, and have always wanted to learn, especially well away from the mirth of your fellow police officers and staff,' Hogarth explained reasonably.

'Good heavens. But why *there*? There must be other dance classes closer to Crouch End.'

'There are. But they lack one thing that the villagers already consider to be a magnet,' said Hogarth.

'What? Hang on! Not …?' came the protest.

'Going undercover isn't always dressing up and assuming an alias, Thomas.'

'Yes, but … well!'

'Think of the mission. Take one for the team. Do it for the cause. Protect the witness, Inspector,' Hogarth intoned solemnly.

'Hmm, if you put it like that,' conceded Trelawney reluctantly.

'Oh I do, I do,' insisted Hogarth, suppressing his amusement at his friend's reaction.

'Yes, but they're all going to think …'

'Does that matter?' Hogarth asked blandly.

'But what if Miss Cadabra thinks ...?'

'Does she?'

Trelawney paused. She'd never given any sign at all that she regarded him as anything other than, at best, a friend and, at worst, an irritant.

'No,' he conceded.

'Well then. You can explain the undercover situation to her when you see her. So there need be no possibility of any misunderstanding of your intentions.'

'Good,' said Thomas shortly, less than delighted with the situation. He retrenched. 'But why does it have to be a *dance* class?'

'Because it's the only community activity several of the villagers will be engaging in regularly as a group. It's a chance to observe and interact with as many of them as possible in perfectly unexceptionable circumstances. The dancers rotate, you know; each leader dances with each follower for a few minutes before changing. Although couples can ask to stay together, but I think that would look rather singular and not suit your purpose as well.'

'I agree, entirely. But, well, … are you absolutely *sure* that there's nothing else the villagers do as a group? No ramblers association or bird-watching or scarecrow-building or … penny-farthing-riding … or …'

'Alas no, Thomas, I am afraid the Sunken Madleyists lack the herd instinct. They are a very individual collection of individuals. The only other thing they do as a group is gossip. And if you win them over at the classes you may become privy to a good bit of it. Some of that might even prove useful.'

Thomas sighed resignedly. 'Oh very well.'

'Now, it will be to your advantage if you are both a desirable partner to the followers and a source of assistance to the other leaders.'

'All right,' Thomas agreed switching to professional mode now that the inescapable was upon him.

'So you need to be ahead of the game.'

'How do I do that?' asked Thomas.

'Get your mother to give you a few lessons and practice with her.'

'Won't she think that odd?'

'Thomas, you can tell her why.'

'Yes, but this is pertaining to a … well, it's not ...'

'You can tell her that there is a potential threat to your witness,' Hogarth replied patiently, 'and you are charged with finding out more about it, and the dance classes are your cover story.'

'Yes. Yes, I can tell her that. It's true, after all,' said Trelawney, getting into the spirit of the thing.

'All right. This weekend then.'

Thomas nodded. 'When do the classes begin?'

'Saturday week,' replied Hogarth.

'That gives me only one weekend. Still, there's always YouTube. I'll ask Miss Cadabra to see if she can find out what dance we'll be starting with. I'll need to make sure I have the right gear … shoes and so on …'

'You can go in a suit with a waistcoat and just take your jacket off. The ladies will like that.'

'Good grief,' said Thomas, reaching for his glass. 'Now I know how a human sacrifice feels!'

Chapter 14

☙

THE GRAPEVINE, AND RECRUITING RUTH

Hi Amanda, please could you pop round after you finish for the day if you're not too tired. Just for a few mins. Would like to show you the space. Jane x

It was lunchtime. The rector had timed her text well. Amanda was relaxing on a silvered white oak bench, sharing lunch with Tempest, when it was delivered to her phone. She had chosen to eat in the back garden of number 12 Priory Lane, to avoid another conclave similar to Wednesday's. But Amanda had reckoned without the determination of her fellow denizens, and forgotten that The Colonel, a life-long civilian but whose bearing and handlebar moustache had earned Henry the sobriquet, lived next door.

'Hello there, Amanda!' came a voice over the garden fence.

'Ah, hello, Colonel,' Amanda replied politely, looking up from her phone.

'Good to see you well.'

'Thank you.'

'Looking forward to getting your dancing shoes out and your best frock on?'

'I won't be dressing up for the classes,' Amanda responded.

'Oh, but for the ball on the Feast of St Ursula, surely?'

'Yes, of course, I will make an effort for that. But a ball? Is it to be anything as grand as that?' asked Amanda sceptically.

'It *is* a special occasion. There's to be a spot of bubbly and some delicacies.'

'Really?

'Yes, indeed,' the Colonel confirmed. 'I do believe our new residents are contributing some rather fine crystal and plate.'

'How kind,' said Amanda sincerely.

'I must say, they seem to be a good sort of couple,' remarked Henry.

'They're brother and sister,' Amanda reminded him.

'So they are. And I do believe will prove to be a nice addition to our little community.'

'I'm glad you think so, Henry. They seem to be generous-hearted people.'

'Met them?' he asked with interest.

'The brother.'

'Good, good. Excellent that you've already hit it off. Very promising. We were all very sorry about your last young man, and the one before that, whom we considered would have been quite perfect for you.'

'Well, thank you for your interest, I really think I'd better be getting back to wor—'

Ding dong! Saved by the bell! thought Amanda.

'Please excuse me, Henry, I must get the door.'

'Of course. Cheerio!'

But Amanda's relief was premature.

It was Pawel, the Royal Mail delivery man.

'Hello there, Amanda. Can you take this parcel for Ruth? Probably another book; you know what she's like.'

'Yes, certainly,' she agreed willingly.

'Just need your moniker.'

'Sure.'

He handed the electronic pad for her to sign, saying,

'So how's your young man?'

'My what?' she responded automatically.

'Your young man at the salon. Sylvia said you two were getting on really well in there.'

'He's not my young man,' Amanda replied with strained civility. 'I was there doing an insurance quote.'

Pawel took the pad grinning.

'If you say so! Your secret's safe with me.'

I doubt it, thought Amanda.

She was about to close the front door when she was pre-empted by:

'Oo-oo!' Joan hurried up to the gate exchanging cheery greetings with Pawel.

'Can you take this for Mrs R, love? It'll never fit through the letterbox.'

'Sure, Joan,' replied Amanda, glad that Pawel, at least, had gone on his way.

'Thanks, love. So how's it going? You know? You and your young man,' Joan enquired.

'I went to the salon in my professional capacity,' Amanda began and then wondered why she was bothering.

'Course you did! That was a professional cup of tea he made for you and a professional smile Sylva said he was giving you too, I expect,' added Joan with a nudge.

'I am very fortunate in my clients, Joan, they usually are friendly. Anyway, I must be getting back to work.'

'See you Saturday week if not before then. Bye, love!'

'Good bye, Joan.' Amanda closed the door and addressed Tempest. 'And now I'd like to get on and build a bunker where I can be sure of having my lunch in peace!'

Most of the banister rail and posts were stripped of their layers of paint. Esta Reiser had said to leave the spindles for now as that would considerably add to the cost. 'Next time I get a windfall,' she'd said.

It was too late to move on to the next stage, and the light was going, so Amanda packed up, and bade farewell for the day to Mr Branscombe. She went out to the car just as Ruth was coming up the lane back from school.

'Hi, Amanda!' Ruth, her hair a couple of shades darker than Amanda's in an echoing plait, hailed her with delight, her brown eyes behind round lenses brightening at the sight of her friend and occasional tutor.

'Hi Ruth,' replied Amanda with pleasure. 'How was it today?'

Ruth sighed. 'OK, I suppose. Got history tomorrow though,' she said, cheering up at the thought.

'Bye, Ruth,' came a shy voice from over the road. The ladies looked around to see a tall, mid-brown-haired teenager waving from the other side of the road.

'Oh. Yeah, bye,' Ruth responded politely but unenthusiastically.

'Isn't he Erik's son, er …?' began Amanda, thinking she'd seen him at her solicitor's office on at least two occasions.

'Kieran. Yes,' said Ruth, rolling her eyes.

'He seems friendly,' remarked Amanda cautiously.

'I knowwww,' replied Ruth in the voice of martyrdom. 'Just another sports moron.'

'Really?'

'Captain of the second XI,' she said scornfully

'Cricketer? Can't be all bad, then,' commented Amanda mitigatingly.

'I prefer brain over brawn,' stated Ruth.

'He didn't look all that brawny.' But Amanda, not wanting to harry her young friend, abandoned the boy's cause. 'Is he in your class?'

'No. Year above.'

'Ah, then don't school social rules dictate that you can't have anything whatsoever to do with one another? In fact, what was he thinking? Actually greeting you in that fashion on the open street and in broad daylight! Your reputations lie in ruins!'

Ruth smiled.

'And I – I whom you have long considered your sister-in-arms who should have rescued you from calumny stood by here.' Amanda pretended to stagger and support herself on the Astra. 'Stood by and did nothing! Alas!' She put the back of her hand to her forehead.

Ruth was now giggling. 'Oh, our school's not like that, and you *know* it.'

Having successfully diverted her, Amanda continued,

'Well, never mind about that. Are you going to lend me countenance and moral support at the new dance classes?'

'Do I *have* to?'

'Of course, not. But the rector wants me to be encouraging, and you know I'm no more the social type than you are. So if we join forces …'

'… we'll make one confident person!' finished Ruth.

Amanda laughed. 'Precisely.'

'Dancing.' Ruth turned the thought over in her mind. 'I don't know,' she said doubtfully.

'How hard can it be?' Amanda asked her. 'I mean after medieval Latin and Middle English?'

'I guess.'

'Thank you. I won't hold you to it if you'd really rather not.'

'No, I'll come along. I'll check with Mum, but I just

know she won't hand me a get-out by saying I can't go! It'll be, "Oh, if *Amanda*'s going …" No it's OK, I'll come along. You off?'

'Yes, the rector wants to show me the dance space, as it hasn't seen the light of day for I don't know how many years.'

'OK, see you tomorrow maybe?' asked Ruth hopefully.

Amanda smiled. 'Yes, I expect I'll be here when you get back from school.'

She looked around to see if Tempest required her chauffeuring services, and found him sitting outside the rear passenger door. Amanda duly opened it.

'If sir would please to mount the carriage?' she asked with exaggerated ceremony. Tempest inclined his head graciously and stepped up onto the seat. Amanda gave way her customary mirth when he took up his place.

Siding into her own seat, she called out, 'And now to the rectory. Drive on, Cadabra!'

Chapter 15

❧

THE SPACE

Amanda and Tempest drove to the end of Priory Lane and turned right into Muttring Lane, then left into the little Vicarage Lane. From there, she could access the few parking spaces behind the church of St Ursula-without Barnet.

Jane, hearing the crunch of tyres on gravel, came out to greet Amanda, as she applied the handbrake and got out of the car.

'Hello, Rector.'

'You got my text?'

'Yes,' Amanda confirmed opening the back passenger door for Tempest's egress.

'Ah,' said the rector, struggling to keep the doom out of her voice. 'I see you've brought …'

'I'm sure he'll behave,' said Amanda quickly but without much conviction. 'Won't you?' she asked her feline companion hopefully. Tempest looked over his shoulder and up at the sky as though he had not heard her speak.

'Well … I've got the keys.' Jane held them up. They took the path to the church hall, but, no sooner had the rector opened the lock of the front door when her phone sounded. She pushed open the portal as she checked the screen.

'Oh, Amanda, it's the bishop! Do excuse me. You go on in.' She hurried back towards the rectory, leaving Amanda to enter the old hall alone. Tempest pushed past her ankles and went in first. The diffused light of a grey sky struggled through the tall dirty windows lining the long sides of the building. It was silent, so silent Amanda could hear her own breathing, even imagine the sound of each mote of dust disturbed by her moving form settling back onto the wooden boards beneath her feet.

Amanda looked anxiously at the floor. It seemed solid enough. She bounced up and down on it a few times. It held. At the other end of the space there was a stage with high, dusty, blue curtains. The hall seemed vast with not a stick of furniture and the high ceiling. It reached all the way to the rafters across most of the roof, but there was an attic space, perhaps for a projection room, a ladder by the long right-hand wall, presumably by which to reach it through a closed hatch. The ceiling had once been white, and the walls too probably. Someone had at least swept.

All of a sudden, Amanda froze. An excited giggle, swiftly cut off, had come from above. She stared upwards. There was the sound as of scuffling, then a small leg appeared … no, it was large … or was it? Suddenly a form fell, at once fast enough to be a blur and yet seemingly in slow motion, both child and adult-size.

As Amanda's eyes followed it down, the music came, singing: 'Roses are shining in Picardy'. The human form seemed to fall into a throng of dancers, waltzing, twirling, a medley of costumes; ladies in long dresses from the First World War, men in dinner jackets, girls in white blouses, bodices and gathered skirts, other men in jerkins and breeches.

The scene vanished at a voice from below.

'What's going on! I won't have it. I demand an explanation, and I demand it be given now!'

The floor had opened at her feet. There seemed to be a man — or was it a woman? — getting up off some sort of bed. The voice and shape were a strange blend of male and female, but, as Amanda shook her head, as though to clear her vision, it resolved into that of a man with a moustache, and wearing regimentals.

All at once he looked up, staring into Amanda's face.

'Here! You girl!' Amanda looked around to see if someone else was present.

'Me?' she asked.

'Yes, you with the cat. Where have they all gorn? I didn't come through The War to be thrown down here and have the whole bally party hide like it's some sort of April Fool's prank.'

'Erm …' replied Amanda, at a loss as to how to respond.

'Come now! Out with it!' insisted the man.

Amanda knelt down at the edge of the hole. 'I, er … you can see me?'

'Of course, I can see you. I injured my arm, not my head.' She saw that he had a sling that he wasn't using.

'I'm afraid I don't know about your —'

'Oh, Amanda!' At the rector's voice, the military man vanished, and she turned her head to see Jane coming back into the hall. 'I'm so sorry to have left you.' Amanda looked back. The floor was intact. Completely. Tempest was looking at it carefully.

'That was the bishop. He most kindly wanted to commend me on the church hall initiative and to wish me all success. Wasn't that kind?'

'Yes,' Amanda agreed vaguely, still inspecting the floor.

'Did you drop something?' asked Jane.

'Er … no,' said Amanda, getting to her feet. 'I just wanted to examine the floorboards up here after seeing the supports in the cellar.'

'Very wise, but I did as you suggested and asked Mr Branscombe, and he came over yesterday evening and said they'd do for now. He said to see how the money comes in, and maybe spend some on proper supports, but they're safe enough at the moment. He said he'd keep an eye on them. Well! What do you think of the space?'

'It's quite magnificent.'

'Yes, large for its day.'

'Probably a lick of paint and clean windows would make it a bit more inviting, do you think?' suggested Amanda.

'That's what I said to Mr Branscombe when he caught a glimpse of it. He said he'd help out.'

'He's a nice man.'

'Indeed. Well, the funds will stretch to a big tub or two of white emulsion. It's an investment after all. Do you think anyone else would give a hand?'

'Yes,' said Amanda with certainty. 'I do. Leo at the salon I'm sure would want to help. And he won't be the only one. All you have to do, Rector, is go down to the corner shop and the offers will be pouring in before the end of the day. Just leave the paint and some rollers and brushes and cleaning materials, and let people come in, as and when then can, and, likely, the job will be done by the end of Sunday.'

'Now that's an excellent idea. I'd better make sure the things are kept in the cupboard under the stage, and I would pop in every now and then to make sure it's all going according to plan. I can wield a paintbrush, myself, of course.'

Amanda nodded encouragingly.

'Thank you, dear,' said the rector. 'Have you had enough of a look round?'

'Yes, thank you.'

Tempest followed them out and Jane locked up.

'Rector?'

'Yes.'

'Were there any … did anyone … do you know about the history of the hall, at all?'

'Only what I told you. It was built at the turn of the century. It was used for years until it became unsafe.'

'There weren't any accidents?'

'Accidents? Not that I know of.'

'It wasn't bombed?'

'I don't think so, dear. You'd really have to ask Mrs Pagely. Why? You haven't seen any evidence of structural damage, have you?' asked the rector with concern, stopping on the path.

'The walls look sturdy,' replied Amanda.

'Well, that's a relief.' Jane recommenced the short walk back to the rectory. 'Would you like a cup of tea?'

'Thank you, Rector, but I ought to pop into the library.'

'Well, give my regards to Mrs Pagely and Jonathan, won't you? Are you quite all right? You look a little pale. Are you sure you won't have some tea?

'I'm fine, thank you, Rector. Just a bit musty and dusty in there.'

'Of course. I should have said to wear your mask,' said Jane apologetically. 'But it had been swept.'

'It's all right. I shall next time.'

'It just needs a good airing before we use it for the class. You *are* coming?'

'Oh yes,' Amanda promised, 'And Ruth might too.'

'Your Ruth?' enquired Jane.

'Yes.'

'Excellent. It would be good to have some of the young people. Well, I won't keep you. Thank you for stopping by, dear.'

Chapter 16

❧

SETTING UP

Amanda got into the car and, with relief, saw that Jane had disappeared back into the rectory.

'Granny! Grandpa!'

Senara appeared in the passenger seat beside her and Perran in the back next to Tempest.

'What's going on in there?' Amanda asked agitatedly. 'Legs coming through the ceiling, bodies falling through the air, and what's with that soldier who could see us?'

'Calm down, *bian*,' said Grandpa soothingly. 'You're doing very well.'

'Yes,' agreed Granny, 'picking up on things nicely. Something even we didn't see. Not that we looked. Aunt Amelia would be proud of you too.'

Amanda was aghast at what she regarded as their inappropriately relaxed attitude to what she had just witnessed. 'Aren't you going to help me at all?'

'We have complete confidence in you, Ammy,'

responded Grandpa. 'You might as well drive home now.'

'So there's nothing you can tell me?' Amanda asked in frustration starting up the engine and pulling out into the road.

'Oh, there's *plenty* we could tell you,' admitted Granny, 'but then how would you learn from experience? This is all part of your training. Look at it that way. All I'll say is, it's complicated.'

'But you'll find a way to unpick it,' added Grandpa.

'So your advice is?' asked Amanda.

'Go and have a bath,' suggested Grandpa.

'Have dinner,' advised Granny.

'Watch a nice film with Tempest,' added Grandpa.

'His purring will help calm you down,' said Granny. 'Personally, he still gets on my nerves, but then he's not *my* familiar. Thank goodness.'

'Don't worry, *bian*, that's very important. Just take the next step.'

'Whatever that turns out to be,' said Granny.

Amanda parked outside number 26 Orchard Way.

They got out of the car and entered the cottage. Amanda had just taken off her coat when Perran remarked,

'Looks like you have a phone call.'

Then Amanda's mobile sounded.

She looked at her grandparents suspiciously as she took it out of her pocket, walking into the living room. There, they sat down, Senara beside her on the chintz sofa and Grandpa in his favourite matching chair opposite.

DI Trelawney, said the phone screen.

'Hello, Inspector?'

'Hello, Miss Cadabra, how are you?'

'I'm fine, thank you. Are you still OK to come to the Feast of St Ursula of the Apples on 17th of November?'

'Yes, indeed. Actually, I was hoping we might be able to meet up sooner.'

'When did you have in mind?'

'Would this Sunday be convenient?' Trelawney enquired politely.

'Yes, I'll be free then. May I ask what the, er ... occasion is?'

'Of course. I was just coming to that. I wonder how you would feel about another trip down memory lane?'

'This is both professional and personal again then, I take it?' Amanda asked.

'Yes. Some fresh information has come to light. No, not regarding the day of the minibus incident specifically. More ... background information, though it is specific to me, and well ....'

Trelawney, usually so articulate, was finding it hard to express himself on a matter so private. Amanda compassionately put him out of his misery.

'You would like me to try to remember some more?'

'That's right. On your previous foray into your memory of the past, you recalled being in the gallery at Cardiubarn Hall.'

'Yes, my chilling great-grandmother showing me ancestral portraits of murderers and victims!'

'I'm afraid so. You recalled that she showed you two groups of paintings, and chronologically left out the earliest ones and a whole load in the middle,' Trelawney reminded her.

'And you want me to try and fill in those gaps?'

'I believe it may be of great help to us both,' he said earnestly.

Amanda wasn't thrilled at the prospect, but, after all, Trelawney, only weeks previously, had saved her life. It was the least she could do. 'OK.'

'Not here,' said Senara firmly. 'I don't want you bringing memories of That Place into our home!'

'We'll need somewhere to meet to do this,' said Amanda.

'Perhaps. And not The Big Tease. We'd better not go to that place again so soon, it's far too public,' agreed Trelawney.

'What about hiring a room at the Asthma Centre? They rent them out to therapists, after all, and you know the manager,' suggested Perran.

'Good idea,' said Amanda. 'But you mean, Bill. But I don't know if he's got the job yet.'

'What idea?' asked Trelawney. 'Although one has just occurred to me. Would it be possible to hire a room at the Asthma Research Centre? After all, you know Bill there.'

Amanda's eyes widened at her grandfather, and she mouthed the words 'What the ...?'

'Would that be an option?' he followed up.

'Excellent. Yes. I tell you what. I'll call Bill now, and see if we can book a slot for Sunday.'

'During daylight,' said Senara.

'During the day?' suggested Trelawney. 'I'll have to drive back to Cornwall in the evening.'

'How about 2 o'clock?'

'Yes, fine.'

'OK, I'll call you right back,' Amanda assured him.

She tapped off and called The Centre.

'Bill?'

'Lassie? How you doin'?'

'Well, thank you, Bill and you?'

'I've got the job. I'm manager noo.'

Grandpa nodded.

'See?'

Amanda smiled in acknowledgement. She said aloud, 'I'm so pleased, Bill. You absolutely deserve it. I have a favour to ask. Could I hire a room for Sunday at 2 pm.? I know I'm not a therapist, but it's for a ... a meditation session for a friend and myself.'

'Gi' us a sec .... I've only got two till three. That long

enough?'

'Oh yes, ample.'

'Right. You're booked in.'

'Thank you, Bill.'

'By the way, we might be back to normal sooner than we expected. Wi' the publicity – goes to show no publicity is bad publicity — we've had a surprising number of applicants for all the positions left vacant by the …. people who were involved in … well, what happened here.'

'That's wonderful.'

'So you just might be able to start your sessions with the healer airlier than we thought.'

'No hurry. I'm still recovering, frankly. In the new year will suit me fine'

'I might not be here when you arrive tomorrow, but I'll leave a note.'

'Thanks, Bill.'

'Bye, lassie.'

Amanda hung up and dialled Trelawney.

'Inspector?'

'Here, Miss Cadabra.'

Amanda confirmed The Centre at 2 pm. 'We can get drinks from the canteen there to take to the room.'

'I'll meet you there then,' suggested Trelawney.

'Yes, that's the most privacy we can expect to get. I know it's in Little Madley, but it's still part of the village and ….'

'Yes, I'm prepared for the consequences,' he answered wryly.

She chuckled. 'Till Sunday.'

'At two. Thank you. See you then'.

Amanda rang off, as her grandparents nodded in satisfaction and disappeared. She addressed herself to her familiar.

'Hm. I take it talking to the inspector is "the next step", but there's another I can take in the meantime. I shall follow Granny and Grandpa's excellent advice and head for the bath. But first: the library!'

* * * * *

'The church hall?' said Mrs Pagely. 'Well, … it was built during the First World War, on land that was part of the Dunkley estate, but was gifted to the church expressly for the hall. Just a moment … I have a … hmm … somewhere here ….' She bustled off to the local history section followed by Amanda.

'Ah. Yes, … here, in *Good Manors of Hertfordshire* by Cecilia Stoan-Mayson written in 1889, it says there was a structure that they called the Big Barn on that part of the land but it was derelict. The Dunkleys were doing less agriculture and more renting, you see, and it was already falling into disrepair. The barn stopped being used as a barn around —' Mrs Pagely turned the book towards Amanda and traced the lines with her finger, as she read aloud —'"1818 following a mishap of a calamitous and embarrassing nature concerning Percy, the youngest son of Sir Edmund and Lady Abigail Dunkley."'

'Interesting,' said Amanda, reading on to see if there was more to the story.

'Oh dear, we have become sidetracked, haven't we!' said Mrs Pagely. 'The point is, that the barn and the land it was on were donated to the church, and the hall was built. It was used as a hospital during the War. But if you want to know more than that, then Mr Hodster is your man.'

'Do you know where I might find him, Mrs Pagely?'

'I believe he is staying at present in Pipkin Acres up the road. He comes into the library at least once a week but not on set days. Miss Armstrong-Witworth is a friend of his. You might ask her about going to see him.'

Back at the cottage, Amanda declared, 'Right, Tempest, one more call.'

'Gwendolen?'

'Hello, Amanda, dear.'

'May I ask a favour?

'Anything,' replied Miss Armstrong-Witworth warmly.

'Mrs Pagely says you're friends with Mr Hodster at Pipkin Acres Residential Home.'

'Indeed.'

'Would you, please, be able to come with me one day to see him, when it's convenient for you?

'Of course, dear. I'll call and arrange it. Are you going to tell me what's it's about or is it a secret mission?' asked Miss Armstrong-Witworth with gentle curiosity.

'Oh, no,' laughed Amanda. 'It's about the church hall. The rector has been showing it to me, and I've become curious about its history. I went to the library, and Mrs Pagely said Mr Hodster is the one to talk to.'

'Yes,' Miss Armstrong-Witworth answered slowly. 'Oh yes …. He would know. Hmm, I haven't thought about all that in years … ,'she added meditatively. 'Before my time, of course, but … yes … he could tell you. Yes, dear,' she said, seeming to return to the present. 'I'll contact him and find out when he's free.'

'Thank you, Gwendolen.' Amanda finished the call and looked at her familiar thoughtfully. 'Hm, Tempest, I wonder what it is that Gwendolen hasn't thought about in years.' He stared back at her. 'OK, I get it. You know and you're not telling.'

He walked in front of Amanda up to the soon-to-be steamingly warm bathroom, thinking, 'She'll find out.' He found it astonishing how humans so often needed to be *told* things.

But his witch was quite a sweet little thing in her way and, at least, quicker on the uptake than most of her sorry excuse for a species.

Chapter 17

෨

PREPARING, AND CAST OFF

Amanda awoke on Sunday morning feeling revived. By Friday, the Reisers' banister had been completely stripped from the top of the house to the ground floor. It had been exhausting, having to rely on manual means when Mr Branscombe or Esta was around, and continually being on the lookout when she did use her magic. Amanda had spent Saturday in recovery. Tempest came out in sympathy and slept beside her on the sofa all day, while she alternately dozed and watched the Margaret Rutherford Agatha Christie box set.

Now it was Sunday morning, and Amanda's chief emotion was curiosity. Whatever was this new information that had come to light that was bringing Detective Inspector Trelawney 400 miles from Cornwall to see her? And what exactly was it that he needed her to dig up from her past? By half past one, she was almost ready to go to the Marion Gibbs Asthma Research Centre to meet him. She was giving her ensemble a last check in the mirror in her room, when the fashion police appeared.

'Orange again?' asked Granny, looking at her granddaughter's choice of a knitted short dress, with straps, that flared from the waist over a cream top and merino orange leggings.

'It's a different orange to last time I met up with the inspector; it's more of a yellow orange, and besides, I'm wearing brown boots with it instead of orange shoes. Anyway, I *like* orange, Granny.'

'I think he'll realise that.'

'It's an appointment, not a date. I'm not dressing to impress, I'm dressing to be comfortable,' insisted Amanda.

'That's right, *bian*,' said Grandpa, sitting on the bed.

'Well, if you're comfortable in that … if you're sure you wouldn't prefer a more sophisticated look? Something more mature?' suggested Granny.

'It wouldn't suit her, love,' Perran protested. 'Ammy can't help it if she looks young for her age. Remember what Bertil Bergstrom always says about her? "Nine years old, ahlvays nine!"' he said, in a fair imitation of their dear friend and magical tool inventor's Swedish accent.

Senara's lips twitched. 'You're quite right, Perran. You look very nice, dear,' she said to Amanda with a nod.

'Thank you.'

'Now don't be nervous.'

'The past that I visited last time the Inspector and I did this, isn't a particularly nice place, though, is it, Granny?'

'Granted. But it is the past. You will be visiting it only in memory,' Senara stressed.

'But it seemed so real.' said Amanda seriously. 'And you weren't there, Granny, when it was actually happening. Not for those times.'

'I know. I wish that I had been. I should never have left you alone in that house for a moment. But they had the power to keep me out. I was lucky that they let me take you away at night since the day when you were born, you know. Though, of course, they didn't want the trouble of caring for you.'

'Really?' Amanda turned from the mirror to look at her grandmother. 'You never told me that. Where did you take me?'

'Back to where your Grandpa and I were staying.'

'Grandpa didn't come to Cardiubarn Hall with you?'

'They wouldn't allow a Cadabra to cross the threshold,' explained Perran.

'They only let me come and go because they needed me,' added Granny. 'I hadn't been back for four decades.'

'How was it that you went back?' asked Amanda.

'They invited me for your birth. Though it was more like a summons!' Senara uttered with scorn. 'And I knew well enough how it would be if you didn't meet their expectations.'

'How would it be?' enquired Amanda with furrowed brow. 'That they would reject me?'

'They did what I hoped,' replied Granny warmly, 'and gave you to me and your grandfather. It turned out very well for us all,' she added putting an arm around her granddaughter.

Amanda nodded with a sigh of relief and an answering gleam in her eyes. 'How right you are, Granny. I have been very lucky indeed. And,' she continued reflectively, 'during the three years I came and went from Cardiubarn Hall during the day, I may have learned some things that could prove to be valuable now.'

'That's the spirit!' Grandpa commended her. 'Now, do you want us to come with you for this meeting with the inspector?' Amanda had turned back to the mirror and now she met her grandmother's eyes in the reflection. They both knew the answer.

'No, thank you, Grandpa. I have to do this by myself,' she said with quiet resolve.

'Rrrowl!' stated Tempest, jumping on to the bed, apparently from nowhere.

'Oh, not entirely alone,' Amanda corrected herself with a grin and went to sit beside her familiar. 'Though how you're going to smuggle yourself into an Asthma Research Centre —'

'— will be of no surprise to any of us!' finished Granny caustically.

'Yes,' said Perran, 'Just as the villagers have always said: he's where he wants to be, when he wants to be!'

The humans chuckled. Tempest preened himself and looked smug.

'Time you were off,' said Granny. 'You want to be on time but not early.'

'Yes, yes, I know, the inspector likes to be the first on the scene,' intoned Amanda.

'Precisely. And you remember how he likes —'

'— his tea. Yes, Granny. Though I still don't see how that's relevant.'

'Got your keys?'

'Yes, I've got everything, thank you.'

'We'll be here when you get back,' said Grandpa.

Chapter 18

∾

HYPOTHETICAL SITUATION

As Amanda drove herself and Tempest up Orchard Row and left into Muttring Lane, she considered that, although it had all turned out for the very best, it was still … well … not very nice to be discarded by one's parents immediately after birth. And a very odd sort of way for them to behave. What Miss Armstrong-Witworth would have termed, 'not at all the thing'.

They turned right off Muttring Lane up Lost Madley Lane. It was not that Amanda felt hurt. She and her mother had never bonded; it was so long since she had looked at a photo of the woman in Granny's album that she couldn't at all recall what she looked like. No, the emotion Amanda felt was … offended.

She parked, took a breath and said aloud to her familiar, 'Well, never mind that. Let's find out what the inspector wants.' She arranged the hood of her soft orange top more evenly and got out of the Astra, to see Trelawney approaching her from his silver Ford Mondeo.

'Miss Cadabra.'

'Inspector.'

They shook hands.

'Thank you for agreeing to this meeting and arranging it,' he said appreciatively.

'My pleasure. Shall we go in?'

They entered, Tempest slinking in unnoticed.

They signed in and were given a room key code. Amanda led the way to the canteen.

'I expect you know this place pretty well after … what happened, and so on,' commented Trelawney.

'You could say that. I'll be back here in the new year to start having healing sessions that may help the asthma.' Amanda had ordered the drinks to be ready for them, Trelawney insisted on paying, and they made the final steps along the carpeted hall to the designated room.

'How apt,' commented the inspector, reading the name on the plaque.

'Rosemary?'

'"That's for remembrance",' he quoted.

'You know your *Hamlet*, I see,' responded Amanda. 'Well, unlike poor Ophelia, I hope to remain sane, at least for the duration of our conversation,' she added playfully.

'And I, for my part,' Trelawney returned with a grin, 'promise not to attempt to see off my mother's latest boyfriend during the next hour!'

Amanda laughed.

'Not that I think she has a current favourite,' he appended thoughtfully.

'She has a number of suitors then?'

'Yes and all far too young,' he said disapprovingly.

'Now,' said Amanda inputting the code and opening the door, 'you're only saying that because she's your mother. You know perfectly well that if it was any other woman you'd dismiss such a notion as prejudice and insist age should be no bar to happiness!'

Trelawney, much struck by the accuracy of this observation, stopped still.

'That's very true, Miss Cadabra. How perceptive of you. Oh my word,' he said, noticing the view through the floor-to-ceiling windows forming the wall opposite the door, 'how wonderful.'

Amanda smiled. 'I'm glad you approve. I asked for one of these especially. That's Lost Madley Meadow, a rare field carved long ago out of the thickness of the Wood. A place for the bunnies to play and where sheep may safely graze.'

'Are those Michaelmas daisies?' Trelawney asked.

'Why yes, I believe so. How nice to meet a man who knows his flowers,' she said, pleasantly surprised.

'Well, not many, only the ones my mother insisted on drumming into my head. Especially the ones she likes,' he added with a chuckle.

'Your mother rises in my esteem every moment,' stated Amanda as they sat down in the mushroom-coloured armchairs, set at 45-degree angles to the window and each other.

Now that the moment to get down to the matter in hand had come, they took sips from their too-hot beverages to cover the brief awkward silence. Amanda set down her cup and invited him to begin,

'Why don't you tell me what's happened? The thing that prompted you to call me.'

Trelawney nodded. 'I've been thinking about how to start.'

Amanda waited patiently.

'Mike Hogarth has a quote he's rather fond of repeating. We seem to keep coming back to *Hamlet* … "There are more things in heaven and earth —"'

'"— than are dreamt of in your philosophy",' Amanda finished gently.

'Is that a view to which you at all subscribe, Miss Cadabra?'

She smiled a little, and said simply, 'Yes.'

He seemed to exhale. 'Well, that certainly makes things easier. What if those "more things" included abilities that were out of the ordinary?'

'Those would seem reasonable to include,' Amanda said amiably.

'Do you remember the last time we spoke like this…'

'In the Big Tease?'

'Yes. I told you about a dream I'd had. I was back in the old family mansion?'

'Flamgoyne,' she recalled.

'That's right. I was with my father, and there were other men and an old woman, and I heard them; they kept asking my father, "Can he …?"'

'I remember,' said Amanda, encouragingly.

'Well, I've had an inkling of what they may have been asking him about.'

Trelawney paused. Amanda sensed how difficult this was for him.

'One of those 'more things?'' she suggested tentatively.

He nodded.

'Tell me,' she invited him gently. 'I promise I won't laugh or disregard what you say.'

Trelawney recounted the strange flashback he had had to when he was a toddler seeing his father's whereabouts.

'Sort of in the reflection of the tea, or like it was a background for a movie projection. I saw my father, not in the *car*, but at *Flamgoyne*, with his mother and the other men in the family.'

'I see,' she responded, understanding his unease.

'I asked Mike about it. And he told me that there's a … a trait that is said to run in the Flamgoyne family: intuition, insight, divination. He said not all have it nor is everyone with the ability a Flamgoyne, but it sounds like I did have it.'

'And that's what the family kept asking your father about then,' Amanda inferred. 'If you had inherited the gift?'

'Yes.'

'Do you think that your father knew that you did?'

'I don't know. I don't remember, but if he did I am certain that he told the Flamgoynes I didn't.'

'Well, that's good. He protected you,' commented Amanda on a positive note.

'Yes, of course, I couldn't imagine my father doing otherwise, but that's not what bothers me. And I said this to Mike. How come I stopped being able to do it? And why don't I remember stopping being able to do it? Is that connected to my loss of memory of most of my early years?'

'Good questions,' responded Amanda noncommittally.

'Well, … you know what your Uncle Mike said?'

'No.'

'"Why don't you ask Miss Cadabra?"'

Amanda maintained a wary silence. Why was Uncle Mike dropping her in it? Finally, she asked cautiously, 'Why do you think that he suggested that?'

'Because, I think … I asked him, if intuition, divination was the Flamgoyne … gift, as you so nicely put it, what was the gift of the Cardiubarns? — their enemies, neighbours, occasional allies, however you want to term it.'

'And he said …?' asked Amanda curiously.

'He said he wasn't sure if your grandmother would ever have told you. May I ask if Mrs Cadabra ever did.'

'No,' Amanda answered slowly. 'And it's strange that you should ask that, because about two weeks ago maybe, one night, just before I was going to sleep … I wondered about that, what was the gift of those houses …. No, no one ever told me. Did Uncle Mike know what the Cardiubarn gift was? Did he tell you?'

'Yes. He said the Cardiubarns were spell-weavers. Oh, it all sounds so outlandish!' exclaimed Trelawney, getting up. Thrusting his hands into his trouser pockets, he walked around behind the chairs. 'And I can't believe I'm using words like "divination" and "spells"! I feel like I've entered a realm of insanity.'

'No, Inspector, just a realm new to "your philosophy",' Amanda said kindly.

His face softened. 'You're right of course. I must say you're taking all of this very acceptingly. Thank you.'

'It's different for me. I've grown up hearing about these things to some extent, but you have no memory of the times when your family may have spoken about them.'

Trelawney nodded. His customary equanimity returned. He resumed his seat and reached for his tea. After a few moments he resumed.

'So then, I gather that what Mike meant when he said to ask you was that, since your family were spell-weavers, you might know whether ….' He shook his head. 'I do find it hard to actually say the words ….'

Amanda came to his rescue. 'Whether I might know if it is possible that a spell was cast on you to remove your power of divination and to cause you to forget?'

'Precisely.'

Amanda chose her words carefully. 'Inspector, as a friend, I want to help you. I hope you believe me.' He nodded. 'However, if I were, hypothetically, to offer an opinion that you might consider to be informed on the question of spells, would that not, in some way, open the possibility of incrimination of my grandparents, regarding the deaths of the Cardiubarn family, when the minibus went over that cliff all those years ago?'

It was Trelawney's turn to proceed with caution.

'While I see your point, Miss Cadabra, and I do admit that, since that conversation with former Chief Inspector Hogarth, such an idea has occurred to me, the fact *is* that both your grandparents were nowhere near the scene of the crime on the day that it took place.'

'True,' replied Amanda.

'Of course, I know nothing of such matters, but I believe it is reasonable to assume that even in the use of … magic … one would need to be in some sort of vicinity of the victim to execute the, er … spell involved.'

'I would concur with that,' said Amanda.

'Then, perhaps you would be so good as to put your reservations to one side, and answer me as a friend, Miss Cadabra?'

'Then my answer would be, hypothetically, and based on stories my grandmother told me, yes, I believe that there would likely be such a spell that could inhibit your powers of divination and remove your memory of that rite, shall we say. Hypothetically.'

'And a person who could perform such … rites would be … a spell-weaver?'

'That would seem logical.'

'And the Cardiubarns were spell-weavers. So why …?'

'Yes, I see,' said Amanda, relaxing after the tension of the uneasy exchange that had preceded and catching the thread of the line of enquiry, 'why would a Cardiubarn help a Flamgoyne?'

'Exactly.'

Chapter 19

❧

INTO THE PAST

'Let's see … who would help a Flamgoyne? …. A renegade Cardiubarn?' Amanda suggested.

'Possibly,' Trelawney agreed.

'But who? And why?' asked Amanda.

'And where?'

'And exactly when?'

'I can't pinpoint it but I'd say, around when I was ten,' replied Trelawney.

'Your parents were still together then?'

'Just about, I think.'

'So then where would you most likely have been? Cornwall?' enquired Amanda.

'Cornwall, yes. So … why?'

'As far as I can tell,' said Amanda wryly, 'no Cardiubarn ever did anything without some sort of angle or agenda, and I'm looking for it.'

'Depriving one of the enemy family of their clan power

would surely have been in the interests of the Cardiubarns.'

'That makes sense. But why make such a secret of it?' asked Amanda.

'Because it was a secret that I had it in the first place?' suggested Trelawney.

'All right. But who among the Cardiubarns would your father have trusted?'

'I suppose,' he answered reluctantly, 'there's only one person who really knows the answer to that.'

'Can you ask your father?'

'The question is, not whether I could *ask* him, but, whether he would *tell* me.'

'Would you wish to try?' Amanda asked diplomatically

'I think I must. It's all linked, the two families, the deaths of the Cardiubarns in the minibus. If it gets us closer to the truth of that day on the coast road, then I must make the attempt,' said Trelawney resolutely.

They stopped and sipped their drinks, looking out over the field towards the trees that bordered it in a protective sweep of golds, russets and greens.

Amanda looked at Trelawney with new respect. 'Well done,' she said. 'I can imagine how difficult it must be for you to come to terms with that memory, and to contemplate there may be a dimension to our human existence that is beyond what is considered to be normal.'

'Thank you. But perhaps it *is* normal, and physics will one day be able to put it in terms that make it perfectly ordinary and acceptable. Perhaps there are thousands of people, especially children, who can do things that ... that are outside the usual range of the physical, the mechanics of the use of the five senses. '

'Perhaps you're just ahead of the game,' smiled Amanda.

'What about you?' asked Trelawney.

She knew what he was asking, and yet it was not as a

detective searching for possible clues of magical assassination, but as a friend, seeking a fellow — not sufferer exactly, quite the opposite, — child, seeking the other child in the class who … was gifted.

'My parents,' said Amanda, 'took one look at me, apparently, and gave up. I think my great-grandmother Cardiubarn kept hoping I'd show a sign of some sort of magical endowment, but in the end even she threw up her hands and passed me onto my grandparents.'

'Who clearly weren't in the least disappointed in you,' observed Trelawney. 'Very much the opposite. That day, when I first met the three of you, I detected nothing but love and pride in you.'

Strangely that brought a lump to Amanda's throat.

'Thank you,' she said with difficulty. 'That means a great deal, Inspector.'

'Not at all. But still, I gather that your grandparents had stories to tell about esoteric matters, shall we say?'

'Not very much,' Amana said truthfully. Her days had been filled with learning the theory of magic. She was never able to get very much out of Perran and Senara about either their own or their families' histories.

'But enough for you to accept the possibility of the existence of things magical?' Trelawney asked.

'Oh yes,' agreed Amanda. She took another sip of her drink and decided that the moment could not be put off any longer. 'So what is it that you want me to remember?'

'The missing portraits,' he replied, coming to the point. 'You said your great-grandmother showed you two lots of family portraits.'

'Hmm. But not the earliest ones.'

'She said they might scare you,' he reminded her.

'That's right,' Amanda concurred, 'and then she showed me a few of the acceptable ones. Then she skipped some in the middle. She didn't want to tire me, she said, and then showed me the ones that almost brought us up to date.'

'Yes.'

'Which ones do you want?' she asked Trelawney.

'Both, if you can get them.'

'This is to do with your theory that you've developed?' Amanda queried.

'Yes.'

'Are you going to share it with me?' she asked hopefully.

'Yes, of course,' he said with a smile, 'but I'd rather not influence your experience of memory with it.'

'OK. So if I can remember then you'll tell me?'

'Of course,' Trelawney assured her.

'We have a deal then,' she confirmed with a gleam.

'We have a deal, Miss Cadabra.' He held out his hand.

They shook on it. Amanda put down her cup resolutely. She sat back in her armchair and gazed out on the meadow.

'You remember being the height of a child,' he said, softly, 'but you're up in the air because your great-grandmother is carrying you.'

'Hmm,' she murmured.

'She is old, dressed in black, a long black dress …'

'… that rustles when she moves. It's smooth …'

'You hear her shoes when she walks,' he continued.

' … on the stone floor … no, the wooden floor.'

'She stops, and on the wall in front of you …'

Amanda was back in Cardiubarn Hall, in the arms of her great-grandmother. She was two years old, almost three. She heard her great-grandmother's voice close to her little ear.

'Now Amanda, you must meet your family. Ours is an old family, an ancient family, a venerable and powerful family, a great clan. Their blood runs in your veins – I hope – at least, somewhere or other,' she added drily. 'Now, you must not be afraid of how they look. Some are perhaps a little unexpected in appearance. Actually the portrait artists toned down the reality a good deal, if all I have been told is true!'

Amanda widened her eyes, but knew better than to vocalize her surprise at the image in front of her.

'This,' declared the old woman, 'is Blunderbore Cardiubarn, founder of our house.' His massive head seemed about to burst the confines of the picture frame, his snarl so pronounced it was almost audible.

'There is no existing portrait of his son or grandson, but here is Morgawr Cardiubarn, four generations on. You see the resemblance.' Amanda nodded mutely. 'Say no more …. Here is his daughter, Ysbore and hers, Endelion. At about this time, the clan became, shall we say, a little over-involved with keeping wealth and power of various kinds within the family. Marriages were kept between Cardiubarns, with some rather unfortunate results. Cormonran was one of them.'

In her two and a half years, Amanda had not seen a great many faces, but a sufficient number to register that there was something outside her experience in the portrait before her. She had grasped the concept of variety in features among her fellow humans, some of which could be extreme. Her grandparents' local baker was a man of advanced years with only two teeth, but, as part of a cheery grin, this held no terrors for her. The fishmonger had an exceptionally large nose but set between two such merry blue eyes that she soon stopped noticing it.

However, the faces that now confronted her, as her great-grandmother reeled off the names, were not just distorted but so cold and vacant of eye, so grimacing, that Amanda could hardly bear to look.

'Finally,' said the old woman, 'they had the good sense to realise that to produce useful offspring they needed new blood. That was the union with a Polgoyne.' She pronounced the name with distaste. 'A rival clan who claimed dominance over the elements, but at least ensured the survival of our blood line. This is the first result of successful breeding: Doombar Cardiubarn-Polgoyne, the last to bear the Polgoyne name. As you see, the union was a wise decision.'

Amanda gazed upon the normal-looking female face with the light of intelligence in her eyes if not goodwill to all men.

'And then,' continued her great-grandmother, 'we come to the beginning of the next era. But we shall save that indulgence for another day. Your grandmother is at the gate. You may go to her now.' With that she placed Amanda back on her little legs. 'You may thank me first.'

Amanda curtseyed. All at once, she saw her feet treading down stone steps. The hand holding her own was her great-grandmother's. Down, down, they went … to a door …. Then she was seeing Cardiubarn Hall over Granny's shoulder as she was being carried out to the car. There was something she had to tell Granny … if only she could remember. The great spiked edifice swam before her eyes into a mist that clouded her vision, then resolved into the white sky outside the Centre.

She gasped as though breathless from running, then put a hand over her mouth, looked down at the grass of the field, at the table in front of her and Trelawney.

'Hm,' she managed.

'You're back,' said the inspector calmly

'Yes.'

'Are you alright?' he asked solicitously.

'I think so.' Amanda put her drink to her lips, but it was cold.

'Wait,' he said, rising. 'I'll get you another.'

'No, please,' she said putting out a hand, 'let me tell you.'

'Very well, but at least have some water,' Trelawney urged her. He filled a cup from the cooler in the corner and brought it to her. She drained it. Amanda related to him, as coherently and completely as she could, what she had seen.

'So there was a union between the two clans?' Trelawney checked.

'For practical reasons,' she added.

'Good, good,' he said, as though to himself.

'This is supporting your theory?'

'Yes but ….,' he hesitated.

'You need more?' asked Amanda. 'You need the other portraits? The missing middle section?'

'Not before you've had a rest. But if you think you could.'

'Does it have to be today?' Amanda was not entirely keen.

'Do you really want to do this again?

'Not really,' Amanda admitted.

'Rest, while I get us some refills,' said Trelawney and went off to the canteen.

Amanda rested her head against the tall chair back and flopped her arm down next to her. Her hand encountered a reassuringly warm and soft surface. Tempest poked his head around the chair and jumped onto her lap. He kneaded her legs, immediately pulling her out of her dreamlike state.

'Here! Mind my dress. Don't you dare pull the threads with your claws. Soft paws, soft paws,' Amanda insisted.

He grumbled and proceeded with ensuring a suitable surface on which to deposit his rear end, and walk around it until he had arranged himself in a tight spiral of cat. He ended with his nose directed toward the window and the grassy stretch, with its possibilities of rabbits, squirrels, birds and other forms of entertainment.

Chapter 20

༄

CAT AND MOUSE

Trelawney, meanwhile, browsed for a snack that might help revive his time-travelling witness, and tried to slow his racing thoughts. Spell-weavers, diviners, ancient clans, giants, the secrets held by Senara Cardiubarn-Cadabra and Perran Cadabra, the mysterious Cardiubarn who had blocked his ability to see … see things others couldn't, his father … his father alone amongst the crows, keeping his son's secret at all costs ….

'Yes sir?'

He looked up into the face of the young dark-haired lady on the either side of the display cabinet. She raised an eyebrow and gave him a glance out of the corners of her eyes, saying.

'Crumpet?'

He suspected she'd said it with a saucy note, and that brought him down to earth.

'Erm, something sweeter, if you have it,' he replied.

'How about a nice bit of Victoria sandwich? We've got dairy-free, egg-free and gluten free or ordinary, and ordinary with coconut cream.'

Thomas had a vague idea that Amanda avoided dairy. 'Yes please, the last one and an ordinary for me, please. Also one hot chocolate with coconut milk and cream, and one Earl Grey tea with milk.'

'Right you are, sir,' she replied with a twinkle.

As Thomas waited then carried the refreshments back to the room, he reflected how kindly Amanda had encouraged and received his confidences. He had meant it when he'd said her grandparents had alibis, and yet, as she had no spell-weaving abilities of her own, how could she know what spellcrafting, or whatever it was called, could encompass? Who was to say they couldn't create some sort of charm that could push a vehicle off a cliff 400 miles away? Although that seemed a bit far-fetched, even to Thomas's imagination.

Well, at least we're in the same boat, he thought. Both from families who are supposed to be magical and neither of us with much to show for it. Both duds. But what if … what if it didn't always work the same way? From what Amanda had said, it seemed that it was expected to show at birth. But what if it didn't? After all, his supernatural aura, or what-have-you, must not have been present at the moment when he was born or how could his father have kept it secret? So then, what if Amanda's 'gift' hadn't been present immediately either? What if she was a spell-weaver and didn't know it?' His eyes were brightening with excitement as he followed his train of thought. As he knocked on the door for Amanda to let him in, the notion came to him:

What if she *did* know it? What if she *is* …. Wouldn't that explain how an asthmatic could cope with what would otherwise be the over-exertion of being a furniture restorer?

'Oh thank you,' said Amanda opening the door and

seeing the tray. 'How kind.'

He had arranged his features into relaxed amiability. 'I thought you could do with something sweet after that.'

'It was a bit of shock,' Amanda admitted. 'You know, it wasn't the features in those portraits so much as … well, they had the look of ill-intentioned giant haddock!'

Trelawney smiled, 'I can imagine how unnerving that would be.'

They ate and drank and talked about the natural world beyond the windows in front of them. There was a pause, and then Amanda, greatly daring, said teasingly, 'So how does it feel to be a witch, Inspector?'

'Great heavens! Am I?'

'Well, the Flamgoynes are said to be a witch-clan. I'll bet Uncle Mike told you that.'

'Yes, but I'm a defunct one.'

'Not necessarily. What if spells can wear off?'

'Can they?' He took a bold step of his own. 'You would know, Miss Cadabra, wouldn't you?'

Amanda looked at him questioningly, exuding an air of innocence that was entirely convincing, and in which she had been trained as a child by Granny. It had its effect. It was more convincing, Thomas reflected, than he had ever encountered from anyone else, and he remembered he'd experienced that from her before …. Yes … that evening ... that evening he'd told her about what the woman had seen on that fatal road, and he had asked her if she could think of any explanation … yes … innocence ….

'Why else,' he continued, 'would Mike Hogarth have said, "why don't you ask Miss Cadabra" how I could have had my gifts suppressed?'

'I supposed I'm the closest thing to a spell-weaving Cardiubarn now that all of the others are dead,' Amanda returned blandly.

'Would you tell me if I asked you … am I the only witch in this room?' Trelawney asked lightly.

'Witchcraft is not a crime, Inspector,' she returned matching his tone.

'True, not since 1956.'

'But murder is,' Amanda said seriously, 'and if saying that I am a witch or my grandmother was, makes us —'

'I would say no such thing, Miss Cadabra,' he forestalled her. 'You were three years old at the time, and in no way implicated, whatever your … your supernatural status, and your grandmother was here in Sunken Madley,' he concluded firmly.

Thomas could see that this was turning into a game of cat and mouse that would get him nowhere and could only weaken the connection that was strengthening between them.

He continued carefully, 'But I have no wish to pry. I feel, in my own case, that this is a very personal, private matter, and I appreciate the help and reassurance that you have given me. Now as to my theory. I need you to make one more trip back …'

'Very well,' said Amanda, relieved that he had backed off. She needed to think and to consult her grandparents before she revealed anything more to Trelawney.

Chapter 21

༒

THEORY, AND COVER STORY

Once more, Amanda relaxed, breathed, and, after only a few words of scene setting, lowered her eyelids and was silent. Thomas waited in stillness. Suddenly he jumped at the sound of a knock at the door, and Amanda opened her eyes.

'Miss Cadabra?' came an apologetic voice from outside. 'Sorry to disturb, but it's 3 o'clock.'

'Oh!' she said breathlessly. 'Thank you! We'll be right out!' She looked at Trelawney. 'Sorry Inspector.'

'Anything?'

'Oh, just a couple more portraits and one of a Cardiubarn who eloped with a Cadabra. By the time they were waylaid, the wife was pregnant and they were persuaded, with the assurance of every wealth and comfort for the rest of their lives, to return and bring up their family at Cardiubarn Hall. They did so. The old woman claimed that "alas, the climate did not agree with the parents and they were much mourned by their 17-year-old son," and then … we were interrupted.'

'Cadabra? What do you know about —' Trelawney asked.

'I told you. A French family who emigrated during the Revolution.'

'So no magical …?'

'Farmers, to the north of the Cardiubarn and Flamgoyne estates,' replied Amanda.

They gathered their cups and plates and left the room. There was a therapist and patient waiting nearby.

'Sorry if we have kept you waiting,' said Amanda courteously.

'Hardly at all,' they responded pleasantly.

Amanda and Trelawney took their litter to the canteen then headed, via reception, out to their cars.

'So … your theory?' she asked. 'Though I think I can guess.'

'Eugenics,' he confirmed.

'They were breeding for a superwitch, yes?'

'One who had the Polgoyne control of the elements, …' Trelawney began.

'The Flamgoyne divination,' Amanda added.

'And the Cardiubarn spellcraft.'

'*But*, breeding with such a limited gene pool would have meant miscarriages,' said Amanda.

'And stillbirths.'

'With every live birth being another roll of the dice.'

He nodded, 'With more and more riding on it as the clans grew fewer and fewer in number.'

'No wonder you were so important,' Amanda remarked.

'No wonder *you* were so important,' Trelawney returned.

'No wonder my parents couldn't get rid of me fast enough. To them I was a loss of face, a reminder of their failure,' she said comprehendingly.

'I can't say I like being shoved on the family discard

pile either by my grandmother and uncles, but it must have happened to other children too,' Trelawney commented consolingly.

'Hmm. Somehow that comforts me,' agreed Amanda.

'Yes, it wasn't personal.'

'No, quite; they were just a bunch of amoral psychopaths,' she observed without rancour.

'But not *all* surely?' pondered Trelawney.

'Yes,' assented Amanda. 'My grandmother wasn't like that.'

'My father wasn't.'

'But he was half Trelawney,' she pointed out.

'Yes, good guys, non-witches,' he replied with the suggestion of a grin. 'And in your case, surely the Cadabra blood would have leavened the Cardiubarn lump.'

'Well, I like your theory, and I don't feel so bad about the way my blood relatives behaved. You can't feel offended by people who don't know any better,' Amanda stated equably.

'Agreed. There was one more thing I wanted to have a brief word with you about.'

'Ok, shall we walk up the lane a little?' she suggested.

'Yes, good idea.' After a few paces he commenced, 'You told Mike that someone let slip that you're being watched.'

'That's right.'

'He's charged me with doing my best to discover who and why.'

He gave her the cover story.

'Your mother's in Crouch End though, isn't she?' Amanda objected. 'I'm sure there are classes closer.'

'Ah well,' he said slowly, 'here the matter becomes a little more delicate, and will require your understanding.'

'Really?' asked Amanda, doubtfully.

'Yes, you see the incentive to attend this particular class would be …'

'Would be …?'

'Yourself,' Trelawney finished.

'Me?' replied Amanda in initial bewilderment, closely followed by unwelcome comprehension. 'Oh! Oh no!'

'I'm afraid so. But let us make use of the kindly concern of your fellow Sunken Madleyists to see you suitably affianced, to our own ends, namely, identifying the person conducting surveillance of you and learning their reasons.'

'Very well,' she said resignedly.

'Thank you.'

'Maybe you can form an interest in someone else once you start attending the classes,' suggested Amanda.

'And I'm sure you have many gentlemen who already have an interest in you,' he responded gallantly.

'Good. Then we can just be friends,' she said with relief.

'Your neighbours should approve of that: getting to know one another before taking things any further,' Trelawney commented humorously.

'Before "walking out together" you mean?' Amanda replied in the same vein. 'And taking tea in the drawing-room every Sunday?'

'Properly chaperoned, of course!' said Trelawney thoroughly entering into the spirit of the thing.

'I'll be sure to arrive at the first class in lace gloves, carrying a fan and smelling salts in the event I should be overcome by the shock of being in such close proximity to so many gentlemen.'

'A wise precaution Miss Cadabra. Shall we turn back to our respective carriages?'

'Thank you Inspector, you are all kindness!'

'Not at all, Miss Cadabra, your comfort is at all times of paramount concern to me.'

'Having been entrusted with my wellbeing by the dear former chief inspector, no doubt.'

'Just so. I shall see you on Saturday week,' Trelawney said, as they reached their cars.

'I shall do my best to avoid a telltale blush at your entrance,' Amanda replied.

At that Thomas's gravity gave way and he laughed outright.

'Thank you, Miss Cadabra, for everything today. See you next weekend.'

Chapter 22

∽

TRUCKLED

'Hello, Bernie,' said Miss Armstrong-Witworth, her diminutive 90-something form, clad in a pale lace-trimmed, ankle length dress under a long coat of lavender, treading lightly towards her friend. Bernard Hodster was seated at one of the window tables in the big living room at Pipkin Acres Residential Home. He rose politely at her words, the sunshine catching his bald crown that was surrounded by still partly dark hair. Though of not above average height, his build still suggested the strength he had had in former years. His grey eyes crinkled merrily.

'Well, if it isn't Gwen, looking lovely as ever. You keeping well?'

'Very well, thank you, Bernie. I've brought a young friend of mine to meet you. May I introduce her?'

'Please do.'

'This is Amanda Cadabra. Amanda, this is Mr Bernard Hodster.'

'Cadabra? Not Perran's granddaughter, are you?' he asked with eyes alight.

Amanda smiled at that. 'The very same, Mr Hodster. It's a pleasure to meet you.'

'And you too, dear. A lovely man your grandpa, always a pleasure to work in the same 'ouse as him. Sit down, the tea trolley will be here in a minute. Tell me what I can do for you.'

'Well, it's about the old church hall,' said Amanda.

'Ah, that. Hm. A bad business, but it was always just a matter o' time. Ever since the place was built!'

'There's something wrong with the building?'

'*Some*thing? *Every*thing I should say. I can remember, to this day, what my granddad used to say about it. He quoted for it, to build it, you know. Hodsters and Sons were the best builders in Hertfordshire back in those days. But the project was "truckled" as they used to say.'

'Truckled?' asked Amanda.

'Miss Truckle, as was,' Mr Hodster began. 'She married the rector. He was a Dunkley, the family that owned Sunken Madley Manor for hundreds of years, where the Poveys are now. But of course, you know that, havin' done the job there not long ago. Anyway, the rector was a Dunkley, though not a main line of descent Dunkley, you understand, but he had the name. All class and no brass. That was the trouble. Then young Dunkley meets Josiah Truckle who was a warm man — oh I mean by that, wealthy — but come up through business, hard graft, and wanting to settle his daughter Lavinia higher up in life than his own working-class roots.'

'So the match was made?'

'Yes, and very happy they both were with it, Granddad said,' answered Mr Hodster. 'Dunkley was pleased as punch with his smart new wife all tricked out in the latest fashion, and full of ideas for the parish, if you please,' he added disapprovingly, 'and her come from all the way over in Warwickshire, knowing what-all about Hertfordshire ways.'

'Really?'

'I should say. My dad, he could remember that Lavinia, always with 'er 'at full 'o ostrich feathers. Well, The Great War was on, see? And she sees how many great ladies was opening their big houses up for the wounded, and she sees herself just like them. But she and her 'usband, they has only the rectory. And she was a great one for the amateur theatricals, with herself always the star of the show, you understand.'

'Oh dear,' remarked Amanda.

'So,' continued Mr Hodster, 'she has this idea to build a church hall. Big, with a stage, and lots of space in the cellar for props and suchlike. I don't know as how she put it to 'im, but she got Josiah, 'er dad, to be more than willing to stump up the readies and no mistake. Good as gave 'er a blank cheque. Then she goes and takes on the whole project.'

'Was Lavinia's family in the building trade?' enquired Amanda.

'No, dear, not a whit. Josiah Truckle was in bicycles. Bi-truckles, the company was called. And very well he did. Whole ones and parts.'

'So how did she manage a construction project?'

'Got an architect, but boasted as how she sketched out the design with her own hand. So then she starts getting estimates, and my granddad — too old for the War, you understand, and my dad too young, in case you was wondering — puts in his figure for building the hall, and well spoken for he and my great uncle and so on were by all around. But then —'

'Afternoon lie-dies and gintelmen. Sorry to interrupt, but may I serve you tea?' came an Australian lilt behind them.

They looked up into the comely and kindly face of Megan, one of the residents' favourite staff members.

'Ah, here she is, our peerless angel,' proclaimed Mr

Hodster.

'Hillo, Bernie. Why it's Amenda, isn't it? And Gwindolen.' They returned her greeting warmly.

'You two do git about. What can I give you? No need to ask Bernie here: builder's tea, right?'

'If you please.'

'I'll take Lapsing Souchong, if I might, dear,' requested Miss Armstrong-Witworth. 'You brew it so well here.'

'Amenda?'

'Trade tea for me too,' she grinned

'Good girl,' approved Mr Hodster. 'I heard you'd taken over the restoration business from Perran.'

'That's right. He was an excellent teacher.'

'I'm sure he's very proud of you, wherever 'e is. I hear you do work that would be a credit to him.'

'Oh, thank you, Mr Hodster. It means a great deal that you should say that.'

'Yes, well, I do still walk into the village, and, of course, Hugh and Sita Povey visit.'

'They do?' asked Amanda in surprise.

'Hugh was born here, you know. That's his great uncle Donald over there. Oh, we don't half like Hugh and his lovely wife. You know they asked everyone for ideas on what they could do with the Manor to help the community? Isn't that nice? Thank you, Megan. Bless you,' he said taking his tea. 'Just 'ow I like it.'

'Yes, it is, and I'd expect no less from them,' said Amanda. 'They were lovely to work for, even though I didn't see much of them.'

'They told us all about the smashing job you done on their banister, and you found a security risk into the bargain.'

'Fig newtons and Garibaldis,' said Megan, putting the dishes of biscuits on the table. 'See you later, Bernie, ladies.'

'Thank you,' they chorused.

They had gone rather off-topic, and Amanda was wondering how to return the subject to that of the church hall. But Bernie Hodster had not lost the thread.

Chapter 23

❧

THE SABOTEURS

'So,' said Bernie Hodster, adding two spoonfuls of sugar to his tea, 'getting back to the old hall. The Hodsters put in their tender to construct the new church hall; an honest sum, said Granddad, for a good and proper job. But then along come the Reckets. Silas Recket with all his oily charm, flatterin' and flirtin' and deferrin' to Lavinia Truckle-Dunkley like she invented the brick, and offerin' her rock-bottom price. Well, she falls for it, doesn't she?'

'Oh no,' responded Amanda.

'And off the Reckets go, cutting every corner in the book. And Granddad said, and Dad too, as how the Reckets had a system. Whenever they built a house, they would riddle it with faults, and make notes on what they done. Eventually, the house would leak gas, or rot, or the rain would come in, and the notes would tell what was wrong. So then they'd make a big show of mending this and that and charging the earth, and, finally, lo and behold, they'd find the problem and pretend to fix it. They'd been doing this for generations, knowin' that every botch would come home to roost and lay another golden egg for the next wave of Reckets.'

'The church hall floor!' exclaimed Amanda.

'That's right,' confirmed Mr Hodster emphatically. 'Charged her for oak and used pine coloured up. Too thin and never treated it neither. And Granddad said he wouldn't have been surprised if they'd set woodworm on it. The hall went up fast all right, too quick for any to see what they was up to. I don't know how they got it past building inspection, but by no honest means, I'd swear.'

'So it was only a matter of time…?'

'Right enough. And it was used as a hospital, all those beds and men and nurses walking across it, and then after the war was over, the ball, with people dancing and well…'

'There was an accident?' asked Amanda intently.

'Terrible it was,' said Bernie sadly. 'And a soldier too. Come through the War and then … went clean through onto Mr Giddins collection of anvils.'

'Anvils?' Amanda asked, to check she had heard him correctly.

'Yes, the Giddins family had been blacksmiths back in days gone by. Well, the poor man who fell through hit his head on the anvils, and that was that.'

'Oh how dreadful!' exclaimed Amanda.

'Fortescue Dunkley, deceased,' concluded Bernie, in funereal tones. 'Though he wasn't a man as was well-liked, and some said it had been contrived, but I don't reckon to that. Not seeing as there was a whole ball full of people dancing away over the same spot that night. Still, who's to say?'

'How come the anvils were in the cellar?'

'They'd belonged to Mr Giddins, as I say, but he got killed in the War, and his widow couldn't bear to sell them but wanted to store them, and asked the rector, who didn't want to say no.'

'I see.' Amanda had drained her cup.

'So there you are. That's everything I can tell you about the hall. Like another cup, dear?'

'No, thank you, Mr Hodster. You've been more than helpful.'

'Well, I expect you must be getting back,' said Bernie, stirring, 'and I have a croquet match soon but before you go ....'

He leaned towards Amanda and Amanda did likewise so catch his whisper:

'If you want to know more, it's not *cherchez la femme*, but *cherchez les notes*.'

* * * * *

As they walked back to the Astra, Amanda was silent at first, mulling over what she had learned. At least, now she understood some of what she had witnessed in the church hall. The soldier falling through the floor must have been Captain Dunkley. But what about the woman? And the legs coming out of the ceiling and the fall from above? And why had she seen it? Was someone trying to tell her something? Finally she said aloud,

'Thank you Gwendolen. That was very informative.'

'You're welcome, dear. May I ask what Bernie whispered to you?'

'"*Cherchez les notes*."'

Gwendolen nodded. 'Find the Recket papers documenting their botches.'

'We need to discover who would be the most recent legatee.'

Miss Armstrong-Witworth pulled on her lace gloves with determination and uttered,

'Cynthia and I will be on the case of finding out who the most likely person is to have inherited them. My dear, you leave that one to the back room boys!'

Chapter 24

୬

FIRST CLASS

Amanda was nervous. She said as much to Grandpa.

'I know you weren't expecting the inspector to join the class when you first agreed to be in on it,' replied Perran, understandingly.

'Or that it was going to be used as an opportunity to catch a spy,' added Granny.

'But just try to relax and enjoy yourself,' he recommended.

'I wasn't expecting to be in the spotlight, is the thing,' explained Amanda.

'Well, you don't have to closet yourself away with him in a corner. Just greet him as a friend and dance with him as you would with any of the other partners, and you won't add fuel to the gossip fire.'

'And you've got new shoes!' Grandpa reminded her. That made Amanda smile naively and look down at her feet, flexing her ankles to watch the play of light on her footwear.

'Yes, I do like my new dance shoes.' They were orange. They matched her orange circle skirt and top, worn over black cycling shorts.

* * * * *

Amanda, parked, approached the open door of the church hall and calmed her breathing.

Just inside was a table bearing a clipboard and a black cash box. An elderly man, with smiling but weary grey eyes, and wearing a white shirt and bow tie was limping towards it. He bade her a cheerful good evening in a gravelly East London accent.

'Good evening, er, Mr Woodberry?'

'Vic,' he replied, shaking her hand. 'And you'd be?'

'Amanda.'

He sat down at the table and looked at his list.

'Amanda Cadabra?' She could see he was wondering if the spelling was correct. People usually did. 'That's right,' she reassured him.

'Int'restin,' Vic commented. 'Is this your first time at this sort of a class?'

'Yes. The rector —,' who had excused herself on the grounds that she didn't want to cramp anyone's style, '— asked me to be as supportive as possible. Is there anything I can do to help?'

'I don't think so. But you can go and introduce yourself to Majolica.'

Amanda paid, then walked the length of the hall toward the stage, catching sight of Trelawney out of the corner of her eye. He was in conversation with the Sharmas.

Majolica, intent on her audio set up, was standing with

her back to the hall holding a pair of headphones to one ear. Amanda stood politely at her elbow. Majolica gave her an unsmiling glance and continued with what she was doing. Amanda waited. The woman went on with her activities. Amanda turned and looked around. There were Sylvia and her husband coming in, then Joan and Jim, Sandra's sister, Vanessa, looking fit in yoga attire with her mid brown wavy hair in a ponytail adorned with a yellow lily, Irene James, jewellery maker and mother to supermodel Jessica, Hugh and Sita Povey, who spotted Amanda and waved, followed by Sandy from The Big Tease, taking a little time off while Alex looked after the café.

Ah, there's Ruth, bless her, thought Amanda, giving up queuing for Majolica's attention and going to greet her young friend.

'Thank you for coming along, Ruth.'

'Hi, Amanda. Not many here yet,' she remarked hopefully.

'More are coming in,' replied Amanda, gesturing towards the door.

'Jonathan!' exclaimed Ruth. The devastatingly handsome but incurably shy assistant librarian was an unexpected arrival.

'Oh, but here's Mrs Pagely,' Amanda said, pointing out his kindly boss. 'I expect she's persuaded him to come and promised to look after him.'

'Who's that?' asked Ruth, seeing an unfamiliar man of medium height with dark brown, carefully windswept hair.

'Leo, the new salon co-owner,' answered Amanda.

'He looks all right,' judged Ruth.

'I think so.'

'What's *he* doing here?' the teenager was staring towards the portal. 'He's a bit celeb for this, isn't he?'

'Yes, I didn't expect to see Ryan. Still, cricketers are

allowed to dance, and perhaps he's showing solidarity with the rector.'

'Oh *no*!' Ruth gazed appalled at the young man at Ryan's side. She groaned. The cricketer had Erik's son, Kieran, in tow. 'I don't *believe* this.'

'Don't worry, Ruth, you'll only be dancing with him in very short bursts, just like with all of the others.'

Amanda suppressed her laughter. Her young friend's martyred expression would have done credit to a portrayal of Joan of Arc in her final moments.

The sea of attendees near the entrance parted as the ladies from The Grange entered. The Misses de Havillande and Armstrong-Witworth waved to Amanda. For once, Churchill, the terrier had been left with Moffat, general factotum and de facto master of the great house and grounds.

The doctors Patel, Neeta and Karan, came in, acting as a buffer between the casually but persistently feuding Miss de Havillande and Dennis Hanley-Page, who was turned out to a T in a striped blazer and cream trousers.

The 'Colonel' sauntered in and handed over his cash as Majolica finally and grandly turned to the hall and, with a gracious smile and gesture of the hand, commenced,

'Good afternoon, new dancers. What a pleasure to see so many of you. Thank you for making the first class of our wonderful new course such an abuhhhndant one.' She had a tendency to draw out her words, which put Amanda in mind of some of the more unfortunate products of the local theatre school a few miles away.

'Now, gather round, gather round. Introductions first. My name is Majolica Woodberry and this … Victor, perhaps you would like to come to the front now?' Majolica pronounced it Vick-tour, to Amanda's amusement. 'Yes, this is my husband and dance partner of many years, Victor.'

'Good evening, all,' said Vic, amiably.

'Next, any questions?'

The hall remained in somewhat overwhelmed silence. Amanda turned her head to her right to see who would be so daring as to speak and Ryan caught her eye and smiled. She nodded her recognition. She looked to the left, to see Leo giving her a little waggle of the fingers. Amanda acknowledged him likewise.

'Very well,' continued Majolica, apparently gratified to see her class so subdued, 'but if you have any, at any stage, please do not hesitate to call upon either myself or my husband.' She paused as though to allow the enormity of this concession to sink in, then went on, 'To begin with, we will learn the very basics of a dance that is probably the most familiar to many of you: the waltz.'

In their serried ranks, Majolica put them through their solo paces, then lined up leaders and followers opposite one another, and had them partner up. Soon Mrs Woodberry considered them ready for musical accompaniment.

'Change partners!' she called, and Amanda found herself standing in Trelawney's excellent frame.

'Good evening, Miss Cadabra.' He seemed to be entertained.

'Good evening, Inspector,' she returned politely.

'How are you liking our gracious instructor?' he asked, leading her smoothly through the steps.

'Overpowering. I don't know how you can chat. Don't you have to mind your feet?'

'No, thanks to my admirable parent's dedicated and, I might add, exhausting tutelage.' They waltzed on, Amanda counting in her head, until she was able to say,

'You do her credit. Spotted any potential spies yet?'

'Only a few,' he replied, playfully.

'Change partners!' came the call.

'Thank you, Miss Cadabra.'

'Thank you, Inspector.' And Amanda passed to her right.

Dennis was an experienced and light leader and gave her a brief respite until she was instructed to move to the waiting arms of Ryan Ford.

Chapter 25

༄

MANOEUVRES

'Finally, we get a moment to talk.'

'I can't, Ryan, I have to concentrate,' Amanda protested.

'Afterwards then. It's for the community.'

'Oh?' she replied suspiciously. But he said no more and let her mind her dance steps. A few moments later, Amanda was in the inexpert hands of young Kieran, her solicitor's son. He appeared to be suffering.

'Not enjoying the class?' asked Amanda sympathetically.

'Oh, it's not that, it's ….. Dad's always spoken highly of you. You have to help me!' he whispered urgently. 'You're her friend. She thinks I'm a moron.'

'Ah. Let's chat afterwards, OK?' He nodded and looked relieved. Amanda had spotted an opportunity that she had been hoping just might open up.

Next, she was received by Leo, who looked delighted.

'Isn't this great?' he enthused.

'Yes, it is,' Amanda agreed. 'It's good to see the village

out in force and doing something together apart from sharing the news of the Sunken Madley world.'

'Have you considered the tea break suggestion?'

'I have,' stated Amanda, having thought it had opportunity to interview a potential spy. 'How about elevenses on Monday? In The Big Tease?'

'Done. I'll be there. I'll let sis know I'll be out of the salon for a short time. She won't mind. I have only one appointment at nine, and I'll easily be finished by then.'

'Good,' said Amanda.

Halfway through, Majolica called a break, and Amanda had another crack at breaking the ice with the lady. This time, Mrs Woodberry paid heed.

'Sorry I was so preoccupied when you came up before, dear, but I wanted everything to be *per*fect for the first class. You understand, don't you?'

'Of course,' Amanda replied politely. 'Is there anything I can do to help? The rector especially wanted me to ask.'

'No, nothing. My husband Vic-tour and I have everything under perfect control. We work together like a well-oiled machine, you know. After all these years, it's really second nature. We have our own studio, you know.'

'So I heard. Very close to Sunken Madley,' remarked Amanda conversationally.

'But, of course, not *in* Sunken Madley. No, we are in Romping-in-the-Heye.' Majolica emphasised this as though it placed her several rungs up the social scale from the village in which she was at present condescending to teach.

'How do you like the hall? Will it do?' asked Amanda civilly.

Majolica glanced around it with pity, but uttered philosophically, 'I've been in worse. Anyway, it's for a good cause.' Amanda having had as much as she could take of Lady Bountiful, excused herself with,

'Well, I'll get some water, and leave you to it.'

'Do that. Hydration. Sooo important.'

Amanda walked away and gasped as though she had been inhaling a too strong scent. Trelawney was now chatting to Vanessa, who was looking a trifle starry-eyed. Leo and Ryan were standing together, each with their hands in their pockets, looking about the hall and apparently commenting on it.

Amanda saw Kieran at the water table, and not only took pity on him, but homed in to acquire a possible ally and extra pair of eyes.

'What can I do to help?' she asked comfortingly, leading him to some chairs at the side.

'Ruth thinks I'm a twit just because I play cricket. It's not even like I'm that good. Well, it's only the *second* XI, and I didn't *intend* to be good at it and picked for captain! It just sort of happened. My thing is French 13th-century history and the Crusades and playing Medieval Melée online, and I *know* Ruth plays it too, but she won't even *talk* to me.'

'All right, all right,' soothed Amanda. 'I understand. I remember at her age taking a rather extreme view of certain things too. You're probably just the same about some yourself.'

'Yes, but I'm fair, I hope,' protested Kieran, in his own defence.

'OK, leave it with me.'

'Thanks, Miss Cadabra. Dad said you were a good sort.'

Amanda nodded, as Kieran went off back to Ryan's side, where he seemed to feel safe.

'What did *he* want?' asked Ruth, returning and indignantly plumping herself down in Kieran's vacated chair.

'To plead his case,' replied Amanda gently.

'What case?'

'The case for being able to be intelligent, a lover of history, an online gamer of Medieval Melée, and, just a little bit, entirely unintentionally, rather good at a sporting activity.'

But Ruth had sprung to attention as if by an electric shock. 'He plays MM?'

'Indeed.'

'He likes history? What history?' interrogated Ruth.

'Thirteenth century French and the Crusades.'

'Hm,' said Ruth, pulled up short in her tracks. Amanda maintained a tactful silence while her friend digested these startling revelations.

Clap! Clap! Majolica's hands commanded attention. 'Let us all assemble, ladies, gentlemen, leaders and followers!'

Jonathan returned to the floor, now carrying a camera, intending to get some shots of this historic first class for the library Community Board. Mrs Pagely had advised him to wait until everyone had warmed up and got their confidence before capturing them in the act. He had intended to be discreet, but had been spotted by the eagle eye of his teacher.

'Oh. Oh dear, no,' bemoaned Majolica, opening her hands either side of her face. 'Gentleman-here-on-the-left … your name? Jonathan? Yes, Jonathan, *if* you wouldn't mind, returning your camera to your bag. You see, my husband likes to be the one to take photographs. Thank you.'

Vic appeared momentarily bewildered but, at a stern glance from his wife, looked helplessly at Jonathan, then walked up to the young man. 'Here, son, I'll look after that for you,' he offered kindly. 'Perhaps once she gets used to you, she won't mind if you do the business.'

'No problem, Mr Woodberry,' replied Jonathan, whose hands shook a little as he gave his camera into Vic's keeping. 'Got lots of things I can practice on.'

'Got your St Ursula festival coming up, and when the new floor gets constructed I'll bet the rector would love some blow by blow photos of that.'

'Yes, the library would put them up on the Community Board too,' said Jonathan enthusiastically. 'I work there,' he added with simple pride.

'Good man. That's the ticket,' Vic commended him and patted his shoulder.

The class practised what they had learned in part one, and more steps were added to create a little routine. This required sufficient concentration to be a bar, for Amanda at least, to any further conversation with any of her partners, beyond the thank you's at each parting.

Finally, the lesson was pronounced over, applause followed, and the dancers headed for their bags and street shoes. Amanda found Ryan at her elbow.

'Have you heard about the new chef?' he asked.

'Erm ....?'

'At the Snout and Trough?'

'Oh yes, Sandra hopes for her Michelin star with this one, doesn't she?'

'Yes, and that's just it. He's doing a grand sort of opening on Sunday week, and she's asked me, in my capacity as local celebrity, to be seen dining there.'

'And are you going to?'

'Of course. But it would look so much more attractive in the press photos if you would join me.'

'Attractive? If you want a trophy date,' said Amanda, practically, 'you'd much better ask Jessica. She's a model after all, and practised at that sort of thing.'

'Actually, she's already going with the local pinup. At Sandra's request and Mrs Pagely's cajoling.'

'Jonathan?' Amanda asked in amazement.

'Indeed. Sandra suggested that I ask you.'

'How about Vanessa?'

'She's got a prospective date in her sights.'

'Then what about Penny? She's pretty.'

'The doctor's receptionist?' he said with a hint of distaste.

'Don't be such a snob,' Amanda teased him.

'Please, Amanda. Do it for Sandra,' he pleaded, 'if not for me. Come on, my treat; I still owe you that dinner.'

Amanda tried not to look or sound like Ruth.

'Thank you, Ryan, that's very nice of you. And of course, anything I can do to help Sandra.'

'One o'clock then?'

'See you there.'

Amanda groaned. She had been planning a nice quiet Sunday lunch with Tempest and *Blythe Spirit* on DVD, digitally remastered. Still, it might be a chance to get a feel for a possible spy.

'Well done, dear!' Miss Armstrong-Witworth commended Amanda as Ryan moved off, mission accomplished. 'You move so gracefully; it's a pleasure to watch you.'

'I do?' responded Amanda in surprise. 'Thank you.'

'Have you observed our dear Sylvia and our new preceptress?'

The two ladies were nodding graciously to one another across the length of the hall, then each turning away, the one to her sound equipment and the other to the door.

Amanda giggled. 'Are they pretending that they've never met?' she asked.

'I think that was the sight of two worthy opponents saluting one another,' replied Miss Armstrong-Witworth, mischievously.

'*En Garde*!' laughed Amanda.

'Indeed. Such an entertaining evening. Ah, I believe the inspector wishes to bid you farewell,' Miss Armstrong-Witworth pointed out, helpfully.

Trelawney was looking in Amanda's direction as he moved slowly towards the exit. She went to join him as they walked to their cars.

'You look vastly entertained,' she observed.

'That was fascinating,' Trelawney replied. 'My first sight of a proper old-fashioned English village up close and personal.'

'Terrifying, isn't it?' quipped Amanda.

'I see what you're up against in the gossip stakes.'

'At last.'

'And how intricately interwoven they all are,' he marvelled.

'Quite.'

'The ladies seem to adore you,' he remarked. 'Every one of them gave me a glowing testimonial. Even Vanessa.'

'I don't know her very well. But she did seem rather taken with you,' said Amanda impishly.

'A charming lady,' Trelawney responded blandly.

'Good. Someone else for you to start a gossip chain with,' she said triumphantly.

'Not sure I want to encourage that. I have the feeling that she wants to drag me off to her cave.'

'Well, I'm sure it's a very comfortable one. I think she's done OK for herself. You could be onto a winner there,' Amanda teased him.

'Thank you so much for your sympathy and understanding, Miss Cadabra,' he replied dryly.

'And what about the spy? Maybe they weren't even here.'

Trelawney was suddenly serious. 'Oh, they were here,' he stated. 'Every instinct I possess tells me unequivocally … that they were present.'

His assurance impressed Amanda. She thought, as she had so often been compelled to, that there was more to the inspector than met the eye or she gave him credit for.

'Any ideas of who it might be?' she asked.

'Ideas, yes,' he replied.

'Are you going to share them with me?' she asked,

hopefully.

'Share? No,' he stated affably but finally. Amanda regarded him speculatively and decided that there was no point in trying to persuade him. He glanced at her, read her expression correctly, and said, 'Good call, Miss Cadabra.'

Amanda laughed. 'Thinking better of attempting to persuade you, you mean?'

'Quite.'

'I seem to remember,' she said, changing the subject, 'that we shan't have the pleasure of your company next Saturday.'

'No, Halloween is a busy time for the station. People do get a bit carried away. But the following week, of course.'

'Will you try to see your father in the meantime?'

'I will. I shall try to have news for you by the Feast of St Ursula of the Apples at any rate, and I very much look forward to your expert guidance around Sunken Madley, past and present.'

'You remembered. Good.'

'See you in a fortnight.'

Amanda waved him off. She now had a new date, an elevenses, and a village tour booked. She noticed Tempest on the roof of the Astra.

'That was exhausting. I want my sofa,' she told him.

He stared back with affront.

'Oh OK; *our* sofa!'

Chapter 26

ↄ

STORM WARNING

During the following week, Amanda asked her grandparents to assist with her dancing practice later in the evenings as well as with her programme of magical training.

'You're coming on, *bian*,' pronounced Grandpa, on Monday, as she gently lowered the second workbench and a chest of drawers to the floor, while continuing to keep the stirring action of the brush in the glue pot going.

'Much better control,' agreed Senara. 'Now. Just the armoire.' Amanda looked doubtfully at the enormous 18th-century French wardrobe that needed new pegs and a strip and wax.

'Remember, love, don't *push* it up; *allow* it to rise,' urged Perran.

Amanda took a breath and deliberately relaxed her shoulders. She pointed her Pocket-wand at the massive piece of furniture and gently spoke the word: '*Aereval*.' It lifted like a cloud.

'Up,' said Perran. 'Good. And hold … now …. without turning around, raise the hammer off your bench behind you.'

'But I can't see it,' objected Amanda.

'Feel for it. Feel for the iron.'

'OK …. Yes! I can feel — ' Thump! The wardrobe hit the floor. 'Oh dear. I was so pleased with locating the hammer I lost my concentration.'

'That's all right, *bian*. I gave you a new thing to do as well as a heavy thing to lift. But you have to be prepared to do unexpected combinations of things without losing your focus. Tell you what: tomorrow we'll practice locating materials separately, all right?'

'Yes, please, Grandpa,' answered Amanda with relief.

'You're coming along nicely, isn't she, love?'

'You are indeed, my dear,' agreed Granny.

Amanda arrived at the Reiser's house as her phone alerted her to a text.

Hi, really sorry but got a panic client at 10.45. Sis says rest of week's jam-packed. Hope to see you Saturday, Leo.

She was slightly relieved, still a little tired from the previous week and the class. The cancellation meant that she could just work steadily through the morning.

On Tuesday, Amanda went, as she often did, for dinner with Aunt Amelia in Muswell Hill, a few miles to the south of Sunken Madley. Amelia Reading was not an actual aunt but a close family friend who had helped to bring up Amanda to be the fine covert witch she was today.

A once famous, but now mostly retired, glassblower, Amelia had been nominally training her de facto niece to 'see possibilities' since she was nine years old. Amanda loved the colours of the globes that Amelia had created, but never saw anything in them but goldfish (whom she had seen so often she had named) or a representation of Paris in the snow. Regardless of this, and more importantly, Amelia had remained Amanda's chief confidante and occasional supplier of titbits of information about her grandparents' pasts that were hard to come by from the horses' mouths.

Amanda had plenty to tell her aunt about the first dance class and her impressions of the teachers. Her impersonation of the overpoweringly gracious Majolica Woodberry had Amelia chuckling heartily. Amanda reported that the Inspector, as she invariably referred to him, was turning up in the guise of a student to discover the identity of the person in the village who was spying on her.

'And does he have any notion yet of whom it might be?' enquired Amelia.

'Yes, but he's not telling. All he gave away was that he was sure it was someone who'd been present at the first class. But of course it could have been someone who was there *unseen.*'

'Hm,' said Amelia, getting up from the dining table and sailing into the drawing room, her long elegant green gown swaying about her as she walked. Amanda followed her to the chairs at a round table where Tempest had chosen to sleep, next to an orb filled with silver stars and a rainbow. Amelia sat down, pushed back her dark chestnut wavy bob, took the globe in her hands and gazed meditatively. Amanda wasn't sure if she actually saw things or it just helped her to focus, but, presently, her aunt spoke.

'I don't like the look of these clouds .... Of course, they might disperse ...' She glanced up at Amanda, 'How is your training coming on?'

'Pretty well, I think. Why?'

'Can you support a weight and perform a minor spell at the same time, with control and accuracy?'

'Yes, Aunt Amelia.'

'Good. Keep training,' said her aunt, sitting back from the globe

'I will.' Amanda got up. 'I must get home, I've got work tomorrow, and I keep having to use manual methods instead of magic with Mr Branscombe around.'

'You *are* careful, aren't you?'

'Of course,' said Amanda putting on her coat. 'It's mainly just setting the cabinet scrapers on the go.'

Amelia rose, put her niece's scarf around her neck and looked into her eyes.

'And you never use magic on humans, do you, sweetie?'

'Of course not.' Amanda was surprised by the question. 'I have no reason to.'

'It is very important, Ammy.' Amelia looked at her seriously. 'You must never … cast a spell on a human … again …. Do you understand?'

Amanda had never seen her aunt look so grave.

'Yes, … I mean, I know about the ripples in the ether that it causes. I know how dangerous that would be.'

Amelia lowered her voice. 'Right now they suspect that there is magical power in your village.'

'They?'

'The Flamgoynes. The spells you have used so far, on people, have shown up on their radar as vague clouds with Sunken Madley as some kind of epicentre. But they will not use their resources unless they are sure. They must *not become* sure,' said Amelia with emphasis.

'OK,' Amanda responded a little bewildered. 'What is it that you saw in the globe, Aunt?'

'All I can tell you is this: one more spell of that kind and the balance will surely tip,' she warned.

Amanda looked solemn and nodded. 'I understand.'

Amelia arranged her niece's scarf more becomingly. 'There now,' she said giving it a final pat. 'Orange always did suit you. No need to worry now. You just need to be a little circumspect. Let your inspector —'

'He's not *my* inspector.'

'*The* inspector then. Let him do his job, and all will very likely be well.'

Amelia opened the door. Amanda kissed her cheek.

'Take care,' said Amelia. And somehow Amanda had the distinct feeling that she meant it as no ordinary farewell.

Amanda returned on Saturday to celebrate Halloween, Samhain, with her aunt, They were to dine as usual, but first, as Amelia said, 'We shall do our remote work.' Amanda nodded. 'Which we keep absolutely secret.'

'Yes, Aunt.' Amelia lit the candle, arranged the crystals, Tempest came to the table to join them, and they began. It was, as always, over far sooner than it seemed. Then Amelia took the nut-stuffed pumpkin, spiced bread and baked apples out of the oven and they feasted.

Amelia did not mention again what it was she had seen in the glass globe. Amanda was relieved, but the memory of her aunt's warning stayed with her. It had been very clear: if she did not want the Flamgoynes to close in on her village, she must never again cast a spell on a human. Surely that was a rule that it would be easy enough to keep?

Chapter 27

⤫

EARWORMS

On Saturday, Amanda, arriving early at the church hall, had been planning to chat to Vic, as he seemed the friendlier of the two Woodberrys, but the front door was locked. She saw him carrying in the various pieces of sound equipment from his van through the side door.

'Hello Vic,' she called. 'Can I help?'

''Allo Amanda. Yes, you can open up the front for me.' He tossed her the key. She applied it and returned to his side, handing it back to him. 'Can I carry anything?'

'No, I'm used to it, but thanks for asking. This is my part, you see. I carry in the equipment and put it out, and Majolica does the fine-tuning and sets up her playlist for the afternoon.'

'I see.' She heard the crunch of tyres on the gravel of the car park, and soon Majolica entered.

Amanda issued a greeting then retired to a chair nearer the front door to await the arrival of the rest of the students.

Within a few minutes, the class began arriving, and Amanda was besieged by dancers asking where Trelawney was. Vanessa, in particular, seemed disappointed. Leo was apologetic about Monday. The salon was taking off, and he couldn't be spared.

'Good,' said Amanda. 'I'm glad business is flourishing.'

'Just a rain check though,' Leo insisted. 'As soon as I get a breather, I still want to keep our tea-break appointment.'

'Of course,' she agreed.

Ruth made no effort to make a get-away when Kieran diffidently approached her. Nor did she issue any complaint about him to Amanda, who diplomatically refrained from questioning Ruth on the subject, when Kieran withdrew to beneath the wing of his cricketing hero, who was on the opposite side of the hall. Good, thought Amanda, if Ruth is Kieran's friend and Kieran is Ryan's friend, there might be a chain of communication there. But also, the teens seem well-suited and could probably both do with a friend.

Once again, Majolica put her students through their paces with her characteristic combination of sharpness and sweetness. However occasionally off-putting her presentation, the class was grasping the basics of the waltz and building their confidence.

At the conclusion of the lesson Majolica made an announcement.

'As you are all aware, next Saturday falls on 11th of November, Remembrance Day, when we are mindful of all who have perished as a result of war. In honour of those who endured the conflict during which this hall was built and in which peace would have been celebrated, after the class, there will be an extra one-hour social. If anyone has any requests of songs or music that were popular in the 1914-to-1918 period, please, do let me know and I shall do my best to play them for us all to dance to. That is all. See you next Saturday!'

During the week, the song, *Roses of Picardy* kept playing

in Amanda's head. She found herself singing it, surprised that she knew the words, as she rinsed off the stripped banisters with methylated spirits. When she found herself dancing to it on the landing of the Reiser's house, she stopped and sent a text.

Hi Majolica, please may I request Roses of Picardy for next Saturday? Will email you the file. Thanks, Amanda.

* * * * *

Trelawney got up to stretch his legs, after a long afternoon of typing, signing, and reading reports after the hectic Halloween week. The morning had been spent in court and had set back his schedule. He was staring out at the oak tree in the car park, now bare of leaves, when his phone provided a welcome interruption.

'Miss Cadabra, what a pleasant surprise.'

'Hello, Inspector, well I thought you wouldn't pick up if you were busy, so that's good.'

'What can I do for you?' he asked genially.

'I was calling to ask if I might claim a waltz on your dance card,' she answered in a jovial tone.

'Certainly, I shall append your name with delight. Any in particular?'

'It's a song that's been going through my head for days on end: *Roses of Picardy.*'

'I don't know it, I'm afr—' Suddenly it was playing in his mind: Roses are shining in Picardy, in the hush of the silver dewww. Roses are flow'ring in Picardy, but there's never a ro-se like you! And the ro-ses will diiie with the summertime, and our roads may be faaaar apaaart, but there's one rose that dies no-t in Pic-ardy! T'is the ro-se that I keep in my heart.

'Actually…, I must have heard it somewhere. It's strange you should mention it. May I ask, do you recall the first time you noticed it ear-worming you?'

'Yes, in the church hall. I was in the cellar, I think ... the first time I was there,' Amanda replied.

'Hmm.'

'Why?'

'Because I heard the song that's been on my brain when *I* went into the hall for the first time. I was there early. It was empty, and I heard this song: "Mademoiselle from Armentières, parlez-vous, …"'

'" … Hinky dinky parlez-vous,"' finished Amanda.

'You know it?' asked Trelawney.

'Apparently,' said Amanda, surprised that the words had just come out of nowhere.

'Did you see anything on that occasion?' he asked.

'Yes, but it made no sense at all,' she replied.

'I saw something too when I heard *Hinky Dinky* ... and it made no sense at all.'

'Let's talk about it on Saturday,' Amanda suggested.

'Yes. Meanwhile, I think I'll ask Majolica for *Hinky Dinky* to be played at the dance. Would you care to take the floor with me for a 2-step?'

'I would indeed. It will cause a scandal, no doubt,' she commented in daring accents.

'Standing up with the same lady for two dances,' he replied in the same vein. 'Quite. I'm game if you are.'

'You're on,' declared Amanda, surprised at how well he knew his dance etiquette history but rightly attributing it to his mother's efforts. 'See you on Saturday. Oh, best to download and email the file to Majolica. Then she's got no excuse not to play it!'

'Roger that,' Trelawney acknowledged.

'Over and out.'

Chapter 28

༄

WHAT THEY SAW

The following week, the reappearance of the new class favourite was greeted with enthusiasm. 'The return of the prodigal,' commented Amanda to Trelawney as he guided her down the room. They were learning the quickstep, at which Trelawney seemed as adept as the waltz that they'd repeated the previous week.

'The novelty, more like,' he responded.

'Still having private lessons at the Mrs Trelawney School of Dance?' asked Amanda merrily.

He chuckled. 'That has a wonderfully Victorian ring to it. My mother would like that, seeing as it's the antitheses of everything that she is.'

'Any news on the other parental front?'

'No, my father was busy again, but I hope to see him this week.'

'Still having ideas about our spy?' Amanda fished.

'Yes. Tell me, was everyone who came to Week One

here last week?'

'Yes. No. Dr Karan Patel was on call, and couldn't come.'

Trelawney nodded.

In the break she saw him helping Ryan and Kieran with one of the step combinations. However during the second half, Majolica taught them all the 2-step, and everyone was confident that they had grasped it. No sooner had the end-of-lesson applause died away than Majolica made an announcement:

'And now, keep your dance shoes on as we go into the special extra hour of our get together on this Remembrance Day.'

The lively conversation in the hall quietened to a murmur. Earlier that day, at precisely 11 o'clock in the morning, a hush had becalmed the streets, shops, cottages and the school of Sunken Madley, as its inhabitants had stood in silent respect for the fallen in general and for those, in particular, whose names were inscribed on the monument on the green. The village, although remote in its way, bore its own scars of war, right back to the Wars of the Roses and the Battle of Barnet that had destroyed the church, wounded The Grange, Sunken Madley Manor, and the Priory, had leveled cottages, and laid low civilians and soldiers alike in the orchards and woods about. In the last century, two more wars had added to the sad roster of the honoured dead, now once again among them in thought.

Miss de Havillande mounted a box before the stage.

'Fellow villagers and visitors. There is not one among us here today whose family was not touched in some way by the conflict that came to its merciful end on this day 11th November in 1918.' There were nods from the crowd.

The Community Board in the library bore what photographs families had of great-grandfathers, great-uncles and great-aunts who did not return: Gordon de Havillande;

Francis Hanley-Page; Arjun Patel of the Indian Expeditionary Force; Hiranjan Sharma of the Gurkha Rifles; Pawel the Royal Mail delivery driver's great uncle Aleksander Mazurek, pilot; George Whittle; Irma Uberhausfest's cousin, 19 years old, German infantry, perished in the mire of the Somme; Ollie Kemp who joined up at 16, lying about his age, then shot as a deserter fleeing the horror for which he was unprepared. The rector back then had risked being defrocked by insisting on Ollie's burial in the hallowed precincts of the churchyard, interred with full honours beside his grandfather. Near him lay nurse Armstrong-Witworth who perished when her ambulance was hit by a shell. The list went on. Amanda knew their faces as well as those of their descendants, studying them as she had every autumn, reaching for some sense of what it had been like to live through such perilous years, how the smiling faces among them found light in those dark times.

'Please take a glass from the table at the front,' Miss de Havillande invited. She waited and then raised her goblet, and, quoting from Laurence Binyon's poem written at the start of the Great War, she spoke the lines, '"*At the going down of the sun and in the morning, we will remember them.*"'

'We will remember them.' the audience responded and sipped.

'Now!' said Miss de Havillande briskly. 'They would not wish us to hold their memory in sadness. They died for our freedom that we might live in peace and happiness. Therefore, let us celebrate life with song and dance. Mrs Woodberry, if you would be so good, strike up the band!'

On cue, *It's a Long Way to Tipperary* began playing. It was followed by the beguiling waltz of *Roses of Picardy,* for which Amanda found Trelawney at her side. She began in proper waltz frame, her upper body rotated away to the left, but as they danced it seem unnatural and she turned to face him. It was as though she had danced every day of her life.

Amanda heard his voice close to her ear. She looked up and he was singing in a light baritone: 'Roses may fade with the summertime …'

For a moment he seemed to have a moustache and be wearing a peaked cap with a badge on it. Then not.

The dance came to an end. Somehow they were both breathless. But there was no time for comment, as Trelawney's request was beginning, *Mademoiselle from Armentières*. They stepped jauntily around the hall. He seemed to know every word. The lyrics, though bawdy, were often funny. He looked down at Amanda as she threw back her head and laughed, and, suddenly, she was clothed differently. He felt her long skirt against his trouser legs. Her hair was short, curling around her ears, and then she was back in her usual gear.

At the conclusion of the dance, Trelawney drew Amanda's arm through his and led her out of the side-door. They looked at one another.

'Did you see…?' they both asked at once.

'I'd have sworn I didn't know all of the words to *Hinky Dinky Parlez-vous*,' said Trelawney.

'And I *know* I can't waltz that well!' stated Amanda.

'And you were suddenly dressed in a long skirt and your hair —'

' — and you had a … it must have been a military cap on!'

'But I don't belie ….'Trelawney stopped. '"There are more things in heaven and earth" … I think *that* I *do* believe.'

'All right,' said Amanda, 'so we're agreed on what we saw?'

'But *why* did we see it?' he asked.

'Yes, why, and why *us*?' she added.

'Yes, no one else seemed to experiencing anything unusual in there,' Trelawney observed.

'Look, we're sharing the *space* with the people who were here back then, just not their *time*. Maybe that's all there is to it. We just happen to be … sensitive to it,' suggested Amanda.

Trelawney was silent, frowning slightly. 'No,' he said slowly. 'That's not it. I don't think this is about the past.'

'That certainly looked like it to *me*,' replied Amanda.

'I mean, I think someone in the past is trying to tell us something.' Trelawney was feeling his way.

'Wars are bad?' hazarded Amanda.

'No, more … more ... local than that …. Specific to us, this place, now…. What if it's ….?

'A warning?' she said finishing his thought. 'But of what? There's no danger here now; no wars, barely any crime, the hall is structurally safe, everyone is medically fit to dance. What could there possibly be a warning of? Or maybe those people were just trying to connect with us.'

'I don't know … yes, but *why*?' Trelawney returned to the question.

'You think they had a message?'

'The first time I was here and heard the song,' he said with a little difficulty, 'I thought I saw beds and … and —nurses they must have been — women with veils, and something was wrong with the floor.'

'Yes, I saw that floor thing too,' concurred Amanda, 'but I've seen the supports in the basement myself. They're makeshift but they're good enough, and Mr Branscombe, who is a builder, has confirmed that they'll hold for now.'

Trelawney sat down on a stone bench.

'Are you all right?' asked Amanda with concern.

'You'll have to excuse me,' he answered, 'I'm not used to being presented with information in this way. I like nice solid witnesses and informants and members of the public who come into the station in modern dress and say things like, I overheard Jason Smith tell Dale Moggin in the fishmonger's that they're planning to raid the till in the bike shop next Thursday.'

Amanda laughed. 'You're doing very well, Inspector.'

'Thank you.' He stood up. 'Well we'd better go back in and dance with other people.'

'Yes,' agreed Amanda. 'You can say I had an attack of the vapours and needed some fresh air in which to recover my equanimity.'

It was Trelawney's turn to laugh. The next time she saw him in merriment, was at the end of the dance, standing with the Patels. Again he looked in her direction as he was leaving and she joined him outside.

'Having fun with my doctors?' she asked, gratified to see how well he was getting on with her fellow villagers.

'We were swapping coroner jokes. I thought I knew them all. But Karan had a new one,' explained Trelawney with a grin.

'Thomas!' came Vanessa's voice from the church door as she hurried towards them.

'Next Saturday at 12, yes?' he asked Amanda quickly.

'Yes, come to the cottage.'

'Oh sorry, Amanda,' said Vanessa sincerely, 'Hope I'm not interrupting.'

'Not at all, I'm just off. See you at the Feast,' she replied with wave and a smile.

Chapter 29

✎

THE SECRET OF SUNKEN MADLEY

Amanda was ready when Trelawney rang the bell at her house. Tempest, fast asleep, hanging like a grey fur stole over one arm of the sofa, was not.

'Cup of tea before we start?' she offered.

'Thank you. I'm good to go.'

'Very well.' She stepped out and closed the cottage door behind her. 'Here to our left, is *The* Orchard, the oldest and most important of Sunken Madley, and where some of our festivities will be held later. But first, let us proceed "in an orderly manner" back up Orchard Row.'

'As a policeman, I would not dream of proceeding in any other way,' he returned with a twinkle.

'Naturally,' she replied. 'This is the house of my best friend Claire Ruggieri, who is a film producer, currently filming in Thailand. You may have seen her name on the credits of such popular movies, and according to Claire, insults to the art form, as *Blockbuster!*About a karate expert who becomes a movie mogul. And *Mindless Dribble*, the tale of an airhead who becomes a soccer star. She's working on *Blockbuster! II* in the hopes that it'll pay off her mortgage and she can make good, if poorly paid, movies.'

'I look forward to meeting the delightfully candid Miss Ruggieri in due course,' remarked Trelawney, remaining tactfully silent on the subject of both movies.

'Yes, she hopes to be home for Christmas. It would be wonderful if she could. Otherwise I'll be watching *Love Actually*, *White Christmas* and *Die Hard* with just Tempest! Meanwhile ...to our left, we just passed the playing fields that back on to Sunken Madley School, founded in 18-something for boys, and then, 50 years later, they happened upon the radical notion of educating females.'

'How shocking. Heaven knows where that will lead,' said Trelawney with a deadpan expression.

'They'll be wanting the vote next,' Amanda responded in kind. 'We are coming to the ingeniously named High Street, and we'll turn right now towards the gateway to the village.'

'Sounds grand,' he commented.

'Oh, believe me, it is … in spirit, that is. On your left, you see the chemist's.' Mr Sharma looked up at that moment and gave a nod and a smile. 'And the next establishment of note is the new salon, Tressed Up, owned by Leo and Donna Weathersby.'

'Leo I have already had the pleasure of meeting.'

'And here is our first coffee stop: The Snout and Trough. Proprietor: Sandra. She won't be front of house at this hour, and Vanessa, her sister, will be physical-fitness-training a private client in the West End most likely.'

'Really?'

'Yes, she's very good, I hear, and much in demand. And she is hot.'

'Something only the shallow-minded person in need

of her services would notice, of course,' he responded with a gleam in his eye.

'Of course,' agreed Amanda.

They found a quiet corner table and brought their drinks there.

'Mind if I ask a question?'

'Fire away,' replied Trelawney readily.

'Have you had a chance to talk to your father?'

'Tuesday evening, I'm having dinner with him. After that I should have some news. Hopefully.'

'OK. Well, then, how about you? Any questions on the tour so far?'

'Yes, the one that has been on my mind since I first came here,' answered Trelawney.

'Oh?'

'How did the village get its peculiar nomenclature?'

'Ah.' This could be a sticky one, thought Amanda. 'That is something few people know, and you won't find it in any guidebook either.'

'I shall treat it as privileged information,' he promised.

Amanda nodded.

'The Wood and the orchards have been here since before records began. Eventually, they were claimed by a baron or a king. About a thousand years ago, the priory — I'll show you that at some point — was built, and the land given over to the care of the brothers, the Benedictines. Over time, these rented to farmers whose cottages sprang up, and so the place came to be called Monken Orchards. Or simply Monken for short.'

'Understandably,' said Trelawney.

'It was a time of fear and ignorance and superstition,' Amanda continued. 'That is the important thing to bear in mind, as we come to this next part in the story.'

Trelawney nodded.

'There had long been a cottage on the edge of the

hamlet, where dwelt a wise woman. She would have had skill in healing, knowledge of herbs and midwifery, practical knowledge, counsel and comfort. Such people were called pellars or wisewomen. Later, they came to have another name; a word that people were taught to fear. One day, in such a climate of terror, the villagers went to her cottage and brought her forth. They led her to the pond, where they conducted a trial by water. As they shouted and jostled and waved the implements of their livelihood, they cast her in. It is said that she did not struggle, but slipped beneath the surface of the mere into the depths below. Some, realising what they had done, threw themselves in after her that they might, at least, retrieve her body. But she had vanished without a trace. When the mob came to its senses, horrified at their heinous deed, they took covenant with one another never to reveal to the outside world what had taken place. But more than that, when they confessed their wrong to one of the brothers residing in the priory, he laid upon them this task, to which they bound themselves in solemn oath of blood: that henceforth, even with their very lives, to protect ever more the inhabitants of the so-called "witch's cottage". In time, the wisewoman's successor appeared there and hers in turn. During the worst of the witch hunts, the villagers concealed her in cellars and barns, and the Dunkley Manor kept her safe within its hidden places.'

'And the name?' asked Trelawney, captivated by Amanda's tale.

'Somehow some breath of the story escaped to the neighbouring hamlets, of the maid who sank beneath the waters of the pond. So that instead of "Monken" it came to be "Sonken"… Sunken Maid … Sunken Maidee, and, perhaps in memory of the moment of frenzy that overtook the villagers on that fateful day: Madley. Sunken Madley.'

Trelawney inhaled, opening his eyes wide for a moment. 'My word. That's quite a story.'

Amanda inclined her head in agreement.

He was silent for a while, then asked, 'And am I to get to see this legendary cottage?'

Amanda stirred her tea, and then looked up at him.

'You already have.'

'I've seen it?' he queried in surprise. 'But I've only been to …' He looked back at her.

Her heart was beating so loudly she could have sworn he must have heard it. Thomas was at a loss for words. He wanted to say something reassuring, and yet at the same time, he wanted reassurance himself. 'I … you …'

Amanda said lightly, 'It's quite all right, Inspector. I'm not going to turn you into a toad. We really don't do that sort of thing any more. It's generally considered vulgarly exhibitionist.'

A flicker of anxiety showed for an instant on his face, then he broke into a smile and breathed.

'Phew! Well, that's a relief.' He lowered his voice. 'So you are a ... a ... witch?'

'My grandmother was certainly a wise woman,' Amanda answered carefully.

'No wonder the village is so protective of you,' Trelawney remarked.

'To be fair, I think they are protective of me because I came here, to live, as an orphan, I am to all intents and purposes alone now, and the village has, in a sense, helped to bring me up.'

'You are in every sense then the village witch,' he observed.

'No, Inspector,' Amanda countered. 'I'm sure no one thinks of me as a witch. Like you, I have some intuition, and a lifetime of stories of things esoteric told to me by my grandparents. The villagers do not come to me for either healing or advice, except on furniture issues. I will admit to being as a much of a witch as you will admit yourself to be.'

'Is it the original cottage still?'

'It's been extended and modernised, but, yes, the heart of it is the same.'

'Does it have anything … unusual about it?' he asked, curiously.

'Like, are bits of it made of gingerbread?'

He smiled. But Amanda spoke with seriousness.

'It's my home. It's just my home. My life began, not when I was born, but the day that my grandparents brought me there for good and adopted me. And you can make whatever you want of this, Inspector,' she said with increasing intensity, 'but the day my family went over that cliff was the best possible day. Because they could never try to take me away from the only *real* parents I ever had, the only family that ever *loved* me …. Perhaps we should go.' She began to rise, but he put out a hand her arm.

'Please. I understand. Really I do.' There was so much sincerity in his voice that she sat down again. 'Your family was dangerous. Then, suddenly, that day the minibus crashed, you were safe. My family was dangerous too, and then suddenly, because something my father arranged and some good fairy did, *I* was safe. At least, that's how it seems to me, in this alternate reality I seem to now inhabit,' he said shaking his head.

Seeing his uncharacteristically lost look, Amanda softened. 'I can see how bewildering this not so brave new world is for you.'

'Thank you. Look. I'm not out to get you or your grandparents. How could I? They are beyond the reach of any court in which I could present any evidence against them. I just want to find out what *happened* that day. Don't *you*?'

Amanda stared at him.

'If it turned out that your grandparents did something to make you safe, would you really think less of them?' he asked her earnestly.

Amanda was silent. He tried another tack. 'Do you think less of my father for… blocking my channels or whatever they call it? For having my memory removed of my … gifts? Do you think he was a bad person for doing that?'

'No,' she said at once with feeling. 'Of course not. He did what he thought was best to protect his child.'

'Then …,' he began.

'Yes, yes I see,' said Amanda, 'But that's different. He didn't —' she lowered her voice '— kill anyone.'

'We don't know that your grandparents did either,' Trelawney replied reasonably.

'Will you excuse me for a moment?' asked Amanda getting up, trying to hide her agitation. She gestured towards the ladies restroom.

Oh dear, he thought, what have I done?

'Of course,' he said, rising politely as she left the table.

Amanda was in desperate need of a private conference with her grandparents. She did her best not to run.

Chapter 30

ᗌ

THE LEGEND OF ST URSULA AND THE BEAR

Mercifully the loos were empty. 'Granny! Grandpa!' Amanda whispered urgently. They turned up, Grandpa leaning with his back against a sink and Granny checking her hair in the makeup shelf mirror. 'Did you hear that?'

'Oh yes, dear,' replied Senara calmly.

'Well?' asked Amanda with emphasis.

'Well, what?' enquired her grandmother, distracted by a loose pin.

'*Did* you? Did you bump off the family?'

'Bump them off the cliff, you mean?' asked Perran jovially.

'Grandpa, it's not funny,' his granddaughter responded severely.

'Finding out is part of your training, dear. Think of it as a puzzle,' said Granny encouragingly.

'A puzzle?' exclaimed Amanda, appalled by her grandparents' light-hearted view of the matter.

'Yes, dear, a team-building exercise,' replied Senara heartily.

'Team? What team?'

'You and the inspector. You're doing very well,' Granny commended her. 'In spite of your trust issues.'

'Trust issues?' protested Amanda indignantly. 'You're the ones who trained me to keep everything secret.'

'Not from everyone,' countered Grandpa.

'Oh?'

'I'm sure you can name at least three people with whom you can share information about your magical abilities.'

'Well ... Aunt Amelia.'

'Good. One,' said Grandpa.

'Bertil and Kerstin Bergstrom,' finished Amanda.

'Well done.'

'See how much more clearly you think when you're not getting all emotional?' Granny pointed out.

'So you want me to go in there and tell the inspector, "Oh, actually I'm a levitant and a spell-weaver and …" Hang on a minute … it was … it was … *you*, Granny! You put the spells on the inspector! *Didn't* you?'

'Did I?' replied Senara blandly.

'Didn't you?'

'Do you think I was the only Cardiubarn who would be prepared to help a Flamgoyne suppress his son's powers?'

Amanda wasn't so sure now. 'OK. Well, do you want me to tell him I can send furniture flying around the room and —'

'No,' interrupted Senara. 'That is for him to work out. He is being trained too.'

'By whom? Ohhh, Uncle Mike? Good grief. This *is* an alternate reality. I know *just* what the inspector is going through,' said Amanda with genuine fellow-feeling.

'Now go back in there and play nicely with the

inspector,' Granny instructed her. 'Stop treating him like the big bad wolf.'

Trelawney, meanwhile, ordered a hot chocolate and an orange Club biscuit, hoping to appease Miss Cadabra with a peace offering. He prepared himself at her approach. Unexpectedly, she smiled and sat down.

'Oh, how kind! Is that hot chocolate?'

'Yes, with coconut milk.'

'Oo, and a Club biscuit. I'm sorry if I became somewhat ... heated,' said Amanda, unwrapping her treat. 'I've thought it over, and I agree. We should work together to discover the truth. I will help you in any way that I can.' She held out her hand. He shook it with obvious relief. 'Though I don't see *how* I can.'

'A trip down memory lane?' he suggested.

'Here? Now?'

'No, I think today is crowded enough, don't you? Maybe we can arrange another session in that lovely room.'

'Don't say that too loudly,' she urged, dunking her biscuit in her tea, 'it'll be all over the village, and you'll be forced to make an honest woman of me.'

'Ah. A pitchfork wedding?'

'Or shotgun. Miss de Havillande has a licensed rifle.'

'Gulp.'

'Although Miss Armstrong-Witworth is accredited the better shot,' added Amanda, fast regaining her sense of humour.

He grinned.

Amanda finished her biscuit with relish. 'Shall we go?' she asked cordially.

'Yes, I'd like more tour.'

They left the pub and, companionably, walked back along the High Street.

'Salon,' Trelawney repeated his lesson. 'Leo and Donna.'

'Good.'

'Chemist, Mr Sharma. Alexander and Julian's The Big Tease, yonder, I already know. Ah, the Sinner's Rue, and over there where Orchard Way turns off the High Street, is the corner shop and post office, Mrs Sharma. And here we have the church, and that shelter is … ?'

'The little covered market for market days.'

'When is market day?'

'Well, we don't actually have one, but it's good for people to stand under if they get caught in the rain, and we do use it for the Feast sometimes.'

'It's the thought that counts,' said Trelawney charitably.

'We think so,' agreed Amanda with a twinkle.

'That, I imagine, is the rectory.'

'Yes, our rector is The Reverend Jane Waygood, who is the model of kindness, goodness and diplomacy. She's like you: keeps the peace.'

'Oh really? Between …?'

'Mainly between Miss de Havillande's Land Rover and Dennis Hanley-Page's selection of vintage, classic and veteran vehicles, in which he pushes the envelope of their capabilities and the speed limit. Except we don't actually have one of the those.'

'Sunken Madley has no speed limit?'

'What I mean is, it has no *urban* speed limit. The 70 miles per hour limit on the A1000 somehow continues to apply.'

Trelawney mentally reviewed the route in the village. 'You're right. There's no 30 or 40 miles per hour sign between here and well … Barnet.'

'Quite.'

'Good grief.'

'Yes, Inspector, you're in the badlands now.'

'So I see. Illegal wood-burning, delinquent drivers, a village with a homicidal history, whatever shall I find next?'

'Time will tell,' replied Amanda.

'May I ask another question?'

'Please do,' Amanda invited him cordially.

'The Feast of St Ursula of the Apples?'

'And right on cue, we arrive at the church, where the story shall be revealed unto you,' she answered portentously.

It was empty of people but abundant in foliage. Holly berries, ivy, and pots of Michaelmas daisies adorned the ends of the pews and the chancel.

'Splendid,' remarked Trelawney, looking around. Amanda led him to in front of the altar.

'Are we allowed to be here?' he asked.

'Of course. Now, behold.' She gestured upward to the stained glass window rising above them.

'Impressive …. The young girl is …?' asked Trelawney.

'St Ursula.'

'Somehow I imagined an older lady.'

'Oh no, when she performed her miracle she was accounted little more than a child.'

'Is that the bear?'

'It is.'

'And a bag or basket of apples. How does all of this fit together?'

'Well,' said Amanda, leading the way to the front pew, 'if you're sitting comfortably …?'

'Do begin,' he requested eagerly.

'Once upon a time, back in the wild days of the Dark Ages, there was a hamlet surrounded by orchards. The apples were its prosperity and its sign of blessedness and abundance. However, they were also the envy of a neighbouring tribe that set its sights, not so much on acquiring the land but, on destroying its pride and joy. And so the jealous rival tribe prepared. Gathering torches, they planned to attack at dawn and burn every tree to the ground.'

'How dreadful,' remarked Trelawney.

'Indeed. However, as the sun was rising, a young girl, Ursula, whose task it was to feed the geese first thing in the morning, was greeting the dawn from the window of her sleeping place at the top of the house. From there she espied a strange and wondrous site. For at that moment, a troupe of mummers, having made an early start on the road to London, were upon the way with their cart and trappings. And one of them was leading a creature such as Ursula had never laid eyes upon before.'

'Aha,' said Trelawney, making a guess at what it might be.

'To her gaze, at first, it had the aspect of a monster. But then, as the mummers came closer to the village, Ursula perceived that it was a young animal. It was, although the name was unknown to her …'

'A bear?'

'Just so; a baby bear. Seeing it led by a rope around its neck, Ursula's tender heart went out to what she thought to be a mistreated orphan. However, at that very moment, the wind changed, and the faint smell of smoke assailed her nostrils. She looked over to the north, and there, her young keen eyes detected the flicker of flame. At once, Ursula slipped down and out of the cottage, darting between the trees until she could see the army massed against her little kingdom.' Amanda paused for dramatic effect.

'So what happened next?' asked Trelawney.

'Without hesitation, she ran to the mummers, grabbed the rope and ran with the little bear towards the line of enemies now coming toward the precious orchards, and took off its leash. The bear did not run but stayed at Ursula's side and roared at the flames and the would-be assailants. The enemy, believing the creature to be a demon from the Netherworld, dropped their torches and fled in terror, never to return to the land guarded by the creature from Beyond.'

Trelawney applauded.

'And so,' Amanda continued, 'Ursula saved her village and the orchard. She encouraged the bear to roam freely but he chose to remain with her, sensing her kind heart, and they remained friends for the rest of their days. And in death they were not divided, for here, beneath our feet, they are entombed in the crypt, side by side.'

'And here in this window they are commemorated,' added Trelawney. 'St Ursula. Ursa: bear, Ursula: little bear. But what a delightful story. Do you think there is any truth in it?'

'Well, this stained glass window is hundreds of years old, and the tombs are there. Perhaps her name wasn't Ursula, but she was so named after the event. Nevertheless, truth or legend, it is *our* legend and *our* feast. To which visitors are welcome,' Amanda added with a smile.

'I expect everyone prepares something, do they?' asked Trelawney.

'Yes. It's not obligatory by any means. The pubs and The Big Tease contribute, and people who like baking and cooking and brewing make cakes and pies and cider and scrumpy and pork and apple stew. There'll be plenty to eat, you'll see. It starts after the service. Well, it's more of a short talk, by the rector.'

'It's not exactly biblical,' Trelawney observed.

'Oh no, my goodness, it's as pagan as they come. But this is old land, old bones, the old religion is deep in its roots. The trees, the water, the wind, the spirit of the orchard.'

'Erm, how does the rector get permission to er …?'

'It's a community thing. And community is good,' explained Amanda. 'It is like an embrace of the village holding it close to the land.'

'What will the talk be about?'

'The story I've just told you. Reminding us who we are, what makes us special, what our story is.'

Trelawney frowned in confusion. 'You say *we*, *our*, and yet … you are a Cornishwoman, are you not?'

'True,' she agreed, 'but anyone who lives here is part of the "us". And it is the only story that is, in some way, related to me that I know. My grandparents never told me of who I was in Cornish terms. To protect me, I suppose.'

'Maybe one day you'll find out,' he said gently.

'I know as much about the Cardiubarns as I want to know,' Amanda countered wholeheartedly.

'The Cadabras then. You said they were, are still, I suppose, farming folk from the north of the Moor.'

'Yes.'

'Perhaps eventually you'll visit,' Trelawney suggested.

Amanda shook her head. Her immediate rejection of the idea surprised him.

'Why not?' he asked.

Amanda saw Grandpa appear beside her. 'You can tell the inspector,' he said.

'You can tell me,' said Trelawney, echoing the words that sounded in his head.

'Granny and Grandpa made me promise never to cross the Tamar without them. I swore a binding oath.'

'Perhaps in time you will feel that that embargo is lifted.' A few weeks ago Amanda herself had resolved that one day she would take the road over the river that divides Cornwall from the rest of England, and visit to the land of her birth and her inheritance.

'Perhaps,' she said noncommittally.

Chapter 31

୧ඁ

FESTIVE SPIN

'Hello,' said The Reverend Waygood brightly, entering from the vestry in splendid robes of red and green.

'Rector, this —' began Amanda.

'Oh yes, Inspector Trelawney,' said Jane shaking him warmly by the hand. 'How very kind of you to join us.'

'My pleasure, Rector. Miss Cadabra has just been explaining the origins of the Feast.'

'Wonderful, isn't it?' remarked Jane happily. 'Probably total fiddle-faddle, but I fell in love with the story at first sight, I promise you. Did Amanda tell you about *The Appel Songe*?'

'Er, no … is it some kind of hymn?'

'Not one that you'll find in any book. It was discovered in the bowels of our very odd library stacks, written in medieval English, although we sing a modern version, together with a melody composed by one of the rectors in the sixteenth century or whatever, to what he claimed were the original verses. Fortunately, we have an able pianist in our midst who has kindly learned to play the organ in her spare time. Ah Neeta, here you are.'

'Hello, Inspector,' called the newcomer recognising Trelawney.

'Hello, Dr Patel.'

Amanda and Trelawney left them to their pre-service conference.

'Is Sunken Madley listed in the Domesday Book?' asked Trelawney.

'No, but the priory is listed in *Holy Houses of Hertfordshire* by Nonius written 1171, only 31 years later, so we're pretty much up there with the longest pedigree villages.'

The congregation was filing in, one or two in high spirits, one or two in *other* spirits, having made a start on the cider, every one with smiles and anticipation of the entertainments to come. They were all, including Amanda and Trelawney, chatting away so merrily that they failed to notice the sight that now confronted the rector who stopped abruptly half-way up the pulpit steps.

Tempest had seated himself upon the lectern and, with benevolent satisfaction, was gazing down upon, what he regarded as, his worshipers,. His witch's first hint of the incursion was an urgent whisper from Jane, who had rapidly descended the stairs.

'Amanda!'

She looked up to see the rector's finger pointing upwards. Amanda gasped, rose guiltily and hurriedly mounted the pulpit, gathered her unrepentant feline in her arms, and, blushing, returned to her pew. Some of the congregation were consumed by fits of giggles.

'Honestly!' Amanda addressed him quietly but emphatically. 'You are the limit!' Tempest wriggled himself into the space between his human and the end of the pew, forcing her and Trelawney to move up. There he sat, regarding the rector with interest, as though he had written her speech himself.

The guffaws and chortles died away and the service began. Sure enough, the rector told the tale, and the audience rose to sing *The Appel Songe*. To Trelawney's ears it was startlingly pagan, with praise for the spirits of the apple trees, the apples, the apple blossoms, the apple peel and the apple pips, the sun, rain, drizzle, wind, mist and fog, earth, earthworms and a species of bird of which Trelawney had never heard. Then came the final rousing chorus,

> *Our foes will ever flee in fear*
> *When Ap-pel spirits do appear*
> *To lend a hand and find a way*
> *To save us as they did that day.*
> *The Orchards rare*
> *They are still there;*
> *Praise Ursula and the li-ttel bear!*

They all applauded loudly and strolled back out and through the rectory, collecting delicacies, some still singing. Trelawney and Amanda waited in their seats for the traffic to abate.

'So, am I to have the delight of tasting your cooking?' he asked gallantly.

'Nope,' said Amanda definitely. 'I am excused on the grounds that I made something else. Something more enduring than apple turnover.'

'Oh?'

'Yes. That.' She pointed to the altar. On it was wooden casket filled with apples. It was the apples that drew the eye, bright rose red and shiny green. But Trelawney went up to examine their container. It had an appealing rusticity to it and was carved with oak leaves and apples, apple blossom, and here and there, a bird.

'You did this?' he asked in wonder.

'I did. With my own fair hand-tools. Old school.' She had too. Back in the days when Perran had insisted she learn the ways of the old non-magical crafters.

'You astound me,' said Trelawney. 'This is extraordinary.'

'Thank you,' replied Amanda, with a smile and a flush of pleasure at his unexpected praise.

'Certainly, no apple pie needed,' he confirmed.

'Shall we go and find Jim's? That's Joan's husband. He makes the best apple pies, and I want to make sure that you have the best!'

'Thank you for the tipoff. Yes, let's go.'

It seemed that the whole village was out in force. Both Alexander and Julian from The Big Tease tea and coffee shop, Sandra and Vanessa from the Snout and Trough, in fact, everyone who couldn't get staff from outside Sunken Madley had, apparently, shut up shop for the day. All of the dance class members were there. Tempest was hanging around the pork and apple stew pot. Someone was sensibly putting some onto a plate for him. Amanda saw Esta Reiser chatting to Erik, her solicitor. Their teenage offspring, as far away from their parents as they could get, were in animated conclave, no doubt about tactics in Medieval Melée. Leo was there, by the apple fritters. Amanda was looking around for his sister, when she felt her phone vibrate. It was a text.

Hi Amanda, I can't get hold of Leo and don't want to spoil his first festival. I wonder could you be an angel and pick up the crystal and plate for the after-dance party? No one else I know has a boot big enough and I have to keep an appointment with a major, very exacting client. If you could pop round? I'll load you up. 5 mins tops promise. Love Donna x

'Inspector,' said Amanda, looking up, 'is it OK if I leave

you for five minutes? Just have a little errand to run.'

'Of course,' he answered readily.

'Joan?' Amanda called out.

'Dear?' said the postlady, appearing.

'Could you take the Inspector to Jim's pies for me? I just have to pop off for five minutes.'

'Oo yes, you leave him with me,' said Joan heartily. 'Can't promise I'll let you have 'im back though, love!' she added with a wink, taking Trelawney's arm. He grinned down at her.

Amanda slid into the Astra and drove the 20 or so yards to outside the salon. Donna was coming out with a crate in her arms. Amanda hastily went to the boot to make space.

'You are a life-saver!' exclaimed Donna. 'You can have a free appointment any time you like!'

'Not at all,' replied Amanda smiling.

'No, I mean it. We'll do your hair for the Christmas ball. How about that? And New Year!' insisted Donna.

'That's very kind, but I really don't mind.'

'Wait here, I'll get the next lot.'

'Can I help?' Amanda offered.

'No no, I'm fine …'

The boot filled up, crate after crate with carefully packed glasses and fine china.

'This is most generous,' remarked Amanda, admiring the quality of the crystal and flatware.

'Oh, the salon I was at before used to give evening parties with champagne and caviar. When they revamped their image, they got all new plate and crystal and said I could take this lot.'

'It looks expensive. Are you sure …?'

'Nothing but the best for the Feast. Look, the church hall will be opening at 6 o'clock to prep for the dance class, that's when I was supposed to deliver this lot. Just go in through the front door of the hall. Here's the key, but if you wait until six, they'll be there to help you carry it in. Put it on the table just inside the door, and that'll be good enough. Take it slowly, getting it from the car, if they're not there yet, don't want to bring on your asthma.'

Amanda, silently agreeing, said, 'That's OK, I'll wait until six, if that's when they're expecting them.

'That's great. Just wish I could be there.'

'Next time,' said Amanda consolingly.

'Exactly. Must rush. Thanks a million. You're a star!'

Amanda drove to the church car park slowly, not wanting to cause any breakages. She found the inspector and kept an eye on the time, as she and Trelawney mingled with the feasters until it was time for the procession.

'Procession?' he queried, looking around for floats and a band.

'It's not really a procession,' Amanda modified. 'It's just a ramble to The Orchard.'

'Your orchard?'

'Yes, well, just *The* Orchard. I don't actually own it!'

'Should I take my, er, whatever this drink is?'

'No, there'll be more food and drink there, I assure you.' The air was cooling with the setting sun. 'There'll be hot apple juice, and cider mead.'

'Cider mead? That's a new one on me. Maybe I should get out more.'

'It is on most people,' Amanda replied reassuringly. 'Don't worry, you can take a sip and still be legal to drive home, but I'd stay away from Mrs Kemp's apple gin if I were you. Oh and Mr Seedwell senior's apple dumplings. Really. On *no* account touch them, however inviting they may look. Lethal!'

As they passed Amanda's house, Trelawney noticed some of the revellers had left a rose or a daisy on the wall.

He wondered if it had anything to do with the old story of the sunken maidee.

Some of the villagers were still singing *The Appel Songe*.

'I don't recognise those words to the tune we sang in the church,' Trelawney remarked to Amanda.

'Those are extra verses. We only sing four of them at the service.'

'How many are there?'

'Forty-one,' replied Amanda.

'My word. You villagers really do love your orchards!' he said. She giggled.

Among the trees, were well-lit tables laid with goodies and steaming pots of fragrant liquid on battery-operated heaters. For the first time, he noticed the village children. They were helping themselves to ladles full of the aromatic drink. Trelawney pointed to it in consternation.

'Is that stuff alcoholic?'

'Yes, why?'

'The children are drinking it!'

'Yes,' said Amanda matter-of-factly. She glanced at Trelawney's alarmed expression and suppressed her mirth. 'It's ok, it's not a school day tomorrow, and I promise they won't be driving this evening. Especially not the ones whose legs are too short for their feet to touch the pedals.'

'That's not what I meant!'

'This is what we folk do in the country, moi good sir. I started on this brew when I were just four year old,' said Amanda in a credible Hertfordshire accent.

'Good grief. That explains a lot!' replied Trelawney with a chuckle.

Amanda saw Leo, and thought she understood why Donna had not wanted to disturb his enjoyment of the day. Some children had drawn him into ring-a-ring-a-roses around three of the apple trees, and his face was alight with joy. This was a taste of the life he'd said he wanted. He seemed so genuine. Surely he couldn't be here in the pay of the Flamgoynes to spy on her, … could he?

Chapter 32

~

DELIVERY

At a quarter to six, Amanda excused herself, this time leaving Trelawney with Sarah and Vanessa. She made her way, at a gentle pace, to the church, and moved the car to half on the pavement at the side of Trotters Bottom, closer to the hall. Taking out one of the crates of glasses, she walked between the trees, around the south side of the building to the front, put the container down and opened up.

The hall was in darkness. However, enough streetlight filtered through for her to see that there was no table by the door where she could put her crate down. She lowered it to the floor. Amanda went back to the car to get the next load. It was on the return from her last trip that the stage-end light flickered on, and a female voice called towards her,

'Donna?'

'Amanda. Donna couldn't make it.'

'Oh, Amanda! Stay there. Here let me take that! They told me about your asthma and exertion.' Majolica bustled across the floor. But, about 10 yards from Amanda, she seemed to lose her footing. Amanda's eye was caught by a movement up on the ceiling; legs penetrated the plaster, then something was rapidly coming down. She stepped back as it plummeted. Her eye followed it down to see the floor collapse, as if made of rice paper, under Majolica's weight. The woman gave a shriek as she disappeared arms flailing. All at once, her cry was abruptly cut off. In the silence, Amanda stood rooted to the spot. She looked at the floorboards, uncertain as to which she could trust. Tempest appeared from the shadows.

'You here?' she said, her voice shaking a little. Her familiar came to her side and nodded towards her feet. Amanda sank to her knees. He stepped forward, testing each piece of the floor before he allowed her to shuffle towards the hole, until she could peer down into the darkness below. She could see nothing. Amanda fished in her pocket and pulled out her pencil wand. It had a stronger and more controllable beam than her phone app.

Amanda directed it downwards. With a quick indrawn breath, she sat back. The wand had illuminated the startled features of Majolica Woodberry, lying on Mr Giddins' collections of anvils, with the point of a stage spear rising out of her shirt.

There was a brief, nervous giggle from above. Amanda looked up. The ceiling showed damage. But it was too high above to see clearly. She stayed stock-still, listening … for what seemed an age …. But there was nothing more to be heard.

Amanda returned her attention to the matter of the deceased below. She reminded herself that being the person who finds the body never looks good. She had to get down there and look for evidence of what might have happened. Floors didn't give way by themselves, and this one shouldn't have. 'I have to get into the cellar, Tempest,' Amanda whispered.

She went back to near the door and then sidled around

the hall to the stage end. '*Agertyn,*' she said softly to the door leading to the cellar. It popped, and witch and familiar entered. She repeated the spell to the door at the bottom of the stairs, and then picked her way through the dusty, cloth-covered props and stored goods between herself and Majolica's deadly couch.

Amanda tried not to look at Mrs Woodberry. Instead, she searched for the supports. They were no longer in place. Rather, they lay in sections on the floor, scattered, the screws in the brackets twisted in situ. Could they really have bent under so little a weight as Majolica's? Amanda picked up one of the floorboards that had fallen through. But it was board no longer. It was little more than a thin veneer. She examined it. It was wet on the underside. Amanda picked up another fragment. She felt her hands burning and dropped the fragile wood. Her fingers tips were red. She grabbed the corner of a cotton sheet and scrubbed at them. The dust gathered on it flew up and made her cough.

'Feels like acid,' she wheezed to Tempest, who was peering at the debris from the collapse above.

She touched the other thinned boards, but they were just damp. The one telltale piece she wrapped carefully in a tissue and put in her pocket. It might be significant. More importantly, it might be incriminating of whoever had been at work here.

Amanda's lungs were stinging from the dust. She flicked her wand-light over the body. Reluctantly, she felt for a pulse, but the open, vacant eyes told their own tale. Here and there, lay flakes of paint and bits of ceiling plasterboard, but no great weight that could have smashed the floor. Tempest also seemed to have completed his inspection.

'Let's get back up and sound the alarm,' Amanda murmured. As quickly as she could, with Tempest lagging behind for some reason, she got them back up and locked the doors behind them with the spell '*Luxera*'. She called Trelawney first.

'Miss Cadabra?'

'Inspector, please come to the church hall at once. There's been a fatal accident. Can you call Sergeant Baker or should I dial 999?'

'I'll take care of it. Do you need an ambulance?'

'No. It's too late for that.'

Amanda returned to the front of the hall and sat on the step. It occurred to her that she and Tempest would have left footprints, if not finger and pawprints.

Within three minutes, Trelawney was there. Amanda stood up.

'It's Mrs Woodberry. She fell through the floor and is dead. Please be very careful.' She led him by Tempest's route to the safe kneeling place. The inspector shone his torch down there and confirmed that Majolica was beyond medical help.

'We'll need the keys to the cellar,' said Trelawney.

'I guess the rector would have them. Shall I phone her?' offered Amanda.

'If you would. Let's get outside. We don't want to contaminate the crime scene. If crime there was.'

Amanda spoke to the rector, then turned to Trelawney. 'I think it had to be. A crime, I mean. I saw the supports myself in place. The floor was safe. Although, I saw something fall from above that might have caused it to cave in. Except I couldn't see any blocks of masonry. Did you, just now?'

Trelawney shook his head. 'Are you all right? Bit of a shock, I'd think. You're coughing,' he observed with concern. 'Is it the asthma?'

'Stress reaction, I suppose. Yes, it was rather a shock,' Amanda admitted.

'Quite understandable. Well done keeping your head and making the call,' he commended her.

The sound of sirens came through the night air. Two police cars pulled up and an ambulance. Sergeant Baker approached.

'Good evening, Miss Cadabra. Found another body, have we?' he asked, with slight disapproval.

'Good evening, Sergeant Baker. Not exactly. This time I sort of saw it, that is, I saw Mrs Woodberry alive and then she disappeared, and next, she was, er …'

'I'll show you,' intervened Trelawney. He took Baker into the hall.

The rector hurried into Amanda's view. 'Whatever has happened?' she asked anxiously.

'It's Mrs Woodberry,' said Amanda. 'She's dead, I'm afraid. In the cellar, and the police need to get down there.'

'Of course. But whatever was she doing in the cellar?' enquired Jane curiously.

'She didn't go down there on purpose, Rector. She fell.'

'Into the cellar? How very odd.'

'The floor gave way,' Amanda explained patiently.

'What! But … but I made sure … Mr Branscombe,' said Jane in distress.

'Yes, I can confirm that, Rector. This is Sergeant Baker,' Amanda introduced him as he came back out of the hall. 'This is The Reverend Jane Waygood.'

'Sergeant,' said the rector, 'here is the key to the basement. You can open both doors with it. I'll show you the way.'

'Thank you, ma'am,' said Baker respectfully.

The police were erecting barriers with rods and tape around the hall. Someone from the ambulance was taken down below, to confirm that there was nothing they could do.

Jane returned and took Amanda into the rectory. 'Come this way, dear, we can get the best view of the action if we sit by this window over here. I'll just put the kettle on.' She was back in moments and peered out into the night.

'Who's that?' asked Jane, seeing a woman arrive and get into a plastic suit.

'Maybe the pathologist?' hazarded Amanda.

'Oh, dear! They'll be coming up soon for the dance,' the rector said in sudden realisation. 'Someone had better tell them.'

'Let's ask the inspector,' suggested Amanda. 'He can assume an air of authority.'

'Good idea. Where can we siphon them off to, do you think? It's better if it's not here at the rectory.'

'I know,' said Amanda and made a call. 'Sandra?'

'Yes, hun?'

'Can you do a quick buffet in your function room? There needs to be an emergency change of plan for the dance.'

Amanda knew she could rely on Sandra not to panic in a crisis.

'I'm sure we can manage,' said the publican calmly. 'How long do I have?'

Amanda checked; it was a quarter past six. 'Fifteen minutes.'

'Right. Can you tell me any more?'

'There's been a fatality at the hall. The police are here now, and it's cordoned off.'

'Who?' asked Sandra.

'Mrs W.'

'Wow. OK, leave it with me. I'll sneak off. OK to tell Vanessa?'

'Yes, of course.' Amanda went outside to Trelawney. 'Are you needed here any longer?' she asked him.

'Why?'

'I need you to do your man-of-the-moment thing and go and head off the party in the orchard. Send them to the Snout and Trough. You can just say there's been a change of plan.'

'OK, will do,' he said reassuringly. 'Did you see Vic Woodberry at the orchard?'

'No. Yes ... yes, but I think he must have gone home. I don't remember seeing him when I left, but there were so many people.'

'Someone has to find him and tell him,' explained Trelawney.

'Leave it to Jane and me.'

'And you'll need to make a statement, Miss Cadabra,' he added.

'Of course. I'll be with Jane in the rectory. I'll let you know as soon as we've located Mr Woodberry.'

He made to leave, then stopped. 'Miss Cadabra.'

'Yes, Inspector?'

'Did you see anyone else at the time of the accident?'

'No, but I heard someone. In the ceiling.'

'Ah yes, there's an attic under just part of the roof. There's a hatch.'

'Yes, you must have seen the ladder at the side of the hall.'

'Indeed. Did you hear anyone come down the ladder?' he asked.

'No. '

'Or see any evidence that the ladder had been moved since you last saw it?'

'None, Inspector, but it was dark in there.'

'OK. I'll go and take care of the party; then I'll come back.' With that Trelawney strode off toward Orchard Row.

Chapter 33

❦

AMANDA'S STATEMENT

'May I use your computer, please, Rector?' Amanda asked. 'I want to find the Woodberrys' dance studio and get some contact details. Someone will have to tell poor Vic.'

'Oh yes, perhaps I could go and see him with one of the police officers,' said the rector.

As Amanda located the information, there was a polite knock on the rectory door. Jane went to answer it and shepherded in the caller.

'Hello again, Miss Cadabra.'

'Detective Constable Nikolaides, isn't it?' Amanda replied with a friendly tone, seeing the familiar face, framed by neat dark hair above the police uniform. 'It's nice to see you again, even though the circumstances are not ideal. You were very kind to me on the last occasion.'

'We try, Miss Cadabra. Are you OK to talk?'

'Yes, I'm fine, really.'

'All right. Why don't you just tell me in your own words what happened.'

While the constable took rapid notes, Amanda explained about the glasses and plate, the time she'd left the party and where she'd parked, what she'd done and what she had seen. 'I knelt on the edge of the boards and, as it happens, I have a flashlight app on my phone.' Amanda described the unfortunate sight that had met her eyes. 'It was clear that Mrs Woodberry was beyond help. I came outside and called Inspector Trelawney, as he was just two minutes down the road, and he called Sergeant Baker.'

'You only touched the floorboards then?' asked Nikolaides.

'I tried not to touch even them, just sort of leaned on my hand so I could look over the edge of the hole and down, in case I could help Mrs Woodberry.'

'OK. Now, can you think of anyone who might have wanted to harm Mrs Woodberry?'

Amanda shook her head at once. 'No. She wasn't the nicest of people, and I think she was probably a bit of a martinet to her husband, but no one kills someone because they're not very nice.'

'So no one in the village, as far as you know, had any kind of a grudge against her?' enquired the constable.

'No, no one that I know of.'

'Do you know anything about her family or friends?'

'No, but Sylvia, our lollipop lady, knew her years ago, before she was married. The Woodberrys' house is in Romping-in-the-Heye; they're not Sunken Madleyists. I only know people there I've done furniture work for, but I know of no one connected to the Woodberrys. I'd never met them before the first dance class.'

'Thank you, Miss Cadabra. Can you tell me where I might find Sylvia?'

'Yes, she'll be at the party. Er, though I think she may be a bit … merry. Probably better to talk to her tomorrow … afternoon. But here are her contact details,' said Amanda helpfully, showing Nikolaides the relevant page on her phone.

Jane came in with tea for the constable. 'Here's some paper for Amanda to write her statement,' offered the rector. 'Save her going to the station.'

'Thank you, but I have some here,' the constable replied kindly. 'Would you mind, Miss Cadabra?'

'Not at all. I'll write it while you drink your tea.'

Jane returned to the kitchen to brew up some more for the police outside. Nikolaides sipped her drink while Amanda scribbled away. When she was done, she read it, signed it and handed it over to the constable.

Amanda had chosen her words with care and precision and told nothing but the truth. Just not the whole truth. Not by a long chalk.

Trelawney presently returned, having herded the merrymakers to the pen of the Snout and Trough, where Sarah had rapidly ordered the upstairs room, cast damask over trestles and set out cups, glasses, bottles, and snacks. Vanessa had commandeered the sound equipment from downstairs and was organising the dance lesson, he reported.

'It was quite a sight seeing the two of them in action. Worthy of Mission Impossible!'

'They are a redoubtable pair,' agreed Amanda with pride in her fellow villagers.

'Have you given your statement?' he asked her.

'Yes, just done. To Constable Nikolaides.'

'Tea, Inspector?' asked Jane.

'Not just at the moment, thank you, Rector,' said Trelawney. He made a gesture to Nikolaides, and she followed him out. He returned several minutes later. 'I have permission to take Miss Cadabra home. I expect you don't feel much like partying,' he said to her.

'True. Thank you. Thank you, Rector, for your hospitality.'

'Any time. I'll take Mr Woodberry's contact details to Sergeant Baker, shall I?

'Yes, please, or Constable Nikolaides.'

Trelawney helped Amanda on with her coat and walked with her to her car.

'Shall I drive?' he offered.

'Thank you, but I can go that short distance.'

'You must have left the door open,' he commented, as they approached the Astra. Tempest was curled up on the back seat. But not asleep.

At the cottage, Trelawney insisted Amanda rest while he made tea. He sat and waited while she settled, then took a folded sheet of paper from his pocket.

'Your statement,' he said.

'A little light reading for you?' she asked.

He regarded her thoughtfully.

'I think, Miss Cadabra, that you are one of those rare individuals who cannot help but always tell the truth. Would you consider that an accurate assessment?'

'Yes,' Amanda agreed levelly. She knew what was coming.

'The question is …,' he said, as he waved the paper, '… is this the *whole* truth?'

'Oh, do you mean, did I leave out the bit where I took the fire axe to the floor, then pushed Mrs Woodberry into the hole, first having ensured that the anvils and stage spear were properly set up to receive her?'

'Miss Cadabra,' he replied sternly, 'I would strongly advise you not to take a jesting tone with either Constable Nikolaides or Sergeant Baker.'

'I'm sorry,' she replied stiffly, 'I did not realise that this was a formal interview, Inspector. I did not intend to give the impression that I take this matter of untimely death lightly.'

Trelawney reflected that she was right. He was not the investigating officer in this case, and he had no authority to question her as he had done. He got up and started making up the fire in the hearth for something to do, forgetting it was not his own.

'No, I'm sorry,' he said contritely. 'I was going into autopilot. I want to help. You found the body, and …'

'I know. That never looks good.'

'You were the only person present when it happened. It may be that everyone else has an alibi. I *want* to help you clear yourself beyond all doubt.'

Amanda felt the urge to confide what she had seen in the basement. But there was no way she was going to tell him the means she had used to get down there, through two locked doors.

Chapter 34

༄

PUZZLE

'Let me put it another way, Miss Cadabra,' Trelawney tried. 'Are forensics going to find your fingerprints on the door handles of the doors leading to the basement? And your footprints in the dust of the floor down there?'

Amanda had already thought about the traces she and Tempest must have left. 'I went down there with Jane, so my finger and footprints will be no surprise,' she answered with a show of unconcern.

'I see. Was that recently?' he asked.

'Not very, but I expect no one except the rector and Mr Branscombe has been down there since, as far as I know. There would be no reason.'

Trelawney essayed another route.

'In your opinion, Miss Cadabra, was this accident?'

Here, at least, Amanda could be forthcoming. 'No, Inspector, it was not. I saw those floorboard supports myself when the rector took me down there. They weren't industry standard, but they were solid and tightly wedged. Mr Branscombe will testify to that effect as an expert witness, I have no doubt. The only way that that floor could have collapsed is if someone had deliberately … damaged it. I thought something fell or was thrown, possibly, from above, but I couldn't see anything when I looked down there. It had to have been sabotage.'

'Could something have accidentally fallen from the ceiling?' Trelawney suggested.

'I don't believe so. I'm sure there was someone up there. I thought I saw a leg — leg*s* — sort of … that is, one was … small and … not clear — but I thought it punctured the plaster. Maybe they unintentionally knocked something down. There is that possibility, of course. In which case, it would be accidental,' Amanda admitted.

He got the fire going, and she attempted a little candour. 'I'm in the soup, aren't I? If my fingerprints and the rector's are the only ones on the basement doors, then either or both of us could have gone down there and meddled with the supports, I suppose. But why would either of us do such a thing?'

'And when?'

'I didn't have a key until this evening when Donna gave it to me. And it could have been anyone walking across that bit of floor that gave way. It could have been me! It makes no sense.'

'I agree. Is there nothing else you can tell me?' he asked her gently.

'Nothing, Inspector. I'd never met Majolica before. I don't know why or how this could have happened. If it was sabotage, it could have been done by someone else with access to the church hall, access to the key. People were in and out of the hall before classes began to help paint it and clean the windows, but none of them would have had access to the basement. All of the decorating materials were above ground. You'd have to ask the rector if any one apart from her was given the keys. Whatever was done to make the floor collapse, it would have had to have been between last Saturday, when we used the hall, and today. As for prints, the saboteur could have worn gloves.'

'You were just in the wrong place at the wrong time. I doubt that you will be considered a serious suspect,' Trelawney said reassuringly. 'But the sooner you can be eliminated from the list, the better.'

'Of course. I'm sorry today has ended like this,' Amanda replied regretfully. 'I'd hoped your visit would be fun for you.'

'It was, I promise you. Don't let this upset you unduly. I think Mrs Woodberry was not a particular favourite of yours,' he suggested diplomatically.

'You could say that. I hope that doesn't push me back up to the top of the suspect list!'

'By no means. I doubt she was a particular favourite of anyone's. Putting that matter aside, we still have a mission. Or rather, *I* still have a mission. This doesn't change the fact that there is still a spy in the camp and your Uncle Mike has charged me with your safety and to discover the identity of the person in question.'

'Well, my guess is that Sandra will offer the function room at the Snout and Trough for the dance classes, and I think Vanessa will be able to take over teaching them. I've watched her, and I reckon she has sufficient knowledge of the technique, plus she loves to dance, even if she doesn't have the Woodberry experience.'

'Do you think the villagers will want to go on with the classes after this?' asked Trelawney, slightly surprised.

'Oh yes,' responded Amanda with certainty. 'They're hooked now. You could see that last Saturday. As you said, no one was attached to Majolica, and I think they'll still want to learn and to support the fund for the new church hall. Perhaps all the more so now. And there's no question about it needing a new floor!'

'Quite,' he acknowledged with a smile. 'I bow to your superior knowledge of your fellow denizens. I shall see you next Saturday then. If you need me, I shall be in Crouch End until late afternoon tomorrow. Will you be all right?'

'Of course. I think I shall have a hot bath, a hot drink, watch something funny on the television and go to bed. And I have my mobile comfort blanket with me.' Tempest had draped himself across her knees and was purring loudly. He now trained his gaze upon Trelawney to convey that the very idea that his human required any more care and protection than could possibly be offered by one other than himself was an insult of the lowest order.

The inspector rose. 'No, please don't get up, Miss Cadabra. I'll see myself out. I'll call you tomorrow.'

'Thank you, Inspector,' Amanda replied with genuine appreciation.

'Sleep well,' he bade her kindly.

'Good night.'

Amanda heard the door close, and, before she could say the words, her grandparents appeared, Senara beside her on the sofa and Perran in Trelawney's vacated chair, each with a cup of tea and plate of scones and jam.

'That's a good fire he's built,' said Perran approvingly.

'He knows his way around the kitchen,' remarked Senara.

'Glad you popped in to talk about the inspector,' commented Amanda dryly.

'Now don't take on. You're not in any trouble,' said Grandpa, cutting a scone in half.

'It's another puzzle,' explained Granny, spreading clotted cream on hers.

'Do you know what happened? Did you see it coming?' Amanda asked urgently.

'No,' Granny replied, 'but then we can't be everywhere at once.'

'And we're not omniscient,' added Grandpa.

'No, that would be frightfully dull!' exclaimed his wife.

'Can you *help*?' Amanda enquired pressingly.

'Naturally. But you have to tell us what you know,' answered Senara, picking up her scone and proceeding to take a bite.

Amanda related the events the evening, while her grandparents gave every appearance of enjoying their cream teas without a hint of being put off by the description of a murder.

'Sabotage then,' said Grandpa, when Amanda ended her narrative.

'Yes. Someone had bent the screws and, I think, painted acid on the underside of the boards then tried to wash it off with water. The piece I picked up stung my fingers like the hydrochloric acid in the workshop.' Amanda looked at Senara. 'You know how Grandpa and I use it very occasionally to make aqua regia for testing the purity of gold?'

'A builder,' responded Granny decisively.

'My first thought was the Reckets,' agreed Amanda. 'But I don't think it's their MO. Mr Hodster never mentioned them doing anything that could cause a fatality or accident or harm to anyone of any kind. The faults they built into their projects were surely just annoying or potentially expensive things. Yes, the joists were too thin and maybe wood-wormed, but they'd have gone rotten and weak over time, no one would ever have fallen through. And the floor was acid-burned away above a very particular set up: those anvils, that javelin or spear shoved in the middle. No, that just doesn't fit with cowboy builders.'

'What about the person in the attic, Ammy?' suggested Grandpa.

'I suppose they could have got up there before I arrived, and then pushed the ladder away and pulled up the hatch. But then how would they get down? And when? The police will have been up there. And there was no chance once I arrived. Even when I was in the basement, I would have heard them, and certainly, Tempest would have.'

'All right, *bian*. So much for the evidence in your dimension, in your time,' said Grandpa. 'What about the things from other times you and Trelawney have seen?'

Amanda thought. 'The man falling through the floor … except…. now I remember! When I saw him, … at the same time, I thought it was a woman, and then it resolved into the man. The woman … I wonder… could it have been Majolica? Was I seeing the future?' she asked in alarm.

'No,' said Granny decisively, handing a newly materialised plate of slightly different scones to her husband. 'No one can see the future. Your Aunt Amelia must have told you that. Ask her.'

'OK,' acceded Amanda. She observed her grandparents with disbelief. 'Honestly, I don't know how you can sit there eating scones at a time like this!'

'These have candied orange peel in them, *bian*,' Grandpa said in an explanatory tone.

'Very good with marmalade,' Granny added. 'It works. You'd be surprised.'

'And we can eat scones and jam any time we like here,' Grandpa continued.

'Yes, it's jolly good,' commented Granny.

Amanda shook her head incredulously and gave up. 'Well, let's get back to the soldier that fell through. Funny …. his hat … cap … whatever you call it; when I was dancing with the inspector last week, for an instant, he was wearing the identical cap …. And that soldier could see me. I wonder …. could he have seen what happened at the church hall? Who sabotaged it? After all, he was down there. He spoke to me once before. If I could speak to him once more …'

'You're going to run into Nikolaides and Baker on that

one though, *bian*, like you did last time, and Hogarth is out of the country, though you could call him.'

'Yes … I've just had a thought. Maybe the Reckets are important in this picture somewhere. Mr Hodster said "*Cherchez les notes*", find the Recket papers. I wonder if the backroom boys have made any progress.'

'*There's* a line of enquiry then that you can follow,' said Grandpa jauntily.

'I wonder,' Amanda went on meditatively, 'if the saboteur was up in the attic, watching to see if the plan was successful. But how did they get down? And ... yes, ... that first time I went into the hall … it was a *child's* giggle I heard. Surely one of the school children couldn't have done such a thing! And yes, I saw two legs: a child's and a man's. At least, it was a trousered leg. I guess it could have been a man or a woman. And then tonight, I saw both of those legs again, except the big one looked solid and the little one looked … see-through.'

Her grandparents continued to sip and eat. Amanda continued, 'There are just so many pieces to this I don't know where to start. I mean, if I could get back into the hall …'

'Start with your backroom boys. But, if were you, Ammy love,' suggested Grandpa. 'I would go ahead with your plan for the rest of the night, and, on Monday, when you've got your overalls on, the next step'll come to you,' he added with conviction.

'Really?' asked Amanda doubtfully.

'Yes, have a rest tomorrow. I expect Jane'll pop in to see you and your Aunt Amelia, too if you let her know. Then ... Monday… you'll see I'm right.'

Chapter 35

❧

THOMAS DOES HIS THING

Trelawney came back to an empty house. It would be too much to expect his mother to be at home on a Saturday night if her son was out. 'Good,' he murmured taking off his shoes. He needed privacy. He sent a text.

Mike. Free to Skype? T

Trelawney made a cup of tea while he waited as patiently as possible for the reply.

On beach. Give me 10. M

Thomas went up to his old room, switched on the desktop computer, and put his thoughts in order.

Finally the Skype alert sounded and the image of Hogarth in his sister's study sprang onto the screen.

'Mike, you got back quickly.'

'Manager's son just passed his motorbike test. Offered to bring me back up the hill. I put life and limb in his hands for your sake, my lad.'

'Thank you to both of you.'

'Now. What's amiss?'

Thomas related the events and conversations of the evening in all of the detail that his detective's mind could summon.

'Well, well,' remarked Hogarth. 'Our Amanda does get herself in the middle of the action, doesn't she? Are you on first name terms, by the way?'

'Certainly not,' said Thomas, firmly.

'Insists on calling you "Inspector", does she, even when you're dancing?'

'Most of the village does too, actually. It's the sort of place where the doctor is "Doctor" and the rector is "Rector", but then they knew me first as the inspector. How, I don't know.'

'It's a village Thomas. You're a small-town boy, you wouldn't understand.'

'You're right. In Parhayle we have concepts like privacy, even occasionally anonymity if you're not there too long, and things like strangers, visitors and tourists.'

'See the difference? Besides which, Amanda has been trained in the art of vigilance, and I'll bet never lets herself forget for a moment that you're there to find out what her family of three had to do with the Minibus Murders.'

'But I've already told her that I'm not there to trap her,' protested Thomas, 'and, anyway, even if her grandparents were involved, it would have been with the best of motives: to safeguard her from being reclaimed by homicidal relations.'

'That will help.'

Trelawney let his exasperation show. 'Every time we have a conversation where it seems that our connection is strengthening, somehow it turns into a cat-and-mouse game.'

'I think you have to concentrate on your shared past, Thomas. Speaking of the past, is there a connection between the church hall murder and the spy?

'Well …. Hard to say … possibly,'

'What does your instinct tell you? Come on, Thomas, do your thing. Is … there … a connection?'

Thomas closed his eyes and saw, as he often did, like the car headlamps in time-lapse photographs, winding trails of light. They were racing beside one another, bending, snaking around and above and below, and, suddenly, in an explosion of white, two collided and crossed.

He opened his eyes and looked at Hogarth's face on the screen before him.

'Yes,' he pronounced without a shadow of a doubt. 'There is a connection.'

'Good lad. Now there's something I need you to do for me.

'Yes, Mike?'

'Find out who the Officer in Charge of the church hall case is.'

'Isn't it your pal, Chief Inspector …?'

'My pal is on leave,' said Hogarth regretfully, 'according to his auto responder and voice mail. It may mean you have to tread carefully. You are a witness of sorts in this case, but you need to follow your own lines of enquiry for both the cold and warm cases.'

'I'm seeing my father on Tuesday. I hope to get some background history out of him,' said Thomas on a positive note.

'That's the way to go,' agreed Hogarth. 'As for the church hall business, remember: be careful.'

The following day, Trelawney went back to the crime scene, where he saw an old friend from Hendon Police College.

'Ross?'

'Thomas? What you doing here, Yokel, in civilized

parts? Don't tell me you've transferred.'

'No, following up a cold case. Are you the Officer in Charge?' Trelawney asked hopefully.

'Chance'd be a fine thing. We haven't all shot up the career ladder like you. No, DI Worsfold is in charge while Chief Inspector Maxwell is on leave, worse luck.'

'Oh. What's he like?' asked Trelawney.

'A nightmare. Thinks he's the salt of the earth like Baker. Two differences though. One: Baker really *is* the salt of the earth, and two, Baker isn't a twerp.'

'Doesn't sound promising.'

'Don't know if he'll welcome your presence, Thomas,' cautioned Ross.

'When's Maxwell back?'

'Four weeks,' replied Ross, in the voice of doom.

'Four weeks?' exclaimed Trelawney.

'Yes, and if we don't solve this case this weekend, don't expect much movement on it until the old man gets back.'

'That bad?'

'Worsfold does get results at times, but it all has to be done his way, he can't think outside the box and he might just arrest any old suspect to make sure it looks like he's doing something.'

'Thanks for the heads-up, Ross.'

'I'd lay low if I were you. Stick to your cold case.'

'What if there's a crossover?' asked Trelawney.

'Then I'll do what I can. Give me your number in case I haven't got your latest and I'll keep you posted. On the QT, or Worsfold'll have my guts for garters.'

They hastily exchanged phone numbers.

'Thanks, Ross. I'll make myself scarce for now then.'

Trelawney sent a text and called in at the cottage, where he was welcomed by Amanda and plied with consoling tea.

'Now, what is it, Inspector? You don't look a happy bunny.'

He gave her the bad news.

'Four weeks? The killer could have killed again by then.'

'That's not the thing that worries me the most, Miss Cadabra. You and the rector are currently at the top of the suspect list, however unlikely you are to have carried out the sabotage, and this temporary man-in-charge is arrest-happy. We have to do what we can to either clear you both or find out who did this.'

'Well, I've been thinking. The rector talked about going to visit Mr Woodberry, in her spiritual capacity, I think. I'm sure she'd take me with her if I asked her. After all, from what you say, the rector and I are in this together to some extent.'

'Good idea. That shouldn't tread on anyone's toes. I think we need to stay away from the hall. '

'You'll keep coming to the classes, though won't you?' Amanda asked anxiously.

'Of course. Business as usual. We have a spy to identify. And we can follow any lines of enquiry we can think of, as long as we're discreet.'

Amanda nodded. 'Yes, we can talk to people as long as it's in the ordinary way.'

'We can't be seen to be interviewing anyone,' he warned her.

'OK. Well, Leo has been wanting to meet for a tea-break and Ryan wants me to go with him to the launch of the new menu at the Snout and Trough. Sandra's got a new chef. I can sound out what Leo and Ryan have to offer in the way of information. They might have seen or heard something useful.'

'Good.'

'Hasn't Vanessa or Madeleine invited you out yet?' Amanda asked practically.

'Actually Vanessa has invited me to the menu launch too. I'd sort of excused myself,' Trelawney admitted. 'I didn't want her to get the wrong impression.'

'Perfect! You can change your mind. And Madeleine?'

'Not really. She's been throwing out hints about various sporting pursuits but I'm really not keen. It would be very difficult to conduct a conversation while engaged in the sorts of things she seems to have in mind.'

'Yes, she is a bit hearty, jolly hockey sticks. Well, never mind, she isn't really in the thick of things. Maybe you can just chat before one of the classes.'

'I'd feel safer doing that,' owned Trelawney.

'Feeling hunted?' Amanda enquired sympathetically. 'You can always call on me. I promise to rescue you from the local wildlife, if necessary.'

'You comfort me, Miss Cadabra.'

'Meanwhile, the church hall affair is going to be the hot topic in the corner shop, the pub and The Big Tease. Gossip won't be hard to come by.'

'Right, well, we'll reconvene here on Saturday, if that's OK with you?' suggested Trelawney

'Yes, after the class. Then we can each do our subtle interviewing at the menu launch on Sunday.'

They shook hands. Trelawney looked worried.

'I'll be fine,' Amanda reassured him.

'I won't let Worsfold lock you up, if I can possibly prevent it,' he promised her.

'I believe you,' she said.

Chapter 36

✑

APPORT, AND KYTTO

On Monday, Amanda, dressed in her overalls, headed out with Tempest to the Reiser's. Come hell or high water, there was still a banister to be polished. Grandpa's words played in her head. Today she would know the next step.

By lunchtime, Amanda was still in ignorance. She took her food into the garden under the awning next to the house to shelter from the downpour. Hopefully the neighbours would either be discouraged by the weather from emerging into their gardens or have gone out for the day. Tempest sat beside her, alternatively looking expectantly at the lunch box and scowling disapprovingly at the rain.

They were finishing up their meal as Amanda began to get cold and felt a sneeze coming on. Quickly she felt in her jacket pockets, customarily stuffed with tissues, but they were empty of anything useful for the occasion. She dived her hands into her overalls and found only a scrap of rag that she pulled out hastily, just in time. There was a flash of gold, and ting! Amanda looked down at her feet to see the forgotten gold thimble she'd found in the crypt that day with the rector, weeks ago. She picked it up before it could roll away.

'Apport,' she murmured aloud. 'Aunt Amelia. I've been forgetting to ask her. This is the next step, Tempest,' Amanda declared. 'The next step!'

* * * * *

'An apport?' replied Amelia. 'Well, an apport is thought by some to be an object that can be in another dimension, that someone there wants you to have, so they find a way of presenting it to you. Why? Where did you hear the word?'

'The rector said it, and said to ask you what it meant. You see, one day, in the crypt, the rector dropped a set of keys, and it went under a sarcophagus, and, when I got my hand under there to get it out, I also found this.' Amanda produced the thimble. 'And the rector thought I was meant to have it.

'Aha,' responded Amelia with interest, taking it from Amanda's palm. 'It's a christening thimble, I do believe.'

'Old, wouldn't you say?' asked Amanda.

'Yes, I would.'

'Something a child could have owned?' Amanda hazarded.

'Yes,' said Amelia.

'Perhaps a child then was in the crypt. Playing maybe?'

'Maybe.'

'It's just that I heard a child giggle in the hall attic. Then the sound was cut off suddenly, or they suddenly had to be quiet. If it was a past thing, I mean, a person who is in another dimension but who keeps visiting a spot here, for some reason, they might be able to tell me what happened that night,' said

Amanda with growing excitement. 'Except,' she continued deflated, 'I can't get into the hall. Not for another four weeks, when Uncle Mike's friend Chief Inspector Maxwell comes back and will let me in.'

'Perhaps,' responded Amelia slowly, 'you don't have to go to the hall. You have the thimble. If the child meant you to have it, maybe you can find her there.'

'In the place where I found it? In the crypt?' asked Amanda, her enthusiasm returning.

'It's worth a try.'

'Yes, and I could ask the rector to let me go down there. She would understand. All right. I will. Tomorrow after work.'

'But think about how you're going to dress. You don't want to alarm the child by looking too outlandish,' Amelia advised.

'What sort of period, do you think?'

'Hard to say. Regency or Victorian perhaps.'

'OK, I've got a maxi skirt somewhere,' considered Amanda, now in high spirits.

'Yes, something long will be fine,' agreed her aunt.

Amanda's eyes were alight. 'Tomorrow!'

* * * * *

Meanwhile, 400 miles away, a dinner was finishing.

'You always liked my shepherd's pie,' said Kytto Trelawney to his son.

'Yes, Dad, and I still do. No one makes it like you.'

Kyt stood up to gather the plates. It would have been easy for anyone to see where Thomas got his height. However, his father was a sparer man, and his hair was more salt than pepper now. The lines etched by stress could not entirely conceal the comeliness of face that had struck a young Penelope when she had first seen Kyt back in their university days. Yet, it was for his kindly ways and depth of thought that she had come to love him, those things that she loved most in their son.

'Sorry I've been so busy,' he said as he took the dishes out to the kitchen.

Thomas waited for him to come back, before saying, 'Actually … I had a feeling that it wasn't just that you were busy.'

His father looked at him with a gentle question in his eyes.

'You know,' Thomas continued carefully, 'how sometimes there are things we don't appreciate about ourselves but that others see in us?'

'I suppose so,' agreed his father amiably, putting a hand on his son's shoulder as he passed his chair.

'Well, lately, I've come to appreciate something about myself that I just thought everyone had in spades.'

'What's that?' Kyt asked sitting down at the table once more.

'Intuition,' replied Thomas. 'My former boss, Chief Inspector Hogarth, said he trusted mine even above his own. I thought that was quite something.'

Kyt smiled. 'I'm proud to hear that, Thomas.'

'Dad, I've got something to tell you. And I need you to hear me out. Will you do that? I've been asking questions for years that you didn't …. weren't ready to answer… and that's OK,' he added quickly. 'But things are different now. There are things I've remembered … things I've found out … things I understand.'

His father sighed, as though something he had been dreading for a long time had finally come to pass. He leaned his head back against his high backed chair for a moment and closed his eyes, as though in relief. Thomas waited. Presently his father opened his eyes and nodded.

'All right, son. Tell me.'

'These are the pieces of the puzzle that I have: I had the Flamgoyne talent, didn't I?'

Kyt nodded again.

'Then, I think, you took me to a Cardiubarn who suppressed it and the memory of ever having had it. But the spells have been wearing off over the years. You knew they would, didn't you? You knew that this moment, this conversation would come.'

'There's no point now in denying it.'

'You did it to protect me; I know that. From the Flamgoynes.'

'They would have taken you, Thomas,' said his father quietly.

'I know,' said his son kindly. 'But they don't know about me now, do they?'

'No, they lost interest in the pair of us long ago,' agreed Kyt on a brighter note.

'So you can tell me. Who was the Cardiubarn who helped us? It was a Cardiubarn, wasn't it?'

His father sat in silent reflection for a few moments before saying, 'You know, I think it would be better for you, if it came to you, that information,' he said thoughtfully. 'I think, son, if you were in the right place at the right time, you would remember.' He got up, fetched his laptop and brought it to the table. 'It might be a bit tricky to arrange … ' He tapped and scrolled.

Thomas leaned over to look at the screen, and saw it was the booking schedule for his father's holiday cottages.

'One of them?'

'Yes, *Marram*. But the changeover from guest to guest is usually on a Saturday when you're up in London. So we need a long weekend booking, and then we can go there midweek … and … nothing until the new year. But maybe there'll be a cancellation. Just be ready, all right? As soon as possible, we'll go there and see if it comes back to you.'

'All right. Dad. You don't have to persuade me. I'll be waiting.'

Chapter 37

৩

BLOCKED

'No,' said Senara with finality.

'What do you mean "no"?' replied her granddaughter in indignant accents.

'I mean, no, not yet. You must stay away from the church. Keep a low profile.'

'Well, when then?' Amanda asked, frustrated.

'I'll tell you when,' said her grandmother calmly.

'Fine. I'll go with the rector to interview Mr Woodberry,' stated Amanda, putting her hands on her hips.

'No. It'll get back to the police. You have to keep a low profile,' insisted Granny.

Her granddaughter pursed her lips in an effort to contain her irritation. Finally, it burst forth in:

'Hrrrm!

* * * * *

'I feel so … blocked!' Amanda told Trelawney, back at the cottage after the class that Saturday. 'It's so *frustrating*. I can't *get* anywhere.'

'I do understand,' he replied sympathetically, stirring his tea. 'When I started out as a detective constable, I felt just like you a great deal of the time. Like a whippet trapped in the starting gate.'

That image of Trelawney made Amanda laugh.

'That's better,' he said. 'But over time I learned patience. Softly, softly. It's like at twilight, waiting for the stars to appear in the sky. That's how the ancient wayfinders knew where they were and the path ahead. At the moment we have to drift a little.'

'OK. I've calmed down. Thank you for that.'

'How's the banister?' Trelawney asked.

'Well, that, at least, is making progress,' Amanda replied cheerily.

'Only three weeks to go, and then Worsfold will no longer be in charge. It's not an eternity.'

'No, it just *feels* like it,' she countered with a grin. 'How about you? Are you edging forward on any front?'

'Yes, I'm learning things.'

'From your father?' asked Amanda excitedly.

'Indeed. But he doesn't want to overwhelm me with too much information at once, I can see that.'

'Did he tell you who did the spells on you?'

'No, he said it's better if I remember. He says he needs to take me to Marram, one of our cottages.'

'Cottages? I had no idea the Trelawneys were property magnates,' said Amanda in surprise.

'They're not; they're fishermen. I mean, holiday cottages. My father's business. But usually, they're only empty on Saturdays when I'm up here. Nevertheless, we do get guests who come for long weekends and leave on Monday or Tuesday. The next chance to go there will be in the new year, unless there's a cancellation.'

'So you're blocked too,' Amanda remarked.

'Well, yes. I just don't feel it quite as intensely as you do,' he said with a touch of playfulness.

She acknowledged a hit with a quick wrinkling of her nose, then asked, 'Did he tell you anything else?'

'I'll see him again this Tuesday. My father said that was enough to start with. And it was. Just to have him open up as he never has before. Finally, I feel like we're playing on the same team, even though it's far from being a sport I would have chosen,' Trelawney added wryly.

'What is your chosen sport?' Amanda asked curiously.

'Well, I have to train for work, and I like to run along the beach but, swimming. I like to swim.'

'In the sea?'

'For preference, but, of course, that's not always practical. So I make do with the pool. Oh, and I like to sketch, not that it's a sport.'

'Not a team player then,' observed Amanda with mock disapproval.

He smiled. 'I can if I have to.'

'Well,' said Amanda, 'dates tomorrow.'

'See what you can get out of Ryan,' replied Trelawney.

She nodded. 'See what you can get out of Vanessa.'

* * * * *

'Negasi is from Ethiopia and trained in Paris and Geneva,' said Sandra enthusiastically, personally attending

Amanda and Ryan's table. 'He's just working here to gain experience. We are very lucky to have him for as long as we have him.'

'Sounds like he's the man to put The Snout and Trough on the map,' replied Amanda.

'I think so. Anyway, I'll leave you with the new menus and get your drinks brought over.'

'Thank you, Sandra.'

They scanned the traditional Sunday lunch options, looked with more interest at the roasts with a twist and then became absorbed in the strange and wonderful dishes from the chef's place of birth. Amanda finally looked up and closed her menu.

'You know what? I'm just going to go with whatever the chef recommends,' she announced boldly.

'Same here,' agreed Ryan.

'So,' Amanda opened, 'what do you do offseason?'

'Training, media stuff, popping down to see the folks, but, look, people are always asking about me and the sport and the celebrity lifestyle. I'd rather talk about you, if you don't mind?' Ryan asked modestly.

'Of course,' she replied, thinking that that was rather sweet, but also just what a spy would say. 'What would you like to know?'

'Furniture restorer. Not the obvious choice for …'

'A girl?' finished Amanda provocatively.

'Well … am I allowed to say, yes?' he asked tentatively, 'without sounding abominably sexist? But not just that. For an asthmatic.'

Amanda nodded. 'That's what masks and ventilation are for. But, fair enough, there do tend to be more men than women who do what I do.'

'Do you do upholstery?'

'No. That really *is* dusty.'

'You know, I'd love to see your workshop, if ever you

have time and wouldn't mind admitting a layperson. I grew up not even knowing how to change a fuse. I'd be fascinated.'

He asked so winningly that Amanda did not want to refuse. It must have been dreadful growing up to be so …. useless, she thought. 'OK. Well, sure, one morning before work. How about that?'

'I'd love that,' he replied thankfully. 'Any time that suits you.'

'Tuesday morning, 8 o'clock?' It was early, but she could then get him out of the way before magical training time at 8.30.

'Wonderful.'

Amanda remembered that Gordon French, the retired headmaster of Sunken Madley School, had told her that Ryan came from Portsmouth, and she said sympathetically, 'I expect you had more interesting things to do than learn DIY, growing up on the south coast.'

'True.'

'Do you miss the sea?'

'Yes and no. Beach cricket's fun but it gets windy, and the bounce isn't the same as on a grass pitch,' Ryan explained.

'The game was more important than the water?'

'Yes, in a word. But then my father's work brought us to Sunken Madley. And I had two happy years here.'

'Why the move away from here?' asked Amanda.

'To get me into a good cricket school that my parents could afford and where they could get jobs to help pay for it all. I was fortunate. I wouldn't be where I am today without all that they did for me,' said Ryan sincerely.

'And now you're back,' Amanda remarked.

'Well, I made a penny or two and could choose wherever I wanted to live, so why not come back to the village where I was so happy and see if I could give something back.'

Amanda was touched. 'That's nice,' she said.

'Ammeee!' shrieked a little voice from knee height, hurrying inexpertly across the carpet as fast as his two-year-old legs would carry him. Little Amir Patel, entering with his grandparents, the doctors Patel, and his parents, had broken away from his family at the sight of his chum. Seeing the object of his delight, the Patels waved, seated themselves and enjoyed some moments of relative peace, confident that their treasure was in secure and familiar hands.

'Hello, Amir,' Amanda responded fondly, smiling at him.

'Up,' he instructed, and she took him onto her lap.

'Hello, there,' said Ryan, but was ignored.

Amir pointed to Amanda's pocket and explained, 'Dat.'

'Oh, shall we see what's in there?' said Amanda. She took out her phone, but Amir shook his head. Next came a packet of tissues, but these were of no attraction either. A pound coin followed, but would not serve. Finally, Amanda took out the one thing she preferred to keep hidden but never left the house without: her Pocket-wand. To all the world it appeared to be a perfectly ordinary IKEA pencil, but was of special interest to Amir. Amanda controlled her breathing and asked calmly,

'Do you want to draw?' Amir nodded. 'Do I have any paper?' She searched her pockets in vain. 'Shall we ask Aunty Sandra for some? Can you see her?' Amanda looked around, and Amir followed suit. In the process of which, what Amanda hoped would happen came to pass. He spotted the waiter's stand, a-glint with cutlery and other exciting items.

'Dow',' he uttered. Amanda put him back on his feet and he staggered off. With every show of nonchalance, she returned her possessions to the safety of her pocket.

'He seems very fond of you,' Ryan remarked. 'You made a charmingly domestic picture, the two of you.'

'Yes, well, I have babysat a village toddler or two in my time, and I confess that Amir is a particular favourite. But that's as charmingly domestic as I get,' Amanda replied crisply.

'Wouldn't you like children of your own?'

'I already have a troublesome two-year-old and a stroppy teenager,' she assured him. He raised his eyebrows in astonishment.

'I had no idea.'

'Yes, both in one. You must have seen him; a weather system on legs with eyes that some say stare into their very soul.'

'Oh!' Ryan laughed. 'I see. Your cat.'

'Yes, those two words don't begin to cover it. He is more than enough for me,' Amanda declared. So, she thought, if you're seeking someone with whom to breed a little cricket team of Fords, you can look elsewhere. But this suggestion of serious interest is just your MO, I'll bet, and exactly what a spy would do to get close to a target. Out loud, Amanda asked, 'You saw what Tempest did in the church at the Feast?'

'Ah. Yes. Yes, I do get your point. He does seem to be a bit of a handful. I take it you have minimal control over him?'

'I have none at all,' Amanda replied airily. 'But then, he's a cat.'

Chapter 38

❧

GRIST TO THE MILL

On Monday, Amanda decided to try her luck, and sent a text.

Hi Leo, got time for elevenses? Amanda

Hi Amanda, yes got a gap at 11.30 if that's not too late? L

Great. Big Tease, 11.30. A

Cool

Amanda spooned extra coconut cream into her hot chocolate and asked, 'How's Donna? She must have been pretty upset by what happened at the hall?'

'Yes, she looked really shaken up,' replied Leo, looking concerned. 'It could so easily have been you or her or me.

And she feels responsible in some silly way, saying if only she hadn't sent the crystal and plate. But I told her that makes no sense. It was an accident waiting to happen to anyone who crossed that floor. It could have been any member of the class.'

'She must have felt better after giving a statement to the police. I expect they asked, did they?' asked Amanda, gently fishing.

'Yes, and the constable was very understanding.'

'Nikolaides?'

'Yes.'

'She's very kind,' said Amanda, 'I suppose the constable reassured her?'

'Yes. It was lucky in a way that, although she had the key, I was with her, or a client was, the whole time from when the rector gave it to her until she gave it to you.'

'That's good,' responded Amanda. 'So at least Donna has an alibi for the day that it happened. That must help put her mind at rest a little, on some score.'

'You're right, but I don't think that's the point for her. It's the fact that it happened at all. Poor thing. She went as white as a sheet. Donna's really a much more sensitive little soul than people realise.'

'She's lucky to have a lovely big brother to look out for her,' observed Amanda with a kind smile.

'Actually, she's the elder of the two us by a few years. I just look more weathered. The effect of life in the City!'

'She just looks youthful,' countered Amanda generously. 'But I meant "big" in the sense of size and presence.'

'Ah, I see. Well, I hope I help. But you, Amanda, you don't seem to be in need of support of any kind. Independent, your own business, and a demanding trade, at that.'

'I enjoy it. It is no hardship for me,' she said pleasantly.

'You know, I'd love to see your workshop. Having been quite involved in the furniture business for some years, I miss the smell of wood. May I?'

Amanda's impish side got the better of her.

'Yes,' she said 'The ideal time would be …'

* * * * *

Amanda brought in the tea tray as Trelawney finished making up the fire.

'Thank you,' she said.

'Thought I'd make myself useful,' he replied and sat down. Picking up his mug he asked, 'So, how did the subtle interview go at the Snout and Trough.'

'OKish. From Ryan, I just got a bit more backstory, and then over tea, Leo told me how upset his sister was … blah blah blah. But the one valuable bit of info he did give is that his sister had no chance to use the hall key from the time she got it from the rector until the time she gave it to me. So she has an alibi, at least for that day.'

'Good data.'

'Oh, and both of them wanted a tour of the workshop, so I booked them in on Tuesday morning at the crack of dawn. You should have seen their faces when they saw that they were not the only one!'

Trelawney allowed his amusement to peep through. 'You shock me, Miss Cadabra. This is a side of you I have not yet seen.'

'Oh, I wasn't mean,' insisted Amanda. 'If I had thought for an instant that either of them was in the least bit interested in seeing French polish flakes and my collections of chisels I would never have thrown them together!'

Trelawney chuckled. 'Then they were justly served, no doubt, though I cannot help but have some sympathy for them.'

'Also, if one of them is the spy or the murderer, I wouldn't really want to be alone in the workshop with them. Anyway, come on. Let me have *your* news,' Amanda responded.

'Well, I got my father talking about the gifts, the particular talents of the … families. You know, Cardiubarns: spell-weaving.'

'Flamgoynes: divination.'

'Yes, he then told me the Cadabra gift.'

'Farming?' asked Amanda, in her best rendition of surprise.

'They are "levitants" apparently,' Trelawney responded.

'Levitants?' queried Amanda in a bewildered tone.

'Levitation, moving objects around.'

Amanda laughed and opened her eyes wide in her innocent look. 'There are people who can actually *do* that?'

'So it would seem, according to my revered parent,' he replied. 'Your grandfather never mentioned this to you?' Trelawney asked her, with every appearance of passing interest.

'I think he was disinherited when he married Granny, or cut himself off, so I guess he put all that family history stuff behind him. They both did. They made a new life for themselves and, in time, for me too, and didn't talk about the past. I think that's generally a good philosophy, don't you? When not so good things have happened?'

Trelawney was about to say that the past can impinge on the present but thought better of pushing it. Instead, he said,

'Anyway, I haven't told you about Vanessa's information.'

'Oo yes, do tell,' said Amanda, relieved by the change of subject.

'She moves about in the West End but gets clients elsewhere here and there. She told me that Vic Woodberry was part of the East End scene back in the bad old days. Went down for robbery a couple of times, but they were never able to convict him for one or two of his more lucrative raids. In Vanessa's opinion, that's what attracted Majolica, who had an eye to the cash and the good life. Anyone could see that was a *marriage de convenance* if ever she saw one. Vanessa actually trained someone Vic was inside with. That man said Vic had turned over a new leaf and made good in the stock market, would you believe?'

'Gracious!'

'Vic was proud of his East End origins and had plenty of stories to impress Majolica with. Vic's chum told Vanessa that Majolica always fancied herself as a "laydee" of exquisite taste, thought herself above her husband, liked men, despised women and generally made, er … good male friends wherever she went. Apparently, Majolica tamed a good deal in more recent years.'

'Well, well. That does fit with what she said about living in Romping-in-the-Heye as though was it was Mayfair and Sunken Madley was the gutter. But that's just irritating and somewhat offensive. Not the sort of thing that would make someone want to see her off for, surely?' queried Amanda.

'True,' agreed Trelawney.

'But it explains why she was a bit frosty with me. She liked you though. I could tell,' remarked Amanda, teasingly.

'Everyone likes me. I am Detective Inspector Trelawney – good cop.'

'Who's the bad one?'

'We try not to have those any more. But I think it's because I'm an OK dancer and she could use me for demonstrations.'

'Possibly,' Amanda said doubtfully. She picked up a gingernut then put it down impatiently. 'Oh, are we *any* further forward?'

'It's all grist to the mill,' Trelawney replied soothingly. 'In the detecting trade, you learn to just write it all down and bide your time. Eventually, some of the dots will start to join up.'

'If you say so,' replied Amanda resignedly. 'Oh by the way, you'd better watch out next Saturday. Donna told me at the class that Vanessa is planning to teach us the Rumba: the dance of lurrrrve,' she added raising her eyebrows.

'Thank you. Forewarned is forearmed!'

Chapter 39

✍

PRINTS

'Possess your soul in patience, Miss Cadabra,' advised Trelawney, the following Saturday. 'You know, if you're going to make a habit of finding bodies, you might as well learn how the professionals deal with investigating a whodunit.'

'Yes, but the professionals aren't *talking* to me!' Amanda exclaimed.

'Ahem,' he said, modestly.

'Oh, sorry, Inspector, of course, *you* are a professional. But it's just you're not on this case. But what about your pal? He must know something,' Amanda remarked, lighting up.

'Well, yes, he has been keeping me in the loop,' Trelawney confessed.

'And?' she asked animatedly.

'It's police business, Miss Cadabra,' he replied levelly. She looked so crestfallen that he smiled. 'Oh very well, I suppose it isn't anything you couldn't find out by hanging out in that Reuters of yours that you call The Corner Shop. But it's confidential, all right?' Trelawney added sternly.

'Of course,' responded Amanda, instantly brightening again. 'And who would I tell, anyway?'

'All right. Some of it you already know, but here goes: the police interviewed everyone at the party, as you would expect, especially those who had been attending classes at the hall. The rector gave a statement. They interviewed Donna Weathersby. Just as her brother told you, she had received the key from the rector in the afternoon, but then she had been with either clients or her brother until the time you arrived, and she delivered the key into your hands. Her brother and clients have corroborated that.'

'OK.'

'The neighbours and shopkeepers were interviewed. Had they seen anyone entering the hall during the last week? Had Mrs Cripps, the cleaner? The ladies who had done the flowers? No, no one had seen anything untoward.'

'A blank so far then,' she commented.

'Next: prints,' he continued.

'They didn't take mine,' Amanda said. 'I suppose because I provided them during the Lost Madley affair.'

'Yes. They found yours, the rector's and Mr Branscombe's.' Amanda thanked her gifts that she had not needed to touch the doors, as they had been opened by her spells. Her footprints down in the cellar were another matter. She had been holding her breath on this one. Surely some of her shoe prints would have been on top of Mr Branscombe's who should have been the last person down there with the rector. But perhaps she had approached the supports by another route on the evening of the catastrophe.

'As for footprints,' Trelawney went on, 'the waters were muddied; by the medic who went down there, in case there was anything that could be done for Mrs Woodberry, and it looked like someone had brushed or smudged the prints left by you, the rector and Branscombe, as well as the builders, Recket and Bogia, who erected the supports. There were scuffmarks where the dust had been disturbed. And … some pawprints all over the place.'

'Oh dear,' said Amanda. Tempest! Tempest, bless him, she thought. That's why he lagged behind when we were coming back up. He must have been sweeping away my shoeprints! I must get him a treat.

'Yes, but practically everyone, including Sergeant Baker,' responded Trelawney, 'has confirmed the presence of a cat in the village who is wherever he wants to be when he wants to be, frequently without his so-called owner, so I wouldn't worry. It's an old building; I expect there are half a dozen ways that an animal could find its way in.'

Amanda tried not to let the extent of her relief show. It appeared that Trelawney wasn't connecting Tempest's presence down there to her. He was pausing for a sip or two of tea. Amanda took one too. Her mouth had become unaccountably dry. He put down his mug and continued.

'They established that the screws in the brackets of the supports down there, keeping up the floor of the hall, had been bent with pincers or pliers, and some kind of chemical had been used to burn away the undersides of the floorboards. Traces of hydrochloric acid were found.'

'Yes,' said Amanda, 'Constable Nikolaides came to ask me if I use it in my workshop. I confirmed that I have only a very small supply because Grandpa bought it years ago and we hardly ever used it. I showed her what I have.'

'Right. Leo and Donna Weathersby were asked if they used it at the salon and they said, no. Mrs Scripps said yes, she sometimes uses it to shift stubborn stains, but it was a fairly weak solution. They've attempted to contact Recket and Bogia, but they are nowhere to be found. No one has seen them for the past month. The police have confirmed the recent presence of someone in the attic. The floor — the hall ceiling — had been freshly broken, most likely by a foot going through it.'

Aha, thought Amanda, so that at least had been happening in the present, at the fatal moment. She asked, 'What about the Woodberrys? They must have interviewed Vic.'

'They had a key to the side and front doors but not the basement. Vic was at home at the time of the incident. He was ill at the party and had gone home to recover before the class. Majolica's relations hadn't seen her for a long time. Apparently, she considered herself above them since she married Vic. Neighbours and any contacts were interviewed. Your summary is correct, though, Miss Cadabra, she wasn't particularly well liked but no one had a motive for killing her.'

* * * * *

The banister was done. Amanda was back in the workshop. The days seemed to be going agonisingly slowly. The inching forward irked her. Each morning she continued to train with her grandparents, but it was difficult to concentrate. She could now lift the armoire, and all three workbenches, while keeping the saw going. Grandpa said that when she could make a cut that didn't resemble a boa constrictor, she could consider that practice complete. Unfortunately, he made his comment mid-exercise, and she broke into a laugh that interrupted the spells and allowed everything to fall to the floor with an almighty crash.

She decided to see if Leo had any more information to yield.

Up for another elevenses? Getting cabin fever. A

10.45? Big Tease. L

See you there.

* * * * *

'Just a few more days to go, Miss Cadabra,' said Trelawney consolingly. 'CI Maxwell will be back on Monday week.'

'Anything more from your pal?'

'Ross? Yes, Worsfold is getting restive. He knows his time in charge of the case is running out and he doesn't have a culprit to show for it. He's put the backs up of everyone in the village, and people are getting reluctant to talk to his team.'

'Are the rector and I still top of the suspect list?'

'I'm afraid so. Apparently, Worsfold wants Tempest's pawprints taken.'

'Good luck with that,' replied Amanda drily. 'Well, I tried talking to Leo again. But as no one is talking to the police, he didn't have anything useful to tell me. Just got him to talk about himself. You know how it is, get the stream flowing and sometimes something useful floats by.'

'What did the stream say?'

'Italian mother. Born out of wedlock, then mother married. Step-father went off with another woman. Family devastated but mother said he still maintained them.'

'How did Wife 2 feel about that?'

'Leo says he thinks she didn't know. Maybe he had his own bank account and paid out of that. Lots of couples do have separate accounts.'

'Sounds well-to-do if he was able to maintain two households.'

'I guess so. Anyway, Ma-maa remarried, this time father of children. Father was horrid. Mother divorced him and eventually met a nice Australian man and, once her children were independent, went out there and has been living happily ever since. Leo sounded quite wistful. I think he'd like to join her but is loyal to Donna, so I think he wants to see her settled first.'

'Good man,' commented Trelawney.

'I think so,' Amanda agreed.

'Are you having a second lunch date as well?'

'With Ryan? Not if I can help it. Too much limelight and I didn't like how he wanted me along just because he's used to having a presentable female in tow when he's in the limelight. But as for Leo, he's OK. I think his outsider perspective on the village could be useful in some way. At least I feel that, in talking to him, I'm trying to do something useful.'

'Well, be careful,' Trelawney warned Amanda. 'This week will be the trickiest. If I were you, I wouldn't leave the house. Don't remind Worsfold in any way of your presence if you can possibly help it. And try and persuade that cat of yours to stay out of sight.'

Chapter 40

❧

WARRANT

It was 10.30 in the morning when the phone rang. Amanda had stopped using headphones and had her work music on quietly. She took one look at the screen and, for some reason, her stomach lurched.

'Inspector?'

'Miss Cadabra. Listen carefully. They've lifted a partial print of a woman's shoe from the church hall cellar. Worsfold is getting a warrant to search your house and workshop.'

'But —'

'No. Listen to me. Don't argue. I know you were down there that night. Don't tell me how, or ask how I know; I just *know*. Now, hide the shoes you were wearing, hide anything you don't want the police to find, do you understand?'

'Yes,' she said instantly.

'Now go!'

Amanda clicked off the phone as her grandparents appeared.

'Get your shoes, the wands and the book,' Granny listed helpfully.

'Mine too,' added Grandpa.

Amanda opened a drawer and pulled out Perran's *Forrag Seothe Macungreanz A Aclowundre*, the Cadabra spellbook. She hurried into the house, gathered her incriminating footwear, her old full-length wand, and *Wicc'huldol Galdorwrd Nha Koomwrtdreno Aon*, her grandmother's Cardiubarn grimoire.

'This way!' said Senara taking the stairs, 'and get The Hat.'

'What about my Pocket-wand?'

'Keep it, it's fine. No one would guess what it is.'

Amanda ducked into her bedroom and grabbed her witch's hat from a high shelf in her wardrobe.

'Up here!' came a call from the attic. Amanda struggled up the stairs with her arms full. 'Quickly,' urged Granny.

She was kneeling on an empty bit of floor. Amanda slid to her knees beside her. Senara intoned: '*Agertyn forrag Senara, atdha mina vocleav*.'

To Amanda's amazement, a section of the floor acquired hinges and open like a lid.

'In here!' Granny instructed her. Amanda poured the items in as fast as she could.

'How will I get them out?' she asked. 'That's a voiceprint spell, isn't it?'

'l'll do it. Never mind that. *Bespredna*,' Granny added to the floor, the hatch shut and all trace of it vanished. 'Lift that pile of suitcases into this space.'

'*Aereval*,' said Amanda to the stack of luggage, making it rise and rapidly sail a few feet until it was over where the magical storage was. '*Sedaasig*.' It lowered into place.

'Good,' said Granny. 'Now then, get back to the workshop, as though nothing is wrong, and when they come, act surprised.'

As Amanda made her way back to her bench, she spoke hurriedly, 'Trelawney knows I was down there. *How* does he know?'

'He's a diviner,' replied Granny. 'And he knows you. Tempest's tracks sealed the deal. He knows that, of course, you'd go down there, if you could, to see if you could help the Woodberry woman and take a look at any evidence, in case you came into the firing line. He knows the Cardiubarns are spell-weavers. Why wouldn't you know a simple spell like how to open a door?'

Amanda's anxious face prompted Grandpa to intervene.

'Don't be vexed, *bian*. You don't have to admit anything to him, and he won't push you. He warned you, didn't he? Doesn't that show he's on your side?'

Amanda nodded and went back to her workplace, stilled her breathing, did some tidying up and waited for the door buzzer to sound.

Constable Nikolaides and another woman constable arrived. They searched, they looked at the soles of Amanda's shoes but found none that matched the print. Nikolaides apologised for the disturbance, and they left.

Amanda closed the door behind them, took a puff of her inhaler and got herself to a chair in the kitchen. She sent a text to Trelawney, saying thank you for the heads up and that they'd departed empty-handed.

Joan knocked on the door on the pretence of delivering a letter and told Amanda, in scandalised accents, that the police had had the effrontery to search the rectory, as if the rector herself had something to do with Majolica's demise. The village was abuzz with indignation and, as far as the police were concerned, shut up tightly as a clam.

Just as Amanda was beginning to relax, Trelawney called.

'Miss Cadabra. It's not over yet. Ross says Worsfold is

brimming with frustration and is determined to make an arrest. It could be anyone. I'll be there as soon as I can. Maybe there's something Mike can do.'

'Thank you, Inspector.'

Amanda wondered what would happen if they arrested her. What it would be like … 'Oh Granny! Grandpa!'

Her grandparents were reassuring and soothing, and she tried not to think the worst.

Forty-five anguished minutes later, as Amanda was taking another puff of her inhaler, the phone showed a welcome name.

'Uncle Mike! Oh, Uncle Mike…'

'Calm down, dear. It's all right.'

'How is it all right?' Amanda demanded.

'It's over. You're safe.'

'How come?'

'Maxwell decided to get ahead on his messages before his flight home on Saturday and saw my email. Trelawney had told me the latest, and, when I let Maxwell know that Worsfold was about to make a fool of his whole team, Maxwell clamped down on him and has thrown him off the case. Baker's in charge until Monday.'

Amanda released a huge sigh of relief and collapsed onto a stool by her bench.

'Thank you, Uncle Mike. You saved me.'

'Trelawney saved you, Amanda. And he was right, wasn't he? You had been down there, hadn't you?'

'Yes but …'

'For the best of reasons I'm sure. But next time be more careful with your feet,' he advised her. 'Whoever went down there to set up the murder was far more thorough than you about messing up their footprints.'

'How did he know I'd been into the basement?' she asked.

'He's one of us, my dear. Maybe it's time you started

putting a few of your cards on the table. So far he's been showing you his entire hand, and you've been just giving him a peek at your two of clubs.'

'I can't. I mustn't tell. I mustn't ever tell. Granny and Grandpa always told me —'

'I bet they're telling you that you can trust him.'

She was quiet, not knowing what to say. She had kept her secret so long. So long it was ingrained in every fibre of her being to say nothing, show nothing, admit nothing. She dared not break silence just because Uncle Mike, whom she had known so short a time and was a close friend of the inspector, told her it was safe.

'It's all right,' Hogarth assured her. 'In your own time. The important thing is that you're safe now. Anyway, I had a little chat with Maxwell on the phone, and, on Monday, he'll get you the all clear to go down to that basement officially, and do your thing, as you've been straining at the leash to do,' he remarked with amusement.

'Fantastic! Finally!' exclaimed Amanda joyfully. 'Can I go and see Victor Woodberry too?'

'Yes, but try not to tread on Baker's toes, OK?'

'Yes, yes of course,' she agreed at once. 'He's such a nice man, I'd never want to upset him.'

'I've turned Trelawney around, and he's heading back to his station. You don't need him now, do you?'

'No, I'll be fine.'

'You'll see him on Saturday anyway. He's done you proud. Give him a big hug.'

'Certainly not!' said Amanda stiffly.

Hogarth chuckled. 'You sound just like him, you know.'

'Never mind that, Uncle Mike. I will, of course, thank him most sincerely for his intervention.'

'You do that.'

Chapter 41

ॐ

WHAT SOPHY SAW

Although Amanda would have to wait until Monday to get a pass to the crime scene, there was now one thing she was free to do the next day. Senara agreed: visit the crypt and call the owner of the gold thimble.

Tempest padded down the stone steps ahead of Amanda. He went to the wall about three feet from the end of the sarcophagus under which Amanda had found the thimble, sat down and fixed a meaningful stare on her face.

'Aha. X marks the spot does it?' She slid down next to him, leaving a space between cat and tomb. 'What do I do now? I don't know the child's name. Oh well, here goes.' She took a breath and called softly:

'Hello? … I think I have a thimble that belongs to you? … Please come and talk to me … and my cat.'

Nothing.

'He's very nice,' — a statement that most of the village would have asserted to be manifestly false, but Tempest thought it touching that, at that moment at least, his witch believed it.

They waited.

Tempest sighed. Clearly, she was getting nowhere. He got up, walked around in the empty space purring and called:

'Mrrrowwwwl.'

The stone steps leading up into the church disappeared. The artificial lights were replaced by lamps in sconces and lit candles on an altar at one end of the crypt. They cast their warm light up onto the low vault. All of the coffins had gone except the one beside them and one other. The flames flickered in a draft coming through a door ajar in the wall opposite the altar. The place had transformed from burial chamber to the chapel it had once been.

A little girl of about eight years of age, with short fair ringlets, wearing a simple pale, long-sleeved dress over pantalets, sat huddled in a shawl in the corner beside Tempest. She looked at him with a forlorn expression, then up at Amanda with large scared eyes.

'Hello. My name's Amanda, and this is Tempest. Do you like cats?'

She nodded.

'So do I. You can stroke him if you like.'

She put out a little hand and Tempest tolerated her fingers brushing over his fur.

'You know,' continued Amanda conversationally, 'he doesn't like just anyone stroking him. So you must be special.' The child looked at Amanda more confidently. 'You can say hello to him.'

'Hello, Tempest,' said the girl, finding her voice at last.

'You can tell him your name,' prompted Amanda.

'I'm Sophy.'

'What a lovely name. It has a soft and gentle sound.'

'Actually it's Sophia, Miss. Sophia Aldenham.'

'I like Sophy best,' commented Amanda warmly.

'Me too.'

'It's not very comfortable here, is it?' Amanda observed.

'It's safe though,' Sophy pointed out.

'Yes, I suppose so. Safe from what?'

'The grownups.'

'Are they dangerous?' asked Amanda in concern.

'Yes, when they're cross!' declared Sophy. 'They shout and go *on* at you.'

'Are they cross with you?'

'No, but they would be if they found out. But, oh! That's not the worst of it,' insisted Sophy, her eyes filling with tears.

'You can tell me,' said Amanda, tucking the little girl's shawl more securely around her. 'I promise not to tell.'

'It was all my fault. If I hadn't got Percy to come with me up into the hayloft, he would never have fallen through!'

'Is that what happened?'

'Yes, you see the servants have their own dance in the Big Barn, and we had been sent to bed after the big house dance, but that was dull anyway, and I went and got Percy, and said let's go and watch the dance at the Big Barn. He said we oughtn't, but I told him it would fun and no one would know. Only the hayloft floor broke, and he fell down,' she finished woefully.

'Was he hurt?' enquired Amanda.

'No, he fell into the trifle,' replied Sophy matter-of-factly.

Amanda bit her lip as her little friend continued,

'And I should have owned up that I was up there too, but I was scared, and I ratted, and now he'll never forgive me!'

Amanda pulled a tissue from her pocket and mopped Sophy's face, then hastily hid it before the little girl could register the strange nature of the handkerchief.

'Have you been back to the hayloft to try and find him?' suggested Amanda.

'Yes, but all I see is the two gentlemen, and they don't

see me, so I can't ask them a thing about what happened,' explained Sophy in a mixture of despair and exasperation.

'What gentlemen were they?'

'A small dark one who comes up the ladder and a tall, fair one who just sort of appears on the pile of hay.'

'I see. Do you remember what happened the next day?'

'We went away. I mean our family.'

'Far away?' asked Amanda.

'India. But I'm here now, and I'm not coming out until Percy says he'll forgive me and I know the grownups won't be cross ... oh dear... ,'said Sophy and faded.

'Oh dear, indeed,' remarked Amanda to her feline. 'I wish I could help her. Meanwhile ... a short dark man — no idea who that could be — and a tall, fair one. Well, I can make a shrewd guess at who *that* might be.' The cat led the way up out of the crypt, as she went on,

'Progress, Tempest. Come on, let's get home. Thank you for your assistance. I was impressed by your tact and expertise in handling the situation.'

He gave her a benign glance and a nod. It did her credit that she had some conception of his worth. Of course, he doubted he could ever reveal the stature of his true nature; it would be too much for the little thing. It always was for humans. But, she was coming along nicely. Perhaps one day ….

* * * * *

On Saturday, Trelawney behaved just as usual at the class. When he came back to the cottage, she thanked him profusely as, unusually, he sat beside her on the sofa and took her hands.

'Miss Cadabra, you don't have to say anything more.'

'Inspector, I owe you this much: I *did* go down there. Please don't ask me how.'

'I won't.'

'How did you know?' Amanda asked curiously.

Trelawney released her hands and went over to the fireplace. He looked back at her, shaking his head slightly. 'I just knew. I know that that's no sort of an answer, but I just knew you had to have been there. It was as though there was a video of it running in front of my eyes.' He became decisive. 'But never mind. If you really want to thank me, make me a cup of tea while I get this burning.'

She laughed. 'That's the least I can do.'

He left soon after, tactfully refraining from asking her what her investigatory plans were for the coming week.

Chapter 42

༄

INDIGNATION

Sure enough, on Monday came the text from Maxwell:

*Baker will be on duty noon till 1 pm. I've told him
to expect you. You'll have a safe window except for the 10
minutes at either end of that. Good luck. M*

Amanda hastily changed out of her overalls into ....
'What should I wear?' Tempest yawned and closed his eyes.
What was this obsession humans had with clothing? He
supposed as they were impoverished in the fur department it
was understandable. Tempest licked one luxuriantly covered
paw smugly.

'Oh, you're no help,' said Amanda to him impatiently.
'Granny? What were they wearing in 1918?'

'Just put on one of my longer skirts and your hair in a
bun. Hurry,' replied Senara, without bothering to materialise.

Amanda had not moved into her grandparents'

room, and Senara's clothes were where she'd left them. Her granddaughter found a grey skirt that came almost to her ankles as Senara was considerably taller than Amanda. She quickly pulled her hair up.

As she and Tempest approached, Baker gave her a friendly nod and greeting, eyed her feline askance, opened the hall front door for them, and walked away.

Witch and familiar entered. The hall was silent. The floor gaped. Amanda crept to the edge of the ragged-edged hole and couldn't help peering over to check that the body had gone.

All clear. She called out,

'Captain Dunkley?'

Nothing.

'Captain Fortescue Dunkley?'

Amanda couldn't see much down there, and looked around the hall in case he was going to appear above ground.

'You, girl!'

She gasped in shock.

'You startled me!' Amanda exclaimed.

'You startled me, *sir*, if you please. Come down here. Come down here at once,' said Dunkley imperiously.

His attitude rankled, but Amanda remembered that she wanted a favour from him and replied accordingly. 'Er, yes, sir. I'll be right there.'

She hurried around the side of the hall, saying to Tempest. 'What does he think I am? A servant?' Her familiar agreed. He didn't appreciate people thinking she was *their* servant.

Amanda used the keys to the cellar doors and approached the scene of the accident.

'Ah. Good,' remarked Dunkley. 'Now. I demand an explanation.'

'Of what?' she asked, then hastily added, 'Sir.'

'Where everyone has gorn and why I can't get back upstairs.'

'Erm, well,' replied Amanda, playing for time to consider the most effective response.

'And who is that woman and those other persons in very odd costume? It seems to me there's been some smoky business going on here. Very smoky indeed, and ending in what I'd regard as a dastardly business,' Dunkley stated.

'Captain Dunkley, I will tell you what I know and do my best to help you. But I need you to tell me exactly what you've seen while you've been here, the people you've seen and what they have been doing.'

'Oh no,' he replied at once with finality. 'I couldn't possibly go into details.'

'Why not?'

'Not the sort of thing one discusses with a lady,' he answered straightening his lapels.

'Lady? But you've been calling me "you girl",' Amanda protested.

'Yes, well. Bad light. Apologies and all that sort of thing. I see now that you are, in fact, a lady, and skullduggery and the shuffling off of the mortal coil and exsanguinations are not the sort of thing with which a chap like me sullies a lady's ears. That's not what I fought a war for,' Dunkley uttered decisively.

'You can't be serious. What about the horrors of the last four years?' Amanda pointed out.

'That was chaps,' he stated shortly.

'Well,' she expostulated, 'what about nurses and so on at the front?'

'Were you a nurse?' he asked, looking down his nose at her with a frown.

'No,' Amanda, incurably honest, admitted.

'Well then,' he replied, as though that settled that.

'But—'

'—please. I beg you will desist from importunities. There is nothing more to be said,' uttered Dunkley indicating with a raised hand that this was his last word on the subject.

Amanda let out a breath of studied patience. 'Fine. What if I bring a man with me next time? Will you tell *him*?'

'Certainly. Man to man. And if your gentleman friend sees fit to share the information that I shall give him with you, that is his affair,' Dunkley stated judicially.

'Gentleman friend ... all right. I'll bring him to see you. When?'

'The Christmas Ball would be best. Nothing unusual about a couple of chaps having a chat over brandy and cigars. Shady business. No saying who might be involved. If the war were still on, I'd suspect a plot. Not but what the Gerry POWs I met were decent chaps to a man. No, this is an inside job,' he pronounced.

Amanda gave it one last try. 'Are you *sure* you can't just tell me about it?'

'Certainly not, madam. Not the thing for a little lady. Bring me your chap. Christmas Eve, 10 o'clock. You can point me out to him. What's his name?'

Amanda had no choice. There was only one:

'Detective Inspector Trelawney.'

'Hm,' replied Dunkley impressed. 'Good show,' he uttered and promptly vanished.

Amanda spluttered her way back up to the open air, repeating under breath, 'I can't *believe* this! I just can't believe this! A ghost who won't talk to me because I'm a woman? I mean ... *seriously*?' Amanda thanked Sergeant Baker, and Tempest, bored by the refrain, fell asleep on the back seat during the very short journey back to the cottage.

Amanda's impulse was to call the inspector on the spot, but decided that this had better be explained in person.

However, she needed to vent her indignation. Senara and Perran bore her rant stoically, occasionally attempting to cool her ire by explaining that things were different in those days. It fell on deaf ears.

'I mean, how *dare* he?' Do I look like I'm three years old or … or a Neanderthal or … or …"

Some 36 hours later, Aunt Amelia bore the brunt of her niece's exasperation.

'I mean … you weren't there … but if you could have heard him! "Little lady!" Little lady indeed! And now I have to drag the inspector into it. At least, last time I had some independence. Now I need … a *man*!'

'Have some pudding,' said Amelia comfortingly, putting a helping of marmalade roll in front of her.

'You probably think I'm making too much of this,' commented Amanda, in passing and with unwitting deadly accuracy.

'Yes, dear. Here, have some custard. You know you like it best with custard,' Amelia replied placidly.

'Thank you, Aunt Amelia. I'm glad you understand.'

'Of course. It's all rather annoying, and I don't blame you for feeling a trifle put out, but you've said that for reasons you can't divulge —'

' —Yes, I have to respect his confidence.'

'And that does you credit, sweetie. But you've said that the inspector will understand and very likely cooperate. So, you are managing the situation admirably. And by the end of Christmas Eve, you'll have all of your answers to who and how and when of the murder. So that's good isn't?'

'Yes, Aunt Amelia,' said Amanda, spooning some of the luscious confection into her mouth and being transported for a moment to sensory heaven.

'I'm sure it's all for the best,' soothed Amelia.

'Hmmmm,' replied Amanda.

Chapter 43

୧ର

A FIRST FOR THOMAS

Trelawney put the other half of his shortbread biscuit on his napkin, leaned back in Perran's favourite chair by the fire opposite Amanda, and said,

'I had the feeling all through the class that there was something you were eager to impart to me.'

Amanda took a deep breath and uttered, 'Yes.'

'I'm all ears,' he said invitingly.

'Well …'

And in that pause, he knew. She's been back down there, he thought. Of course, she has. That's what she did last time. Went back to the scene of the crime where she was — what was it she and Baker said? — 'sensing things'. Maxwell got her a pass again, but … this time… it hasn't gone according to plan …

'It's a bit awkward,' she muttered.

'How about,' Trelawney intervened, coming to her aid, 'if I tell you about a conversation I had with my father on Tuesday? Perhaps it might help.'

Amanda, glad to have the dreaded moment of revelation forestalled, eagerly assented.

'Thank you. I mean, please do, Inspector.'

'I was telling my father that you are a furniture restorer like Perran was ....'

* * * * *

'Was?' queried Kytto Trelawney

'Perran and Senara are dead,' Thomas explained.

Kyt shook his head with a slight but knowing smile. 'Transitioned, you mean. There is no way in which those two are going to leave Amanda by herself.'

'Transitioned? To another dimension, you mean? But they're still around?'

'Exactly.'

Thomas went quiet again. His head was buzzing. Partly he had a sense of the surreal, having this outlandish conversation with his father after all these years, partly a sense of closeness to him that he'd never felt before. But right now, it was as though his eyes were opening to who it was, who he … could be.

'Is it possible, Dad, that, as someone with this intuition talent, I would be able to hear them?'

'Entirely, son,' said his father with conviction.

'Then … I think I can.'

'I'm not surprised.'

'You see, there have been times when I've been with Miss Cadabra, and I've heard voices in my head, and found myself repeating the same words as though they were my own, and then realising that I hadn't actually *thought* those words myself.'

'Yes, yes, that's how it would be,' confirmed Kyt.

* * * * *

'So,' continued Trelawney, 'it turns out that, not only can I can see future possibilities and present events in my tea, but … I hear dead people,' he finished on a rueful note.

Amanda nodded slowly.

'Does that help you at all with what you want to tell me?' he asked.

'Yes. Actually, it does.' Emboldened, she commenced, 'You see, last time I found a body —'

'No need to go into that,' said Trelawney, helpfully. 'I think I know what happened when you revisited the crime scene.'

'Ah. All right then. Well, you see the first time I went to the hall with the rector, she left me alone there for a few minutes and, even though at that time, the floor was intact, I saw the hole, much as it is now, only there was a man who'd fallen down it. He was in regimentals; I think, First World War. He was blustering about how he hadn't come through the War to end up in a hole and where was everyone, and he wanted to get back upstairs.'

'He was someone who'd … transitioned?'

'Yes. And he fell through in the same place as Majolica, and, for an instant, I did see a woman and him at the same time, falling through. So I thought maybe he saw what happened to her and what and who caused it.'

'Logical.'

'So, as soon as I got the text from Chief Inspector Maxwell giving me the go-ahead, I went back to the hall and called the man and he appeared.'

'So far so good. And did he see all that happened?'

'Yes, in fact, it's been pretty busy in that hall. He mentioned people in what must be modern dress coming and going and engaging in acts of "skullduggery" that ended in such distressing events that …. and you're not going to believe this! …'

'Try me.'

'He won't *tell* me!' finished Amanda in exasperation.

'Oh. A secretive ghost,' remarked Trelawney.

'No,' she corrected him. 'He wouldn't tell me because I'm a woman!'

'Really?'

'He said it wasn't fit for a lady's ears.'

'Dear me. I'm beginning to see where my humble services might be of use to you, Miss Cadabra,' Trelawney commented, his lips twitching.

'Well yes, I was coming to that. I asked if I brought a man if he'd spill the beans then. And he said he would. But only to you, and, if you chose to tell me, that was your affair,' explained Amanda, with a toss of the head.

'Outrageous.'

'Antiquated!'

Trelawney was struggling to keep his countenance. The absurdity of the situation was overcoming his self-control. He manufactured a coughing fit and masked his mouth.

'Are you laughing?' asked Amanda accusingly. 'It's not funny.'

'I'm sorry, Miss Cadabra. But are you sure it isn't?'

She managed the smallest of smiles.

'I suppose, just the tiniest bit. Snookered by a stuffy ghost. But what if you hadn't been available? What would I have done then?'

'Has it occurred to you,' he asked reasonably, 'that this has happened to bring us both a little more into the open with one another, and that, one day, that may be especially important?

Amanda hadn't looked at it that way.

'Well,' she said slowly. 'I suppose so. So you'll do it then?'

'Of course. Er, what exactly do I need to do?' he asked uncertainly.

'Hm … I suppose it would help if you dressed for the period. It's a bit short notice, but I could ask Sandra and Mrs Sharma and Joan to put it about that the Christmas Ball is optional black tie. I think it's actually the New Year's Eve Ball that's period costume, but black tie would certainly cover 1918 evening dress, I'd imagine.'

'All right. I'm sure I can rustle up something,' Trelawney agreed.

'And then, you have to meet him. His name is Captain Fortescue Dunkley, by the way —'

'Fortescue?' he asked with a shade of amusement.

'Yes, I know! Anyway, you have to meet him at 10 o'clock. So we'd have to slip away from Sandra's party, at the Snout and Trough function room, just before then. I am to point him out to you, and then you go and introduce yourself to him as Detective Inspector Trelawney. I could see that your title impressed him no end, the nincompoop,' Amanda added scornfully.

'Thank you, Miss Cadabra.'

'Oh, I don't mean … anyway …'

'Yes, you will lurk somewhere within earshot, and I will get the goods. Is that the idea?' he enquired cordially.

'Exactly,' Amanda confirmed.

'Understood,' responded Trelawney, unable to banish the twinkle from his eye. Amanda observed it and remarked,

'I'm so glad that you're enjoying all of this.'

'It's a first for me, Miss Cadabra,' he replied apologetically. 'My first time interviewing a witness from another dimension. The sense of the surreal is overwhelming, and may be making me feel a little light-headed.'

For the first time that evening, she smiled properly

and shook her head. 'I can hardly believe you're the same person I met that day in this room when you came to see my grandparents and me for the first time.'

'Neither can I, Miss Cadabra,' Trelawney replied with sincerity, 'neither can I.'

Chapter 44

❧

THE SCENT IS UP

All of the shops in Sunken Madley were cheerful with Christmas lights and decorations. Leo had done the salon proud with a tasteful bough stretching across the window, from which snowflakes and white and glass baubles were suspended. It was charming.

The Snout and Trough was equally elegantly attired in festive décor of gold. By contrast, The Sinner's Rue was festooned with every light in its attic in every colour, and huge tissue stars were suspended from the ceiling, linked with coloured paper chains in the most garish colours available. But it was tradition. And the villagers liked it, in spite of their expressed horror.

Amanda had ordered all of her presents and nearly every one had arrived. One special gift was carefully packed in its red box, wrapped in marbled paper, tied with gold ribbon and hidden away upstairs on the bed in Granny and Grandpa's room. Cards from Aunt Amelia, the Bergstroms and her fellow villagers jostled for space on the mantelpiece and every available surface in the sitting room. Mince pies, gingerbread biscuits and Christmas puddings crammed the cupboards. Cranberry-and-nutmeg-scented candles stood ready for the big day, stacked by the fire. The Christmas tree was up; a live one, chosen by Amanda and delivered by the nursery up the road: Muttring Breeze Trees and Plants. She had decorated it in traditional red and gold, and Tempest was being heavily bribed not to climb it.

Amanda was putting the star on the top, when the phone rang.

'Gwendolen?'

'Happy Christmas, dear'.

'Happy Christmas,' Amanda replied enthusiastically.

'In fact,' said Miss Armstrong-Witworth, 'I may have an early present for you. Can you come over? I think it's best if you see it in person.'

'Of course. I'll come right away,' said Amanda, in cheerful anticipation.

Tempest perked up. A chance to annoy Churchill and an opportunity to woo the enchanting Natasha, she of the ice blue eyes, dark points and luxurious cream coat, was too good to pass up.

Minutes later, Gwendolen was ushering Amanda into the dining room, where Miss de Havillande was stretching out a large sheet of paper.

'Good afternoon Amanda,' she greeted her heartily.

'Good afternoon, Miss de Havillande.'

'Now, I shall leave this to dear Gwendolen, as this discovery owes more to her able research skills than mine. Do go ahead.'

'Yes. We'll have tea afterwards, shall we?' suggested Miss Armstrong-Witworth.

'That's fine,' said Amanda.

'Come here, dear. Now as you can see, this is a family tree, I have drawn it up to simplify matters. It has taken a while to get these facts, but here we are. Now. We have been researching the Recket family, in an attempt to discover who might be holding the Recket notes on the sabotage of the church hall that Mr Hodster described. So, for the first time, the Recket line was failing, as this tree shows. You can here see various members perishing without issue.'

Miss Armstrong-Witworth, indicated them on the diagram. 'The last of them, Ronald Recket, the one that our dear rector had dealings with, went into partnership with a non-family member: Filippo Bogia, whom Jane also met. Now, we went in search of victims of Recket building methods, and discovered a couple who had sued Recket in the county court over work he'd done on their property, but settled out of court. I contacted them, and, fortunately, Mr and Mrs Crumbleigh-Howse were willing to talk to us. They were just over in Potters Bar so we paid them a call. Now, it turns out that Mrs Crumbleigh-Howse's sister lives in the same village as Ronald Recket, and knows for a fact that the man is such a persistent toper of spirits that he developed cirrhosis of the liver and she doesn't know how he's lasted this long. Now, what if, fearing his days were running short, and having no heirs, Recket gave the papers to Bogia?'

'OK.'

'So we decided to investigate his partner, Mr Bogia, instead. And this, as you see, is what we found: Filippo — or "Phil" as he is known — Bogia is, in fact, of Italian extraction. He had a daughter, Bella. Now a year ago, he had a health scare, with his heart. What if — and I know that this is a lot of "what ifs"— Bogia, in the Recket tradition, gave the papers, or sent them, to his only child?'

'And where is she?'

'We were able to find some contact details for her, but

unfortunately, it seems that she had gone to live in Australia. But we were able to discover that she had married again and subsequently divorced, but, perhaps for the sake of her children had retained her second married name: Weathersby, and has two children who still live here in the UK.'

'Leonardo and Donatella Weathersby,' exclaimed Amanda excitedly.

'Indeed. Now, if I were Bella and I had those papers and had left behind my ne'er-do-well relations and made a new life in another country, what would I do with the papers?' asked Gwendolen.

'Destroy them so no one else could use them?' suggested Amanda.

'Or?' prompted Miss Armstrong-Witworth.

'Use them to put things right. It is possible she may have left them to her children, and for that reason,' Amanda replied.

'But what if her children used them for sabotage instead?'

'But why would they do that? They didn't know Majolica.'

'We shall continue to dig,' said Miss Armstrong-Witworth.

'Hm,' mused Amanda, 'I wonder if Vic would see me if I called round.'

'I don't see why not, dear. Give it a try.'

Amanda was not given to making impromptu visits and didn't much like receiving them. She preferred her guest appearances to be arranged in advance. However, the scent was up. Tempest, who was having no success with Natasha but furnishing her with considerable entertainment alternately luring and repulsing him, was more than ready to leave.

He sat beside her on the passenger seat, indicating that even his interest was engaged. Amanda set off out of the gates, turning right into Grange Way, left into Trotters Bottom, heading for the road to Romping-in-the-Heye and the Woodberry Dance Studio.

Amanda's heart beat fast as she rang the bell. The door opened. Vic came out, looking surprisingly well.

'Hello, Amanda, isn't it?'

'Hello, Mr Woodberry,' she said a trifle tentatively.

'Vic. Come in. How nice of you to call on an old man.'

'I wanted to see how you've been these past weeks.'

'Oh, I'm fine.' He was smartly dressed in crisp pale blue shirt and light khaki trousers, shaved and fragrant.

'You're walking better,' Amanda noticed.

'Yes, I'm getting physio for my leg. I don't think my dancing days are over after all. Got to keep up the studio. Hiring Vanessa to help me out.' He led the way to the conservatory at the back of the house.

'That's wonderful news.' Vic seemed to have got a new lease of life.

'Yes, well, it was all a shock but …. life goes on,' he said philosophically, gesturing to Amanda to sit down on one of the rattan chairs.

'I heard that you weren't well at the feast,' commented Amanda, to open the subject.

'Oh, that's right. Something I ate.'

'Do you remember what it was?' she asked. 'So you know to avoid it in future.'

'Do I! Those apple dumplings. Oh, my favourite, haven't seen them in years, and there were so many, and no one else seemed to want them, and Mr Seedwell said, 'Oh, dig in!' So I did. And the next thing, oh, my stomach! I just had to come home for a bit, you know, and then the next thing was I got a call … ah well. It's done. And however it happened, she's gone.'

'The police are still working on it,' said Amanda.

'But life doesn't stand still, does it? Anyway, sooner or later, they'll catch up with those rogues,' Vic stated with conviction.

'Those rogues?'

'Recket and Bogia. Oh yes. Sometime they'll have to come out of their hole in the wall.'

'You're sure it was them?' Amanda asked.

'Course,' stated Vic. 'I knew them back in the bad old days when I were a rascal. Long behind me now. Majolica helped me a lot, you know. Made a new man of me in a lotta ways. Bit dominating and she liked the lolly, if you know what I mean. I'm grateful, but not sorry to have my freedom. I can say that to you, can't I?' he added confidingly.

'Of course,' Amanda reassured him kindly.

'Come and have a cuppa, and let me show you round my little kingdom.'

* * * * *

Amanda mused on the drive home. The memory of that strangely blurred fall replayed in her mind. The soldier and the woman. The woman had to have been Majolica, and, if so, had Amanda been seeing the future?

'Aunt Amelia,' she said into the phone, 'can I drop in?'

'So,' asked Amanda, seated in Amelia's kitchen while her aunt made tea. 'Was I seeing the future when I saw Majolica fall before it actually happened?'

'No sweetie,' Amelia answered her calmly, 'no one can see the future.'

'What was I seeing then?'

'You were seeing a possibility … even a probability.'

'How come?' Amanda was a little at sea.

'Trace the train of events,' Amelia encouraged her. 'Think about traps. The very first traps were animal traps. Go from there.'

'Well, let's see,' said Amanda thoughtfully. 'For a trap to work, the hunter would have to be able to predict where the animal would come. By laying bait. Or by observing its movement or its runs.'

'Next step?' said Amelia.

'So for a trap to work on a human, the assassin would have to learn that person's routine. So … the murderer knows there's a dance class every Saturday. He knows the teachers come to prepare … wait! *Vic* always preps, but *that* night, Vic ate the dumplings, got sick and didn't turn up! If the murderer knew Vic well enough to know his food tastes, then it would have to be a villager, because who else would know the dumplings were certain to upset the strongest stomach?'

Amelia nodded.

'Makes sense.'

'But,' continued Amanda, gathering impetus, 'what if they *weren't* from the village? Then they wouldn't have known about the dumplings, or they didn't know Vic that well to know he wouldn't be able to resist them and then they would have been expecting Vic to be at the hall. But Vic goes home, and Majolica comes instead! What if we've been looking at the wrong person all this time?'

'That is all together a possibility,' agreed Amelia.

'Excuse me while I make a call?' asked Amanda.

'Go ahead. I'll get the gingernuts out.'

Chapter 45

❧

TEMPEST GOES FORTH

Amanda dialled.

'Gwendolen? What if Vic was the intended victim and not Majolica?'

'Yes, we're on the case, my dear. We should have some information for you by the morning.'

'If I'm right, it wasn't anyone who is what Mr French calls "Village" and it wasn't someone who knew Vic intimately.'

Back home Amanda with a furry, purring bundle on her lap, was processing what she had learned.

'Tempest,' said his witch, scratching him behind his right ear, 'who was at the Feast for the first time? Let's see: Ryan, Jonathan Sheppard, Leo and Donna, Vic and Majolica. If only we knew definitely if Leo and Donna had the Recket papers. I can't see them inviting me in to search their premises, but ... Amanda looked down at her familiar speculatively. He sighed wearily.

It was Friday night. Bound to be busy for Leo and

Donna, thought Amanda. They were doing lots of fifty-percent deals on hair for the Christmas Eve Ball, now to be held at the Snout and Trough.

Amanda had to make sure that they were both in the salon. She needed a pretext. There must be someone in the village she hadn't sent a Christmas card to. How about someone in the salon, having their hair done at this moment?

She headed for the corner shop and struck gold: the postlady.

'Oh Joan, I'm sure I've forgotten to put someone on my Christmas card list. I keep thinking if I wander around I'll see them and remember. You don't happen to know who's in the hairdresser's at the moment, do you?' Amanda asked, with an air of helplessness.

'Yes, love, Irma's in there, Pam ... and oh yes, Maddy Hinch is in there too.'

'Oh, Maddy Hinch, of course,' replied Amanda, feigning relief. 'I did a restoration job for her.'

'Wasn't that about five years ago?' remarked Joan dampeningly.

'Good marketting policy; to remind customers that you still exist, Joan,' Amanda replied merrily.

'Of course. See you at the party, dear. Happy Christmas!'

Amanda walked home at a reasonable pace, pulled out her Christmas card box, and hastily penned best wishes to Maddy. She returned to the High Street and walked into the fragrant, hot and crowded salon. Leo and Donna looked up in surprise.

'Hiya,' called Leo.

'Sorry to interrupt,' said Amanda, 'Just wanted to give you this,' she said leaning across and offering the card to a bemused Maddy. 'I've been a bit remiss, but I'm on the ball this year. Happy Christmas, Mrs Hinch!'

'Oh well ... that's very nice of you, Amanda. Well!

Very sweet. Actually, I do have … but I'll call you in the new year. See you at the party.'

Once they were on their way home, in the deserted Orchard Row, 'Right,' said Amanda to her walking grey cloud of a companion. 'Leo and Donna's whereabouts confirmed. Time for a bath.'

Tempest was more than Amanda's companion, or, from his point of view, she was more than just his witch. They had a unique bond that, in certain conditions, allowed her to see through his eyes. The conditions were a meditative state on Amanda's part, and the enjoyment of an, occasionally extortionate, bribe on his.

Tempest's delicacy of choice was caviar. If Amanda were lucky, he'd accept the lumpfish recipe. If she wasn't, it meant handing over the contents of a costly sturgeon variety. Amanda considered that if her career as body-finder general were going to continue, this would have to be factored into the budget.

Presently, Amanda was relaxing in hot water under a quilt of lavender-scented bubbles, and Tempest, waving aside his treat for the present, set out on his reconnaissance mission.

The trouble with winter was that people had an irksome tendency to close their doors and windows. Tempest preferred to stick to normal methods of entry. Magic left a trail, and leaving a trail was careless, and Tempest, being perfect, at least in his own estimation, was never careless. He toured the perimeter of the premises. In the end, he decided there was only one way in. If it was good enough for Old Father Christmas, it was just about good enough for him.

Amanda, looking at the view through her cat's eyes, was alarmed at the sheer dark drop down the chimney. But Tempest was an able climber on any axis. He came to earth in the fireplace, stepped to one side and cleaned himself of any trace of soot, while Amanda tried not to be overcome by a fever of anxiety. Tempest was right, of course, she told herself.

The Weathersbys would be down in the salon for some time to come.

This was a two bedroom flat; with two occupants, there was no space for a study, but there was a table in the living room with a small drawer, and a 1960s-style sideboard on legs with cupboards. Tempest, with the dexterous application of a claw here, an incisor there, soon had them open and explored.

Nothing.

Then again, precious papers were more likely to be in a bedroom. A careful and systematic search of drawers, wardrobes and bedside cabinets revealed … nothing. Hm.

'What if,' thought Amanda to Tempest, 'they were taped underneath something?'

He returned to the living room, glanced around, then slipped under the sideboard and looked up. Bingo. Taped in place, was an A4 sized envelope. Deftly, Tempest got his claws under the Sellotape, and soon the manila packet was on the open floor. It was not sealed but also taped. He was no ordinary cat, and as adept with his teeth, tongue, claws and paws as any human with their hands. He got a paw inside the envelope and pulled the papers out.

Together, witch and familiar read headings, addresses, and lists of purposeful faults. There were houses, offices, churches, even schools. It was on the fourth page that they came to Sunken Madley Church Hall …. Joists undersized, woodworm … beams … rafters … purlin incorrectly positioned, missing roof tiles … persistent leak ... rot .... Suddenly, there was a sound of a key in the door. Tempest swiped the papers and himself under the sideboard.

Feet trod up the stairs, the door opened, the light switched on. Trousered legs with turnups came into view. Must be Donna, thought Amanda. There was the sound of a drawer opening above. She saw legs going to the table, and heard a pen scribbling.

'"Deck the halls with boughs of holly, tra la la la",' sang Donna softly, as she wrote what Tempest next saw in her hand as she crossed the room to the door: a Christmas card, probably for a client. The light went out, the shoes descended the stairs, and the street door shut.

'Tempest, put them back and get out of there,' said Amanda nervously. 'We've seen what we need.' He replaced them and pushed the tape into place. Laying on his back, the feline sleuth pressed the envelope onto the sideboard underside with his paws.

Tempest walked over to the chimney and looked at it with distaste.

'You owe me,' he thought to Amanda. 'Spectacularly.'

Amanda knew this would cost her. Having risen from the bath waters, dried, dressed and descended to the kitchen in time for his return, she got out the £17 pot of caviar without regret and served it to him at the table. 'Thank you, darling, wonderful, Tempest, whatever would oor Ammy do wivout oo?'

True, he reflected, taking the first taste of his just reward. So true.

* * * * *

On Saturday morning, Amanda was summoned to The Grange.

'I've found out that, yes,' she told the ladies, 'the Recket papers are in the Weatherby's flat, which means one or both of them had the means to dispatch one of the Woodberry's. But motive?'

'We can't supply one,' replied Gwendolen, 'but we do have a link between the Weathersby children and Vic. Bella

Bogia's first marriage was to a Victor Woodberry, but soon after they divorced. Then she remarried. Her new husband's name was Weathersby. Donna has no father named on the birth certificate, and Leonardo's father is recorded as Weathersby.'

'Well! So Bella Bogia's marriage to Vic was the marriage Majolica broke up! It was for her that he left Bella, Donna and Leo. But Leo, at the classes, didn't seem to recognise either Vic or Majolica.'

'I expect he was too young at the time. And I expect he never met the woman. And Vic wasn't his father, why would he hold a grudge against either of them?'

'Of course. I suppose *Bella* might have a grudge against Majolica. Only she was on the other side of the world. That's pretty much the ultimate alibi. And Donna wasn't free to come to any of the classes until Vanessa was teaching, so she would never have seen them. Oh, poor Leo and Donna,' said Amanda compassionately, 'they do seem to have had a rocky road. No wonder they're so close. I wonder, though, if their mother could have been using them to punish Vic or Majolica?'

'We found her Facebook page,' answered Miss Armstrong-Witworth, 'and based on that, I don't think she is at all that sort of person. She seems to be very positive and kind and lives in the present. She's engaged, you know.'

'Why complicate her life with a crime after all these years?' Miss de Havillande chipped in.

'Well, what about the children themselves?' asked Amanda. 'Though I can't see that they would hold a grudge against a man who was once married to their mother. And even if we can establish a motive, they still didn't have the means: no keys to the hall or the cellar.'

'There's probably more to the story. Somehow, we have to talk to Bella Bogia,' said Miss Armstrong-Witworth intently. 'I think I may have to pull in a favour from the old days …'

Chapter 46

✃

CHRISTMAS EVE BEGINS

Amanda had got an Edwardian dress off Amazon. She knew she might well end up in a dirty, dusty cellar and had no intention of blowing a small fortune on it. It was a short-sleeved, calf length, V-neck, black lace affair, over a sleeveless orange underdress that fell to just above the ankles. She consoled herself with the knowledge that she had something far better for the New Year's Eve Ball, thanks to Claire's contacts in her film company's wardrobe department.

Amanda got some volume into her hair then piled it into a loose bun. Next, and most vitally, she pulled on a pair of Falke cream holdups. It was a sacrifice. They were expensive and would probably get snagged to death in the hall basement, but she needed the efficient elastic and deep lace band to house the one thing that she never left home without and that could not be concealed in her dress: her Pocket-wand.

She added some orange earrings; not expensive, in case they got lost down there. Finally, she threw on a long jacket and orange pashmina, and headed out into the night, Tempest keeping close. The wind was rising, and she hastily put her scarf around her hair to protect it and got into the car as fast as possible.

By 8 o'clock, the Snout and Trough was already filling up with merrymakers. Amanda made her way upstairs, already a little overwhelmed by the press of humans. But there was Dr Patel, taking her hand.

'You look lovely, Amanda. Well done. Vanessa is going to give a little lesson for half an hour before the ball gets going. I've saved you a seat. Come.' She took Amanda's hand and, knowing her young friend and patient was not at her best in crowds, steered her across the floor to a quiet spot near a table, with a carafe of water and glasses on it.

'Hiya, Amanda,' said 15-year old Becky Whittle, whose physical attributes gave the misleading impression that she was considerably older, and was seated on the other side of table.

'Hello, Becky,' replied Amanda, in a friendly if surprised tone. This wasn't the sort of event at which she'd expect to find Miss Whittle. 'Going to try out some dancing?'

'Yeah, why not? Might be some hot guys. Thought I'd check it out. I can always go downstairs when I get bored.'

Amanda was pouring herself a glass of water when Becky abruptly stood up.

'Oh … my….,' she uttered. 'Eye-candy fest, or *what*?'

Amanda followed her gaze. Ashlyn Seedwell, captain of the Sunken Madley cricket team was in conversation with Chris Reid their spin bowler and Trelawney. All fit, all unquestionably good looking in evening dress; they certainly made a trio at which the ladies in the room were struggling not to stare.

'All ancient, of course,' commented Becky, 'but, not bad, I mean *reeeeally* not bad.'

'Yes, Ashlyn must be, oh what? 28?' asked Amanda.

'Yeah, don't get me wrong. I prefer older men. See Jay

Kemp over there? He's *nineteen*.'

'Ah, he meets with your approval, does he, Becky?' asked Amanda, amused.

'Sooo meets,' replied her youthful companion.

'Why don't you go and ask him to dance the next two-step while he's still young enough to make it around the dancefloor?' she suggested. 'Here, the music's changing. You can both do this one.'

'I guess,' said Becky, standing up and rearranging her décolletage in a practiced manner. 'Oo! Comin' this way! Yum-mee. I mean, not my style, but … yeahhhh, like … for an old guy,' remarked Becky, nodding encouragingly at Amanda, whom she regarded in the light of a maiden aunt, then making a bee-line for her quarry.

Amanda saw the 'yum-mee' 'old guy' who was approaching her. She could see that Becky, for once, had a point.

'Good evening, Miss Cadabra,' Trelawney said, shaking her hand. 'You look charming.'

'Thank you,' answered Amanda, 'You look very … nice … I mean, appropriate.'

'I'm glad you approve. I was just chatting with Ashlyn and Chris about the Feast. Just casually, but especially about when the crowd arrived at the orchard. I asked them whom they remember seeing. Neither of them mentioned Ryan.'

'That is a bit odd,' Amanda remarked. 'He seems to have been pretty pally with them both since his first cricket match here in the summer. You'd expect him to hang out with them. I'm not sure he's made that many close friends, on account of being away so much, perhaps. And he and Ashlyn and Chris do, at least, have the sport in common.'

'Speaking of which,' said Trelawney modestly, 'they've asked me if I'd consider being a reserve for the Sunken Madley XI.'

'What!' exclaimed Amanda, almost knocking over her glass. 'But … but …. you're not Village!'

'That's what I said,' he replied diffidently, 'but erm, they seem to regard me as part of the furniture, and, seeing as I can catch a ball and can still, at need, chase down the average delinquent Parhayle teenager, they seem to think I could, in an emergency, be a useful player at the crease and in the field.'

'Well! Behold me all astonishment. Wait till I tell Uncle Mike. He'll probably present you with The Golden Mata Hari, or whatever they award infiltrators.'

Trelawney chuckled, but said, 'Seriously, though. It could be useful. It would certainly get me closer to Ryan Ford.'

'I don't know how you do it, Inspector, but I take my hat off to you,' remarked Amanda admiringly.

'Thank you. I try. Your friend was not able to make it back from Thailand?'

'No, Claire called to tell me they've gone over-schedule. The cast and crew are gutted but the cost of bringing everyone back here and then out there again isn't to be thought of. She won't be back until the new year, alas. But Claire is very upbeat, you know. She said she's just thinking of the money!'

'Good for her. No Ryan here tonight, I see.'

'No, the glitterati are required elsewhere. But I know that Jessica James, our very own homegrown supermodel, don't you know, would much rather be here. But duty calls.'

'Jessica James? The Ice Queen?'

'That's right. There's her mother Irene, a talented jewellery designer and crafter standing with Irma Uberhausfest, fêted party-planner extraordinaire for the over-70s, many of whom she regards as wild young things, by the way, and Gordon French the retired headmaster of the Sunken Madley School.'

'And the CEO of the Asthma Centre?' enquired the inspector.

'Up the road, in Lost Madley, you mean? Damian Gibbs?'

'Yes, and his troublesome daughter.'

'Samantha would rather a die a thousand unfashionable deaths than be present at a homely little do like this, and they don't live in the village,' responded Amanda. 'But I'll bet wherever she is, her father will be too. I understand, from Bill — he's over with The Grange ladies if you want to say hello — that Damian's now keeping a much closer eye on her since … well, you know.'

'Indeed, I do. It is still alarmingly fresh in my memory,' he answered.

Vanessa was saying something into the microphone.

'Shall we take our places? I think the class is starting,' suggested Trelawney.

Amanda nodded and accompanied him onto the dance-floor. Throughout the lesson, she was distracted by two things: partly, the inspector's unexpectedly appealing appearance — which she'd considered rather ordinary, if she'd considered it at all — but mostly by the approaching 10 o'clock appointment, on which so much depended.

Trelawney appeared unconcerned, but then he was good at that, she thought. He danced with her a great deal.

'Why are you partnering me so much?' Amanda asked curiously.

'Do you object? You can say no, you know,' he replied amiably.

'No, no, I like it. I mean, you're a very good lead, but…'

'I thought that if we were seen dancing together so much, it would not be thought odd if we should be seen slipping away,' Trelawney explained.

'Surely we don't want people thinking …,' she began to object.

'Take a bit of gossip on behalf of the cause, Miss

Cadabra,' he said bracingly.

'I suppose so,' Amanda agreed reluctantly.

As 9.45, she told him, 'It's time.'

'Yes,' Trelawney replied. 'I'll get your coat and meet you by the entrance. Make out that you need some air.'

Amanda gave him a few minutes, then flapped one hand in front of her face fanlike and put the other to her chest. She made her way to the door of the function room.

'Are you OK, Amanda?' asked Donna solicitously. 'You look a bit overcome. It is a little crowded, isn't it?'

'Yes, just need some fresh air,' Amanda answered with a smile.

'Hair looks great,' Donna remarked kindly. 'Did you do it yourself?'

'Yes.'

'Nice job!'

Chapter 47

❧

1918

Amanda descended to the ground floor of the Snout and Trough, and, sure enough, Trelawney was by the door. He helped her on with her coat.

'How did you know which one was mine?' Amanda asked.

'It was the only orange one,' he replied.

They moved out into the street. The wind was now so strong that it was a struggle to walk the few paces to the car. Once inside the vehicle, Amanda asked,

'Has your friend Ross said anything to you about the builders? The Recket family notes on the builds they scuppered?

'Yes, and the connection with the Bogias, and the link to Leo and Donna. If those two are in possession of the papers, it would give them the means, if they were able to gain entry to the building, to effect the sabotage that resulted in the death of Mrs Woodberry.'

'Wow.'

'Yes, Miss Cadabra, the police are not as slow as Conan

Doyle's Sherlock would have had people think.'

'No … right …. ,' Amanda agreed. And here comes the delicate bit, was what she was thinking. 'Well, what if I said that I have reason to believe … that the papers are in the Weathersbys' flat?'

'Then I would be careful not to ask you what that reason might be,' said Trelawney, choosing his words. 'Are you sure the papers are there?'

'I am sure that they were there last night,' she replied.

He nodded and got out his phone. 'We'll call it a hunch, shall we?' Trelawney said, tapping out a text.

Amanda drove towards the church.

'There's no one on guard there,' she remarked, taken aback.

'I know. I cleared it with Maxwell. He said they'd got everything from the crime scene they that they could. The tape is really just for security. Don't want anyone going in and falling down.'

'How will we get in?'

'Ross has the front door key for me.'

'Does he know about this expedition?'

'No, but Maxwell told him to give it to me,' Trelawney answered.

'Where is it?' asked Amanda.

'Under the mat, so to speak.'

They left the car in the church car park and got out with an effort. Trelawney was looking around at the gravestones.

'Ah,' he suddenly called out. 'Over here.' He slid his fingers down behind the headstone of one Truvella Clay and drew out a key.

They strained against the wind as they started up the path to the hall. There seemed to be a mist before them, and what was far looked close, and what was close looked far.

'A time boundary,' murmured Amanda. And on this occasion, there was no spell needed in order to cross it.

The trees in the churchyard were bending, the empty twigs scraping and rustling, and yet …

'Do you hear that?' Trelawney asked her.

Music was coming from the hall. And voices. Singing. 'Roses are shining in Picardy …'

'Yes,' answered Amanda. They entered, and found the hall awhirl with dancers, laughter, people nibbling, sipping, chatting, gentlemen elegant in evening dress and ladies in ankle length dresses of softly draping chiffon and silk. Before they had gone more than a few steps, Amanda was approached and relieved of her scarf by an attendant. 'I'll keep my jacket, thank you,' she said. They moved to the side of the hall, out of the way of the waltzers, to get their bearings.

'What's that?' asked Amanda, looking up at the tall window above and behind them. Tiny balls of ice were hitting the panes. 'Hailstones?'

'Looks like it,' Trelawney concurred.

The song ended, and the dancers clapped. Then, in the brief lull before the next song, they heard a creak from above. The roof seems to be slightly swaying. Or was it just the perspective effect of a time border, wondered Amanda.

'It's 10 o'clock,' Trelawney said.

Amanda peered around the dancers until she saw Dunkley by a table halfway down the hall where drinks were set out. 'This way.' She approached the man confidently. 'Captain Dunkley.'

He turned. 'Ah, Miss er … '

'This is Detective Inspector Trelawney.'

'Ah, good show. Come this way, sir,' said Dunkley.

He led Trelawney, with Amanda following, across the floor towards the stage end, until they reached a doorway to a room apart, where supper was laid out. Dunkley appeared to have found the only quiet spot in the building. He glanced back at Amanda, and she heard him ask,

'Is she your, er …?'

'My secretary and chauffeur, yes,' Trelawney answered him smoothly.

'Oh quite, quite,' responded Dunkley, somewhat abashed.

'In fact, as an employee of the Metropolitan police force, there is no reason why she should not be present for this exchange between us. I do assure you, that her experience makes her more than equal to tolerating the unpleasant details of such situations as, I understand, you are about to describe.'

Dunkley clucked like a chicken, but in the face of Trelawney's air of ease and assurance, responded 'Well, I suppose, Inspector …'

'Miss Cadabra is very discreet and will not intrude, I promise you.'

'Hm, well, as you wish,' Dunkley conceded.

'Miss Cadabra,' Trelawney called to her.

'Sir?' she answered, in keeping with her assigned role.

'The captain has kindly agreed to allow you to be in attendance.'

'Would you like me to take notes?' she offered, hoping her fictitious boss would say no, as she had no means to write. The captain looked uncomfortable.

'No, I think we can rely upon your excellent memory. Thank you, Miss Cadabra.'

Amanda took a step back, standing slightly apart, at what she hoped looked to Dunkley like a respectful distance.

'So,' began Trelawney to the captain, 'when, in your opinion, for I should imagine during your war experiences you must have developed something of a sixth sense for this sort of thing, would you say that things started to look …?'

'Smoky?' supplied Amanda, using Dunkley's own word.

'Yes, thank you, Miss Cadabra,' said Trelawney. He

turned back to Dunkley. 'Smoky? Fishy?'

'Hrrmmm. I would say, the day those chaps appeared with the, er, odd sort of lady. She was in trousers and a jumper and, well, what looked for all the world like a clerical collar.'

'Ah, the deaconess,' Trelawney responded calmly.

'Really?' queried Dunkley, doubtfully. 'In a dog collar and … trousers?'

'The collar just has that appearance, and, I daresay, the lady was in work clothes.'

'Oh very well, if you say so, old chap.'

Amanda was impressed at the way in which Trelawney was swiftly winning the man's trust.

'Anyway,' Dunkley went on, 'she brings in these two chaps, rather shabby-looking, I'd say, not shirt and tie or workcoat; in faded blue trousers. I remember that. You can tell a man by his clothes, don't you know.'

The immaculately dressed Trelawney inclined his head in agreement, and Dunkley continued:

'The lady took them downstairs, and I followed them. Bit reluctant because, for some reason, I keep getting stuck down there. Anyway, thought I should keep an eye on things. Because, you know … lady… even if she was got up like some sort of Vesta Tilley.'

'Commendable, Captain,' commented the inspector.

Amanda's attention was again caught by the weather. Were the hailstones getting bigger or was it just that she could hear them more clearly here?

'Well,' explained Dunkley, 'once down there, she shows them one of the beams and some floorboards above it. And I must tell you, Inspector, these floorboards are dashed odd. One minute they're there, and the next they're not. Frankly, I think, it's something to do with those two chaps.'

'Quite possibly,' agreed Trelawney.

'At any rate, the two chaps assure her that they will take

care of it and they leave. Only to return shortly with some short lengths of timber and some brackets. They assemble them into poles and shove them into place. Jammed between cellar floor and the underside of the boards above. Next thing I know, the Tilley-looking lady —'

'Miss Jane,' interpolated Trelawney gravely.

'Er, yes, Miss Jane and your secretary are down there looking at the poles and your secretary —'

'Miss Cadabra.'

'Miss Cadabra — says they're safe. Then Miss Jane brings down another chap that I thought was rather more the thing, and he confirms.'

'So far so good,' commented the inspector.

'Ah, but then,' Dunkley went on, more animatedly, 'another lady, again in trousers, comes along to the hall and sets up the ladder up to the hatch in the attic. Then she goes up carrying a rope with a grappling hook attached slung around her for all the world like a mountaineer. I hear a rattle and then back down the ladder she comes.'

'Can you describe her?'

'Short, with darkish hair tied back.'

'Slim?'

'Yes. And dark eyes, red lips,' added Dunkley.

'You remember her well?' asked Trelawney.

'Yes, because I saw her again.'

'Where?'

'Down below by the poles!'

'What was she doing?'

'Something with pliers, and, before I knew it, the poles were on the floor in pieces. Then up she climbs on the anvils with a white sort of can and starts painting the underside of the boards. Very odd. I thought, perhaps she was trying to put some sort of varnish or something to kill woodworm or such like. She kept prodding the wood with a screwdriver and then painting some more, and, finally down she comes. Then she goes over to the javelins; props, you know. Takes one out and sticks it in the middle of the anvils. Odd, I thought.'

'Indeed.'

'Looked smoky. Dashed smoky. Little did I know,' Dunkley added portentously. 'Next thing I remember is, I hear your secretary, then another woman's voice, then footsteps up above and, next thing I know, I see this other woman coming down through the floor and then it's all a bit of a muddle, you see, because I'm here at this party and I'm falling through the floor at the same time. And we both seem to end up on the anvils with some bally javelin sticking out of us, but somehow we're all right! Except she sort of comes and goes, though I haven't seen her lately. It's all a bit much for a chap really,' he concluded, rubbing his forehead.

Amanda's attention was drawn upward again. There was a ceiling above this room, but she could swear she could hear the roof timbers creaking.

'I see,' Trelawney was saying. 'Would you mind showing me this, in the cellar?'

'Of course,' agreed Dunkley. 'Just get myself another drink. Would you like one, Inspector?'

'No, thank you, Captain.'

'Meet you down there,' said Dunkley, with a wave of the hand. 'Doors are all open.'

Trelawney nodded, and Amanda led the way to the cellar entrance.

Chapter 48

❧

ACID RAIN

'Thank you for getting me in on the act,' Amanda said, as they reached the door to the basement.

'Least I could do. And I see what you mean about him,' responded Trelawney.

'Yes, and thank you for giving me a professional role. I could see where his mind was going!'

'I just hope you don't mind that it had to be a subordinate one to fit these less enlightened times,' he apologised.

'It's fine.'

Trelawney followed Amanda through the cellar entrance, down the stairs and through the door at the foot of the flight. As they crossed the unfamiliarly neat, prop shop of a basement, they heard a cry and the crunch of splintering wood. They ran forward, seeing Dunkley flailing through the rotten boards above and impacting with the anvils. As they reached him, preparing for the gory sight, his ethereal form sat up, very much in one piece.

'See?' he said indignantly. 'That happens all the time!'

The music had stopped, and the dancing feet stilled, but Dunkley lingered. In the silence, they heard the click of a door behind them. The cellar door at the foot of the stairs had shut. Amanda hurried to it.

'Locked,' she said, looking back at Trelawney. Dunkley was standing on the anvils looking up through the hole. They heard a key turn in the door at the top of the stairs and footsteps sounding above.

There was now no mistaking it, the wind was louder than ever, and as it changed direction, was hurling the hailstones alternately against the walls and the fragile roof.

'Well, as I live and breathe,' Dunkley declared inaccurately, 'that's *her*, that's her …' His words faded with his form.

Amanda and Trelawney heard the front door close, then presently open again followed by thumping, as though the woman was putting down something heavy. She must have made trip after trip.

They tried, during her short absences, to climb up out of the basement, but the wood was too friable and would not support even Amanda's lesser weight. Finally, they heard the main door open, shut, and lock.

Then a female voice sounded matter-of-factly. 'I know you're down there. This is your scarf.'

'Donna?'

'Yes, Amanda. Amanda the snoop. You've got your tame copper down there with you, haven't you? Two birds with one stone,' she said in a sing-song voice. 'Talk to me, Amanda. You like to talk, don't you? Talking to Leo, talking to Ryan, talking to dad. What did he tell you, Amaaanda?'

'Your dad?'

'Don't act stupid,' said Donna scornfully. 'I know you're not. Now let's test this, shall we? I've only tried it with a paintbrush so far. Let's try a little splash, shall we?'

Amanda and Trelawney heard the sound of liquid hitting the wood above and saw it fizzle away a small hole. They backed off from it.

'That works nicely. Time for a bigger test.' Splash, sizzle. They could see Donna looking down through the gap. 'Hiya, you two,' she called happily. 'The trick is … not to splash it on the joists, or where will I walk?' She laughed.

'That would make sense,' agreed Amanda, matching her hearty tone.

'Now,' uttered Donna, suddenly stern. 'Talk, Amanda. Dad.'

'Vic is your dad?'

'See? I knew you were smart.'

'I thought Douglas Weathersby is your father,' said Amanda.

'How could a vile maggot like him be my father?' Donna snarled. 'My father was Victor Woodberry. I should have been Donna Woodberry. I never liked the name Weathersby. I wasn't his! Not like my poor brother.' She suddenly sounded tender. 'He couldn't help it. I don't blame him.'

'Then why try to kill your dad?'

'He left me,' Donna said in a low, intense, distracted voice. 'He left me like my husband left me. Like my mother left me. Like they *all* leave me. He had to be punished. It took time to find him, yes, but I tracked him down and then,' and her tone lightened, 'I found out he was a dance teacher.'

'It was you? You who recommended him and Majolica to the rector to teach our villagers?'

'Well done, Man-dee,' Donna sang.

'Thanks,' replied Amanda, conversationally. 'How about rewarding me by not throwing any more of that liquid down here?'

'l'll think about it,' Donna replied chattily. 'Say something interesting.'

Amanda rapidly searched her mind. 'You have the notes. The Recket papers.'

'I knew you knew,' Donna said with satisfaction. 'I heard something in the flat. I checked under the sideboard, and I knew they'd been pulled off and opened. Then I watched you tonight. Saw you leave, followed you here. Because this is where it ends, you see …. You won't be leaving ….. *No* one is leaving … *ever* … again.'

'Well, that's not entirely accurate,' countered Amanda pedantically. 'Just maybe not leaving so alive.'

This time the acid was flung over a wider area. It caught Trelawney's sleeve and Amanda's collar. They hastily removed their jackets.

'Is there any other way out of here?' he asked Amanda, in an urgent whisper.

'No, not that I know of. Phone?' she suggested.

'Can't get a signal. You?'

Amanda shook her head.

The splashes and holes were becoming more random. Amanda and Trelawney were dodging and moving around the basement, trying to keep under the remaining floorboards, out of Donna's sightline, listening carefully for her footsteps, trying to anticipate where the next lethal onslaught of fluid would fall next.

Suddenly Donna said, 'You know what? This is taking too long. I'm getting bored.'

'Why don't you let us out? There are more interesting things to do outside this building,' suggested Amanda helpfully.

'No, it's OK. I'm going to try something fun. I've got all this lovely crystal up here and these nice big plates. And you've got all that dust down there, haven't you?' she said in a teasing voice. They backed up so they could see her through a gap, going to the wall by the door where Amanda had stacked the crates. Donna unpacked a platter, then walked to the floorboard gap nearest them.

'Try this!' she called with a smile, and hurled the plate down onto the cloth-covered pile beside them. The dust flew up and sent Amanda coughing.

'Result!' Donna sang.

'She's off her chump,' wheezed Amanda.

'Donna!' called Trelawney. 'Why not phone your brother? He must be angry too, deep down. Why don't you let him help you?'

She paused. 'Hmmm.'

'He's been loyal to you, Donna, … hasn't he?' said Amanda, between coughs. 'He's a good brother, isn't he?'

'Yes, but he likes you. *That's* disloyal,' pronounced Donna, picking up another can and destroying another piece of floor. 'I like this game; it's like Whac-a-Mole.' She giggled.

Amanda made a spiral motion with her finger next to her head, mouthing the words, 'Lost the plot.' She turned her face up again.

'Why don't you go after Vic, Donna? It was him you wanted to kill, wasn't it?'

'Yeah, I know. I had to wait before I had another go. After all, it should have been a … floorless plan!' She laughed merrily. 'Get it?'

'Hilarious.'

'But, you know what? Killing *her* will do. It was *her* fault. And now she's left him like he left our mum. Now he's all alone; that's his punishment,' she adjudicated with satisfaction.

'But he isn't sad, Donna,' said Amanda.

'Yes, he is!'

'I talked to him, and he said he isn't.'

'You're lying.' Donna threw down a glass. It shattered and threw up more dust. She hurled down another and another. Amanda's airways were swelling. Trelawney took off his tie, waistcoat and shirt.

'What are you doing?' whispered Amanda.

'Here,' he replied, and tied the shirt over her nose and mouth. Acid suddenly sloshed through the gap over where they were standing. Trelawney quickly got them both out of the way of the deadly waterfall.

There were plenty of gaps now in the floor above them, through which to look up and see the roof. A blast of hailstone suddenly seemed to hit one particular spot. As if in slow motion, a beam detached itself, frayed and splintered and descended towards the floor. Trelawney pulled Amanda away and shielded her with his body, as it smashed through the joists above them and down into their bear trap. The dust mushroomed.

The hail, now turning to rain, was pouring in.

'See what you've done,' said Donna, wearily.

'Me?' called back Amanda, between short breaths. 'Those beams must be rotten. If anyone's to blame, it's your grandfather and his friend.'

'Oh, been doing some reading, haven't we?'

'This whole place is going to come down, Donna. At least, get yourself out. You can leave us in here.'

'And let you get out like mice? Besides, *I* don't leave people.'

'You can leave *us*,' said Amanda encouragingly. A brief coughing fit followed. 'Really, we won't mind a bit.' She turned to Trelawney remarking quietly, 'Serious abandonment issues, here, wouldn't you say?'

'Yes, but I'm not sure if this is the moment for a discussion about it!' he replied, putting his waistcoat back on.

'Let me think about it,' said Donna. She sloshed more acid toward them. This time Amanda felt a splash on her hand.

Trelawney hastily tore off his waistcoat again, and wiped the liquid off her skin, but she didn't feel it burn.

Amanda looked up. 'It's OK,' she whispered. 'It's rain!

The rain's coming through.'

'We have to get out,' said Trelawney, 'The floor will be gone soon! We can't dodge the acid forever and we're running out of places where we can safely tread.'

'Donna!' It was a voice from outside. 'Donna! Donna, it's Leo!'

'Go away! I'm busy,' she replied in a scolding tone.

'What are you doing in there? Let me in!'

'No.'

'Leo, she's got acid,' Amanda called back to him. 'She's throwing it around!'

'Donna, open the door. Let's talk,' Leo entreated.

'No more talk,' stated his sister.

'Then listen. I've been Skyping with Mum.'

The splashing paused.

'You've got it all wrong, Donna. About Vic. He wasn't your dad. He didn't leave you; he left *me*. He was *my* father.'

'You're lying,' she shouted back.

'Let me bring in the phone; you can talk to Mum. I've got her, right here. She can tell you. Doug was your father.'

'No! She lied,' stated Donna.

'Trust issues too,' Amanda murmured.

'Let her tell you,' Leo pleaded.

'Go away. I'm busy. Go back to the salon. You've got appointments.'

'I think she's completely batty,' Amanda whispered to Trelawney.

The inspector crept to the door of the cellar and tried it again, put his own keys to the lock, put his shoulder to the panel, and, finally, looked around for something, anything to smash it open. Donna, hearing his manoeuvres, tossed some more lethal liquid his way, chasing him back towards the main entrance end of the cellar and Amanda's side. He looked up toward the front doors and shouted, 'Leo! Call the police!'

'Now *that's* not nice,' said Donna between gritted teeth. There was just one spot near the door to the stairs that was covered now, but open joists between them and it. Donna was walking along a spit of remaining floorboard, struggling under the weight of a full can of acid.

Amanda now knew she would have to use a spell to get the doors open. But they would have to get to them first. She took her IKEA pencil from her pocket and pulled out the tiny wand.

More roof timbers were falling. Donna shook off the fragments that were landing on her and gathered the can ready to swing it. 'Bath time!' she sang out.

Amanda had no choice. There was, in fact, no normal way out of this. Only magic would save them. Magic against the human running amok above them. And yet, one more spell and the Flamgoynes would know, know that the epicentre of the power they were tracking was Sunken Madley. Amanda was ready to die for her village, but Trelawney… she could not sacrifice him. He was not part of this … She just had to buy them a few seconds to get to the door …. If only there was some other way … But she knew of none. Her time and her options had run out.

Amanda flicked the wand up and spoke the word: '*Understeppith.*'

At once, Donna's legs seemed to wobble under her, sending her off-balance. As she struggled to regain it, Tempest, lurking unseen by the wall, took a flying leap from behind, onto her head, his weight dragging her back and down toward the floor. He leapt away as she fell, spilling the can of noxious liquid over herself and the support below her. Her scream was cut off as a beam plummeted down from above, and silenced her.

Amanda felt the tell-tall magical blast sweep outwards. 'Come on!' she shouted over the wind and rain and falling timbers.

She grabbed Trelawney's arm, and, running for the door, called out, '*Agertyn!*' It flew open. The roof was collapsing, as she, wheezing, tugged him up the stairs. '*Agertyn!*' Amanda shouted at the next door. They rammed their way out into the tiny gap before the hall side door, wood, plaster and masonry cascading like rain. '*Agertyn,*'she choked out to the final side door as the building collapsed. Amanda buckled, coughing, starved of oxygen and Trelawney pulling her free, tumbling, stumbling, falling amongst the gravestones. Amidst the crashing and thundering, the sound of sirens was heard. Two police cars and an ambulance flew into view. Leo was on his knees before the wreck, calling his sister's name, in vain.

Trelawney supported Amanda as she lay on the grass, and removed his shirt from her face. The paramedics ran up bearing a stretcher, got a mask on her, and lifted her up and away to the ambulance. Baker hurried to the inspector's side. He looked at Trelawney's shoulder where acid was burning away his t-shirt.

'Go with Miss Cadabra,' said Baker. 'There's nothing you can do here. Go on, sir!'

Trelawney ran and jumped into the ambulance just before the door was shut and it whisked through Sunken Madley High Street. 'Better take that off, sir,' said one of the paramedics, seeing the cloth's capillary action spreading the acid.

The last thing Amanda saw was Trelawney's final layer of clothing being removed, before she passed into oblivion.

Chapter 49

༄

BACK FROM THE DEEP

The sea was warm and soothingly dark. Amanda let herself drift down. The further down she floated, the warmer and darker it was. So nice, so gentle, so cradling.

'Amanda.'

The voice was faint.

'Amanda.'

Who was that? Oh ….

Amanda was five years old. Doctor Tahami was calling her. It must be the doctor calling her now. Oh dear, it was so comfortable down here, so restful, and yet, she had promised. If only she hadn't promised, but a promise was a promise.

'Miss Cadabra.'

What had she promised?

'Amanda. Please.'

Oh yes; to swim.

'Amanda, come back.'

The voice was pleading.

Swim where?

'Please, Amanda, come back.'

Oh yes. Up.

'Amanda!'

Up as fast as she could. And with all her might. She began to swim. It was so hard. She was so tired. But she had promised.

'Oh please. Please… Amanda…'

It didn't sound like the doctor … but she had promised. Up. Swim. Up.

Suddenly she broke the surface.

Amanda opened her eyes. There was the inspector. He looked so intense, so … tender? And he was holding her hand … He was looking at her eyes, and suddenly his face was relaxed and professional. He seemed to let out a sigh. He spoke calmly:

'Miss Cadabra. Well done.' He patted her hand in a perfunctory manner and released it. 'I'll just let the nurse know that you're awake.' He left the bedside.

'Well, hello,' said a cheerful voice. A friendly face framed in black curls came into view. 'Glad you decided to rejoin us. I'll tell the doctor.'

Trelawney took the nurse's place.

'Where have I been?' Amanda asked him.

'You passed out.'

'The hall … oh!' she breathed, remembering. 'Donna!'

'She didn't make it,' Trelawney answered levelly.

'Leo?'

'He's fine.'

'You called me … I thought it was the doctor.'

'Yes,' said Trelawney matter-of-factly, 'the staff seemed to think it might help you to regain consciousness, if a familiar voice encouraged you to do so.'

But, thought Amanda, he had sounded … quite unlike the inspector ... but then she had been delirious; no doubt his voice had been distorted.

'Well, thank you,' she said.

'How do you feel?'

'Sleepy.'

The nurse returned, checked Amanda's vital signs and conferred with the medic who had just turned up.

The doctor came to the bed.

'Hello, Miss Cadabra. I see you've been a guest here several times in the past. Not for quite a while though, I'm glad to say, at the risk of sounding inhospitable.' He chuckled. 'Sorry. Medical humour.'

Amanda managed a wan smile.

'That's the way,' he continued. 'You're going to be fine. I'm sure you know the ropes. A few days rest. We've called your listed next of kin, who will be here in about an hour. In the meantime, just get some rest.' Nurse and doctor departed.

'Well, thank you, Inspector, for getting me out of the hall.'

'No, Miss Cadabra,' he said seriously. 'Thank *you*. You saved us both. You saved my life.'

Amanda closed her eyes. The spell. She had done the one thing she had been warned not to do on any account. She had cast against a human.

Never mind. She was alive. The inspector was alive. She would face the music when the time came.

And there was the other matter: he had seen her do it, seen her wand, seen her use it, heard her use the spellwords.

Amanda opened her eyes.

'You're welcome.'

'We don't have to talk about *how* you did it,' he said gently.

'But we shall. If only to stop it being the elephant in the room!'

He smiled. 'When you're ready.'

'You always suspected, didn't you?'

Trelawney shook his head. 'No. Not at all. It was a possibility that I was entirely unable to contemplate, I assure you.'

'And now?'

'I seem to have travelled an inordinately long way since then,' he admitted ruefully.

Amanda grinned weakly. 'You're dealing with the culture shock surprisingly well.'

'Thank you.'

'I expect you have to be getting back. Your mother … your station.'

'No,' Trelawney replied firmly. 'I'll stay with you until your next of kin arrives. I've let my mother know I'm safe, and I have the Christmas holidays covered.'

'Thank you,' she said drowsily and sank into sleep.

And there he was, still there, when Amanda awoke some 45 minutes later, pulled herself into a half-sitting position and stretched her arms.

'How long was I out?'

'Well … it's Christmas Day now. Happy Christmas, Miss Cadabra.'

She smiled. 'Happy Christmas, Inspector. What time is it?' She saw a faint light through the window. 'It's dawn.'

Trelawney checked his watch. 'Yes, it's ten past eight.'

'You must be exhausted!' said Amanda, concerned. 'You've been up all night.'

'I slept in the chair a little.'

'Any news?'

'Just that Baker's team searched the Weathersbys' flat and found the Recket papers.'

'Where were they, as a matter of interest?'

'Stuffed into a sleeve of a coat in Donna's wardrobe.'

'Ah.' She'd moved them then, thought Amanda. 'What

about you? You're not going to get into trouble over all of this, are you?'

'No. Actually I wrote my report while you were asleep and sent it to Ross. Of course, I may have to produce it as a written statement,' Trelawney said. 'But he says that Maxwell says there'll be no question of any poor reflection on either of us.'

'I'm glad.' Amanda leaned her head back on the pillow and sighed. 'You know, it's just occurred to me, no wonder Donna only came to the classes after Majolica had kicked the bucket and Vic was too distraught to make an appearance. She couldn't afford to be recognised by either of them, especially Vic. And once she'd sprung her trap and caught the wrong rabbit, it was too risky to try again, at least straight away, as she said. And in the meantime she was going quietly round the bend.'

'Quite,' agreed Trelawney. 'Just a moment.' He disappeared and presently returned with cups of tea.

'Oh thank you, how kind.' Amanda took a sip. 'You know, Vic was right all along. He said it was Recket and Bogia, and, sure enough, it was a Bogia descendant that was responsible for his wife's demise.'

'Shrewd man,' Trelawney observed.

A familiar voice was heard at the entrance to the ward. 'Thank you, nurse.' A lady with a dark wavy chestnut bob, and wearing a long sweeping dark red velvet gown under a matching coat, was sailing towards them.

'Aunt Amelia!' said two voices simultaneously.

Amanda and Trelawney looked at one another in confusion.

'Aunt Amelia?' they both asked.

'What do you mean, "Aunt Amelia"?' asked Amanda, taking umbrage.

'She's my Aunt Amelia,' he explained mildly.

'She can't be your Aunt Amelia. She's *my* Aunt Amelia. You can't have her,' insisted Amanda.

'Peace, my sweeties,' said the lady in question, intervening diplomatically. 'I can be both. Ammy, I am Thomas's father's sister. And Thomas, Ammy is my de facto adopted niece.'

'But … but…,' stammered Amanda. 'Why didn't you tell me he was your nephew?'

'Because I didn't know, my love.'

'Didn't you ever mention me?' asked Thomas, a little put out.

'Yes, but …'

'Amanda never mentioned you by name,' explained Amelia. 'She only ever called you "the inspector".'

'But you must have told her that you had a nephew who was a police detective,' persisted her nephew.

'Thomas dear, immensely proud of you though I am, I am not so far gone that I assumed you were the only inspector on the Devon and Cornwall police force,' said Amelia gently, with a gleam in her eyes.

'But didn't you gather it from what Miss Cadabra told you about me?' he pursued.

'Amanda told me very little. She said that your conversations were in confidence, and she kept yours.'

Trelawney was touched and impressed. He turned from his aunt to Amanda. 'Thank you, Miss Cadabra.'

'Not at all, Inspector.'

'Listen to you two!' exclaimed Amelia. 'You sound like you're trapped in a Victorian time warp!'

'I know the inspector only in his professional capacity,' explained Amanda firmly. 'He is investigating the —'

'Ah yes,' Amelia acknowledged.

'Miss Cadabra,' added her nephew, 'is the sole remaining witness.'

'All right,' Amelia conceded, 'I understand. As long as you don't start calling me "Ms Reading". Well, you can be off now, Thomas, to your mother. You can't hang around collapsing buildings in a hailstorm and not expect the local press to get hold of it, followed immediately by your mother.'

'I have called her.'

'She'll have been waiting up then. Best go home now. And I must get Ammy home too.'

Trelawney held out a hand to Amanda. 'Thank you again, Miss Cadabra.'

'You're welcome, Inspector. Glad to see that you've got your clothes on again,' she said playfully. 'It's not every day someone gives me the shirt off their back.'

'You are also welcome. I'll call you tomorrow.'

Amelia regarded her nephew thoughtfully as he left the ward. She turned to her niece.

'Well now. I went to the cottage and got you something to wear. Let's get you dressed.' Amanda had become aware of a warm mound under her knees.' I think,' added Amelia, 'that that leg pillow is probably getting short of air, too.' She drew the curtains around the bed as a small nose, and two livid yellow eyes appeared out from under the bed covers.

Chapter 50

༽

AN APOLOGETIC VISITOR, AND THE RECTOR'S NEW PLOT

Amanda rested. After a couple of days, Amelia went home. The rector dropped in. Constable Nikolaides came by for her statement. Baker came to see how she was. Perran and Senara were always nearby.

Trelawney phoned to check on her and said he was looking forward to seeing her at the New Year's Eve Ball and had requested a particular song for them to waltz to.

Amanda got some good news. A text:

On my way home. Uncle Mike

Leo came. He was subdued.

'Let me make you some tea,' said Amanda kindly.

'Are you OK to do that?'

'Oh yes. I'm much better. I'll be fine for the dance. Will you be there?'

'I don't think so. Actually, I came to say how much I regret what happened,' Leo said contritely.

'It wasn't your fault,' replied Amanda. 'Come with me to the kitchen.'

'But it was,' he insisted, following her. 'You see, I knew Donna was setting something up. Only she said it was just a joke. She was just going to make a couple of floorboards a bit wobbly so Vic would fall on his face or something. She was so … insistent that she owed him one for leaving her. She's always said she was his daughter. There was no father listed on her birth certificate, but Mum always said she was Doug Weathersby's daughter. Only Donna didn't want to believe it.'

'So, I gathered.'

'Donna was always a bit obsessive about it. I tried to get her to have counselling or therapy. And then her relationship fell to pieces, and she got worse. She manoeuvred us to Sunken Madley. I didn't realise she planned it. Donna made out that Woodberry, *my* dad, just happened to be up the road. I didn't recognise him. I was just a baby when he left.'

'Have you told the police this,' asked Amanda.

'Yes.'

'How did Donna get into the cellar without the keys?'

'She visited the rector, swiped the keys, took an impression and put them back. Our grandfather was in the building trade; a bit of a crook. She picked things up off him. I didn't know she was still in touch with him.'

'The Recket papers?' Amanda enquired.

'Mum gave them to us. Asked us to find a way to make things right. Let the building owners know. Donna kept telling me to leave it to her, that she was working on it. And I was busy winding up my business and learning hers. I suppose I let it go when I shouldn't have. I'm so sorry. You could have been killed. I would never have forgiven myself.'

'Well, no use crying over spilt milk,' said Amanda

bracingly. 'I wasn't, and it's over.'

'Yes, the inquest decided it was accidental death, and Vic isn't pressing any charges against me.'

But it wasn't accidental, thought Amanda, remembering Tempest's flying leap, pulling Donna to her doom.

At that moment, the Lord High Executioner himself sashayed into the room and gave Leo a long, hard, head-to-toe stare, then sat down and glared at him in a purposeful manner until Leo became so uncomfortable that he stood up.

'I think I should be going.'

'Finish your tea,' Amanda urged him, then followed Leo's gaze. 'Oh, I see. Stop that Tempest.'

Leo took a hasty sip but sat down.

'There is one thing I'm wondering about,' said Amanda casually. 'How could Donna resist the temptation to be there when it happened? I mean, see her plan come to fruition.'

'Oh, she had someone up in the attic who was supposed to be filming it for her, like she was going to post it on YouTube or something. I guess they must have done a runner as soon as they saw what was really going on.'

'I don't suppose you have any idea who it was?'

Leo shook his head regretfully. 'No. To be honest, I didn't want to know too much about it. I just wanted her to get it over, and, well ... get over it.'

'Yes, I see.' He finished his tea. 'Will you keep the salon going?' she asked him.

'I don't know. I need a little more time to think. I'll let you know what I decide to do, but I've closed it for now.'

'OK,' Amanda said understandingly, but thought, bang goes my New Year's Eve Ball hair appointment! And after I'd psyched myself up to it, too. Ah well.

'By the way,' Leo was saying, 'if you see Miss Armstrong-Witworth and Miss de Havillande, please thank them again for me. They contacted my mum and she called me and told me … well … what I told Donna. I don't know how exactly they got Mum's number. It's not like she's listed anywhere but … Miss Armstrong-Witworth said something about dear Sir Reginald Carpetworthy being so kind.'

'Probably,' commented Amanda. 'Those two ladies have a lot of friends in all sorts of places, I understand.'

'Well, I'm glad they have.' He sighed, then noticed the ferocious feline had inched closer, and rose. 'Well, I'll leave you to rest. Take care. I'll let myself out,' he said, edging around Tempest.

She heard the door shut.

'Naughty kitty,' Amanda scolded mildly.

The front doorbell rang. It was Joan with a large, flat, rectangular parcel.

''Ello dear. This must be it, eh?'

'Er …?'

'Your dress! For the New Year's Eve Ball. Oo, we are all so excited!'

It was clear that the villagers' enthusiasm for the festivities had not been dimmed by the collapse of their church hall over their new hairdresser.

'And your inspector will be there!'

'He's not *my* inspector,' Amanda corrected Joan automatically.

'Didn't he look proper 'andsome on Christmas Eve? Oo he's lovely! If I didn't have my Jim! Shame you two missed the party. We did 'ave a laugh. And the music! Still, you were off detecting that Donna. Each to their own. One thing I will say: you two brought the house down!' Joan went into a peal of laughter.

Amanda smiled and nodded, acknowledging the joke. She spotted the rector, who was hurrying along Orchard Way, in the direction of number twenty-six.

'Amanda,' Jane cried, waving a sheaf of notes.

'Hello, Rector.'

'Oh Joan, Amanda. I've had such news!'

'Come into the cottage both of you,' said Amanda, shepherding them into the living room.

'Oh, I can't sit down. I am so excited!' exclaimed the rector. 'I have just come off the phone with the insurance people. And it turns out we were insured for criminal damage as well as rot, and it means we should get enough money to pay for the new hall!'

'Jane, I'm so glad,' said Amanda, hugging her, and Joan joined in.

'Can you believe it? And you know what I've decided?' The rector paused dramatically.

'No,' said Amanda expectantly.

'I'm going to have a Huf-Haus. No more old stuff. The church is old enough. No. For the church hall: new and modern. It's shielded from the road by trees if the old fogeys don't like it. But that's what I want, and that's what I'm going to ask for,' said Jane with determination. 'Will you back me?'

'Yes,' cried Amanda and Joan in unison.

'Get those lovely boys back,' enthused Joan. 'We'll see Hugo again and Yanek and all of them!

'It'll take time,' warned the rector. 'It has to be passed, and then designing and building it but ... it'll be grand!'

'Yes, it will,' Amanda agreed.

'We can put all of this behind us,' added Jane.

'That's the spirit,' said Joan.

Amanda smiled, but thought ... if only it were that simple ... if only I had not had to cast that spell ....

Chapter 51

❧

HIDDEN CARDS

'I've been thinking something you said, Dad.'

'Oh yes, son?' responded Kyt, passing Thomas the roast potatoes.

'Well, you said, "There's always hope", and optimism is always a healthy thing, but I'm a realist, Dad. If the Flamgoynes have the greater numbers and the malice aforethought to stop at nothing, and the Cadabras won't fight, and Amanda is all alone, how on earth are they to be defeated? They're a law unto themselves and they seem to hold all of the cards.'

Kyt carefully spooned horseradish onto his plate, and very precisely cut up his carrots. Thomas spotted thinking-time manoeuvres.

'Not quite, son,' his father said at last.

'Oh? Something you haven't told me?'

'Yes. You see, it's not something I think you would be at all comfortable with, and you've had so much to take in already.'

'Now you're making me nervous,' said Thomas.

'I tell you what. Let's wait until pudding, and, while we have our main course, you can tell me what became of Uncle Elwen's jacket, waistcoat, tie and shirt studs. How about that?'

'Agreed. Well … it was … you see, I got acid on the jacket, so I had to remove it. Then Donna was making a lot of dust to set Miss Cadabra's asthma off, as I told you. I knew that some sort of mask would help with keeping it out of her lungs. Miss Cadabra had left her scarf upstairs, and every scrap of textile around us was deep in dust so …'

His father was grinning. 'So you ripped your shirt off, sending studs flying, and wrapped it around her nose and mouth?'

'Yes,' said Thomas apologetically, catching his father's humorous take on it.

'Well done, son. Of course, every hero needs an excuse to take his top off.'

Thomas chuckled. 'In my defence, I was wearing a t-shirt underneath. That is until …'

'Until?' prompted Kyt with lively interest.

'Well, some acid had got on it and the paramedic in the ambulance said I should …'

But the rest of the sentence was drowned out by mirth.

Presently, Kyt Trelawney went to the bookshelves in the corner by the fireplace, drew out a volume and took from between its pages, a single sheet of paper. He brought it to the table and put it before his son.

Thomas studied it, then said, 'I've seen this … no, I've *read* about this ... wait… Mike showed me a passage in a book describing this. It was on a wall that some cave divers found. The carving was thousands of years old. Yes, the man with the stag's head mask, holding a wand in one hand and a staff in the other, standing by an oak tree.'

'A man?'

'Yes, I think so.'

'Good,' remarked Kyt with satisfaction. Thomas was taken aback. It wasn't like his father to be sexist. 'Did Mike give this figure a name?'

'No.'

'It was a while ago that he showed you the book?'

'Yes.'

'Well, that makes sense.'

'So who is this man?' asked Thomas.

'It is more a depiction of an office than a person. You see, this is a position held by many over the millennia, but the actual identity of each person who held it was never known while they were in office. It would only be revealed to one other person.'

'So what is the office?'

'The word was … Wicc'Lord.'

'Oh come on, Dad!' his son responded incredulously. 'What is this? *Star Wars*?'

'Now you see why I haven't spoken of this to you before? Just open that realist's mind of yours a crack and stick a wedge in it long enough to hear me out, and you might learn something useful,' chided Kyt gently.

'Sorry,' said Thomas contritely. 'All right. Yes. Open mind. Please go on. Wicc'Lord.'

'The Wicc'Lord is a person with great magical power who subtly works for good. They never enter conflict openly but move in the shadows, tipping the balance at great need toward the light. They are our ace.'

'OK. Let's just say that such a person exists,' conceded Thomas sceptically, 'any idea who he might be?'

'You assume it is a man, but more often it has been a woman. The gender assumption from the depiction and the word "Lord" have been great sources of protection for her.'

'All right, who do you think she, he … to pick a pronoun, *she*, then, could be?

'I have no notion, Thomas. That's the whole point. It could be anyone.'

'But you said that each Wicc'Lord revealed his or her identity to one other person.'

'Yes, their successor, and so the baton of the office and secret are passed down.'

'So not necessarily a daughter then?' queried Thomas.

'Not necessarily, but could be.'

'Then we need this person on our side. How are we to find them, recruit them?

'We can't. We must just trust that they know and somehow will help.

Thomas mused. 'Wicc'Lord … a shadow ….'

'Of course, we do have another card whose value is yet to be revealed,' remarked his father slowly.

'Which is?'

'You,' said Kyt simply.

"Me?' His son was astonished. 'All I can do is intuit and see things in teacups occasionally.'

'You, Thomas, are like the vintage motorbike discovered in a long-forgotten shed.'

'Erm … not sure how to take that,' he responded uneasily.

'Look. Say you found such a motorbike in the grounds of … a property you'd inherited … what would you do with it?' asked Kyt eagerly.

'I don't know… see if it would run, clean it up, tune it up and …'

'Take it for a spin?'

'Well … yes.'

'See what it could do?'

'Yes,' agreed Thomas.

'Well, we don't know yet *what* you can do. What you might be capable of. With a little tuning up,' explained Kyt.

'Ah, I see. You're hoping I'll turn out to be a Harley or an Enfield,' his son quipped.

His father smiled. 'No, Thomas, I think you might turn out to be … a Triumph.'

* * * * *

Amelia leaned back from the crystal ball in front of her.

'I'm afraid not,' she said seriously.

'No way of stopping them?' asked Amanda.

'It's done, sweetie. They know Sunken Madley is the epicentre. I warned you. One too many casts against humans: The Manor, Lost Madley and now the precincts of a holy place.'

'Why didn't they react the other times? Why was this one so crucial?'

'Because the spell was loosed and then a presence in this dimension vanished,' explained Amelia.

'But I didn't kill her!' insisted Amanda.

'But it looks like you did,' Amelia replied softly.

Her niece looked around the room, as though for answers. 'What am I to do? When will they come for me?'

'They are not coming for *you*, my darling; they are coming for your village.'

'How do I fight them?'

'You do not fight them,' Amelia responded patiently. 'You are a Cadabra. Cadabras do not strike out, they defend.'

'All right,' said Amanda more calmly, her strategic mind beginning to click in. 'How do I defend the village then?'

'You will have help. The crystal shows that clearly,' said her aunt encouragingly.

'Who? Who will help?'

'That is not shown. But I think I know where you can start.'

'Where?' queried Amanda eagerly.

'Do you remember the story I told you long ago when you were, oh, about thirteen? When you were asking about your grandparents' past?'

'You called Grandpa and Granny "Romeo and Juliet", yes, I remember.'

'And do you remember how Juliet came to know that Sunken Madley would provide them with a safe refuge?' Amelia asked.

'There was a friend of Juliet's — Granny's — that she met during the war…. Yes… her name … you called her Viola.'

Amelia waited for her niece to process this.

'Viola – Viola is still there?' Amanda continued. 'In Sunken Madley? Viola must have been a witch, or, at least, a magical person, or how would she have known the village was safe? Although, all she would have had to have known … was the legend about the cottage … but she helped Granny and Grandpa back then and might help me now. You're saying, find Viola?'

'Can you think of a better starting point?'

'Who is Viola? It could be anyone … anyone old enough … Let's see. Mrs Uberhausfest said she and Granny had been friends for over 50 years and she's always looked out for me. Gwendolen? I don't think Granny was a particular friend of hers. Cynthia de Havillande? I often thought she and Granny were as like as two peas in a pod! I don't know …. If I had to put my money on one, … I'd say … Miss de Havillande.'

'All right.'

Amanda looked hopefully at her aunt. 'Do you know who it is?'

'No, sweetie. Your grandparents never told me.'

'Well, I have an open invitation to The Grange practically. Maybe I can somehow intimate to Miss de Havillande that I know who she is? Although … what if it's Irma?'

'Then I expect Cynthia won't know what you're talking about,' replied Amelia.

'I suppose so. You know,' said Amanda, reflectively, 'I really like Irma, she has that get-up-and-go spirit that I admire about Granny, although it can be a bit much at times. Hm … I will have to think about this … and tread carefully. But it's a start.'

* * * * *

Vera and Harry walked along the beach at sunset.

'So did young Mikey get off all right?' Harry asked. 'Airport run pretty clear?'

'Yes. He was glad to be going home, I think, in spite of his fondness for your cooking, my love,' replied his wife affectionately.

'Hmm … do you think he's going to be OK?'

'I think so. But what do *you* think?' she asked, watching his face.

'Hard to say but …. my feeling is yes.' Harry shook his head ruefully 'He treats everything as though it's one huge game organised expressly for his amusement.'

'I know,' agreed Vera.

It was getting dark. They tacitly agreed to turn back. The lamp outside their house glowed invitingly.

'But yes,' said Harry reassuringly, 'I think he'll be all right. I think she will too …. in the end.'

They smiled at one another, and, linking arms, walked towards the light.

Chapter 52

✑

CATCH AND DISPATCH

'So, young niece. You've been busy,' said Hogarth, as Amanda, in the guise of cabbie, on his orders, drove Claire's lime green Audi Sportback out of Heathrow Terminal 3.

'Yes, but I have a feeling that I've just messed things up,' Amanda replied regretfully, 'and made no progress in the one area I should have. If anything, I've gone backwards. I'm bringing the Flamgoynes down on my people, and don't know who's spying for them, if indeed it *is* them that the spy is spying for. We still don't know who sent my horrid family over the cliff, and, oh yes, I played a part in the destruction of my village church hall.'

Hogarth chuckled. 'I think you take an unnecessarily bleak view of the situation. Let's go to our luxury lair, shall we? And I will endeavour to show you that you have done far better than you think.'

Presently they drew into Britain's worst motorway service station: the notorious Watford Gap, Eastbound on the A4 highway linking the main airport to London. Seated in relative privacy with hot chocolate and coffee respectively before them, Hogarth began.

'The Flamgoyne incursion has been waiting to happen ever since the Cardiubarns were reduced to you and Senara. And, I'm sure, they've only just decided to risk all on one throw of the dice, so you have time to prepare.'

'Gather my army?' asked Amanda.

'Army: no. Home Guard: yes,' Hogarth corrected her. 'The source or sources of the magical power that they know exists in and around Sunken Madley, is an unknown quantity to them. They are taking a risk. There will be dissent in the ranks, regarding moving against the village. All of which gives you a number of advantages.'

Amanda felt slightly more optimistic.

'As to the spy,' continued Uncle Mike, 'how far have you got? You do know someone was watching that day in the hall.'

'Yes, the little girl I told you about —'

'Sophy?'

'Yes. She said there was a small dark man and a tall blond one. I have no idea who the small dark man could be, but surely the tall blond has to be Ryan. He's the only tall blond in the village, except the Colonel, and I can't believe he'd be the spy. Besides, Ryan is the only one fitting the description who's recently moved in. Except he was at the party and, like everyone there, has an alibi.'

'*Does* he?'

Amanda stopped and reconsidered. 'Well … there were a lot of people there. I looked at the assistant librarian's photos but they only showed the lit areas just around the tables. I would have said Ryan's number one fan Kieran, my solicitor's son, would have known if he was there, but, thanks to my intercession, which I'd hoped might make him a useful tag of

Ryan's movements, he and my teenage friend Ruth are now thick as thieves. A plane could have crashed into the orchard and I doubt Kieran would have noticed.'

'Don't despair, my dear, it takes time to develop a mole, especially if they don't realise that they are intended to be one. Those two young people may still turn out to be helpful in the future. Meanwhile, tell me what you remember seeing before you left the orchard for the church hall,' said Hogarth.

'We'd all walked down from the church to the orchard,' Amanda recalled, 'like we do every year. There was singing, of course …'

'Singing what?'

'*The Appel Songe*,' replied Amanda.

'You sing that every year?' queried Hogarth.

'Of course. We sing a whole load of apple-related songs.'

'The same ones every year?' he checked.

'Yes, there's actually an order to it. Silly maybe, but we sing them in a sort of chain one after the other as we eat and drink and go around blessing the trees and tying pretty things on the branches.' Amanda stopped.

'Uncle Mike! There's an order to the songs. It *isn't* written down. Only people who are Village would know it. If Ryan is the spy, he won't have been present for one of the songs. He won't know that it was sung …. Let's see … it was a quarter to 6 when I left ... and there were a few verses of *The Appel Songe* left. He would have needed time to get up there, into the hall attic. The song after *The Appel Songe-* is *Don't Sit Under the Apple Tree* … He wouldn't know that they sang it … But how do I catch him out?'

'You'll find a way,' said Hogarth confidently. 'See? You're making excellent progress.'

'And, I think I know why he was really up there. Leo said someone had agreed to film Vic falling over, which is what

Leo thought Donna had planned. Why would someone like Ryan agree to be in on something so silly? But what if Donna told him she was planning something more dramatic? Not murder, but something more risky. If she was setting me up to be the person who'd witness it, he might have been expecting me to use a spell to save Vic, thus exposing myself as part of the source of the magic that has been radiating from the area of the village!'

'Very good. And of course, if he had hung around ...'

'He would have seen me open the basement doors without a key. Yes. But I'm sure that as soon as he saw that Donna meant murder, he was out of the skylight as fast as he could climb, taking the rope with him.'

'Indeed.'

'But then, why *Ryan*? He has no connection with Cornwall, he doesn't need money, why would he spy for the Flamgoynes? But then, what if he's watching me for someone else? Some other reason? Something about me that I don't know about. I can't make sense of it. He's successful at a sport he loves and he's an OK-ish sort of person. And yet, I do think it was him up there.'

'You've actually come a long way. Are you sure you've made no progress on the family minibus affair?'

'Well, I'm sure it's narrowed down to either Granny, for the best of reasons, or one or more Flamgoynes. Both had motives, but I'm not sure about means or opportunity. How would the Flamgoynes have known about the vehicle or its route, for example? How could Granny have set it up, seeing as she was in Sunken Madley on the day that it happened? Whoever did it, they've got away with it for 30 years. The flawless plan. The perfect murder. The perfect murd*ers* .... So far.... The inspector was 12 when it happened, and his father was still taking him to Flamgoyne, I think. My instinct is that he saw or heard something that has some bearing on that day. I need him to remember!'

'You're sounding more and more alike, you two,' remarked Hogarth, amused. 'But to return to your list of imagined woes: as for the hall, that was an accident waiting to happen. It was built that way.'

'That's true. And the rector is thrilled actually. She's plotting revolution: a modern church hall!'

'There you are then. Well done, my niece.'

'So…,' Amanda said, idly stirring her hot chocolate. 'Once I establish Ryan is the spy, … I expect the Inspector won't need to …'

'Oh, Trelawney's job will only be beginning,' replied Hogarth. 'We need to know why you're being watched. And then, once we know, we start feeding in the information that we want his masters to have. Trelawney has his work cut out for him.'

'Ah. Right,' said Amanda, with carefully studied nonchalance.

Hogarth leaned back, enjoying himself. 'Yes, I'm afraid you're going to have continue to endure his presence. Glad to see you're taking it so well.'

'Inspector Trelawney has been of great assistance,' she declared. 'I am pleased to hear that his visits to Sunken Madley will be ongoing.'

Hogarth grinned. 'Well, well. He's gone from being National Irritant to "of great assistance". There must be a medal for that. Good. Let's drink up. You have a train to get me on, niece.'

* * * * *

'So Captain Dunkley helped you out in the end. Have you helped him in return?' asked Amelia casually.

'No. Oh ... no, you're right,' answered Amanda, conscience-stricken. 'I haven't. But ... well, I've never tried to help anyone like him move on. What if he won't go? I mean, he wants an explanation for what happened to him, and an apology, I expect ... aha!'

* * * * *

'Sandra?'

'Hi Amanda. Everything OK?'

'Yes, thank you. I need a small favour, but in the strictest confidence. No one must know that I asked you.'

'Of course,' Sandra answered warmly. 'Anything.'

'Do you have the playlist for the Feast?'

* * * * *

'Hello, Rector, how are things?'

'Oh, fine, Amanda. You know, I thought of another good thing about having the old hall in ruins; I shan't have to get new keys cut!'

Amanda laughed. 'Do you mind if I take a last look at it?'

'You'd better do it soon; the site's being boarded up tomorrow, for health and safety.'

It was quiet, until Amanda struggled up the shifting debris to where she thought the hole might have been.

'Mr Recket? ' she called.

'Another one, eh?' said a voice behind her.

Amanda jumped and disturbed the jumble of wood beneath her feet

'Mind yerself, love.'

She turned to see a man with a round cherubic face and blue eyes, dressed in a jacket and cloth cap, seemingly waist high in the pile of what had been the roof.

'Ah, hello. Mr Recket?'

'The very same. I take it this is the scene of a disaster, down, in some way, to yours truly? Though I never seen one this bad before. They usually repairs it long before it ends up in a heap. But I'm here to do the business as usual,' he replied readily.

'What business it that?' asked Amanda curiously.

'I learned the error of my ways, Miss. I come to say sorry and help the person on their way what is stuck in the place where they has the accident, see?'

'You mean other people have died because of your sabotages?' asked Amanda, shocked.

'Not necessarily, but often they keeps coming back to it and can't get on, see?' explained Mr Recket.

'Can't move on to the next …?'

'That's right. So I 'elps,' he stated virtuously.

'That's what I was hoping, Mr Recket,' replied Amanda. 'That if you explained to Captain Dunkley what happened and said you were sorry, he might be able to get on his way.'

'Give it a try, Miss,' Recket said encouragingly.

Amanda looked towards the spot where she had last seen the captain and called his name. Presently he appeared, also waist high in the ruin. He looked Amanda up and down, and demanded to know what she was doing floating up there, but then listened to Mr Recket.

'I see,' he harrumphed. 'Well, I don't know about all this. Where's your employer, Miss Cadabra? Why isn't he here? And you, man, I demand to see your superior. '

'I'm my superior, cap'n; I works for the family business.'

'This is all very irregular,' replied Dunkley, much put out.

They were getting nowhere. Finally, Recket whispered to Amanda, 'Leave this to me.' He turned to Dunkley. 'Cap'n, you know what? That's just what your Nanny Smith used to say.'

'Nanny Smith? Nanny Philby, you mean,' replied the captain, as though Recket was an idiot.

'That's right. Of course. What was her first name, now? Daphne?'

'Geraldine' Dunkley corrected Recket crossly.

'Geraldine Philby. That's right. 'Scuse me for coupla minutes,' said the builder, and melted into the ether.

Amanda patiently heard Dunkley out as he exclaimed and spluttered about his situation, until Recket reappeared with a white-haired bonneted lady of upright mien but kindly disposition. She interrupted Dunkley's diatribe with a carrying call.

'Master Fortescue!'

Dunkley turned, and his face went from affronted to disbelief to joy.

'Nanny!' he cried, apparently hurrying through the rubble 'Oh, Nanny!' He hugged her with relief.

'Now, Master Fortescue, none of your nonsense,' the lady instructed him. 'Mr Recket has explained everything to you and ...'

'But that woman was saying it was 2018 and there's a queen and a … a *female* prime minister —'

'I hope you haven't been impolite to the lady, Master Fortescue.'

'Well, er,' he muttered sheepishly.

'Come along now.'

'Where are we going, Nanny?'

'Where everything will become perfectly clear to you, Master Fortescue.' She took his arm and steered him towards where the side door at the other end of the hall had once stood. It was now a bright rectangle of white light.

'Oh, all right, Nanny,' Dunkley said meekly.

'Say goodbye to Miss Cadabra now.'

He turned and flapped his hand, saying politely, 'Goodbye, Miss Cadabra.'

'Goodbye Captain,' answered Amanda, 'and thank you for your help.'

Nanny led her charge through the portal. Recket stood for a moment before it, looked back at Amanda, raised his cap and winked. Then he was gone, and with the sound of the door sliding shut, the light went out.

'Hm,' said Amanda. 'Job done.' Tempest looked at her meaningfully.

''Yes, of course, your Highness.' She swept a curtsey. 'Luncheon!'

* * * * *

'I'm glad you were able to make it,' said Amanda, smiling sweetly at the man opposite.

'I'm glad you asked me,' he replied warmly.

'You gave me such a wonderful treat last time, it was the least I could do, and I was thinking, I'd like to try the hot chocolate here with coconut milk, and maybe write a little review for the dairy-free community?'

'That's very thoughtful. But then you are,' he said admiringly.

'Thank you. Sandra is Village, you see, and she's worked so hard on this place, and I'd love to see her succeed.'

'Of course,' he said, regarding her glowingly. Ryan Ford looked around for a waiter to take their order.

At that moment, the song that had been playing ended, and a new track began.

'Oh, I do like this one, don't you?' enthused Amanda. Ryan stopped to listen.

'Ah yes,' he responded.

'Come to think of it,' she said, 'it would have been an obvious choice for the Feast.'

'Yes, I can't think why they didn't play it,' Ryan Ford agreed.

'Next year,' Amanda said, cheerily, and began to sing along, '"Don't sit under the apple tree …."'

Chapter 53

ༀ

NEW YEAR

'You did well to be dancing again only a week after being in hospital,' Trelawney said, as he made up the fire. It had become a routine with them, after the Saturday dance class to come back to the cottage; Amanda made the tea and he lit the kindling in the hearth to set the blaze alight.

'Thank you, but I sat down as much as I could.'

'Will you be all right for tomorrow?' he asked solicitously.

'I wouldn't miss the New Year's Eve Ball for the world!' she replied enthusiastically. 'But I shall pace myself.'

'Good.'

'Oh, your evening clothes must have got ruined on Christmas Eve!' Amanda exclaimed.

'Yes, but I have something for tomorrow night, so no worries there,' Trelawney responded calmly.

'Was it insured? With the place you hired it from?'

'It wasn't hired. It belonged to my great uncle, who

won't be requiring it back,' Trelawney replied gravely but with a telltale twinkle.

Presently they were seated opposite one another as usual on either side of the fire with their mugs of tea; Trelawney with a plate of shortcake at his elbow and Amanda with gingernuts beside her.

'I helped Dunkley on his way,' she said.

'To the ... next dimension?' he asked hesitantly.

'That's right. Well, that's what we call it. I don't really understand it, but anyway yes.' Amanda told him how Recket had managed Dunkley, and Trelawney laughed heartily at the tale.

'What about the little girl in the crypt?' he enquired.

'Sophy? Of course, I shall help her, but there's one thing I need to talk to her about again. A part of the puzzle that still remains unsolved.'

'Tell me,' Trelawney invited her.

'Well, Dunkley said a woman went up the ladder to the hatch carrying a rope with a hook on it.'

'Yes, the police found a skylight up there in the attic and scratches on the window frame,' he replied. 'So I think we can gather how Ryan Ford got up there and back down on the night of the murder.'

'Aha. OK. But here's the riddle that's been bothering me. Now, we know that during Sophy's time, there was a barn on the site of the church hall, and she and Percy, the young Dunkley of those days, were hiding up there watching the dancers of their time, but she could still see what happened 200 years later on the night of the murder. Now, Sophy said she saw a small dark man and a tall blonde one. The latter is easy: Ryan Ford. But the first man? And how come she didn't see the woman whom Captain Dunkley saw going up the ladder?'

Trelawney said thoughtfully, 'It's as though the woman became a man when she entered Sophy's time-frame.'

Amanda stopped still, biscuit half-raised to her mouth. 'Time-frame … history … in Sophy's time … men wore their hair short, but some men, older men and military officers, still wore wigs with curls and often a ponytail. If what Sophy saw was a woman in trousers with her hair like that, she may have assumed that maybe it was a sailor or a soldier. Small, dark, hair tied back, and add the dark eyes and red lips from Captain Dunkley's description, and you have … Donna Weathersby.'

'That makes sense. Well done.'

'Good. Then I will do my best to help Sophy on her way.'

'Two hundred years is a long time to be stuck in a crypt.' Trelawney remarked sympathetically.

'Well, according to my Aunt Amelia —'

'*Our* Aunt Amelia,' he replied teasingly.' Amanda could not help but smile.

'*Our* Aunt Amelia — people in other dimensions don't necessarily experience time in the same way as we do. Sophy may be unaware of the passage of so many years.'

'I certainly hope so.'

They sat and sipped and crunched away for a while, enjoying the crackle of the fire and a companionable silence.

'Oh,' said Amanda, suddenly remembering something important. Trelawney looked up. 'There's … I … I'm not exactly sure how do to this. I know that we have a professional … juxtaposition … You are …. I mean, I am a witness in a case that you are investigating, and so, I think, you can't accept any presents from me because that could be perceived as … something that could affect your judgement, have-I-got-that-right?' she finished in a rush.

'Yes, Miss Cadabra,' he replied kindly. 'And it's thoughtful of you to consider that.'

'So … it's Christmas, and I wanted to give you a present, and then I thought I didn't want to make it awkward for you or have you say you couldn't accept it. So I thought, you can accept a present from Aunt Amelia. Yes?'

'Of course.'

'So I asked Aunt Amelia to arrange it. If you go and see her, she'll give it to you, with Happy Christmas from us both. If that's all right, Inspector?'

'That is most thoughtful. Thank you. I shall look forward to seeing what you have cooked up between you,' Trelawney said with genuine pleasure.

'Cooked up?' repeated Amanda playfully. 'Oh very apt.'

'Is it a cake?' he asked, his curiosity aroused.

'I'm not saying any more,' she replied impishly. 'You'll see!'

* * * * *

The following morning, after an exchange of texts with his aunt, Thomas presented himself at Amelia's house to receive his Christmas present. Wreathed in smiles, she sat him down on the living room sofa.

'I won't make you wait while I make the tea. Here you are.'

With that, Amelia put an eight-inch cube on the table before him. Thomas looked at it, then at his aunt then back at the object, frowning with perplexity. Finally he undid the gold ribbon, drew apart the marbled paper and opened the red box inside.

Laying in folds of black velvet, was a crystal ball. Within, it seemed to swim and flow with blues and turquoises and peaks of white.

'It's beautiful,' Thomas marvelled.

'Good,' replied Amelia with satisfaction.

'You made it?' he asked.

'Yes, did me good to see the old furnace again,' his aunt

responded heartily. 'Nice to know I've still got it.'

'It's like you've given me the sea. Is this for me to … divine with?' Thomas asked uncertainly.

'It can help you focus, yes,' Amelia confirmed.

'What do I do with it?'

'Play with it, get to know each other, look at it, and … just see what you see.

The following day, Amanda dressed for the New Year's Eve Ball with butterflies in her stomach that she was unable to explain.

'Aw, I'm *pur* proud of you. You do look a lovely sight, *bian*,' said Grandpa. 'I think the inspector will think so too.'

Amanda blushed slightly. 'I hope so. He looks very grand in evening dress. I want to look like I have, at least, made an effort,' she said, gazing uncertainly at her reflection.

Claire had performed her own brand of magic and nailed 1918 high fashion that would suit Amanda. A bodice of cream lace hung from her shoulders and matching fabric cascaded to her ankles. It was clasped at the waist by a deep corset black belt from which fell lengths of black chiffon at the sides of the skirt and a long train behind.

Amanda's hair was drawn up and back in a loose bun of soft curls, and the amber earrings her grandparents had given her on her 18th birthday, dangled glinting from her ears. She wore cream Mary Jane's, that were dressy enough for the occasion but comfortable enough for dancing, over a precious pair of cream Falke holdups, into the top of which went the indispensable Pocket-wand. The perfume that Grandpa had had made specially for her in France, from the herbs and flowers in the garden, hung about her.

Senara put her hands lightly on her granddaughter's shoulders.

'You'll do,' she said nodding. 'In fact, you'll *more* than do!'

The New Year's Eve Ball, which this evening was

commemorating the hard won peace of 1918, was held, as it had been a century previously, not in the church hall, but where many a party had been celebrated over 400 years: in the Sinner's Rue. Cleared of tables, and chairs pushed to the edges of the room to make as much dancing space as possible, the dear old pub had been spruced up. Sandra had been allowed in to replace the garish decorations with white, silver and blue. Every surface had been scrubbed, the bar shone with polish and the brassware gleamed.

The programme was to begin with a short class to teach everyone the two-step that was popular at the time, and was a dance anyone could quickly learn and enjoy. Amanda entered, found a chair and took off her coat. She was greeted by Joan and Sylvia, and Dr Patel came over to see how she was faring. It wasn't until Sandra called the dancers to order, that she saw him. Trelawney, attired in more modern evening dress than the previous ball, came over to her as she rose from her seat, and, leading her short distance away from the other ladies said,

'I am not sure if the rules governing the behaviour of an inspector towards the chief witness in his case permit, but I must say, you look stunning this evening, Miss Cadabra.'

Amanda beamed with delight.

'Thank you Inspector. Let's keep it off the record, just in case,' she said conspiratorially.

'You are too kind. Shall we?' he asked gesturing towards the dance floor. 'By the way, thank you for prompting Aunt Amelia's thoughtful gift. It is greatly appreciated. I look forward to working out how to use it!' he added ruefully.

After the lesson, the lights were dimmed and DJ Bill MacNaire struck up hits and requests from the First World War years. Trelawney danced with Amanda once or twice but she had to rest frequently. She watched the clock moving towards midnight, to that moment when the old year would become the new. When *Hinky Dinky Parlez-vous* came on, she and the inspector shared a knowing look.

It was a quarter to midnight. Amanda got up for a little air and stood by the door, looking on as the coloured lights were sweeping over the couples moving across the floor. There they were, Karan and Neeta Patel, Mr and Mrs Sharma, Jonathan and Mrs Pagely, Dennis and Aunt Amelia, the inspector and Gwendolen, the Colonel and Miss de Havillande, Joan and her Jim, the rector and Iskender, Joe from Madley Cows Dairy and his daughter Olivia, Penny and her fiancé, Sylvia and her husband, Hugh and Sita Povey, Sandy and Vanessa, Julian and Sandra, Gordon French and Irene James, Erik and Esta, even Ruth and Kieran. And then she began to be aware of more pairs amidst the couples: Granny and Grandpa … men in regimentals, ladies in dresses like her own, all singing, laughing, talking.

''Scuse me, Miss.'

Amanda looked to her right, and there was a young man in neat soldier's garb standing at her side. There was just the veriest hint of transparency about him.

'Fancy a dance?' he asked. Amanda rather liked the idea of two-stepping with someone from 1918, but knew it would look odd to the people of her own time if she were moving around the floor by herself with, to them, an imaginary partner.

'I'm just taking a breather, but thank you for asking me, sir.'

'That's all right.'

'May I ask you a question?'

'Course.'

'How come you are in uniform. I mean it's over, isn't it? The War?'

'Oh yes, long, long ago, but it's nice to wear it all in one piece. Lot of us here, our kit didn't come out of it whole, if you know what I mean, and neither did what was under it.'

'So how come …?'

'Costume party, Miss. It's nice to dress up and remember the *good* times we 'ad, us lads together. It wasn't *all* bad. And what *was* bad, well, that's long behind us now. You must know that. Same for you too, eh?'

'I'm not actually from …'

'Ah, you one of the currents, are you? Oh well, you'll see.' The song playing was ending. 'Ere, my girl's free. 'Scuse me if I go and ask her for a turn about the floor.'

The new tune was beginning, it was two minutes to midnight, and here was the inspector holding out his hand to her.

'Our dance, I think, Miss Cadabra.'

And there it was, playing as though at once from the past and in the present: *Roses of Picardy*. And as they waltzed, it was as though all the villagers over the centuries who had rejoiced on this night were dancing with and around the two of them, and all of the people Amanda loved most.

The music paused and the dancers with it. It was almost midnight. The countdown began and crowd chanted 10 … 9 … 8 … 7 … 6 … 5 … 4 … 3… 2 ... 1… and the shout went up. A flicker of light caught Amanda's eye and drew her gaze upwards as Trelawney's attention too was pulled towards it; they were standing under a sprig of mistletoe. In fact, the hall was so thus bedecked with them, hidden amidst the white and blue decorations, that it would have been difficult not to have been. Thomas looked down at Amanda, smiling up at him, and felt an unaccountable desire to kiss her. Amanda saw it, and, suddenly, for no apparent reason, hoped he would.

Trelawney reminded Thomas that before him stood the sole witness in the case he was investigating, and it was his duty to maintain a professional relationship with her. Miss Cadabra reminded Amanda that here was the policeman on the trail of, possibly, her grandmother. The conflict was brief. A tacit agreement on each side was reached.

Trelawney leaned down and kissed Amanda's cheek.

'Happy New Year, Miss Cadabra,' he said.

Amanda reached up and hugged him. He held her briefly and they released one another.

'Happy New Year, Inspector.'

Chapter 54

✍

A GIFT, PERCY, AND HOPE

It was dawn. Trelawney was running along the beach in Parhayle. He slowed to a walk and sat on a rock to watch the sun rise over Cornwall and the inshore fleet of fishing boats heading out. He needed to think, and this was where and when he thought the most clearly.

This Wicc'Lord his father had spoken of … who could she be? How would she help Amanda in her hour of need? When would the Flamgoynes, those whose blood, for better or for worse, flowed in his veins, strike? And the tantalising promise of a memory to be regained in a holiday cottage, not far away. The memory of the day that his gift was buried deep within him, and, with it, so much of his own record of childhood, and the identity of the spell-weaver, who may have saved his life. And what if that very person turned out to be the murderer of a busload of Cardiubarns sent crashing to their doom at the bottom of a Cornish cliff?

He resolved to talk to Amanda about this strange shadowy figure whose role stretched back to antiquity. Perhaps together they could find a way to work out who she might be. They were, after all, quite an effective team. Although, Thomas reflected, next time she asks me to accompany her to a derelict building, I'm taking a hard hat!

* * * * *

By later that Wednesday morning, it had become cold but sunny with only a breeze, and, consequently, Amanda had decided to give herself some time off and lunch with Tempest at her favourite retreat; up on the ruins of the thousand-year-old Priory. First, however, she had an errand. One last piece of unfinished business. Amanda brought the flat, stiff, gift-wrapped parcel that had arrived in the post under brown paper and string that morning from Aunt Amelia. Even Joan had not been able to deduce what it might be, and Amanda had decided to unwrap it once she was up in her eyrie.

Tempest installed himself on the back seat of the Astra, and Amanda drove them to the church car park. As she got out, Leo emerged from his car too.

'Hello,' she said pleasantly.

'Hello, Amanda,' he replied hesitantly, but with new life in his eyes. 'I hoped to see you before I went.'

'Went?'

'Yes. I'm going. And I'm leaving everything in the salon. I want the rector to have it, to sell, for the new church hall. It's the least I can do.'

'That's very kind of you, Leo,' Amanda said sincerely.

'I never meant…' he began.

'You don't have to say any more. I take that you are free to go?'

'Yes, no charges. I was fool but not a knave.' He took a deep breath. 'So I'm off.'

Amanda saw a suitcase of the backseat of his car. Leo noticed and explained,

'I'm going to join Mum. I only really stayed here for Donna, and now she's gone, well … Mum's getting married … she's going to live out there, and, maybe, if I can make myself useful, Australia will take me too.'

'I'm happy for you, Leo. I think you're making a wise decision.'

He paused. 'Look … Mum says Australia is a wonderful country. Just the place for making a new start. I don't suppose it's something that … you'd ever consider …?'

'Sunken Madley is the place for me. But it's always nice to be asked,' she answered him warmly.

Leo nodded. 'I understand. So, anyway, would you give these papers to the rector for me, please? I've seen Erik, made it all legal. And thank her, for the welcome she gave us both. And you too.'

Amanda held out her hand. 'No hard feelings.'

They shook on it. 'Well,' he said, his mood lifting. 'Better be going. Don't want to miss my plane!'

Leo got into his car, and she waved him off until he disappeared with the bend of the road.

Amanda walked back to the rectory calling for Jane.

'Hello, dear.'

'Rector, I've got good news,' said Amanda, waving Leo's papers.

Twenty minutes later, Amanda and Tempest entered the crypt.

Amanda went to sit down next to where she'd last seen the little girl.

'Sophy,' she called softly. The artificial lamps and all but two of the coffins vanished as the old door to the outside world reappeared. It was open and daylight streamed in. The child materialised next to her, looking timid. 'It's Amanda. Remember me?' Sophy nodded. 'How would you like to leave here, be with your family and them not be a bit cross with you?'

'It's impossible,' said Sophy sadly.

'Well, what if you could say sorry to your friend? Would that make you feel better?' Amanda asked.

The child nodded mutely, tears springing to her eyes.

'All right,' said Amanda kindly. 'What's his name? Your friend.'

Sophie sniffed and managed a barely audible, 'Percy.'

'Percy Dunkley?'

'Yes.'

'I think, if we both called him he'd come.'

'He'll be cross with me,' protested Sophy anxiously.

'I don't think he will, but even if he is,' Amanda reassured her, 'I'll be right here and I promise that nothing bad will happen to you. All right?' Sophy nodded. 'Let's call him.'

'Percy?'

'Percy Dunkley.'

He appeared, a boy of about nine years of age, wearing an apron over his clothes. At the sight of Sophy, he gladdened and sat down next to her.

'Hello, Sophy, what are you doing in here?'

She broke into a tearful and muddled explanation of why she had abandoned him when he had plummeted into the Big Barn party dessert, expressing her deep remorse, interlarded with self-recrimination until Percy interrupted her.

'Don't be a ninny, Sophy. Of course, I forgive you, if it's all that important to you, but the fact is that it's all worked out splendidly.' She looked at him in amazement. 'After I fell in the trifle,' Percy explained, 'and half of it had gone and it was huge bowlful so no one was that upset and I didn't hit any part of the Christmas pudding, the servants cleaned me up and weren't going to say anything, but it got back somehow to my father and mother. They were so cross, it took them two days to decide how I was to make up for it. Well, cook's scullery maid had gone off to get married, so Mama said I was to help cook for a month, because, if I was going to destroy dinners, I should jolly well learn how to create them.'

'Oh no!' commiserated Sophy.

'Papa wasn't sure because he thought I might pick up low ways, but Mama persuaded him, and I'm glad she did because, Cook is a right one, and I found I had a turn for cooking and baking, and I know what I'm going to be. I'm going to be a hotel owner and serve the best dinners in London! And if you want to, Sophy, you can come and help me.'

'Truly?' she asked, brightening.

'Truly! But we can't do it in this draughty crypt, so let's go, shall we?'

'No one is cross with me?' she asked cautiously.

'Not a soul,' promised Percy.

He got her to her feet and they walked toward the bright rectangle of light that was the door of the crypt.

Sophy turned, and finally, showed her first smile.

'Thank you, Amanda.'

'Goodbye, Sophy.'

As the pair reached the portal, Amanda heard Percy ask, 'So how long were you in the chapel there?'

'Nearly a whole half an hour, I'll bet,' said Sophy with feeling.

Then came the whish of the door closing, and the usual electric glow returned to the crypt.

Amanda and Tempest climbed the steps that the Victorians had installed when they got tired of clearing the path to the chapel after each storm. At the top of the flight, all was just as usual. However, it seemed to Amanda, that her familiar was a trifle put out, as he proceeded with her to the rectory to return the key.

Of course, thought Amanda. The children had failed to notice him!

The two of them had barely started up the road toward the priory, when they were intercepted.

'Oo-oo!'

Amanda turned, thinking it could only be one of two people.

''Ello dearie,' said the lollipop lady. 'You recovered from your ordeal?'

'Yes, I'm really all better, thank you, Sylvia.'

'I thought so when I saw you at the ball, dancin' away. You and the inspector. You lookin' so luvely and 'im ever so 'andsome. Who'da thought it, eh? 'Im bein' a policeman 'n all. But I was wotchin' you. Oo, you do dance well together, you and your inspector.'

'He's not my inspector,' replied Amanda robotically.

At which, abruptly, the lollipop lady stood still. Amanda halted in surprise.

'Oh,' said Sylvia, and patted Amanda's cheek kindly, 'I rather think he is, dearie.'

The lady departed briskly across the street, leaving her young friend standing, staring after her.

'See you later,' called Sylvia with cheery wave behind her.

Amanda gave a moment's consideration to the lollipop lady's assertion, then dismissed it, shaking her head in wonder at the incurably speculative nature of her fellow Sunken Madleyists.

'Ah well,' she said to Tempest tolerantly. 'If it makes them happy.'

After a few more paces, Amanda heard another voice

behind her calling her name and turned to see the librarian hurrying up the road.

'Mrs Pagely, please don't rush. Do you need me for something?'

'No, no, dear. It's just that Joan said you were heading for your crow's nest and I thought you might like to take this with you.' The librarian was holding out a faded black, cloth-bound book. 'Just be careful with it and bring it back when you've finished with it.'

Amanda looked at the title. *There's a Small Hotel - obscure hostelries of London 1820 -1870* by Laurence Heart and Richard Rojers. Somewhat mystified, she looked at Mrs Pagely. 'Erm?'

'It mentions Percy Dunkley, the one that the Big Barn incident was about, do you remember? In *Good Manors of Hertfordshire*?'

'Oh yes.'

'See? Jonathan has marked the page. He found the book in the stacks. Both of us would swear blind that we've never seen this book before, but Jonathan always says that the library basement is a very odd place. He keeps meaning to tell you about it, but something else always comes up. But never mind. You take it with you.'

'Thank you, to both of you! I'll drop it back after lunch.'

Amanda and Tempest continued their progress up to the ruins, and climbed to a place above the old night stairs that Amanda had shored up to make a little platform. From here, she looked over the village and the trees to the countryside around.

They shared their midday meal, enjoying the mild warmth of the sun. Finally, Amanda moved the lunchbox off her knees, and replaced it with the book from Mrs Pagely.

'Let's see what this is all about.' She opened it at the bookmark and at once the relevant paragraph caught her eye:

One hotel of particular note is that opened in Thiberton Street by Percy Dunkley in 1836. It was celebrated locally for its excellent dinners and assiduous maintenance of the building. This establishment was remarkable in that preparation of the meals was overseen by the owner himself who was a chef of considerable skill. The successful running of the hotel, Mr Dunkley attributed to his wife, Sophia Dunkley née Aldenham, whose business acumen was learned in India from her father during his work there in an administrative capacity. Mr and Mrs Percy Dunkley eschewed naming their enterprise after the family and, instead, called it The Golden Thimble Hotel.

'Oh how wonderful, Tempest! And yet … this book seems to have just appeared … as though … it had just been written? … How very, very strange … Never mind, the fact is that Sophy and Percy were happy and fulfilled their dream.' Amanda put the book aside.

'And now for the parcel from Aunt Amelia.' She carefully undid the orange ribbon and opened the matching wrapping paper. Inside, was a board-backed envelope. Curiously, Amanda pulled up the flap and drew out a thin, A4 booklet, yellowed with age and printed upon the cover: *Roses of Picardy*, 1916. Lyrics by Fred E Weatherly. It was signed by the composer, Haydn Wood and priced 1/9, one shilling and ninepence.

'It's the song,' she declared to Tempest with delight. 'The one we danced to at the ball and kept hearing. How thoughtful. What a lovely present!' Amanda continued to study the pages. 'Oh he's signed it … what?' She laughed. Thomas had written on the back, in the lower right hand corner:

To my esteemed secretary and chauffeur. T.

At last, Amanda put it back in the envelope and laid it on the seat. Tempest sat close to her. Somehow both he and the song brought comfort as her mind turned to matters that could not be ignored.

The mystery of the murder of her blood relations on that day their minibus plummeted over that cliff on the Cornish coast. Could Granny really have been responsible? Or was it a Flamgoyne plot to assassinate every Cardiubarn with a magical gift?

Why did she have this sinking feeling about her sessions with the healer that would begin soon? There was a chance his skill would bring a cure for her asthma… the possibilities that would open up ... but why did she have this profound doubt that it would make her well?

Then there were the new memories of the Cardiubarn portrait gallery, the inspector's theory of eugenics, and that recurrent vision of walking down those stone steps with her great-grandmother and the something she needed to tell Granny ….

On top of all of this, there was Ryan … spying … for whom? And why? The answers were most likely the least palatable ones. He could be annoying, but Amanda had associated him with normality; his golden hair and easy smile, summer days, cricket. And now … she would have to be careful … far more careful, about him, about everything. For the Flamgoynes, they were coming, coming out of the West, out of Cornwall, for her village, her people.

And yet, Aunt Amelia, Granny, Grandpa, Uncle Mike, they all seemed to have faith in her that she would find a way to defend all that she loved from the approaching onslaught. And there, somewhere down among the houses and cottages and shops and lanes, was Viola. Viola who would be the beginning, the beginning of those who would gather to the standard.

There is always hope, thought Amanda. But now she had more than hope. She would draw her army — no, her

Home Guard — to her. She would find a way to defeat the Flamgoynes.

Tempest climbed up onto her shoulder and she stood and faced the West.

'Bring it on,' said Amanda Cadabra.

THE END

Author's Note

Thank you for reading *Amanda Cadabra and The Flawless Plan*. I hope you enjoyed your visit to Sunken Madley both present and past.

Whether this was your first time in the village or your second or even third trip, I would love you to tell me your thoughts about your journey through the book. And if you could write a review, that would be of tremendous help. You can post it on the e-store where you bought the book (if you're not sure how to post a review on Amazon, there is a how-to on my website) or on Facebook, Twitter or your social platform of choice. It would mean a great deal to me.

Best of all would be if you dropped me a line at HollyBell@amandacadabra.com so we can connect in person. If there is a character you especially liked or anything you would like more of, please let me know. Amanda Cadabra Book 4 is in the pipeline, and I want to make sure that all of the things that you liked about the first three books make an appearance for you.

For tidbits on the world of Sunken Madley and to keep up with news of the continuing adventures of our heroes Amanda, Tempest, Granny and Grandpa, Trelawney and Hogarth, visit www.amandacadabra.com, where you can also request to enter the VIP Readers Group or sign up for the newsletter to stay in touch and find out about the next sequel. The VIP Readers is a limited numbers group. Members are invited to receive and review an advance copy of the next book. If you are one of that treasured number, thank you for reading, evaluating and giving your precious feedback.

If Tempest has endeared himself to you and reminds you of your cat or one you know, in any way, you are invited to enter a photograph in The Tempest Competition. Details are at http://amandacadabra.com/the-tempest-competition/

You can also find me on:

Facebook at https://www.facebook.com/Holly-Bell-923956481108549/ (Please come and say hello. It makes my day when a reader does that.)

Twitter at https://twitter.com/holly_b_author-

Pinterest https://www.pinterest.co.uk/hollybell2760/

Instagram https://www.instagram.com/hollybellac-

Google+ at https://plus.google.com/u/0/110373044289244156044-

Goodreads at https://www.goodreads.com/author/show/18387493.Holly_Bell

and Bookbub at https://www.bookbub.com/profile/holly-bell

See you soon.

ABOUT THE AUTHOR

Cat adorer and chocolate lover, Holly Bell is a photographer and video maker when not writing. Whilst being an enthusiastic novel reader, Holly has had a lifetime's experience in writing non-fiction.

Holly devoured all of the Agatha Christie books long before she knew that Miss Marple was the godmother of the Cosy Mystery. Her devotion to JRR Tolkien's Lord of the Rings meant that her first literary creation in this area would have to be a cosy paranormal.

Holly lives in the UK and is a mixture of English, Cornish, Welsh and other ingredients. Her favourite animal is called Bobby. He is a black cat. Purely coincidental. Of course.

Acknowledgements

Thanks to Flora Gatehouse, for constant support, keen-eyed and intuitive editing and publicity, to Judes Gerstein, my Canadian gem of an advance reader, for noticing issues and offering ideal solutions, to Katherine Otis for her invaluable fine-tooth-combed proof-reading of the manuscript, to Dana, Mary and other wonderful VIP Readers Group members for their supportive comments and suggestions, and to Katherine DeMoure-Aldrich for round-the-world inspiration and feedback from wherever her travels take her. Thank you to Joe for his loyal support on Facebook. Thanks to Pravin Jootun and Philippa Shallcrass for their encouragement during the writing process.

Thanks are also due to the rector of St Mary the Virgin, Monken Hadley whose fund of information helped me to shape the village of 'Sunken Madley', and to Stephen Tatlow, the Director of Music there and the churchwardens for their kind welcome and delight at being fictionalised.

Praise and thanks go out to my talented and immensely patient illustrator Erik Patricio Lúa (Instagram: tripaciolua) for his beautiful book cover art. Your dedication to the project was truly remarkable. Thanks and admiration are also extended to my map maker Methmeth who skillfully turns my sketches and mockups into exquisite works of art.

Thanks to Marcus Sands of Parliament Hill Roofing for his indispensable advice on the structural integrity of the fictional Sunken Madley church hall.

Greatly appreciated was the generous advice and research leads provided by Dr Susie West and Matthew Steele for the design of the church crypt and the secular uses of the church hall.

Also due are thanks to Tanja Slijepčević of Books Go Social for her expert advice and unfailing assistance with spreading the word about both this book and the Amanda Cadabra series.

Thank you, in fact, to all those without whose support this book would not have been possible.

Finally, in whatever dimension they are currently inhabiting, thanks go out to my cat who inspired Tempest, and to my grandfather and brother for Perran and Trelawney. Your magic endures.

ABOUT THE LANGUAGE USED IN THE STORY

Please note that to enhance the reader's experience of Amanda's world, this British-set story, by a British author, uses British English spelling, vocabulary, grammar and usage, and includes local and foreign accents, dialects and a magical language that vary from different versions of English as it is written and spoken in other parts of our wonderful, diverse world.

QUESTIONS FOR READING CLUBS

1.   What did you like best about the book?
2.   Which character did you like best? Is there one with whom you especially identified?
3.   Whom would you like to know more about and why?
4.   If you made a movie of the book, whom would you cast and in what parts? Have you chosen any recasting over Book 1 or Book 2? Would you still have the same actress play, Amanda, for example, as you did in Book 1?
5.   Did the book remind you of any others you have read, apart from the first and second books in the series, either in the same or another genre?
6.   Did you think the cover fitted the story? If not, how

would you redesign it?

7. How unique is this story?

8. Which characters grew and changed over the course of this book, and over the first two books and this one, and which remained the same?

9. What feelings did the book evoke?

10. What place in the book would you most like to visit, and why? Any additional ones to Book 1 and Book 2?

11. Was the setting one that felt familiar or relatable to you? Why or why not? If you read the first or first and second book, how at home did you feel revisiting the locations?

12. What did you think of the continuity between the first book and this sequel?

13. Was the book the right length? If too long, what would you leave out? If too short, what would you add?

14. How well do you think the title conveyed what the book is about?

15. If you could ask Holly Bell just one question, what would it be?

16. How well do you think the author created the world of the story?

17. Which quotes or scene did you like the best, and why?

18. Was the author just telling an entertaining story or trying as well to communicate any other ideas? If so, what do think they were?

19. Did the book change how you think or feel about any thing, person or place? Did it help you to understand someone or yourself better?

20. What do you think the characters will do after the end of the book? Would you want to read the sequel?

GLOSSARY

As the story is set in an English village, and written by a British author, some spellings or words may be unfamiliar to some readers living in other parts of the English-speaking world. Please find here a list of terms used in the book. If you notice any that are missing, please let me know on hollybell@ amandacadabra.com so the can be included in a future edition.

British English	American English
Spelling conventions	
—ise for words like surprise, realise	—ize for words like surprize, realize
—or for words like colour, honour	—our for words like color, honor
—tre for words like centre, theatre	—ter for words like center, theater
Double consonants for words lik traveller counsellor	
Mr Mrs Dr	Mr. Mrs. Dr.
A1000	A Road - a main road that is not a highway
A4	8.26" by 11.69"
Biscuit	Cookie
Boiler suit	Coveralls
Bonnet	Hood
Brickie	Bricklayer
Boot	Trunk
Car Park	Parking Lot

Coffin	Casket
Coupla	Couple of
Corner Shop	Small grocery store
Cornish pasty	Disk of puff pastry filled with meat and vegetables then folded and sealed at the edges.
Crumpet	Cake with holes in, served toasted with butter
Cuppa	Cup of tea
Curtains	Drapes
Defence	Defense
Different from	Different than
Elevenses	A tea break at around 11 am
Eyrie	Aerie
Fridge	Refrigerator
Garden	Yard
Gastropub	Pub that serves high-quality food
Glammed up	Dressed up
Grey	Gray
Headmaster	Principal
Hun	Short from of 'honey'
Jam Roly-poly	A flat layer of suet pudding, spread with jam and rolled up
Jewellery	Jewelry
Jumper	Sweater
Lolly	Slang for money
Loos	Restroom
Marmalade Roll	Cake dough spread with marmalade and baked in the oven

Minibus	Van, minicoach seating 8 - 30 people
Mobile phone	Cell phone
Moggy, Mog	Slang for 'cat'.
Momentarily	For a moment
Motorway - M	Expressway, Highway
Ninepence	Nine old pennies - UK pre-decimal currency
Pavement	Sidewalk
Practise	Practice
Pub	Quiet, family friendly, coffee-shop style bar
Publican	Owner of a pub
Real-deal	Genuine
Pyjamas	Pajamas
Scone	Smaller, lighter and fluffier than the US scone, served with cream and jam
Sceptically	Skeptically
Scrumpy	Rustic, local cider
Shepherd's Pie	Minced lamb with mashed potato topping
Solicitor	Lawyer
Spotted Dick	Steamed suet and dried fruit pudding.
Tap	Faucet
The ladies	Ladies' room, restroom
Tin	Can
Torch	Flashlight
Trainers	Tennis shoes

Trifle	A dessert of layers of sponge, custard, fruit, jelly and whipped cream
Tyre	Tire
Van	Delivery truck
Victoria Sandwich	Sponge cake with jam and cream filling

Cornish Accent and Dialect

Bian	Baby
Pur	Very

Scottish Accent

Airly	Early
Gi'	Give
Noo	Now
Wi'	With

A Note About Accents and Wicc'yeth

One or two of the villagers have a Cockney accent indicated by the missing 'h' at the beginning of words such as 'hello' becoming ''ello'. There is also a character with a Scottish accent and another with a Cornish accent. These have been renedered as closely as possibly using English spelling conventions.

Wicc'yeth, is a magical language peculiar to the world of Amanda Cadabra., and is the language in which the two spellbooks mentioned in the story are wriiten If you are curious about the meaning of individual spell words, you will find a glossary at http://amandacadabra.com/wiccyeth/ and Amelia's Glossary with Pronunciation.

THE LAST WORD .... FOR NOW

Thank you once again, dear reader, for allowing me to share Amanda's story with you.

Best wishes,

Holly Bell

http://amandacadabra.com/contact/
http://amandacadabra.com/come-on-in/

42498749R00218

Printed in Poland
by Amazon Fulfillment
Poland Sp. z o.o., Wrocław